I0535440

# About the Author

Bob was born in Bristol. His career was in the marketing, retailing and distribution of a broad range of technologies, and latterly the event management of technology exhibitions. More recently he has been providing event research for the launches of a number of overseas exhibitions for others.

He has been writing for the last seven years, both fiction and non-fiction.

Bob is married, with two children and five grandchildren, living in rural Oxfordshire.

'Still Water' was Bob's first published novel, here it has been revisited and extensively updated. It was simply stunning how much has happened since it was first written and therefore needed to be changed.

The key protagonists in this thriller feature again in the sequel 'Gene Genie'.

For more information visit www.BobDenton.co.uk

# STILL WATER

**Bob Denton**

# STILL WATER

## Dedication

To Jane, my wife, friend and best critic!

## Acknowledgements

To family and friends who supported me in my literary aspirations.

To Mark Elliott who asked for his name to be applied to a character.

# TABLE OF CONTENTS:

PROLOGUE
BOOK ONE
Chapter 1 - *Pacific*
Chapter 2 - *Pacific*
Chapter 3 - *Galápagos Islands*
Chapter 4 - *Moscow*
Chapter 5 - *Pacific*
Chapter 6 - *Pacific*
Chapter 7 - *Moscow*
Chapter 8 - *Pacific*
BOOK TWO
Chapter 9 - *Moscow*
Chapter 10 - *Kazakhstan*
Chapter 11 - *London*
Chapter 12 - *Similian Islands, Thailand*
Chapter 13 - *Russia*
Chapter 14 - *London*
Chapter 15 - *Kent, UK*
Chapter 16 - *Novosibirsk, Russia*
Chapter 17 - *Novosibirsk, Russia*
Chapter 18 - *Lhasa, Tibet*
Chapter 19 - *Brighton, UK*
Chapter 20 - *Novosibirsk, Russia*
Chapter 21 - *Lhasa, Tibet*
Chapter 22 - *Novosibirsk, Russia*
Chapter 23 - *Lhasa, Tibet*
BOOK THREE
Chapter 24 - *Novosibirsk, Russia*
Chapter 25 - *Novosibirsk, Russia*
Chapter 26 - *Nadym, Russia*
Chapter 27 - *Novosibirsk, Russia*
Chapter 28 - *London, UK*
Chapter 29 - *Odessa, Ukraine*
Chapter 30 - *Novosibirsk, Russia*
Chapter 31 - *Istanbul, Turkey*
Chapter 32 - *London, UK*
Chapter 33 - *Oxfordshire, UK*
Chapter 34 - *Democratic Republic of the Congo*
Chapter 35 - *Kinshasa, D R of the Congo*
Chapter 36 - *Novaya Zemlya, Russia*
Chapter 37 - *Iraq*

Chapter 38 - *Kurdistan, Turkey*
Chapter 39 - *Cizre, Turkey*
Chapter 40 - *Cizre, Turkey*
Chapter 41 - *London, UK*
Chapter 42 - *Oxfordshire, UK*
Chapter 43 - *Novaya Zemlya, Russia*
Chapter 44 - *Virginia, USA*
Chapter 45 - *Oxfordshire, UK*
Chapter 46 - *London, UK*
Chapter 47 - *Odessa, Ukraine*
Chapter 48 - *Virginia, USA*
Chapter 49 - *Belgrade, Serbia*
Chapter 50 - *Vidin, Bulgaria*
Chapter 51 - *London, UK*
Chapter 52 - *Virginia, USA*
Chapter 53 - *Odessa, Ukraine*
BOOK FOUR
Chapter 54 - *Jinghong, China*
Chapter 55 - *Moscow, Russia*
Chapter 56 - *Novaya Zemlya, Russia*
Chapter 57 - *Moscow, Russia*
Chapter 58 - *Novaya Zemlya, Russia*
Chapter 59 - *Virginia, USA*
Chapter 60 - *Jinghong, China*
Chapter 61 - *Beijing, China*
Chapter 62 - *Moscow, Russia*
Chapter 63 - *Ho Chi Minh City, Vietnam*
Chapter 64 - *Novaya Zemlya, Russia*
Chapter 65 - *Jinghong, China*
Chapter 66 - *Vientaine, Laos*
Chapter 67 - *Mekong riverside, Laos*
Chapter 68 - *Roadside, Laos*
Chapter 69 - *Ho Chi Minh City, Vietnam*
Chapter 70 - *Kent, UK*
Chapter 71 - *Litke, Russia*
Chapter 72 - *Virginia, USA*
Chapter 73 - *Oxfordshire, UK*
Chapter 74 - *Moscow, Russia*
Chapter 75 - *Virginia, USA*
Chapter 76 - *Arctic Circle*
Chapter 77 - *London, UK*
Chapter 78 - *Novaya Zemlya, Russia*
Chapter 79 - *Novaya Zemlya, Russia*

Chapter 80 - *Matochkin Shar, Russia*
Chapter 81 - *Oxfordshire, UK*

# PROLOGUE

**From Moby Dick by Herman Melville:**

*'Why did the old Persians hold the sea holy? Why did the Greeks give it a separate deity, and own brother of Jove? Surely all this is not without meaning? And still deeper the meaning of that story of Narcissus, who because he could not grasp the tormenting, mild image he saw in the fountain, plunged into it and was drowned. But that same image, we ourselves see in all rivers and oceans. It is the image of the ungraspable phantom of life; and this is the key to it all.'*

It looked just like a whale as the nose of the nuclear submarine suddenly surfaced off their port side.

The pale sea had been like a highly polished floor, the Captain, with little to do but wait, had been day-dreaming that he could slide across it like a skater all the way to the horizon.

The crew had been wondering why they had been ordered to this desolate location. It had no redeeming feature unless you liked quiet; the only noises had been the normal shipboard ones that they had long since learned to ignore.

Their base of operations was located at the river Lena's delta-like estuary and they had been heading there after almost three months aboard. They had been looking forward to being back in port well before winter set in.

Absolutely nothing had been visible in any direction before this leviathan had broken the calm and their waiting.

The Captain had been ordered to this location, told only that he was to collect two people, then take them on to a place that the pair would specify. As a good Russian should, he never questioned these instructions, nor did he give thought to who had given them, or if this was an appropriate use of his vessel. The fact that they had received them through the normal channels was quite sufficient for him.

They had ducked south and then west of the Severnaya Zemlya Island group to avoid the limits of the pack ice and arrived at the coordinates in good time. The orders had been quite clear, if more brusque than was usual, and particularly thin on detail.

They were in the Proliv Vil'kitskogo channel off the south-western shores of Ostrov Bol'shevik Island in the Arctic Ocean.

Once the sub's sail had emerged all he wanted was to fulfil this inconvenient order and get back on course for home and a deserved leave. The promised two people and a number of cases of equipment were despatched towards them.

Everything was handled with military efficiency, not at all surprising given that both craft were fully manned by military personnel.

However the two, very heavyset, men being transferred were very definitely not military; more resembling what they clearly were, a pair of thugs. They strutted across the deck with complete indifference to the crew.

After these newcomers had safely passed by, those closest wrinkled their noses in distaste at the distinct and unpleasant smell of submarines that they had brought with them; a noxious cocktail of stale air, body odour and diesel oil.

The pair reached their quarters managing not to talk or to catch the eye of anyone aboard. Down below they held a short meeting with the Captain. The submarine wasted no time in diving, moving off to wherever.

The crew knew there were two distinct sorts of outsider. There were those they need not fear and thus would suck dry of useful information, though of course never quite accepting them into their close-knit community. Then there were those they feared, and these were best avoided. These two were quickly assessed by all as being definitely of the second variety.

All crew members had plenty of stories of their close encounters with thugs while ashore, but thugs who came out of the blue, well in fact out of a nuclear sub, and with the sort of connections that allowed them to divert and annexe their vessel, were certainly to be avoided like the plague. So the crew returned to normal duties. Good Russians, they knew that an inquisitive streak was invariably unhealthy.

The Captain had emerged morosely, abruptly issued the new coordinates. It became obvious they were not headed back to port, in fact they had some distance to go. He offered only that they were investigating an 'event' at these new coordinates, his answers making it clear he knew no more than this.

As the Captain and crew went through the steps of getting under way, the visitors emerged and summarily annexed the radio room for some time, ejecting the ship's operator while they used his equipment, then returning directly to their quarters. Here they stayed, accepting their meals at intervals without comment, emerging only when the Captain sent a junior officer to advise them they were approaching their destination.

They had turned into a narrow channel between the large island of Ostrov Oktyabr'skoy Revolyutsii and the much smaller Ostrov Pioner, entering a three-way junction formed by these islands and Ostrov Komsomolets. The charts were vague about the channels and none aboard had been through them before, so the Captain picked his way cautiously to the location that had been indicated.

Those who were on watch had again been expecting to see some other vessel and were therefore concentrating on the horizon, not particularly taking notice of the waters directly around them.

It was something in the engine noise, a different tone, something odd about the way the ship made its way through the water that made them all look down.

The surface was unusual, almost as if there was ice forming, but it was just a little too glutinous to be that. Regulars in the Arctic, they instinctively knew that this was out of the ordinary, something strange and unfamiliar. Perhaps some form of weed or organism then? But in these waters they had seen almost every form of both, this was clearly something new.

The Captain only became concerned when it grew more obvious that they were applying far too much power for the forward speed that was actually being achieved. He ordered that they cut the engines to investigate.

He reviewed and dismissed the usual reasons for this sort of effect. It could have been ice, but it was not that. Perhaps they were caught up in some sort of tough weed, no sign of this though. Maybe they were pushing against a gradual sand bank, but they would have heard that. Though any of these might have caused a similar reaction he knew instinctively that it was not the case here.

He walked to the edge of the bridge to get a better look over the side. The water was grey, still, and something about the way it looked made the hairs on his neck tingle.

The Russian research ship Captain watched as the small dinghy was lowered on to the surface and the selected crew members reluctantly climbed down into the boat. The sense of something being out of kilter had spread throughout the crew. There had been no volunteers. One moment they had been deservedly on their way back home after a long tour of duty and now they were in this godforsaken place where the sea was not behaving normally.

Earlier his 'guests' had offered no comment or advice when the Captain exercised his command in sending down a diver to investigate what it was that was fouling the hull of his ship. The duo had not interfered but had shown a good deal of interest in the actual process and they were the only ones who appeared unsurprised when the diver had not resurfaced.

After an hour beyond the diver's air reserves it was clear he was not coming back and, as no one seemed terribly keen to go and investigate, the Captain had tried with limited success to restart the engines. They made some headway but they were under immense strain to achieve only a fraction of a nautical mile per hour.

The Captain was on the bridge pondering his next course of action when he was approached by a delegation of junior officers. They were unhappy that they had been put in harm's way in this manner by their high command. They pointed out that the submarine that delivered their visitors could just as easily have investigated whatever this 'event' was. The meeting was heated.

'It's clear that they didn't want to risk their precious submarine. No, let us be the guinea pigs, we don't count.

'Just like Chernobyl. They sent out unimportant people like us to shut it down and clear it up. Perhaps this weird water is the site of another nuclear accident.'

'We can't expect any help if anything goes wrong. Look how they delayed in getting assistance to the crew of the Kursk out in the Barents. The largest attack submarine in the world, the pride of our fleet, a top crew, yet they wasted valuable time and let Lieutenant Captain Kolesnikov and twenty-two others die down there.

'It wouldn't have happened in the West, they even offered to help us, but we were too proud to accept. So what chance do we have, this ship is of no importance to anyone, who even knows that we are here...'

The main speaker, Andrei Korkin, realised that in the middle of his sentence he had lost his audience, and turned to see the two visitors were standing behind him. He involuntarily took a few steps backward.

The taller of the two wore an open-necked shirt that revealed a tattoo on his neck which most of the crew recognised as the crest of the White Guard. They would also have known from their school days that it was the White Guard that had fought the Red Guard during the Revolution.

Today this tattoo had nothing to do with those earlier days of their glorious Soviet history, nowadays it was a sure sign that the man had served a prison sentence. In the harsh prisons there was a distinct pecking order and this was the tattoo that defined it. Whatever else he might be, this crest identified him as a high-ranking Mafiya member.

Lev Solonik looked hard at Andrei, his eyes piercing and threatening, yet he was wearing a cynical smile. He was a hulking guy, with muscles on his muscles, but as he crossed the bridge he was surprisingly light on his feet. Like a prizefighter he appeared to be perpetually balanced, ready to strike.

Lev's smile was at once both dismissive and menacing. It was as if, while cataloguing the many places where he could effortlessly inflict pain, he was also considering whether this simple effort was in any way worthy of his time or attention.

Andrei crumpled under this scrutiny. It was as if he had mentally adopted a foetal curl. He appeared to shrink visibly as his shoulders both drooped and turned inwards to make clear that he posed no threat, that he was certainly not worthy of any aggression – although he still clearly expected some.

Lev snapped his eyes from Andrei, 'Captain, your duty is clear. We need samples of this water. We have brought the containers that will allow you to do this safely.'

'Then how will we get away from here? Is something going to come and pull us out?'

'If you cannot do it under your own power then we will evacuate you and your crew by helicopter.' Clearly Lev's patience was lost. He gave Andrei a further withering look as the thugs both left the bridge.

It had been no surprise at all that it was Andrei who was ordered with two other crew members to descend into the small boat filled with the Mafiya man's many containers.

These were a selection of vessels each capable of holding around twenty litres. Some were made of glass, some plastic and some metal, and they had a variety of different sealing mechanisms. Clearly some thought had gone into this selection. If whatever was in the water was able to breach some, the notion, or perhaps hope, was that it would not breach them all.

Andrei and his team had donned weatherproof gear, large wader boots and thick rubber gloves. This made the descent more difficult but it did not fully explain their slow progress. They plainly did not want to be near that sinister sea. Their shipmate, the diver, had entered it and disappeared. Clearly something was very wrong with the water around here.

No amount of dawdling stopped the inevitability that they had to reach the boat and start obtaining the required samples. Once down there one of the men went to the bow and steadied the boat, clearly wanting no part of the task itself. The second man quickly took out and unscrewed the first container and held it out, leaving Andrei the task of collecting and transferring the water.

No way was he going to lean out over the side. By now he had an ever-growing feeling that there was something sentient about the water. It was so still and unnaturally smooth and yet the reflection one would expect to see of the ship and those crowding the side was somehow swallowed up by the surface, becoming more like a shadow. He would not have been surprised if some watery hand had reached out of the depths to pull him to his death.

Part of his mind was shouting that this was totally irrational and he was making himself look stupid in front of the whole crew. But another part said, 'To hell with that, they're all safely up there. If they're so clever let's have them come down where I am and see how stupid they look.'

Andrei reached out over the side with a tool supplied by the visitors. It looked like a large serving spoon, over two metres long. He was careful to keep his arms and hands well within the confines of the boat. As he scooped the water it proved very viscous. The surface tension stopped the spoon cutting through the water. His first attempt crabbed off it like some amateur oarsman but without the usual accompanying splash.

Several more half-hearted attempts met with much the same result and made it apparent that he was going to have to stand in the boat to get some real purchase. In this way he managed to get the spoon to cut down into the water. Struggling to free it again made the boat swing and when it finally emerged at pace it cast several globs of the stuff into the bottom of the boat.

He and the crew member jumped out of the way and watched as the material found the lowest level and coalesced. Its movement reminded Alexei of mercury from his school chemistry lessons.

He decided to pivot the spoon into a rowlock so that he could be more careful in applying the required effort and thus he succeeded in getting the first sample. The work was hard and each container required one whole scoop or more. Taking comfort from the fact that so far no denizen of the deep had emerged, the three seemed to relax into the task. The other two men eventually rotating with Andrei when they saw him tiring, they took turns to get this business over and done with.

The mission completed, they painstakingly transferred the containers in a sling up to the ship. As the last container was swung aboard they were beginning to see an end to their discomfort. Suddenly the line securing the boat to the ship was thrown down and they looked up to see that their shipmates were no longer gathered at the rail.

Instead Lev was there with a Kalashnikov which he used to fire a burst into the bottom of the boat. The crewman at the bow was still close enough to the ship to jump in an attempt to reach a crawl-net on its side but was picked off with a single shot and disappeared beneath the surface.

Andrei looked down into the boat and was horrified to see water coming up through a mass of holes in the hull in a creeping or rolling action rather than a seepage. The water appeared to be joining up the dots rather than flowing.

He called up to the rail, 'Why?'

'You contaminated the boat and it's not safe to come aboard. You are honoured. Your sacrifice is for the greater good of Mother Russia.'

The other crewman shouted 'Fuck the greater good!' and dived towards the ship. He cut the surface expertly with the first few arm strokes of a rapid front crawl and then no more, he simply slipped below the glasslike crust on the sea without leaving even a ripple.

Andrei watched as the level in the boat reached up the side of his boots. He looked up to the rail to see his tormentor idly watching him.

Lev was reminded of times from his childhood, peeling the legs off a spider and watching what it would do. Would he jump in and try his luck? Or would he meekly succumb? Lev thought he himself would always go out trying everything and anything but he guessed this wimp below would stay frozen to the spot and die without any fuss.

He was wrong. Andrei walked the boat as it went down at the stern and stood at its highest point. There was a glorious moment when he thought the viscosity of this bizarre water might hold the boat near the surface and not reach the top of his boots. It hung there for what seemed like minutes without sinking further.

Lev ponderously reached over the rail to add a little encouragement with another burst, but before he did the boat gradually started to move slowly and steadily downwards as though someone in the depths had pressed a button to call it.

Andrei watched as the hateful stuff rolled into his boots. It was not as cold as he had expected. It felt as if there was a film insulating his flesh from the inundation. He was already on tiptoe and with his body arched like someone from the Bolshoi, but there he froze and, clinging on hoping for a miracle, he watched the water's remorseless rise.

It was at the very moment that the level reached his groin that things changed for the worse. He felt he was experiencing an alien intrusion, he sensed its impingement, his blood vessels and innards were accepting and spreading the fearful fluid throughout his body.

As a very last thought he realised that his groin was the first place where the water encountered a mucous membrane, a direct aqueous route to his vitals. His last image was perplexing, something lanced into his lower body but by then there was no sensation, just vision without interpretation. There was no nervous system function to alert his mind to the injury as it approached shutdown.

For nanoseconds he felt the stream continue its rush through his body, seizing up arteries, shutting down organs, so fast that he had no time to register pain. Then his brain just stopped.

The weakly Arctic sun sat out on the horizon, simulating a dawn, but then it had never really gone down. It had skimmed across the horizon to climb lazily and half-heartedly, offering pale light but with an absolute minimum of heat.

The noise of the rotors physically bounced off the structure of the research ship, the din and the downdraft like a sudden squall in this otherwise bleak and currently preternaturally calm wilderness.

The crew was still assembled where the Mafiya men had directed them to stand as the containers had been loaded on to the insectile helicopter, but this had not been what had held their attention or raised their anger.

Their eyes were on the partially concealed body of Andrei Korkin poorly wrapped inside a tarpaulin shroud, poorly wrapped because he was virtually impossible to conceal. The long harpoon that had impaled him and then been used to haul him aboard made the shape too irregular for even the most imaginative packaging skills of these two thugs. The combination of the awkward shape and their efforts to avoid any direct handling of the corpse had made their attempts extremely cursory.

As a result the crew could see their shipmate cruelly impaled, misshapen by the close-quarters impact of a harpoon designed to penetrate the thick sides of a whale at distance. They dismissed the fact that he had been dead before the bastards had decided to capture his body in this horrific manner. It wasn't any religious belief regarding defiling the dead that made their faces angry, it was the realisation that these bastards were not only happy making your life a misery for you, they would not show you any respect even after your death.

If it had been only the two visitors they might well have taken their chances and rushed them. The flight crew had been 'invited' on to the deck after the helicopter had landed and now these gangsters were supported by four others, each heavily armed with guns. There were few doubts that they were ready, willing and seemingly pretty keen to use them.

It was with some relief that the crew finally saw the helicopter rise from the deck because there had been a growing belief that these six would turn the guns on them before leaving. Their emotions were in turmoil. There was hate that they had been brought to this place, anger at their lost shipmates, horror at the state of Andrei and yet an overwhelming relief that they still lived to experience this cocktail of emotions.

They watched it climb and then pause perhaps a kilometre away. It turned to look back at the research vessel hovering just a few hundred metres aloft. Thirty seconds passed as it hung there like some vulture, waiting for something.

The crew gathered along the rail, knowing that it wasn't over. Their elation at still being alive was just a false dawn: their precise fate exercising one part of their minds while the other part was contemplating how to run, where to hide. Yet their bodies showed none of this frantic mental turmoil. They stood passively accepting the fate that was already written for them somewhere far away in Moscow.

Death materialised with a clap of thunder as a military aircraft swooped to supersonic speed somewhere out there, but as yet unseen. When it appeared, it came at breath-taking pace and then jinked as two tiny objects fell from beneath its wings, ignited and two contrails appeared. In fact these weren't smoke trails but rather impressions where the hot missiles had passed as they headed straight for the research vessel.

The crew realised how futile it would be to do anything and watched as the two missiles struck at the water line front and rear. The captain in any other circumstance would have called them to order and set about saving their vessel but he stayed silent as the ship lurched to port and then settled back on to starboard and took on a list.

As the ship slowly descended all they could hear was the aircraft circling and the helicopter hovering. As the awful water rose to consume them some appeared to find a religion and prayed, some ranted, the Captain just looked up at the distant helicopter transmitting as much malevolence into his stare as he could manage.

He assumed that cameras rolled and he hoped to reach from beyond his approaching watery grave and curse whoever might review the material. Perhaps his last grain of hope was that his stare might compel someone to seek justice for his crew.

The radio antennas were all that showed of the vessel when the aircraft ran over the location three times dropping napalm on to the waters. Lev, in the helicopter, filmed the flames until they died and then ordered the pilot to turn and hasten away from the event.

# BOOK ONE

**Thales of Miletus** (624 – 546 BC)
Considered as the first Greek philosopher, the 'father of science', he sought to replace the early myths and anthropomorphic gods and heroes, by stating that the world all originated from and consisted of water:

*'It is water that in taking different forms, constitutes the earth, atmosphere, sky, mountains, gods and men, beasts and birds, grass and trees, and animals down to worms, flies and ants. All these are different forms of water. Meditate on water!'*

**Marq de Villiers,** 'Water – the fate of our most precious resource'
Published in 2000

*'The trouble with water – and there is trouble with water – is that they're not making any more of it. They're not making any less, mind, but no more either. There is the same amount of water in the planet now as there was in prehistoric times. People, however, they're making more of – many more, far more than is ecologically sensible – and all those people are utterly dependent on water for their lives (humans consist mostly of water), for their livelihoods, their food, and increasingly, their industry. Humans can live for a month without food but will die in less than a week without water. Humans consume water, discard it, poison it, waste it, and restlessly change the hydrological cycles, indifferent to the consequences: too many people, too little water, water in the wrong places and in the wrong amounts.'*

# Chapter 1 - *Pacific*

The young American made his way across the lava blocks as speedily as he could manage. He was not alone; in fact it was almost impossible to find a place to step among the jostling creatures that teemed across this shoreline. There were hordes of different sizes and shapes that basked or scuttled over the rocks. He was in a hurry, had no time to appreciate their diversity, he had to get to the rendezvous.

He had no wish to hurt any of the creatures, could rely on the fact that none of them would want to harm him either. He just wished they would get out of his way; he had only fifteen minutes or he would be missed.

This area had been declared by UNESCO as the 'universal nature heritage of humanity'. Control of any developments was therefore a minefield of legislation which was every bit as tough to negotiate as his ponderous trek across these slick, sharp black rocks.

He had to get back to the main island and to the expedition team's inaugural meeting; he should not have been here on this tiny volcanic island. He certainly should not have been supporting, and worse, paying the mercenary team to be plundering its shores. But he had been sent here because he would be perfectly deniable, irrelevant – provided he made it back to the meeting undiscovered.

Tom Carter entered the meeting area quietly without being noticed, and used the opportunity to assess the American-led crew that he would be joining for the next month or so. Tom looked around at their body language, it was clear that the atmosphere was edgy, tetchy somehow.

His impression was right. Each of those present was a specialist in an active discipline of one sort or another. None had ever claimed any particular expertise in sitting and listening to the sort of red tape nonsense that was being delivered here; they wanted to be outdoors, but their team leader had insisted they were here.

The local official's poor English had created an assumption from the crew that he was none too bright, but it was the message he laboured that really confirmed it. He had lectured them on the peculiarities of the conservation legislation for the area. He stressed that some 95% of these islands were designated as a National Park and went into a stilted and detailed review of the regulations that Ecuadorian civil servants had woven around this initial decision. Given so many years unfettered at their task, this had become a labyrinth of red tape directives.

Tom was confused because if there had been one thing he felt these islands represented it was absolute nonconformity. At no stage of the islands' formation or history had they ever been connected to any continent. All the life found on them today had been there from the very outset or had flown, swum or been washed up on to them. They had developed in glorious isolation from the rest of the world and in a spectacularly diverse way. There were only a few thousand species, but half of these were only found right here on these islands and absolutely nowhere else in the world.

That the Incas had regularly visited these islands was easily established by many pottery finds, but that had not stopped European history claiming that the islands 'were first discovered' by the Spanish Bishop of Panama in 1535. Tom bridled at the thought that not only were the Incas wiped out but it seemed that every one of their achievements had been systematically deleted from history too.

The name given to these islands derived from an old Spanish word for the extremely long-lived giant tortoises that they had found here. With time it contracted from *gaur pagos* and became the Galápagos.

Charles Darwin arrived three hundred years after the bishop. It was based upon his cataloguing of its fauna that he later compiled his theories of natural selection, resulting eventually into the much-delayed publication of his controversial 'Origin of the Species'. This was precisely Tom's preferred sort of science, the extreme unorthodoxy of the Galápagos meeting up with Darwin's doggedness. His very ordered scientific approach in this remote corner of the world had led to the need for a total reassessment of the established wisdom. As a result the age of the Earth had to be recalculated based upon Darwin's new principles of how animals had evolved and how we came to be what we are.

Tom noticed a young guy down near the front. Mark Elliott was still sweating profusely from his headlong rush to make the meeting from his side trip. The team had been advised that the young American was still training as a biologist and botanist. They believed that he had used his father's connections to get this internship with them, that apparently the father was a senator or some other big political hitter. None of this was true. Mark had worked hard on his research of the local oceanography and the region to justify this role, but he knew he could always fall back on the excuse that he was training rather than qualified if, or perhaps more likely when, his knowledge proved deficient in any manner.

Mark's deliberately heavy Oklahoma accent meant he was assured that any fellow Americans instinctively treated him as somehow inferior. This and the fact he looked only to be in his early twenties, though he was in fact much older, routinely assured that he would be underestimated by others. He found this a very useful advantage and milked it regularly at times like these.

The official was describing the local concern for the flightless cormorants, birds that to Mark sounded a lot like the infamous dodo. Flightless too, the dodo had been unable to avoid the hungry seafarers on Mauritius, so, Mark thought, it became extinct, dead, it had ceased to be, it was an ex-dodo.

Though Mark was also finding the guy's presentation pretty nauseating, he made sure that he was the only one providing any form of obvious feedback. One, it gave him something to do, and two, it added to his geeky image with the others.

The official had paused for effect. Tom watched as an African-American began to ease herself from her chair to take over the session but was forced to sit back down under a withering stare from the speaker. He realised with a start that this must be Ellise Walker, he had been given her name but not her ethnicity.

The official paused only to wait for a minion to switch on a battered old slide projector and then impatiently nodded each time for the assistant to cycle manually through a very tired set of slides showing the many subspecies of Galápagos finches, or what he referred to as '*los finches de Darwin*'.

Tom continued to scan the room from the safety of his position and noticed his fellow Brit, Paul Wells, sitting towards the centre of the room. He frowned at the discovery; he had not realised he would be there. He noted that as usual he had sought comfort by locating himself in the middle of the crowd, never a leader, too needy to lurk at the edges.

Paul was beginning to nod off; he couldn't work out whether it was the effect of the extreme age of the slides or whether the birds actually were truly dull and uninteresting. To him the comparison of slides, supposed to show the variety in beak size and shape from island to island, was not at all obvious and certainly not very gripping.

The official droned on showing each minor difference with enthusiasm and in far too much detail. After each slide he sought some form of feedback from his audience before proceeding. Paul noted thankfully that some sweaty young guy up front obliged each time, so the progress painfully continued.

It subsided into a succession of nods from the official to bring up the next slide, a brief description of the differences, a nod from the young guy and then on to the next. Tom smiled as he made the mental note that he was gaining a 'nodding' acquaintance with Darwin's finches.

However, Tom fully appreciated that these minor beak-shape differences were vitally important. For a finch the shape of the beak during food shortages was literally the difference between life and death. Not the 'survival of the fittest' but survival of the best adapted. Those best able to grub around in roots and trees for vital traces of food during shortages survived. They were the ones that made it through to procreate. Aptness, not fitness, was the key to survival.

The official was trying to explain that for Darwin it was the isolation of the islands and these beaks that provided him with clear evidence of evolution through selection. If Tom had been presenting he felt he would state that at its simplest, human written history was a record of winners and survivors and so too, Darwin established, was evolution.

'Our islands honour Carlos Darwin, but no all believe heem.' The official smiled revealing his uneven and discoloured teeth. 'We believe in God, as you

Yankees say "in God we trust" and we thanks God for Carlos, without heem no turismo.'

The team had established its field station here on Isla Isabela, the largest of the island group. Isabela had been formed by the gradual output of four major volcanoes, one of them named after Darwin. From here the team's main distraction from the official's diatribe was the sight of Volcan Santo Tomas. There was no doubting this Thomas, it completely commanded their view from the large picture window of the building.

The atmosphere in the room was hot and humid, the ceiling fans failing to do more than simply circulate the turgid air. More significant than the temperature and humidity was the growing impatience of the team; they wanted to be out there, exploring this amazing place and not listening to a bunch of petty-fogging regulations.

Mercifully the official rounded off his set-piece presentation with a further nod following which two more minions bustled around to hand out material to the group. He waited until there was a desultory round of applause then he finally gave the stage over to Ellise.

'Of course, I want to start by underlining that we will respect our hosts' rules very carefully.' Ellise took the time to make fierce eye contact with each of those in the front rows to show that this was to be taken as an order. 'This truly is a special place and we will all help make sure that it stays that way. Yes, we'll want to soak up the local colour while based here, but our real role, of course, is away from the islands where an entirely different set of rules needs to be observed.'

She was talking more to their hosts than to the team itself. 'Our task here is to review and maintain the systems that will help to protect these and other shorelines.' Clearly a high-flyer, she worked for the OAR, the Office of Oceanic and Atmospheric Research, but Tom had read that she was more a computer specialist with oceanography as her current application.

Indeterminately late 30s, perhaps older, she was quite reticent about her past; there may have been a husband, quite probably children too, but nothing of this would be forthcoming from her.

From Atlanta, Georgia she had a very melodious accent that held her team's attention. She was tall at around 175cms, with well-defined musculature, dressed today in light-blue Levis and a cut-off tee-shirt that showed this off to full advantage. Her bare midriff, broad shoulders and strong arms made it obvious that Ellise worked out, regularly.

She had made it clear from the outset that she was well used to managing a team of guys who would first see the woman, many the black woman, and only later, the manager. She had also shown that she was not afraid to use her femininity where it suited her purposes. She seemed to mesmerise the tiny Ecuadorian with her hands-across-the-ocean pitch.

'We understand that the islands have very little animal life.' Ellise counted out her points to stress them. 'No amphibians, few reptiles, under ten mammal forms, and fewer than a hundred species and subspecies of birds. The fauna here is therefore ALL at risk and we shall not add to its precarious position. All our eating and drinking needs have been brought here with us.'

Paul too was enjoying her presentation when suddenly she stopped and rushed to greet someone behind him. When he turned he just could not believe what he saw. Rising to meet Ellise and dressed in what Paul would later describe as designer-jungle, was Tom-bloody-Carter.

Her whole demeanour switched as she shook Tom's hand and air-kissed both his cheeks. She was no longer the demanding boss with a tough duty to dispense, now her body language and the tone of her voice showed real enthusiasm. Paul felt that she revealed much more than just a scientific interest. She and the official instantly danced to Carter's attendance, ushering him to the front of the room.

She announced to the room, 'Here's my big surprise. We were all delighted when Tom Carter agreed to join our team. So glad you could join us, Tom. So sneaky of you to hide away at the back here!'

'Not at all, I was enjoying the presentations, keen to immerse myself in the team.'

She led him to the front of the room. 'You should know that your best-selling "Eden Re-charted" was required reading for all of us before we set off on this mission. Perhaps you'd like to offer us a few words?'

Paul grimaced, 'Why on earth did he have to be here?' He could hardly hide his reaction when Tom shook her hand again by cradling it inside both of his, holding on rather too long for Paul's taste.

Paul believed his life to have been routinely blighted by Carter. Perhaps it wasn't terribly surprising that they should bump into each other in that they were both active in the relatively small world of oceanography. But while Paul struggled to maintain his grasp on the lowest rung in their vocation, Tom appeared always to scale the heights, seemingly always in the right place at the right time. Better published, he seemed to move effortlessly from successful project to even more successful project.

Worse, he had authored or co-authored many significant technical publications, hailed and promoted by the 'establishment' within their science, yet he was at the same time acclaimed for having the 'common touch'. He had published a succession of populist books on various subjects, not just oceanography.

He had become a much-used TV expert to be wheeled out whenever something within the broadest scope of the earth sciences caught the media's eye. He could always be relied upon to turn up, smile for the camera, trot out some crafted sound bites and thus his appeal just carried on expanding.

Tom was not particularly tall, but he carried little fat and there was something about his proportions that suggested height. Paul thought it might just be the skilful tailoring of his outfit, for tailored it certainly was. Tom always seemed to eat and drink well but managed to remain annoyingly lean. Though hardly toned or particularly muscular, he always appeared quite fit and sporty. Small but perfectly formed, Paul had once said scathingly when asked to describe Tom.

Fairish eyes, fairish hair, fair complexioned, in fact Paul thought 'fair' was a good word to sum up Tom. Nothing remarkable to look at, nor did Paul feel his papers or books were particularly earth-shattering; he would rate them as just a 'fair' too.

But annoyingly there was that something, or was it a series of somethings, that seemed to stamp him out. Whatever it was, he always appeared to be assured of success.

On top of all that there was a vulnerability about him that seemed perfectly designed to attract female interest. Paul couldn't understand it. To him he was flat, featureless, forgettable, and he knew from personal experience that the guy was a coward.

Yet this certain something always marked him out, propelled him forward, and, each time it did, it felt as if part of the effect was arranged very deliberately to mock Paul, to ridicule his own slow and painful progress, highlighting his own shortfalls in the success department.

He watched him now, unable to take in his words, quietly seething that once again his progress might be blocked by this bastard. The man he knew to be worthless, the same man who exhibited no shame about that at all. If their roles had been reversed he would not have been able to look Carter in the face without remembering that day, yet he watched him now weaving a spell over this audience. He had them enthralled with his tales of these islands. Paul reluctantly realised that he too would have enjoyed the content if he hadn't known him for the fraud that he was.

Tom said, 'You have to appreciate that when Darwin visited these islands the world's population was around a sixth of what we have today and of course international travel was still in its infancy. Travel to these islands back then was by sailing ships and that took time, time that made the traveller more appreciative of, less damaging to, the local environment.

'Today, we rush around burning up resources, polluting with our waste and our noise, barely seeing what's around us. We pause only to see if things we find are either edible, a suitable gift for friends and family or can be applied to something useful for us, useful today, right now. We dash about not noticing, plain ignoring anything that has no apparent immediate value to us. Today's traveller wouldn't have had or even thought to have made the time to notice the inexorable course of selection, nowadays he'd just take a few snapshots and move on to the next island.

'We choose to ignore Darwin's clear message at our peril. All of life is interconnected and constantly changing. The changes are mostly painfully slow, but they are mighty steady too. These changes are remorseless, yet still, they are very evidently affected by everything that we might choose to do, or choose not to do.'

Tom paused as the audience pondered this, then bestowed a broad smile on them, 'I don't want you all to think I'm some sort of extremist tree-hugger, but it's not often that you can go somewhere that is so geologically recent, so zoologically different and so philosophically challenging.'

He turned to the official. 'We truly are most fortunate to be allowed to make our base here. Thank you. I know we're all keen to respect the unique nature, with a capital N, in this truly wonderful place.'

The meeting over Paul noticed that the previously restless team was now slow to move off with several members, including Mark, keen to gather round Tom and sycophantically ask him questions. Paul pointedly wandered over to Ellise instead. 'So how're we going to house all of his ever-present TV crew, speech-writers and hairdressers aboard?'

Ellise was surprised by his obvious venom, 'I thought you two Brits would be best of pals. Do you guys know each other or something?'

# Chapter 2 - *Pacific*

While the American team spent some days setting up their operational base and checking their equipment, Tom and Mark seemed to have stepped up to become the PR squad for the team, for many of the local politicians appeared to need constant attention and appeasement.

Ellise realised early on that their project was viewed as having deep pockets and a number of the officials seemed to be looking at inventing ever new ways of picking them. Local licences appeared to be required from every lowly branch of government and she had given up trying to find any rhyme or reason for their demands. Then, of course, they were securely located in male-dominated South America and not only was she a woman, she was black, and politically correct principles hadn't even begun to dawn in these backwaters.

This was where Tom really came into his own. His 'celebrity-status' seemed to somehow psych out the locals. They had clearly been briefed that here was someone in touch with the global press, someone who was able to command column centimetres and gain worldwide notice for his opinions and observations. Though Ellise had seen no sign of a central controller of these many bureaucrats, they did all seem to have reached the same conclusion, that Tom must leave the islands with a very positive view to report.

By fielding Tom at most of her formal meetings, Ellise found she was able to deflect the rather blatant appeals for some form of payment or other. The two of them developed an easy understanding, never talking over each other, seeming to understand naturally when Ellise should provide the steel in the negotiations and when Tom should provide the glitter to deflect their protagonist's attention.

Ellise enjoyed their 'partnership' and boasted of its benefits and smoothness to the other team members. She realised that Tom never seemed to be prepared to reveal anything of his personality or his own beliefs and enthusiasms; he seemed to hide behind an armoury of ready stories. While she could not deny that he had a wealth of truly interesting and varied anecdotes, where was the man at the centre of these events?

When she looked at him she saw a fit guy, very much within what her best friends would describe as her type. He was successful, confident and physically competent but there was some sort of underlying vulnerability too. These were the minimum attributes that she would list to her friends as essential for her to show any interest in a guy. And yet there was no real feedback that she could latch on to. He exuded plenty of empathy, but perhaps if you project that much sincerity then you had by definition to be basically an insincere sort of guy. The fact that he appeared uninterested meant she wondered if perhaps he was gay. Certainly she considered him neat, tidy and meticulous enough.

Mark too had become a key member of their PR squad. If anything he appeared to express a more thorough appreciation of the unique nature of the islands; obviously his research had paid off. Ellise found that she was unsure of Mark, there was something beneath his Okie persona, something a little smarter and more knowing, but she couldn't nail it down.

She also quickly accepted that Mark was one of those people who would look untidy in anything. Even if she arranged for him to be rigged out in the best that designer labels could offer, she knew he would somehow manage to look scruffy; dressed in the very coolest of gear he would still be lukewarm.

His almost naïve enthusiasm made up for all of that. Scruffy he might be, but somehow he was able to make people like him. She had begun to realise his success was not just the consequence of short-term charm such as Tom managed to weave. This was more a lasting camaraderie that made people really like him, want to spend time with him, seek him out, tell him their thoughts and as a result they showed genuine pleasure when he entered a room.

A six-footer he was probably fitter than he looked, his scruffiness added pounds to his appearance. Dark haired and brown-eyed, he was a good-looking guy but there was just something that made her feel he was someone to become a firm friend, good company, but that it would never go any further.

Tom on the other hand was an attractive guy, certainly fit too. He had this great smile that lit up his face but there seemed to be a certain something lacking that she could not yet fathom. Very eager, very keen to please but it appeared to no particular end. Anyway, she had concluded that she was wasting time and should concentrate instead on getting the project under way and not contemplating the available guys. She was their manager for God's sake!

Tom had always been uncomfortable around powerful women, which was just how he thought of Ellise. She was brisk, competent and urgent in her negotiations with the officials and he felt the need to deflect what he viewed as her underlying aggression. He found himself leading the conversation off into tales of other places and projects to reduce the tension in a situation. He was fully aware of her femininity and realised that she was showing some interest in him but he always preferred to make the running and be predator not prey.

When Mark came up with a proposed field trip, Tom pressed that he and Ellise should also take a break from the bureaucracy and was delighted when she freely agreed. Neither of them noticed Mark's reticence. He had planned on inviting Ellise but hadn't counted on Tom wanting to tag along too. Why were American women such suckers for a British accent?

# Chapter 3 - *Galápagos Islands*

From their map Tom could see why the shape of Isabela was usually described as a seahorse, but there was a big blob at the base that he felt ruined the effect. In his notes he remarked that it looked more like an italicised number three with little Fernandina perched before it like a decimal point.

Virtually a cone, Isla Fernandina had at its core Volcan La Cumbra it was the youngest of the Galápagos Islands, probably less than 100,000 years old, and also currently the most volcanically active. As recently as 1968 its crater floor had collapsed some six hundred metres, a huge explosion sending fumes and ash kilometres into the air, prompting hundreds of follow-up earthquakes.

On the way between the two islands they were pursued by a huge pod of dolphins careening through the wake and speeding alongside their powerful boat. The dolphins showed an incredible blend of outright curiosity and downright fun.

Mark entertained the others by quoting a concept from Douglas Adams *Hitchhikers Guide to the Galaxy*. It had suggested that the two most intelligent animals on Earth were humans and dolphins, with humans claiming they were the smartest because all the dolphins did was fool around in the sea all day, while the dolphins felt they were the smartest for precisely the same reason!

As they landed at Punta Espinoza and confirmed their return arrangements, Ellise looked around and thought that the black volcanic rocks were moving, but as she focused more carefully and realised that there were hordes of different-sized lizards and crabs, scrambling over each other or riding piggy-back. She couldn't help scratching her waist at the sight of what she instantly considered an infestation.

Mark explained, 'Those "large lizards" are in fact marine iguanas, they're found only here in the Galápagos Islands. You'll see that they regularly swim out through the surf, dive to feed, staying down for perhaps twenty minutes at a time. Once they've fed, they need to warm up so they climb out on to the rocks to catch the sun. When fully warmed, you'll see them turn away from the sun into the cool breeze. So all that twisting and turning isn't just random, it's their way of maintaining a regular body temperature.'

The three of them walked on in silence as they moved away from their landing point, spotting some of the flightless cormorants that had apparently 'unlearned' the art of flying as there were no predators to bother them on these islands. Mark once again thought of *Hitchhiker's Guide.* 'Do you think they forgot in the same way that Arthur Dent learned to fly by simply forgetting to hit the ground?'

Ellise puzzled aloud, 'Sorry but I can't imagine how that works. OK, I haven't ridden a bicycle in ages but I'd still know how to get back up on to the saddle. I'm pretty darned sure that if I ever managed to learn a skill even half as amazing as flying, then I'd sure as hell never forget it!'

They walked on and she watched Tom and Mark ahead of her, quietly assessing them both. They appeared at peace here, each finding joy in what she was already feeling to be just a little too much of the same. The prehistoric-looking iguanas didn't look very appealing with their habit of snorting out salt water leaving a crusty deposit around their nostrils. She felt if you'd seen one beachful, you'd seen enough to last a lifetime.

'Is there anything else to see?'

'Tell you what, if Mark doesn't mind, I'll race you up the side of the volcano, see what we can find, what sort of view there is from up there – fancy that?'

Mark masked his relief and nodded assent. They struck off for the interior leaving him to his coastline. As they added distance he mumbled to himself, 'Go on, don't mind me. I don't mind being your wingman just this once.'

Mark had a meeting along the shoreline that had to be handled alone. His 'father' had funded a full geological survey of the area around the islands, pretty sensitive stuff given the global attention on leaving the area unblemished. He was here to collect the latest results.


Tom and Ellise found the going was tough. Their route had to be picked carefully across rough volcanic debris that had not had any human or animal traffic across it to create anything that could be considered a useable trail. What plant life there was proved to be coarse, spiky and all over the place, making it difficult to make headway as every step had to be carefully tested before anything like their full weight could be applied.

The early conversation, more a relaxed banter really, started to wane as the heat and the physical effort of the climb began to take its toll. But neither was going to be the first to call a halt.

Both had failed to come properly equipped for this climb. Their shoes were more suited for aboard a boat or on a gentle sandy shore. Of necessity they could not avoid leaning on each other over the difficult terrain and were forced to join hands on occasion to clamber over obstacles. Initially they had set out unconsciously maintaining space between them, but increasingly they did nothing to stop physical contact.

Both had earned multiple superficial and several deep scratches on their legs, then Ellise stumbled and caught her bare ankle on a sharp rock and gouged it deeply. Tom bent to look at the damage.

'You'll live,' he pronounced and pulled out a tissue, spat on it and cleaned the area as best he could.

Ellise laughed, 'I hope you have no certifiable diseases, swapping body fluids with me like that!'

They caught each other's look and he reached across to kiss her. A kiss that started out gently but rapidly became demanding. They stood and pressed urgently against each other, tongues first softly, then penetratingly, exploring each other's lips, teeth, mouth, tongue. Their hands were initially around each other in an encompassing embrace but they quickly became more exploratory too.

They broke off from that first long kiss and it was Ellise, with her head looking over his shoulder, who first realised that there was not a single place in sight where they could lie down nor any smooth rock that they could even lean against. She giggled, 'Looks like we need to get ourselves a room.'

The laughter broke the mood somewhat and Tom asked, 'Is this such a good idea anyway?'

She looked deeply into his eyes, ignoring his comment, then quickly removed her T-shirt and shorts, 'Well, what do you think now?'

He answered by gently caressing her, then kissing her nipples until she became impatient and bent down to unfasten his shorts. She placed his hand on to a relatively smooth rock so he could steady them and then carefully wrapped her thighs around him, using her arms over his shoulders to raise herself first above and then down on to him.

It ended with more laughter as both realised the ludicrous picture that they must have made. He trying desperately not to fall over or to brush against anything sharp, with his clothes tangled around his ankles further restricting any movement, and she therefore having to provide most of the action, clamping him with her thighs, elbows pressing and releasing on his shoulders, moving insistently until she rode him to her climax and, impressively she thought, on to his.

Only he knew that it was his sincere fear of falling among these lethal rocks that had probably earned him 'a personal best' in terms of staying power. He hadn't really been able to concentrate, until he just had to.

'Great sex,' she said, keen to define it, contain it, now it was over. 'God I needed that after all those god-awful meetings.'

Tom was dressing himself and passing her the discarded items. He wasn't sure whether her comment meant intimacy was now over or whether he should post-coitally seek to hug or kiss her. He chose not to. 'Sorry, I don't know what came over me.'

'It was me,' she laughed. 'Don't get all serious on me now. That was great, let's just accept it for what it was, honest-to-goodness, great sex. It was just what the doctor ordered – thanks!'

He pondered this, accepted it, 'So do we press on up to the caldera then?'

She grabbed him and kissed him, 'Honey, I've had all that I came up here for, how about you?'

On the way down to the shoreline she was on a high, chatty, giggly, trying to make it into something of a race back to the shoreline, but the terrain made it next to impossible.

As they reached the beach, they saw Mark with a snorkel and mask in his hand; he was up to his waist in the water talking with some guys in an idling, but evidently fast, launch down at the shoreline. He saw them coming, waved, finished off his conversation and carefully worked his way across to meet them. Tom thought his shoulder bag looked a little heavier than earlier, but assumed he had collected some samples.

Ahead there was a large rock pool and Ellise scrambled down to the side of it with warm memories of her childhood spent with a net at just such a place. She scaled the rocks nimbly and turned over stones in the pool, careful not to disturb the sand and silt. Searching for anything that might be lurking beneath, after a few attempts she found a strange crab. She quietly called them over to identify it.

Mark joined her and excitedly started to describe what it was. They were just like a pair of kids together and it would have been nigh on impossible for Mark not to hazard a guess at what had happened earlier by her unusually high spirits alone. Any doubts were dispelled when his innocent comment, 'You can't possibly have gone all the way in this time,' was greeted by her collapsing with laughter.

The rock pool was deep and dark enough that reflections were mirror-quality. Tom had just come up behind them and was looking over her shoulder to see what was so funny. As she looked into the pool she caught his reflection in the surface and watched as a look of wide-eyed, absolute horror spread across his face. He turned ashen and then suddenly stumbled away across the beach, ignoring both of their calls after him.

# Chapter 4 - *Moscow*

Lev Solonik was a very serious *chainik*, a prison bully. This proudly proclaimed title was, for some piece of serendipity, derived from the cheap teapots used in Russian prisons; despite this it still managed to maintain a menacing sense to the other inmates. His presence and his indifference had very effectively terrorised the research ship crew but now back in Moscow and here in Kabitsin's presence, he was the one who was fearful.

For Kabitsin was someone who could, at a whim, cause pain and death, not just to Lev himself, but more disturbingly he would usually extend his punishment to even the remotest family members. On many occasions it was not just death that was dealt out, Kabitsin would not rest until he had ensured the complete elimination of his victim's gene pool.

He took every opportunity to spread his own seed, eschewing any forms of birth control, angrily insisting any mistresses must become impregnated. It was something of a fetish for him – that while he worked hard to expand his own lineage, he would be just as diligent in eliminating the DNA of his opponents, to erase them in the longer-term competition that would stretch on down through ensuing generations.

Kabitsin started out in a not too dissimilar manner from Lev. Originally he too was a gang youth, but where Lev had simply and mindlessly matured into the role of adult thug, his boss had brutally battled his way past his peers and used his intellect to become a powerful black-marketeer. Gathering a strong crew of 'Levs' around him, he had used his position to catch the attention of local aspiring politicians by delivering them the 'grey' services that gave them their popularity and forwarded their progress.

He concentrated particularly on those things they did not want attributable to them or ever publicised. It might just be the supply of girls and/or boys as sweeteners, or perhaps torturers as looseners, or even contract killers as silencers – it could all be left to Kabitsin. Forward progress was assured as soon as Kabitsin was awarded the contract.

What they had not perhaps counted upon was that he was never a one-time contractor, he managed instead to follow them in their political progress, dog them into their better future that he had enabled. He worked to make sure that he became inextricably tied to the development of their careers and they relaxed as they realised that with his help they would expand more rapidly, significantly and assuredly.

The way Kabitsin evolved beyond a thoughtless thug was by maintaining good records, incriminating records of all the favours and services he had supplied, so that with time he was able to turn the tables on his employers and use this information to broaden both his role and status. He had illustrated many times that to cross him meant death and complete familial extinction, so he was seldom refused.

Kabitsin was sitting behind his desk, did not even look up as he demanded, 'Have you delivered the merchandise?'

Lev stood almost to attention as he said, 'Yes, just as you asked.'

'And what have you done with the body of the sailor?'

He was surprised to be questioned further. Of course he had done as was required of him, 'Yes, all as you said has been delivered to the research laboratory.'

Now Kabitsin did look up, 'Not quite all I hope?'

Lev was desperate to reassure, 'No, the majority of the flasks were brought here as you ordered. We have carefully placed them in your storage facility. And, we made sure that these were only the flasks that have shown absolutely no signs of any seepage. Those we had any concerns about went to the labs.'

Kabitsin had merely been an opportunist, but as the old Soviet system imploded he discovered, somewhat to his own surprise, that he had developed a fervent patriotism. Not for him the move towards the West, the espousal of capitalism, market forces... No, he worked his way alongside those wanting to reinstate the past ways, the old Soviet strengths.

He showed his new friends that he could go into places they could not, he could find out things they needed to know and most importantly that he could change those things as required. In this way he edged ever closer towards the centre of real power. Called upon to fulfil the necessary off-the-record dirty work, he proved to be a safe if somewhat bloody pair of hands, and became the preferred fixer to the great and the not-so-good.

He and his new employers had watched with dismay as the oligarchs emerged on to the Russian scene. Yeltsin and his administration were in decline; he was an alcoholic with heart disease, only managing to work a few hours each day, the state in essence being run by his daughter and his bodyguard.

Few in the post-Soviet Russia had any appreciation of the opportunities presented by a country that had moved within less than a century from feudal state under the Tsars, via communist state under the Commissars to suddenly espouse the West's market economy. All this happened without any control and with no real understanding of business, or at least the business techniques as evolved by Western Europe and America.

Unsurprisingly to Kabitsin it was the Jews who saw the opportunity best and earliest – they who managed to steal Mother Russia's precious resources. The oligarchs bought up all the oil, the natural gas and other minerals for a fraction of their true value, then used this strength to buy up TV channels to promote themselves further.

They despoiled Russia with their financial and media muscle, working their way deep into the fabric of the political system and creating private armies from among the disaffected ex-Soviet republics in order to keep their status.

Kabitsin felt powerless as he watched them import American election experts and gave Yeltsin unopposed airtime to guarantee the re-election of their 'lapdog'. They couldn't believe their luck when almost immediately another heart attack meant Yeltsin spent this new term of office in hospital while they, the oligarchs, could rape and pillage the mineral wealth of Rodinya. Mother Russia.

To Kabitsin, the emergence of Vladimir Putin was a much-needed breath of fresh air and none too soon. While Putin engineered his takeover from the top and at the heart of the system, it was essential that down at the grass roots individuals like Kabitsin and other 'patriots' fought the virus that was crippling Mother Russia.

Putin was able to wrest control of the media and imprison or chase away the oligarchs, but he owed much to the change of public opinion that was created by people like Kabitsin. As a result of this invaluable service Kabitsin's status now knew no bounds.

From this strong position Kabitsin had been able to learn very early of this peculiar water. He had seen the reports of a small vessel becoming caught up in it and its increasingly frantic calls for assistance. His unique experience helped him to comprehend its true potential and his new status helped him to reach deep inside the military to have Lev arrive at the right place at the right time.

His political colleagues would be delighted by the delivery of the water samples and the body. They could do the costly research, they could establish the science of this strange substance, but Kabitsin had his own plans for this water.

If it truly had the capabilities that he thought, and that Lev had apparently witnessed, then there was a real opportunity for him to strike back at those who had damaged Mother Russia.

'*Spashiba*, thank you. I'll call you when I need you.'

'*Do svidaniya*,' Lev happily took his leave, surprised at being thanked, not something he judged to be a Kabitsin trait in the past.

Kabitsin pulled out a map and ran his finger across his first target, the ninth largest country in the world, extremely rich in natural resources, but pitifully poor in loyalty to its teachers and rightful leaders.

# Chapter 5 - *Pacific*

'This wasn't what I signed up for,' Paul whinged. 'I'm not a bloody service mechanic! I didn't spend all those years of learning to become a maintenance man. It's bloody Boxing Day for heaven's sake, I should be looking forward to cold turkey sandwiches and "Great Escape" on the telly.' He sat forward and rubbed some more blocker into his face, took a deep swig at his water bottle, before lying back with a sigh on to his lounger.

Ellise was beside him on the small forward deck. She hardly stirred. 'God, you're like some annoying insect, shut up or I'll swat you. Here we are, in one of the most tranquil and beautiful parts of the world, and better still, both being paid to lie here and sunbathe. So do try to show a little more gratitude.'

Paul wasn't normally prone to grumbling aloud, but this time he felt he had perfect justification. A series of six-week missions they'd said, based on the Galápagos they'd said, it had sounded like a series of exotic paid holidays. Most of these days had proven to be so long with absolutely nothing at all for him to do. He was a pretty good all-rounder, able to tackle anything he set himself, but he had never shown any capacity whatsoever for this sort of enforced relaxation.

He had been lecturing part-time at Florida State University's Department of Oceanography when this offer had come up. It all happened in something of a hurry, and a little too late in the process he realised that he must have been a last resort to complete the team. Now he realised that he had been stupid to jump at it.

He was desperate to make any sort of progress with his work, he just had to get some recognition, and soon. Lack of any published research meant he had dropped into an existence where he had to seek out work and that was never easy. In his world they seemed to believe in the old adage that 'if you want something done, ask a busy man', and here he was, once again, not at all busy.

Mark, who made up the third of their tanning team, mumbled, 'Thought that's what you oceanographers did, look at the sea?'

Paul sighed; he wasn't sure whether Mark was deliberately obtuse or whether what the Yanks said about Okies was true. 'No, it's the whole system! Not just the ocean, but its moods, its chemicals, the life it contains, the effects of the tidal flows, the shorelines, the seabed. Certainly not aimlessly looking out across the swell like on some pleasure cruise around the bay.'

To add to his professional frustration they were floating directly above the point that forged two active tectonic plates, the Cocos and the Nazca, two of those plates that steadily shape and define the living planet, shuffling continents and oceans around the Earth's surface, painfully slowly yet completely relentlessly. Their progress went virtually unnoticed within any human appreciation of a timeframe, and yet their impact was significant.

The Cocos and Nazca are both spawned from within deep mid-ocean ridges running well over a thousand miles along that imaginary line invented by humankind, the equator. The Nazca plate plies its way south and east, until it disappears into the Peru-Chile Trench. It might disappear, but it is far from forgotten because the reaction caused by its being crushed downwards builds up enormous pressure that just cannot be contained. Its release causes eruptions that form part of the 'Ring of Fire', a long line of active volcanoes that runs the length of the South American continent.

Paul groaned as he thought about these features. 'Just imagine, studying the rock out in the centre of the abyssal plains that stretch away from this ridge. It was spewed out about the time the dinosaurs were starting to take over, and, unlike those big lizards, it's still going strong. Here we are bobbing along like some gin palace, a bunch of bloody weekend sailors applying factor 35 to our noses!'

Ellise threw a cushion at him, 'Look, don't make me get up from here to come and swat you.' He knew that Ellise was certainly fit enough and strong enough to do just that. Paul realised that he was intrigued, interested, but hadn't she shown rather too much interest in bloody Carter?

The really annoying thing about what he had just been describing beneath them was that of course absolutely none of it was visible. They could be on any ocean anywhere in the world. He peered over the side, trying to look down deep but with no hope of seeing at all far down the umbilical that connected them with the submersible, with Hal – and of course Mr-Bloody Wonderful, Tom.

Deep down in the submersible Tom was peering into the gloom via a video screen; he noticed something suddenly come into view as it entered the range of their intense lights. He recognised immediately that the lights had picked out the peaks of the mid-ocean ridge itself, a huge rent in the crust of the earth that stretched away either side of them, the same chasm that had spawned the volcanoes that had created the Galápagos Islands.

This sort of feature was relatively new to mankind. It had originally been seen not too far from their current location and only as recently as 1979. Tom had written an article saying that it was remarkable that so much of the current received wisdom of the way the planet Earth itself 'operates', had in fact only been defined and discerned in the few decades since then.

This was the real joy of oceanography. He believed that it was still very much in its infancy. Now the world was post-cold war the massive investments into arms and space had slowed; increasingly there appeared to be more ready-funds for exploring the depths.

This was his very first direct look at a mid-ocean ridge and there it was, right up close and personal. He found he was dissatisfied with the quality of the video image; if he'd wanted to watch it on television he could have done that from the surface or from someone else's video. When he turned to peer out through the 18cm thick glass window he realised just how good the camera technology must be, as the direct view was much cloudier and indistinct than on the screen.

Hal steered them along parallel to the line of the ridge and in the light of their lamps pointed to an outflowing straight ahead, a series of dark cloudy flumes that issued from a series of 20m to 30m high funnels along the ridge. 'Look, directly ahead, your first black smoker.' This was a very hot hydrothermal vent that they had to avoid passing through at all costs.

Tom was honing his thoughts into developing some imagery he might use in one of his books or regular TV appearances. His first instinct was that the mid-ocean ridge put him in mind of looking down on to a northern industrial town from a nearby fell, then realised that he had mentally added a sound track to the image, the sound of a choir singing of William Blake's 'Dark satanic mills' spoiling 'England's pastures green'.

He opened his mental notebook as he picked out features and had already started the process he privately called his 'word-smithing'. This was a particularly appropriate term for here, because it felt just like the Earth's foundry, some medieval blacksmith's barn. He was still seeking the apposite description to capture a reader and to impart the sensation of this place.

The obvious term was the demonic landscape summed up in Blake's 'mills', but Tom never liked to use anything too obvious. He had spent several hours looking out at featureless views punctuated only by the gently falling 'snow' of dead matter; suddenly here was life, movement, purpose, colour. Very deep blues and blacks, highlighted by yellows and ochres, while all the time there was this constant flow of black 'smoke' belching out of the funnels from some infernal underground. His description needed to capture all this feverish activity and somehow that ever-present feeling, within this tiny craft, of being weighed down by the mass of water above them, but most particularly the visceral pressure he felt pressing in from all sides.

Hal manoeuvred as close as he dared and explained, 'I must make sure we keep well clear of those flumes. The crew that first discovered them inserted a thermometer, shoved it directly into the flow, and it promptly melted. Must have been very sobering, because the thermometer had been built to withstand temperatures of up to around 300 degrees-C and the material of their craft was only rated for just a little more than that itself. It must have caused quite a panic.'

Tom agreed. 'Not really that surprising when you appreciate these vents are direct routes through from the crust; they reach down directly into the Earth's molten mantle. Just one kilometre further down and the temperatures would be well over 1,500 degrees-C, two kilometres deeper and it's as near as damn it 4,000 degrees-C.'

He explained, 'It's these ridges that help to control the Earth's temperature. They create the movement of continents. In effect they mould the very world in which we live. And, they've been doing it since the beginning of time. And just look at us, for all our pride in our discoveries we've only known about it for just a few decades!'

# Chapter 6 - *Pacific*

The Pacific Tsunami Warning System employs a whole series of deployed buoys that feed, via satellite, data on the seismological events they encounter. With some 75% of its warnings being false alarms, there was currently a huge sum in research bucks being applied in the chase for a better solution. But for now the buoys were the main data source and they used batteries, batteries that need to be replaced periodically, and this was one of the team's tasks.

Paul grumbled, 'A bloody monkey or better still a trained dolphin could do the job!'

Ellise propped her head on her arm and smiled at him, 'OK, so we've all got the message. You want rough seas and poor weather. They'll be right along soon enough, but for now, learn to relax, chill out. This constant bickering is destroying you, not to mention what it's doing to me!'

Ellise watched him through scrunched up eyes. She thought Paul was quite good-looking, at least a six-footer, good body, great thighs. His dark hair was a bit of a downer though. It was undeniably receding a tad at the forehead and he wore it a little too long at the back for her taste.

Men who spent time worrying about their hair bothered her a lot, but at least he didn't have a pony-tail. Her brother had once told her that under both sorts of pony-tail you find a horse's ass, and she agreed. But then there were those striking blue eyes, she could almost forgive even a pony-tail for those.

Perhaps it was just that Paul was a bit obvious, a little too much of a letch. She had seen him looking at her, assessing, but never quite daring to make any approach. She realised that her way of relieving the boredom was this sort of sexual appraisal.

Paul started up again. 'But is this what my profession has come down to, eh? A series of drones and machines chuntering back data to a lab for you computer nerds to number crunch?'

'What do you want? Have some poor mother sit out here with a cellphone?'

Paul smiled at her response and used a heavy British accent. 'Heaven forbid, I wouldn't wish that on a dog. Just the few weeks I've spent here is quite long enough, ta very much.' Then in his normal voice, 'I picked oceanography during and after my stint in the navy as the only profession that might keep me away from the desk and securely in the field.'

Paul constinued, 'Surely all this technology should be just the tools of the trade? It's the insight and experience of the human being that will provide us with any sort of progress.'

Ellise smiled across at him. 'Nah, if the batteries fail, what sort of insight can even a genius like you offer?'

Paul chose to ignore this, glancing at his watch, 'Hal should be ready to start up again.' This meant the end of the blissful twenty or thirty minutes of peace while the winch had been still. The next two hours would grind away as they reeled them back in.

'Hal, how's it going down there at your end of the yo-yo? Over.' Paul slipped into a seat beside Mark at a long bench in the control room of their vessel.

It was Tom who answered, 'We very much appreciated the side trip to the trench, but I still don't really understand why we can't just haul the buoys up to our ship rather than us dragging all the way down here? Over.'

'Because the equipment is oh so sensitive,' Mark smiled, 'and you, you're, well, just so not, Tom. Have you finished?'

Ellise had followed Paul to the control room and watched Mark in action.

Hearing Tom on the radio, she once again muddled over what it was that caused Tom's reaction on the beach? He wouldn't talk about it and it was as if what had happened on the island between them was already some sort of dream. Perhaps he woke up and thought it more a nightmare?

She had undeniably made all the running. Maybe her best friend was right and she did have streaks of scarlet woman in her? Hadn't it caused her enough trouble? When would she grow up? No man is going to refuse sex when it's offered on a plate, especially from someone as hot as this momma, she smiled.

But that look! She couldn't erase it from her memory. She'd heard and read the expression a 'look of horror' but now she'd actually seen one. It was just so extreme. No one could have that reaction to sex, or to her, surely? Perhaps it was best to leave him behind his façade? Perhaps there was madness lurking in there somewhere? His loss!

Tom's voice came over the loudspeaker, 'Yes, haul away and we'll twiddle our thumbs until we see you. And, don't forget skin cancer while you lounge around up there. Over and out.'

Paul started the winch and then decided to check his monitors before returning to the lounger. Coincidentally he was looking directly at the screen just as the alarms sounded. Their insistent tones brought Ellise to his side. There had evidently been a seabed earthquake and this was what the alarms were for, but Paul's thoughts were immediately moving beyond the quake to wonder whether there was the potential for a tsunami.

When movement occurs along the abrasive contact of two sub-ocean tectonic plates this does not always result in a tsunami, but this was the focus of Paul's current research, so his first instinct was to look for one.

Tsunamis move across the surface of the sea twenty times more slowly than the vibration travels through the solid rock at the seabed. Fortunately this time-lag does create the opportunity to provide a warning to any coastal communities in their way, and this had been Paul's current centre of attention.

He sought to do more than just define when any such coastal impacts might be expected. Yes, knowing when they would hit was important, but forecasting the likely height and ferocity, both initially and for any follow-up waves, was much more important so that the warnings could be appropriate. It was this quantification that currently proved elusive.

All three of them were now feverishly looking at their individual screens, running various models and predictive routines to define the location and the likely outcome of this seismic event. Paul had been working single-mindedly for almost a year on this particular issue of prediction and he had all his latest notions, original, borrowed and plagiarised, buried deep into one piece of early prototype software. This finally was his chance to test his theories, perhaps now he could see his breakthrough become a prospect for publication.

Paul had been originally 'attracted' to the subject when he had read the details of a 7.1 magnitude earthquake that had killed over 2,000 on Papua New Guinea. The original quake had shaken some thirty kilometres of coastline along a peaceful spit of sand, home to a series of doomed small villages.

More significantly it had also deformed the sea bottom beyond their lagoon twenty kilometres out into the ocean. The normally flat sea surface there had suddenly been thrust upwards perhaps thirty metres, creating a noise that sounded like thunder. Along the coast the tide was seen to recede well below the normal low-water marks, uncovering large areas of foreshore as all the surrounding waters were rapidly sucked in to replace the void that had been created beneath the displaced water.

Survivors had said that there was then a four to five minute silence; perhaps modified by some strong hindsight they commented that it was a particularly threatening and unnatural hush. This was suddenly broken by a sound like a low-flying jet aircraft. The disturbed water had collapsed and pressed the tide back to the shore.

The first wave was only three metres high but the force of it was strong enough to carry many of the villagers, tossing them around for a full kilometre, back deep into the mangrove swamps behind their villages. Many were lost there, impaled on broken mangrove branches, the dead and the injured falling easy prey to the surviving saltwater crocodiles and wild dogs.

This was nothing compared to the fifteen-metre high waves that followed to flatten the villages. The area today is just a barren sandbar; no-one is interested in rebuilding the life that had been there.

This was just one example of the power of tsunami waves and had been just a relatively local affair, considering that the reach of a tsunami can be truly awesome. Over the past century around 500 tsunamis had claimed more than 50,000 lives but during the previous decade more than eighty tsunamis had been reported, a significant increase, the record books had previously shown just fifty per decade.

It was difficult to establish if this was because of better communications and record-keeping or whether it was a disturbing new trend. Paul was attracted to the topic; perhaps he was literally catching an early wave.

However the Sumatra-Andaman earthquake and tsunami struck on Boxing Day 2004without warning; the sector might be vogue but no tsunami warning systems had been deployed in the Indian Ocean.

The Indian and Burman plates had clashed along 1,600 miles for almost ten minutes. It was the third largest earthquake ever measured. It made the whole planet move one centimetre and set off further earthquakes, one as far distant as Alaska.

Satellites did record the Indian Ocean rising by 60 centimetres but these were not connected to any warning software, the data was only seen many hours later. The resulting tsunamis threw up thirty metre waves that killed over 230,000 in fourteen different countries.

Paul knew that the knowledge base was so short-term within geological timeframes and hoped that he would be coming up to publishing his ideas just as tsunamis were growing in frequency. This would help to make his proposed book sell, perhaps now he might get on to the TV circuit too?

Ellise and Paul had both independently used their equipment to establish in seconds the location, the strength and the depth of the earthquake – the features that made up what was termed the 'generation phase'.

Having the basic data of the generation phase was important and it was vital to know these facts. They were just three of at least ten factors that were required if some basis was to be established for guessing the height and ferocity of any resulting tsunami waves. That was currently what it amounted to – a guess – and a guess that might underestimate the likely effect by a magnitude of as much as five to ten times.

Mark interrupted him, 'Should we advise the submersible team what's happening?'

'They'll be fine, I'm trying to establish which coastlines are at risk.' His fingers chased across the keyboard and his monitor was a mass of open dialogue boxes which he shunted around the large screen so they could be watched simultaneously.

*Tsu-nami* is a Japanese word meaning 'harbour-wave' as the effect of these waves is not really felt out at sea. They don't run deep but instead spread their energy across wide areas. It is only if and when they reach stretches of shallow water, particularly harbours, that they can wreak their havoc.

The waves are slowed up as they encounter the shallow waters so that the following waves catch up and combine to increase the height and volume. They can then either run ashore like a tide-like flood or through refraction and shoaling become funnelled into a very high and dangerous wall of water. Neither is particularly pleasant.

Tsunamis have been formed by meteor impact and by volcanic eruptions, but most often they are created by undersea earthquakes. The earthquake deforms the sea bottom and pushes up a water column above it to create distinctive waves. But these earthquakes vary in both speed and effect. The variation is created by the erratic impacts between the Earth's tectonic plates, plates just like the Cocos and Nazca deep beneath their current location.

None of these plates is uniform in shape or in its basic material, so when they clash they jerk and stagger rather than have one simple impact. These impossible to forecast staggers and variations are categorised by oceanographers as either slow or rapid. Recent research has established that perversely it is the slow variety that causes the worst tsunamis.

With these the sea-floor deforms relatively slowly so it does not score highly as an earthquake, but its effects in terms of the tsunami it creates can be much more devastating than more highly Richter-rated events.

Though lagging behind the earthquake they were plotting, these waves would move across the surface of the sea at speeds faster than a modern aircraft, so time was very much of the essence for those in the vicinity. On board they could expect to have absolutes on only a few of the ten factors. Their first conclusion, from the seismic data they had established, was that the closest landfall had probably already been hit. But they might still be in time to warn other shorelines further afield.

Paul's screen showed a cascade of data as the software was streaming information it received about the event.

Ellise snapped, 'We have to alert someone.'

Paul agreed, 'The blokes in Seattle will have a procedure, but it won't do any harm for us to call it in too.'

Ellise commented, 'I'll dig out the contact data we have for the islands and countries located around us.' Mark was already making the necessary connections.

Ellise was surprised as she noticed that Mark dropped the Okie charade as he worked with what was virtually a complete television studio of equipment that could be used to broadcast to almost any point of the globe.

Mark jacked in to Inmarsat to provide him with an uplink, a live feed of a video image of the three of them working at their stations. On audio he had first called their base and advised that they should expect to see their material being streamed via this route and he also activated the microphones at their workstations to a separate uplink. Ellise had no time to wonder about this sudden burst of skill.

Their base had alerted a news channel in Australia and they were therefore the first with the report the impending disaster. It would take many days before the impact and extent of the event was fully realised and for the World's press to get there to show the pictures, seek out the human stories and glean the images captured on personal cameras and phones.

Until this could all unfold, the only game in town was the feed that Mark had established. More channels were switching in. Using their studio equipment and the onshore team, the three were being asked for more and more individual interviews. Paul rose to the occasion and was waxing lyrical to anyone who cared to patch in to their feed. He had already perhaps achieved his sought-after moment in the limelight by virtue of Mark's quick and deft use of their on-board kit but then something happened to make his brief fame assured.

He was in the midst of tailoring some comments for a Hong Kong based channel, having to listen carefully for the heavily-accented interviewer's questions, when his screen began to report new data and just as quickly the sea around them started to become violent – all hell broke loose.

The turbulence dragged them off station, alarms sounded and the horizon visible in the video shot was all over the place. As all was captured in close-up on screen, Paul looked in charge and unflustered throughout this turmoil. In truth he was struggling to interpret both the interviewer and the data on his screen simultaneously. It was an illusion that he was calm and in control. To the eventual millions who saw these images, he looked a hero.

While Mark worked the studio equipment, Paul sat with his attention-grabbing look of sangfroid.

It was left to Ellise to ponder the fate of the submersible. They did not want to jerk it across the seabed so she decided to sever contact. Her first instinct, as the budget-holder for the project, was to reel in the cable which was now running free without the weight of the submersible at its end.

'Uh, uh cable's down.' Hal was instantly all business.

Tom was confused, 'What's happening up there? Is this Paul's idea of some kind of joke? Perhaps it's a drill of some sort?'

Hal shook his head pointing out a warning light on his panel, 'No drill, no idea what it might be, but we're not able to talk to them up there, all cable functions are down. Now I really get to earn my money.

'Relax, we have an eight-hour reserve in stand-alone mode, plenty of time to reach the surface. Now excuse me while I become the pilot I was born to be, not some sort of highly-paid crane driver!'

He took a more proactive stance with the controls, moving away quickly from where the tumbling umbilical could descend and potentially ensnare them.

# Chapter 7 - *Moscow*

Kabitsin wanted to use his new weapon, let loose its havoc, demonstrate his new power. Alone in his study he was concluding on the most suitable and worthy target.

The early years of the third millennium had proven very kind to Kazakhstan. It had one of the fastest growing economies in the world, it accounted for a sizeable majority of the GDP of the central Asian region. And it was only going to get better. Its resources, such as the massive oilfields in Tengiz, Karachaganak, and Kashagan, held impressive reserves well beyond their current highly profitable production levels.

Although its President looked and acted like one of the old-time Soviet dictators, Kabitsin had looked on with disgust as he ignored his old friends, seeking out instead new connections with the EU countries, despite their geographical remoteness.

Of course these greedy western European states chose to brush aside the President's extreme actions, anything in order to get their hands on his resources. Didn't they always? The past list was endless, where the West initially supported a dictator in order to allow themselves to rape and pillage resources, until much later when that dictator became too carried away by his power and powerful friends. Didn't they always?

These were resources that Kazakhstan had gained merely by happenstance, by the accident of geography, resources that rightfully of course belonged to Russians who had found and exploited them, financed and built the rigs, the refineries, the pipelines.

Kazakhstan, so far as Kabitsin was concerned, had been given untold advantages by Russia. It had gained employment and revenues from the many nuclear, military and space research stations that the USSR had set up there too.

He dismissed as Western propaganda the claims that back in the 1940s Beria had lied when he declared that the Semipalatinsk region was uninhabited or that many had been irradiated by the USSR's early nuclear tests.

Hadn't Kazakhstan one of the worst records for waste of its natural and mineral resources? Who's to say that they did not cause the problems in Semipalatinsk themselves? Always easier for them to blame the old Soviet system, something the West had a vested interest in demonising too.

When it came to water Kabitsin knew that Kazakhstan was a mess. Didn't the whole world know about the Aral Sea disaster? The sea had been reduced to a saline shadow of its former self through Kazakhstan's redirection of the Amu Darya and Syr Darya Rivers for its own industrial use. Once it had been the world's fourth largest lake but now some eighty per cent of its volume had been lost and the quality of what was left was dire.

It had taken no time for Kabitsin to research the water position further and to learn that more than fifty per cent of Kazakhstan's water supply was not local but instead came courtesy of its neighbours, Kyrgyzstan, Uzbekistan, China and Russia.

It was time to teach them a lesson, for them to learn that they deserted their erstwhile friends and mentors at their peril.

For his demonstration of the real potential of his special water he had selected one of the world's largest lakes, Ozero Balkhash. It was all so elegant. The lake had all sorts of useful qualities, half fresh water, half salt water, and this would become his own very special approach to provide invaluable field research.

At the same time it would clearly be a righteous act of retribution and teach those central Asian black-arses that their deceit and lack of loyalty had consequences.

**Mid-Pacific**

Ellise slowed the winch that was now running wildly without any tension against it. She just had to hope that this turbulence was at the surface. She hoped it treated them kindly, she assumed that the submersible team was able to handle its own end; Hal was a good guy.

The crew had already started the engines and were turning the craft to face this unexpected swell. Ellise crossed to stand behind Paul and rested her arm on his shoulder. He ignored her but realised that it felt good, comfortable somehow, full of promise, but he tried to dismiss that feeling and concentrated on his computer model.

The first event was almost forgotten as he sought to establish what had happened locally and of course here he had all sorts of data being fed from buoys and satellites to satisfy his computer model. It was a separate event, perhaps some sort of secondary? Was it some sort of response to the bigger event? Masses of data were being received so the output was currently rather slow and ponderous.

It was a smaller event and therefore had to be very close to their position for them to have been hit by the waves at almost the moment the alarms had sounded. His immediate conclusion was that it must have been a slow earthquake, the very sort that would herald a tsunami.

He had designed his program to establish just how big and just what risk there was to the nearby islands. But was it ready? Was he ready? He felt the tension of the moment but shrugged it off, concentrating on the facts he had.

Paul's 'dull tool' was delivering its initial forecast and concluding that this could be a serious threat to Vanuatu and, if his predictions were correct, it was right at the top of his scale of devastation.

He turned full face to the cameras and explained, 'My projections show the first landfall will be Port Vila on Vanuatu. The first big waves will reach it by

13:50.' He looked back at his screen, 'I'm still trying to gauge this properly but the waves should arrive at Suva on Fiji by 15:22. Some of the power will have started to dissipate by then. It will reach Funafuti on Tuvalu by around 15:37, will get as far as Honiara on the Solomon Islands by 15:44.'

He smiled directly into the camera again, 'You should be able to see some sort of impact on the swell in Jackson Bay in New Zealand by about 7pm tonight, and in Honolulu, Hawaii around 9pm.' Boy was he enjoying all of this, 'By tomorrow morning any late-night revellers fancying a skinny-dip at 2am while on their way home from that party or a club in La Jolla, Southern California could also notice something of a swell.'

Was his projection correct? After all these days of inactivity Paul now found it difficult to get his mind in gear, particularly with the warmth and promise of Ellise stood right behind him. He didn't want to make any mistakes so he rechecked the model, instinctively not doubting his own work, but it was best to be sure.

Computers were of course only as good as the data you fed them – GIGO, garbage in, garbage out. His mind was now fully up to speed and he was confident he had not put garbage in. This was good work he'd done and the conclusions were therefore sound.

He turned, a little disconcerted by how close her face was to his. 'I hope Vanuatu is all set to meet this bad ride.'

She removed her arm and he found he was missing it already. 'You are sure about this?'

He snapped, 'Of course I'm sure.' It was fine for him to doubt himself but his pride would not allow someone else to challenge his findings. 'It should be the maximum alert. This will be a big one.'


Hal allowed the submersible to go into free-fall, to be sure that they were clear of the cable. They were currently some 2,750 metres below sea level.

Tom felt the depth was something tangible, always there looking for any sign of weakness that it might exploit. Of course the submersible kept the environment acceptable but he could sense the tremendous weight of water, already several hundred atmospheres, all seemingly with one simple desire; to crush this tiny, fragile craft.

Tom knew that the titanium hull on this craft should be reliable and his trepidation was more created by the cold from outside that seemed to reach inward. He felt as if it was bypassing the life support systems, chilling his mind while perversely raising the temperature of his body.

Commercial fishing had already depleted everything from sharks to sea cucumbers in this area but right now Tom found neither of these losses terribly distressing, sat here virtually on the bottom in this oh-so flimsy submersible. By now he assumed they were quite deep enough not to worry about any known predator of the sea but still the unknown kept him on edge. Now more than three kilometres down from the smooth surface that had been provoking Paul's frustration, that very same surface was now for Tom a dream location, a treasured goal: would they reach its safety again?

He was snapped out of his thoughts as he realised that Hal was now using the controls and their descent had been gradually halted. None too soon, as he realised they were approaching the seabed.

'Why have you gone so low?'

'I wanted us to be just a few hundred feet off the bottom,' Hal laughed, 'and first you need to know precisely where that is!'

Hal had in mind a course that would take a steep climbing curve away from the ridge and any chance that they might become entangled with the cable for he had no means of assessing where it might be, whether it was snaking its way down from above or being reeled in by the vessel.

He switched the screen to look forward where it showed the sea bottom stretching out away from the ridge. Just as Hal was applying power Tom noticed a sudden cloud rushing toward them. The sea floor seemed to shudder and the submersible instantly became a spinning nightmare. No seat restraints were supplied with a craft that normally only ever alternated between a sedate lowering or raising. These two prime manoeuvres were only ever planned to be relieved by a gentle rotation when using its arms to perform very deliberate, accurate, never hurried tasks.

The craft did have a 'dead-man's handle' and so shut down its drive as soon as Hal's hands left the controls. The first five or six rotations of the craft tossed both occupants around so violently they lost all sense of which way was up. Tom instinctively tucked his body into a tight ball and realised much later that it was he who had probably broken Hal's flailing left arm as they collided several times during the mêlée.

After the first series of violent spins Tom found he could gain some degree of control, slowly able to predict and therefore ride with the rotation, and he started to match his movements to meet those of the careening craft. As he became better at predicting the rotation he carefully managed to crab himself into more of a slinging action across the axis of the spin until he was able to grab for the chair. The momentum was still strong so his hands soon lost their grip but he managed to hook his legs over the chair and anchor himself in this way around the back of it.

He gradually edged himself around the seat and towards the panel but, still out of control, Hal cannoned off him grunting in pain. They both crashed into the instruments and this plunged the craft instantly into darkness.

Tom threw out both arms in a desperate grab for Hal and that seemingly malevolent aspect of fate ensured that his first attempt connected with Hal's broken arm.

The excruciating pain from Hal's upper arm fracture combined with the terrifying and absolute black enveloping them. Hal heard an explosive primal scream ring out and only vaguely realised that it was he who was making the noise. To him it was as if a switch had been thrown that flipped between his conscious and his subconscious. Surely it was his conscious mind that was feeling the pain, the tumbling, and the impacts, so who was issuing that scream and the sobbing that followed?

Hal felt time slow perceptibly, so it seemed endless inside this human tumble dryer. With no vision at all there was no opportunity to prepare for the impacts. A part of his mind could sense two distinct and invisible forces, one drawing him ever onward and another spinning him around as he progressed to that unknown destination.

He struggled as a new horror came out of the dark. As he felt that talons were raking his body he struck out at them with his good arm, missing, and rapping his wrist painfully on some unseen obstacle.

The invisible claws struck home again and this time managed to get a purchase that rapidly turned into a bear hug from behind as Tom sought to get him under control. Hal himself had by now lost all restraint and struggled violently to get free. Tom appeared to be making some progress until suddenly it felt as though an express train came silently up and hit all of the life out of him. He became part of the all-encompassing black and slowly slipped down into unconsciousness.

Hal was shielded from most of the impact by Tom's body and somewhere outside his panic his deeply trained instincts identified both the impact and the ensuing noise as a grounding. After the recent frantic movements some order descended as the craft crashed into the seabed and scrubbed off all of its rotation. With Tom unconscious there was now absolute silence and Hal strained through the dense darkness to hear the moment when the hull would collapse, as surely it must. He waited for the instant that it would take for the outside pressure to stamp out his life.

He strained his eyes to make out anything in the funereal cabin but there was no light at all. It was as though he'd joined those life forms that eked out a chemical existence at the vent. No light, no sound just an all enveloping pressure and heat. But they had air in this vehicle's body. What had Tom said? If those things at the vent had air in their bodies they would be crushed by the pressure?

His ears were at full strain and he could hear no noise at all. Instantly he realised the craft could not be circulating any air, the rhythmic pump noise had stopped. It was becoming very hot and clammy.

Then he heard it. The sound he had been expecting. His straining ears were assaulted by a sort of shuffling noise. He envisaged the gradual peeling away, a crumpling of the hull around him but this was nothing compared with the pressure clutching at his chest.

Up at the surface the video feed was switched off. Paul had run his calculations three times now and having successfully convinced Ellise to give the highest warning condition to the affected areas, he sat back watching her, trying not to be impressed with the smooth manner in which the procedures had been set up and were being followed. Not to mention the smooth line of her thigh that protruded from her wrap.

'You realise your butt is really on the line here?' Ellise turned to him and caught him looking at her legs; she smiled. Strangely embarrassed by this, he turned back to his screen. She added, 'Ashore all hell is breaking loose. Shoreline evacuations, other emergency procedures, they are all springing into action. Perhaps you should be rechecking your model again?'

Again his pride kicked in, 'No need, it's a big one and we're doing the right thing.'

'Nevertheless, humour me, run it again and again. Keep running it until the wave hits, then measure that, then run it once more just to be sure. I'm not getting any confirmatory data from anywhere else as yet.'

Paul humphed but interrogated his model to look at the base data and the assumptions. It was a slow event. It had all the features that he had assumed added up to a tsunami and he could see no error in the conclusions reached by the model. But as he ran his models once more he spotted something of an anomaly, there appeared to have been a third event, surely just an echo? He tried to isolate the three events but found their effects difficult to separate within his software.

Just then the vessel appeared to settle down, the turbulence had fully subsided. Paul sought to reassure himself by running the analysis one more time. It was preternaturally quiet: the only noise was the tapping of keys on his terminal.

Paul realised that the software had been somewhat addled by the proximity of three apparent events but he felt sure that while the timings might change a little from his earlier forecast he was now even more certain of his conclusions. He just could not consciously accept that his forecast might well have been wrong, but a deep-rooted sense of self-preservation had him already trying to marshal the data to defend his original expectations.

Mark watched them both. Clearly Paul was disturbed. He was becoming verbally more confident of his forecasts while his body language shouted his uncertainties. While Ellise was challenging him in the privacy of the boat, she was already preparing to defend him and her team against the outside world.

# Chapter 8 - *Pacific*

Tom woke. His first thought was that he hurt everywhere. Although he already believed he must be at maximum pain, when he tried to move he found it flared to even greater heights in so many places. Breathing too was difficult, the air turgid. It felt there was nothing that his lungs could use from what little air he was raspingly taking in.

Finally becoming aware of the absolute darkness, panic overwhelmed the pain and screamed at him to run but something very heavy was pinning down both of his legs to make that completely impractical. He tried to ignore the pain that flared as he reached out towards whatever it was. The lack of air was not helping, he felt dizzy and disoriented, and was lying at a strange angle, but of most concern was that numbness in his legs and lower body.

He touched something, cold and clammy, and closed his fingers around a hand. His mind exploded, part of it wanting to let the hateful object go and the other throwing all of his final reserves into grasping it, as if life itself depended on his grip.

His mind had no idea whose life was hanging in the balance but his body struggling for air, for anything vaguely reassuring, eventually made it clear that it was his own. He tugged at the hand, the effort being mostly in mental energy and not physical. This was not muscle memory. It was instead a strong buried mental memory from years before. The memory also carried with it an overwhelming feeling of defeat.

**Home Counties, England**

It had been the first truly spring day after what had seemed like a very, very long winter. The sort of day when everyone felt uplifted, suddenly alive for the first time in months. It was great to have weathered the winter, to have borne its cold short days and now to get back to some real sense of living.

He and his brother found this sudden feeling of unfettered physical and mental freshness was positively euphoric. Not a single cloud in the sky. Just enough wind for them to have their first outing of the year. Excited to be outside again, without the need for heavy clothing. Breathing the crisp fresh air they went through their practised rituals of preparation.

They paddled away from the lee of the boat-house until they could catch the wisps of wind which seemed to be all that would be available to them on that day. He noticed the way in which the water on the lake seemed so languid. As he looked back across the lake the surface was perfectly still, despite the wind. Even the ripples raised by their dinghy appeared to subside rapidly in their wake. It was as if the lake was filled with some sort of viscous oil.

Coming from a long line of yachtsmen, the young twins had been sailing from the age of five and the lake was one that they knew intimately well. It was in fact their grandfather who had landscaped the grounds, diverting a river that crossed the estate to create a large ornamental lake that commanded the view from any part of the front of their large house.

So soon after winter the lake was perhaps just a little higher than normal, but as they glided through the water lilies and weeds that abounded at the farthest side from the house, they were revelling in the exhilaration that came from their unconscious yet skilled handling.

Identical twins, they appeared to others to have an instinctive understanding, some thought almost telepathic, an assumption they chose to do nothing to contradict. But he knew that, at least where sailing was concerned, it was more about the fact that they had worked hard at their technique and spent years on the water learning through trial and many errors. Summers passed on this lake and elsewhere had honed their skills. Skills that were being challenged by these very light wind conditions; trying to make the most of these available, pretty meagre, breezes was thoroughly engaging them.

The lake was quite shallow, and as they were both good sailors, equally good swimmers, they had chosen not to wear preservers.

It just happened as they broke free of the weed into an area of crystal clear water. Suddenly it was as though a switch had been flicked so that everything occurred in slow motion, just as it would be in the 'replays' he would experience down the years.

He glimpsed their mother waving to them from the house, but he knew they had to effect their turn and so he concentrated on making the manoeuvre. As he completed the move his first instinct was to laugh aloud as he saw William, intent on waving back to her, being swept overboard by the boom. But something suppressed his laughter. It was the way in which William appeared to be swallowed up all too readily by the water.

A few slow frames further and he realised that William was struggling hard to keep on the surface. It looked so odd; the day was so beautiful, the lake's surface so still, William such a strong swimmer. What could possibly be causing his distress? However it was evident that William was indeed in trouble. Had he been stunned? No, he appeared to be swimming perfectly normally, yet making no progress at all.

These rapid impressions cascaded through his mind as if it was working on another timeframe. Yet his body operated in what felt like ponderous slow motion. He turned again to manoeuvre back towards William to help him.

As he drew level he could finally appreciate the reason William was not calling out. He was in a virtual whirlpool, pulling him towards the sluice. Of course, he thought, father must have opened it to drain the surplus water from the lake. He could see that there was a gap in the sluice of about fifteen centimetres right down at its base, probably at a depth of a metre or so. It was the current of the water exiting here that had William firmly caught in its pull.

His mind, still racing, recognised that the water was simply seeking out its own level beyond the sluice and he physically shook his head to control his thinking. He shouted inwardly, 'Stop spectating and do something!'

In the background he was aware of his mother and father calling from the opposite side of the lake but he concentrated on William who was beginning to lose his battle against the force of the sluice.

He reached over the side and stretched for his brother's hand. Something in the quality of the lake water had a distinct sliminess about it. It made the water feel more than a liquid and it took several attempts to achieve a reasonable grip which they needed to keep adjusting.

Now that he had a firm hold he assumed it would be a simple matter of heaving his brother aboard. He pulled hard but that was when he realised the force that William had been fighting was too strong for him too. He anchored his knees against the side of the dinghy to seek more leverage but still could not overcome the incessant, invisible pull of the sluice.

He realised instinctively that his brother was too big to pass through the gap so if he lost his grip he would be sucked against the gate's boards where he would surely drown.

By clinging on to him William had now lost what had been his most potent resource, his flailing arms. His legs were down deep within the focus of the whirlpool and now he had insufficient strength with these alone to make any impact upon the pull. He slowly, inexorably, subsided beneath the surface. On the boat the panic of what was happening to his twin lent his brother additional strength as he continued to pull.

The effort was by now really hurting and he had been screwing up his eyes to assist with the single-mindedness of his purpose. When he finally opened them and looked down it was as if he was looking directly into a mirror. There was the still, smooth surface of the water with William as a virtual reflection of himself, arms stretched in front of him inside the glass, pulling with the same force that he could feel. It seemed interminable until he slowly became aware that someone, his father he assumed, was splashing across the lake towards them.

He just could not tear his mind away from the tableau, nor could he shake off the feeling that he was looking into a cold blue mirror. They were two ten-year-olds at the limit of their strengths. He knew his father was coming so he locked on to the side of the boat, arms at full stretch against the pull of the water which was ever so slowly winning.

He was looking straight into his brother's eyes and saw the precise moment when he gave up the fight. All expression and character simply left them. They did not close or flicker, they just stared straight ahead right through him, apparently perfectly calm and relaxed. The grip however continued for appreciable moments before relaxing too, as the glue of their two-way pull came apart.

The mirror disappeared as his lifeless brother was swept rapidly down to the gap in the sluice gate while he continued to stretch out in a forlorn effort to rejoin hands. Through the water he felt the thud as his twin crashed sideways across the gap, his arms splayed out either side. William was firmly lodged against the boards facing in to them. Through the gap the force pulled at the main part of his body, but his legs and arms halted his progress through the sluice.

He knew there was nothing he could do to help and slumped back exhausted into the boat hoping that this nightmare would end. But it never did.

**Pacific seabed**

Perversely it was this horrendous event from his childhood, its re-living of that sensation of impending defeat that now galvanised him. He was not going to fail, not again.

Everything shifted in his mind as he was jolted back to the present, realising it must be Hal who lay across him, Hal's hand that he was gripping.

Finally, reluctantly, he felt able to release Hal's hand and move his legs slowly, alternately pulling and relaxing until he had developed a rhythm. Eventually he was able to roll Hal off him in fact relatively easily, though even this rather limited effort had left him gasping for air.

He crawled over to Hal finding every breath increasingly difficult, each was unpleasant, unsatisfying. He felt for Hal's neck, failing to detect a pulse, but when he held his ear down to Hal's mouth he believed he detected some shallow breathing. He carefully tried to shake him awake but gave up when he accepted this was having no effect.

Fumbling around him he eventually found the pilot's chair. Though it was at an odd angle, he eased himself into it and tried to remember the various controls and switches he had watched Hal using. Pushing and prying all that he could find, he was rewarded with a red light on the panel and from this meagre source he found he was able to discern some outlines along the panel surface.

He recalled that the life support systems were at the top left hand edge of the panel. His left arm felt numb so he fumbled across his body with his right hand to reach that area. The movement made him begin to slip from his precarious perch and he almost passed out from the pain as he grabbed at the chair with his left hand. His instinct was to take deep breaths to control the pain but this only served to remind him that there was all too little air in the craft for him to take in.

So this was the right area of the panel, but suppose there was a button that would vent the air and worsen his position further? Surely there must be fail-safes to avoid that possibility? He knew nothing about the craft and cursed himself for his lack of curiosity. In almost every part of his life he had studied remorselessly, never comfortable until he thought he had the item or the process defined and bundled away in his memory. Here he had allowed someone else to take him to these dangerous depths and he'd come along as a blissfully ignorant passenger trusting in Hal's skills – and immortality!

There was still no sign of life from Hal, so it was up to him. Inaction was not an alternative. He tried out a few buttons and switches and on the third attempt heard a pump start up and the sound of air movement. He tried to assess which way it was pumping and gradually became aware that the air temperature was improving. A few more thumping heartbeats and it was clear that the air quality and volume were rising too.

Breathing deeply he tried still more switches and was rewarded with a light that instantly blinded him. His pupils had been so fully dilated trying to discern any details from that one meagre red warning light that this relatively low cabin light flooded his optic senses and etched an image on his retina that was intense, like a very vivid migraine.

Once he was able to see beyond the flare in the centre of his vision he assessed his own condition; nothing life threatening just darned painful. He then climbed carefully from the chair to examine Hal. He couldn't be sure with his impaired vision but there was a distinct ashen look to Hal's face and his lips were blue.

He recalled that the doctor had called this blueness cyanosis when his father had been struck down with a heart attack. But wasn't asphyxia also shown up by blueness? No that's the skin not the extremities Tom thought. By now his eyesight was improving appreciably and he reconfirmed that it was pale skin, blue lips.

He carefully arranged Hal into the recovery position, remembering his ABC observations from his navy days. Airway, well Hal was now in the recovery position and there was nothing blocking the airway and the air was back on. Breathing, it seemed that there was still some shallow breathing so he did not try mouth-to-mouth. He concluded this with relief as he thought it potentially embarrassing if Hal suddenly woke up and had only been knocked out!

With some difficulty, he recalled that C was for Circulation, but couldn't remember what that meant, particularly in this circumstance. He decided his best course of action was to get them both to the surface, if he could!

Tom looked around the instruments and established where the drive system was located. Logically it appeared to work in three dimensions labelled as X, Y and Z. He grabbed the yoke control and switched on.

There was a lurch as some automatic process appeared to right the craft and he found the chair move beneath him to the horizontal. Then came a distinct shuffling noise as the craft moved a little across the soft-packed sea-bed, the very same noise that had triggered off Hal's coronary as he imagined the hull had been collapsing.

He pushed the stick forward and there was a sense of something dragging across the underside of the craft which then seemed to come loose as it rose from the bottom. Once clear he tried a few gentle moves to the yoke in each direction to see what effect each movement had. The screen was useless as the craft's external lights showed only the mist of disturbed seabed matter, it provided no outside reference at all. He could only guess at what was happening by the pressure of the seat against his backside. He realised, with his first smile since the accident, that this must be the origin of 'flying by the seat of your pants'.

Just two or three attempts completed his picture of the control of the craft and he tried some more determined thrusts to be sure. With relief he began to climb up and out of the murk that clouded the screen and viewing port.

# BOOK TWO

**Sir Peter Blake KBE** (1948-2001) His last journal entry before he was shot dead by Amazon River pirates, known as the 'Water Rats' at Macapá, Amapá, Brazil:

*'The quality of water and the quality of life in all its infinite forms are critical parts of the overall, ongoing health of this planet of ours, not just here in the Amazon, but everywhere...'*

**Kofi Annan** while Secretary General of the United Nations

*'Fierce national competition over water resources has prompted fears that water issues contain the seeds of violent conflict.'*

*'As I travel around the world, people think the only place where there is potential conflict [over] water is the Middle East, but they are completely wrong. We have the problem all over the world.'*

**Queen Noor of Jordan**

*'War over water would be an ultimate obscenity. And yet, unfortunately it is conceivable... Water has been a source over so many years of erosion of confidence, of tension, of human rights abuses...'*

# Chapter 9 - *Moscow*

The lush north-east of Kazakhstan had prompted Khruschev to define it as 'virgin lands' and his officials had promptly formed massive state farms as part of their initiatives to increase the grain production for the Soviet Union.

In this initiative they had completely failed, but it was the resultant Russification of the north of that country that had made Kabitsin look further south for his 'lesson'. At one time almost a quarter of Russian ex-patriots were based in Kazakhstan and he did not want to be attacking his own kind.

His original target for the insertion of his special water had been Ozero Balkhash, a lake of around 20,000 square kilometres. This had attracted him as it would have an undeniable and major impact, but further research had left him concerned about containing the potential for damage.

Would it spread to Ozero Alakol and from there into China? An attack on them must wait, he planned for that to come much later.

Of course currently he had no real information as to what the characteristics of the new water might be, or whether there was any means to stop its spread or counter it. This was what the academicians were being charged to do with their samples, though he had retained the bulk of what they had taken from the Arctic within his control.

He had to call in favours from some of his more murky contacts to establish the whereabouts of three very secretive locations he knew he had to avoid – Stepnogorsk, Kurchatov and Baykonyr. He knew that these never appeared on Soviet maps but he was well connected enough to know they existed.

Stepnogorsk, the centre of uranium mining, he learned was in Akmolinsk Oblast and so was situated well north of where he was planning his demonstration.

Baykonyr, the main location for space exploration, he discovered was in Kyzylorda Oblast to the west and up near the Aral Sea. He'd already dismissed the Aral Sea as unsuitable, as it had already been so badly destroyed that no one was likely to notice if he used it for his 'example'. He needed somewhere containable and yet able to demonstrate the power of his new weapon.

While he was a little worried to learn that Kurchatov, the nuclear testing area, was close to his area of interest he judged it was far enough away from his chosen insertion point.

His attention became focused upon the lake, Ozero Zaysan. While the result would not be nearly as impressive, it did appear to be contained securely by the Altai Mountains. He saw that it was fed from China by the Irtysch River and then flowed northward past Semiplatinsk and from there on into Russia where it passed through Omsk and onwards to join the slow-moving Ob.

But the region local to the lake, known as Vostochnvy Kazakhstan Oblast, was relatively small in population at around 1.5 million so this was encouraging.

Surely if the river flowed through the old nuclear test area there was already enough damage done, his demonstration could not make it any worse?

What finally confirmed the choice for Kabitsin was his research uncovering the local legend of *Belovodye* or the 'White Waters'. High above his target lake in the Altai Mountains, one of the highest is Mount Belukha. It is located within a region of year-round snow so perhaps not very surprisingly had inspired a number of religious myths.

He read that the local Buddhists had a holy place there known as *Shambhala*, described as a natural source of radiance and brilliance in the world and a kingdom that was an enlightened society of fearlessness, dignity and compassion.

The legend of *Belovodye* appeared to Kabitsin to be rather similar, but in its case it was said to be some sort of perfect subterranean civilisation located deep below Mount Belukha. Apparently it was a place you could only find if you had enough faith and were sufficiently spiritually developed – what complete and utter bollocks he thought.

If there was anything Kabitsin disliked more than the black-arses, it was any form of religion. He despised it as being one of the key diseases that interfered with the rightful re-establishment of his Mother Russia.

So a chance to hit out at both the break-away republic and its religion was just unmissable. He chuckled to himself at the thought that these legendary White Waters were destined to meet a new reality and completely change their nature. He called Lev into his office to give him his final instructions.

**Mid-Pacific**

Heading back to base, the noise from the rain lashing against their ship would have made it necessary to shout even if tempers had not been frayed. El Niño had arrived and was giving of its worst.

Ellise had proposed that any meeting of the 'protagonists' be held back until they were all safely at Isla Isabela, back in the Galápagos. She was hoping that a delay would take the steam out of any arguments, but she reckoned without the ferocity of feeling between Paul and Tom.

They had all been following news of the first and larger event. Ellise had been moved to say to Paul, 'You really do have to be careful what you wish for!'

But, horrific though it was, they were in the eye of their own storm. Paul's alarm had led to panic in many of the Pacific islands that they had alerted – panic that had led, so far, to six reported deaths.

A mother and child had been trampled to death as a crowd left a sports stadium, two looters had been shot by local police officers trying to supervise a shoreline evacuation, and the final two had been killed in a road accident as panicked drivers sought to make good their escape through those on foot.

And no tsunami had arrived!

However for some reason, perhaps best categorised as kismet, Paul had retained all the kudos from his earlier broadcasts and, probably because of the severity of the first event, had as yet received no knocks for his local error. That was perhaps all about to change.

Tom asked, 'Maybe there were further events beyond the first quake and the one that just about flattened Hal and me? Perhaps that could have thrown out your models?'

'No, nothing on my read-outs shows any third event, just an echo. Hal must have gone too close to the ridge as the quake hit it.' Paul wasn't having Tom whittle away at his success.

'Isn't that just like you? Blame anyone but yourself. Blame someone who may never be in a position to contradict you.' Hal had been airlifted to a hospital and as yet had not regained consciousness. 'This all has consequences and we must be clear as to what actually happened.'

Ellise tried to intervene, 'I don't think that it much matters, Tom. Two events, three events, there can be little doubt that Paul's model predicted the tsunami incorrectly but the science is in its infancy and errors will occur.'

'Of course it matters. He gave out a warning that spread undue panic, rioting, looting and deaths. We can't ever trust his model again.'

Paul shouted, 'You won't let it rest, will you? See how he is Ellise, Mr God-Almighty Carter. Mr, always right, TV Pundit. He just can't accept that while he was fooling around down there chiselling off his next sound bites, writing his blurb for his next work of bloody fiction, we were both up here trying to save real lives. So we got it wrong this time, I bet they would have preferred twenty false alarms rather than sit there unaware to be swamped and washed away.'

Ellise stepped between them, 'Guys, I declare the meeting closed. I want you both to go to your quarters and calm down. Now!'

Tom watched as Ellise turned and went to calm Paul down, stroking his arm to pacify him. He looked knowingly at Paul and then at Ellise and calmly walked from the cabin.

As he left Ellise said quietly so that Tom could not hear, 'Don't worry Paul. My report will be quite clear on this matter. It was an honest error.'

Paul was still bristling, 'It was just the same in the navy, always putting me down.'

### Arabian Gulf

They had both served in the First Gulf War, posted close to the Shatt-al-Arab, literally the 'river of the Arabs', a marshland area that many claim as the site of the Garden of Eden.

Whether the Shatt-al-Arab was the Garden of Eden or not, it was at one time certainly a lush land of plenty, civilisation there dated right back to the

Sumerians, one of the earliest civilisations, credited with developing the first written language. But its more recent history was far less fortunate.

First it unhelpfully became embroiled within the history and beliefs of three major religions, Judaism, Christianity and Islam, and these of course proved routinely and regularly argumentative.

Then, back in the 17th century, the Ottoman Empire and Persia defined the current borders in a peace treaty that could not have been better designed to generate ongoing conflict – conflict between the two subsequent modern nations, Iraq the inheritor of the Babylonian empire, placed cheek-by-jowl with Iran, the heir to the Persian empire.

Finally, sprinkle oil, as in oil discoveries, across these troubled waters and it had, far from its proverbial calming effect, guaranteed that the area was to become a global hotspot.

The 20th century had been no more helpful. Heavy damming of the Euphrates and Tigris for agricultural irrigation by Iran, Iraq, Syria and Turkey meant this once-fertile wetland area had been decimated. It was the centre of the dispute between Iran and Iraq throughout most of the 1980s and later Saddam Hussein brutally persecuted the area's inhabitants, the *Shi'a Ma'dan* or Marsh Arabs, direct descendants of the ancient Sumerians.

If that were not enough it was the fact that the modern arbitrary borders gave Iraq just a sliver of land reaching out towards the Gulf, a narrow access surrounded by its most recent enemy Iran on one side and by Kuwait, independent only since 1961, on the other.

Not only had Kuwait opportunistically been pumping oil from Iraq's Rumalia fields while it had been preoccupied with Iran, but also its oil overproduction crashed the world price just at the time that Iraq needed to recoup the billions of dollars it had accumulated in debt from its wars. Sadaam's invasion of Kuwait had set off the next conflict in this region.

Paul and Tom were both serving on HMS Gloucester, the ship that became known as the 'Fighting G' for its use of two Sea Dart missiles to knock out Iraqi Silkworm missiles just seconds before they would have hit the major US battleship Missouri.

This was not the origin of the friction between the two men. It started just a week earlier than this. Both of them had been attending meetings with their American peers and had a 'sleep-over' aboard another ship, the USS Tripoli, part of a group of ships sat off Faylakah Island.

Tripoli, operating as the command ship for a minesweeping operation, ran into a moored mine, probably one that had been left over from the earlier Iran-Iraq War. It ripped a huge hole below the water line.

Two other ships, the USS Avenger and USS Leader, arrived to assist while the USS Princeton provided them all with air defence. But during these manoeuvres the Princeton hit another mine and this then in turn set off yet a further mine a few hundred yards away.

While the other ships hurriedly searched out any further problems that there might be in the area, the fires and flooding aboard Tripoli took quite some time to get under control. Trauma enough for two young men at the start of their naval careers, but they had a very personal encounter that had defined their relationship for the rest of their days.

Somehow fated to have careers that would ceaselessly intertwine, both during the navy and subsequently, they seemed constantly to cross each other's path and these regular encounters ensured that the scars would never quite heal.

# Chapter 10 - *Kazakhstan*

Lev and two of his team had travelled to Kazakhstan in a very slow, extremely uncomfortable, small cargo charter from Moscow's Domodedovo airport. It hadn't so much landed at Ust' Kamenogorsk airport, it had felt much more like a semi-controlled crash that had jarred them all badly.

All hard men, they'd shown the bare minimum concern about the impact upon their bodies and spines. Instead they each stared in alarm at the base of the crate that they had brought with them, fearfully looking for any signs that the container had been damaged, terrified of any of that awful water being spilled.

The hired, and very tired, Toyota Hilux had carried them and their crate through Serebryansk and on until they reached Kabitsin's target lake. The tension that had started in the aircraft was sustained by each and every impact from one of the numerous potholes along these poorly maintained roads. This constant fear, for men who believed they had no fear, had taken its toll on Lev and his team.

Lev had no wish to show his concerns to his men, but this water was completely outside his previous experience; unlike them he had seen what it could do up in the Arctic and his anxiety was catching. He decided that he was not prepared to put himself at risk any longer than was necessary, so opted to discharge it in an area where the lake constricted to form a relatively narrow channel and not to go press on to the far end of the lake as Kabitsin had directed. Kabitsin was not here sharing the journey with this toxic package. What he didn't know couldn't harm him, or them.

It was only when they pulled over to the lakeside that they realised none of them had given much thought to how they would manage to issue the contents of the 100-litre container into the lake, while maintaining their own safety in the process.

Lev's accounts of the danger of the water were replayed in their minds so that even the unloading of the crate became slow and laborious. Not one of them wanted to do anything hasty, nothing that might lead to a spillage; not one of them had ever been accused of volunteering for anything in his life, and now was definitely not the occasion to change these deep-rooted self-preserving habits.

Lev naturally adopted the role of supervisor and so made sure that he supervised from a safe distance; safe and comfortable himself, he pressed the others to offload the container and manoeuvre it towards the lake.

The team couldn't fail to notice his lack of proximity and this led to a great deal of grumbling, mostly under their breath so Lev could not hear them, as they manhandled the crate up to the shoreline. They then had a very heated debate as to quite how they could empty the contents without putting themselves in danger.

It was resolved very simply in the end. Lev got them to roll the still-sealed container right into the lake and to push it out into the waters where it bobbed on the surface, albeit mostly submerged. Then, from the furthest extent of the range of Lev's hand-gun, he peppered the container with shots.

The three stood well back from the shore as the container sank, issuing its contents into the lake. They stood and watched for a while; when nothing appeared to be happening they lost interest, latched the rear of the Toyota and set off on their return leg, relaxed now they were free of the vile stuff.

Deep inside the lake, unnoticed by Lev or his team, the chemistry was in fact steadily taking its course.

Lev, with the benefit of distance and several beers, loudly explained his theory to his colleagues inside the rather more comfortable commercial flight to Novosibirsk where Kabitsin had diverted them.

He believed that their water was simply being diluted in the lake and would have no effect. He felt that the Arctic conditions needed to be present for it to show its murderous characteristics. In fact it was reacting, albeit slowly; it was creating an effect upon the adjacent waters.

Water is the most abundant compound on Earth and yet it really is quite odd. For instance, ice floats because somewhat counter-intuitively its solid state is less dense than its liquid form. It is in fact around 10% less dense, that's why icebergs have 90% of their mass below the waterline. Without this characteristic of course the life expectancy of fish and other pond life would be very drastically reduced.

This 'water' they'd added to the lake was much more dense than normal water and it promptly sank to the bottom.

'Normal' water both freezes and boils at unexpected levels too. For its measurable physical structure the physicists would expect that it would both boil and freeze at lower temperatures than it in fact does. It reacts differently because of the strong hydrogen-bonds within the water molecule; these prove to be extremely 'clingy'. If water were more as expected then it would in fact be a gas at room temperatures and we would have a very, very different world.

This same clinginess is what makes water slow to warm up and yet causes it to hold on to a temperature once it has been heated. But this new water on contact with the cold water of the lake promptly turned to a form of ice, although the lake water would have needed to drop in temperature by a further 4 or 5 degrees Celsius to be able to have managed the same feat by itself.

Water is $H^2O$ and, as any school child has been drilled to know, this means it has two atoms of hydrogen and one of oxygen. Though in its various natural forms it clearly and radically changes in physical appearance, its inherent chemical properties do not change as it phases from ice to liquid to steam. It is just the packing of its molecules that changes. They become much closer when they are ice than when they are water and even more spaced out when the water turns into steam.

This new water was not simple $H^2O$. It wasn't even formed from the simplest and most common 'protium' form of hydrogen. Instead its basic structure was based around hydrogen's more complex isotope of deuterium, $^2H$ or D. The vast majority of deuterium atoms in the universe were formed shortly after the big bang, though most of it fairly soon after that event moved on to be converted into helium. Deuterium atoms can also be created when cosmic rays pass through atmospheric gases.

This material is perhaps best-known as the basis for the WWII 'heavy water' used in the early rockets that were developed by German scientists. Though its origins make it seem like a pretty exotic material, in fact one in every six thousand drops of water on Earth is deuterium oxide or $D^2O$ and not the plain old stuff we know as $H^2O$.

Water is also recognised for its pretty effective capability of dissolving a whole host of substances because of its chemistry. Plain rainwater tends to be somewhat acidic in its straightforward natural form, acidic enough to dissolve limestone for example. If it falls through some heavy air pollution then this can convert it into a much more damaging format that falls as the heavily corrosive 'acid rain'.

It's not just in the atmosphere, other natural processes can and do add all sorts of solutes. By passing through the ground, water often collects calcium and magnesium traces. These then turn it into hard water, making it tougher to lather up soap for instance, leaving stains on taps, sinks and kettles from its deposits.

Water also contains electrolytes, biological matter and viruses, and fragments of DNA or RNA that simply hang around waiting to meet up with host cells so that they can reproduce.

Then of course mankind has been excreting, dumping and pouring all sorts of stuff into the sea, lakes and rivers for many centuries.

By any sort of scientific assumption it would have been pretty implausible for this special water to have been pristine and clean of any solutes. Though deuterium oxide itself is not as good a solvent as simple $H^2O$, but this water was to prove not a simple and straightforward $D^2O$.

Tests made upon deuterium oxide have shown that humans liken its taste to distilled water referring to it as similar to a de-aerated water. In small doses it proved not at all harmful to humans and as a result is often used today as a trace element in medical investigations.

Laboratory tests on rodents are not quite so reassuring. When up to 15% of a rodent's body water is replaced by $D^2O$ there is little obvious effect except that the creature does not gain weight normally. As the $D^2O$ percentage of body water rises the rodent gets more excitable, until at the 25% level it may convulse and become very aggressive. By the time the $D^2O$ content reaches 30% it refuses to eat and can fall in to a coma. If the substance continues to be increased until it reaches 35%, then it dies. The only good news is that if the researcher stops before the 35% point is reached and places the rodent back on normal water, then it will recover very quickly.

This was no laboratory. The tainted water in its glacial form reacted with the lake water and initially it appeared to subsume it. The ice spread steadily across the bottom of the lake killing all forms of plant, fish and microscopic life that it encountered. The process was not speedy but was very steady and remorseless. The cumulative effects of the chemical reactions heated up this new water so that it eventually ceased to remain in its ice form. As a liquid its growth picked up pace.

The northward current in the lake ushered the changed water downstream at first, but by the time it had spread across the narrow neck of the lake its more viscous nature acted a little like a moving dam. The fresh waters coming down from the Altai range tried to usher it on, but were pressed back by the new water without being changed. If a scientist had been watching, he or she would have concluded that it seemed as if a pair of surface-like menisci was formed between the two.

The concave meniscus of the normal water netted perfectly within the new water's convex one, touching but not apparently joining, the surface tensions in the menisci keeping the two forms apart. In this way the mass of new water was pushed before the greater pressure of the arriving mountain waters.

On the downstream side the same effect would not have been apparent, the conversion process continued unchecked and the mass of changed water became ever larger as it crossed the north-western part of the lake destroying all life that it engulfed. The lake had previously teemed with fish but the approach of the new water gave no warning of its arrival; no instinct was triggered for the fish to make their escape downstream. Absolutely nothing remained after its passing.

It was shunted onwards towards the only outlet for the lake, the White Irtysh River. When it encountered the Bukhtarma River, which flowed into the lake from the east. The inflow here proved to be much slower and the waters warmer than had been encountered at the narrow neck of the lake, back where it had been inserted.

For some reason no meniscus formed here, so that the conversion to the new form of water was able to travel up the Bukhtarma. Several hours later, it reached the Zyrianovsk Mining Complex. Here the Kazakhs had spent heavily to clean up the mine and sewage water that used to be allowed to flow unchecked into their water system. The release of effluent mine water into the river had been halted and a concentrator using the fresh water from the river had been installed. This concentrator ingested the new water and promptly seized up. The pressures built up in the stalled equipment until a release valve blew and started to dump the chrome-polluted mine waters into the river where they too were converted readily into this strange new form of water.

Whilst the 'sideshow' unfolded the bulk of the changed water left the lake and entered the Irtysh, soon reaching a hydro-electric dam where it passed through the intakes, was forced down through the narrow penstock where it met, and eventually seized, the turbines there.

The vast majority of the altered water was now in a sort of frail stasis, contained between the dam and the fresh water pressing down from the mountains. But enough of it passed through the turbines and this headed on downstream to continue its course.

Its next major 'victim' was the Ust' Kamenogorsk Metallurgical Complex where again the measures that had been taken to reduce pollution from the plant were the very things that allowed the new water in.

The river swept on downwards towards the steppe known as Semipalatinsk 21. Here in 1949 the Soviets had carried out what they called 'Operation First Lightning', what the Americans labelled as 'Joe One' – their first nuclear explosion. In this area, around the size of Wales, there had subsequently been more than 300 underground and over 100 atmospheric nuclear tests carried out from the 1950s right up until the late 1980s.

Suddenly, as the strange water reached this fearsome place, it just ceased to be. Having dropped from the lake situated at 400m above sea level down to this lush grassland area, the sun here was unfettered by clouds and it was therefore much warmer. Perhaps that might have been what halted it?

The river was passing through a once heavily-irradiated area so maybe that was the cause? It was moving much more slowly here, perhaps this lower speed might have had an impact too?

Later investigators reasoned that it must have been one, a combination, or all of these factors that meant that the rampage was over and the flow reverted to the more conventional mix of $H^2O$ and $D^2O$.

Up at the dam the contained special water there also began gradually to revert to the more usual form of water. No observers or investigators were there to understand what had taken place, no one had been there to impassively observe and record this whole process, Lev and his team were long gone.

Although anyone who had been there along the damaged section, had noted the unusual changes and effects, had at some stage been drawn to approach it, eventually to touch the water – had died.

# Chapter 11 - *London*

The Foreign & Commonwealth Office building in Whitehall clearly displayed its great history and past power. It was still a place that inspired one to make calm and considered, statesperson-like, judgements from what had once been the heart of a considerable empire.

The Foreign Secretary's office was not particularly comfortable, a little too old-world for her taste, she had not yet found a way of making it at all personal apart from two simple family pictures that sat on her desk.

'We need to put together a strong, but most of all a reliable, team. This is the first time they have ever admitted that they need our assistance. We need to go in there and show why they should invite us in much more frequently.' The Foreign Secretary leaned back in her chair feeling that she had set the scene well enough and could now sit back and watch the testosterone blizzard that was sure to hit whenever Russia was in any way involved.

She was amused that the Wall had been down for so long, the Cold War had been effectively over within months of that, but still the intelligence and military services saw Russia as a prime enemy. The West had fought all sorts of other foes. They'd attacked Slobidan, faced Saddam twice, met threats from Bin Laden's group and its successors, invaded and occupied Afghanistan and faced the potential of threats from Iran and north Korea, the mess that is Africa, the global expansion of China in terms of its rush for resources, yet still it was the 'Soviets' where a considerable part of their 'defence' resources, assets and spends seemed to be directed.

She instead looked at the way the Russians had fully participated in the peace-keeping force in Kosovo. The way they had assisted in the transfer of power from Milosovic when he was reluctant to give up the reins even after election defeat. But years of planning with Russia cast as the Evil Empire, the arch-enemy, added up to an avalanche of momentum that was not going to stop for some time yet.

The Foreign Secretary had established that one of her prime tasks for her period in this office would be to seek to adjust that focus at every opportunity. Here was just such an opportunity. Her counterpart in the Russian government had called and requested that the UK send a team to investigate what they had called their 'event' in the Arctic Ocean.

She realised she was really rather looking forward to this meeting and was immediately rewarded by the head of the Secret Service, Sir Joseph Maudlin, who leapt in grumpily. 'And perhaps a little earlier next time! We have been tracking unusual activity in the area for months. It's been driving our analysts crazy. It's not been at all clear what they were up to, there has been all sorts of traffic up there, mostly military, and no rhyme nor reason given as to the apparent cause or objective.'

Admiral Bracewell, the Chief of Staff, was keen to doubt their intentions too. 'Can we entirely trust their motives? There is so much firepower amassed in that area currently that it seems to belie the scientific issue they have outlined. We had assumed that they'd had another nuclear sub go down there and I still wonder if that might be the real issue here. They asked for us to loan one of our best submersibles. We know theirs are not up to such a recovery.'

'Nonsense, they have very similar capabilities. It's our scientific personnel they need. They've no shortage of superb theoreticians but their ongoing lack of funding has meant that appropriate practical experience is somewhat limited.'

Sir Joseph's riposte was just a little too hearty for the Foreign Secretary's taste. As she watched the exchange she made a mental note to look at some way of tethering him in the very near future. He was just too overpoweringly confident and too evidently disparaging of his military peers. She needed people around her table who could deal with the issues and not simply exercise their bulging egos – a team that could provide her with the evidence, identify potential solutions, not go over the same old tired arguments.

The discussion proved not to be as amusing as she had hoped and it was already in great danger of descending to the level of an argument when she interrupted, 'Professor Groves, what have you gathered from their first communiqué?'

Groves had been her tutor at Cambridge and on her appointment she had readily created a role for him in her advisory team. This had caused some concern with her officials because of his reputed communist leanings during his early years, but she insisted that it had been just something in the air at Cambridge in those days; when nothing could be proven in either direction they had given in to her, something she wanted to become a habit for them.

To her he was just like a favourite uncle. His way of expressing himself was familiar, warm and comfortable. He had the habit of speaking only when asked, and then only of what he felt he had properly researched and prepared.

He replied, 'It's almost impossible to say. They suggest that it is something about the quality of the water but give us no hard facts to appreciate quite what they mean. Apparently they are calling it 'still water' because one of their team had said he did not know what it was, yet that it was still water.

'Of course that area is one of the most polluted in the world. The Ob and the Yenisey Rivers stroll into the Kara Sea after wallowing through their industrial heartland. Their inefficient gas, oil and coal industries have been dumping all sorts of materials for years, and those rivers are so languid that they have plenty of time to coalesce and fester. Then, the part of the Arctic they have mentioned is virtually a lake with no real outlet so even more opportunity for noxious compounds to form. Add all that to the effect of long-term changes in the ice and permafrost and we have all the requirements for brewing up an amazing chemical stew. Heaven knows what concoctions have been created in those waters, or what may be created and crawl out from their soup.

'The area certainly has high levels of almost every pollutant known to mankind – PCBs, pesticides and even DDT. Their farmers continue to use the stocks they'd accumulated, before their banned usage, to fight their massive, persistent insect problem.'

Sir Joseph commented, 'My vote is still with something nuclear.'

The Professor ignored him, 'Look, be assured, this is no Green Party scare story. The pollutants are very clearly and securely in the food chain of the Arctic. One Greenlander in six is shown to have harmful levels of mercury in the blood, and they get it from their diet of whale and seal meat. So we're not talking of a little damaged pondweed. This pollution has reached the very top of the food chain.'

'Nuclear!'

'In deference to Sir Joseph, I guess we do have to consider the significant nuclear pollution both from their loosely-maintained nuclear power stations and also from the residues of their atmospheric nuclear testing back in the 50s. The latter still shows up in higher than normal radiation detected in reindeer herders in the region. It's…'

Sir Joseph interrupted abruptly, 'Interesting though this description may be, surely the point is that they have asked us to send a team to investigate what it is, so conjecture without the collected evidence is perfectly pointless until we get there and see it for ourselves. Aren't we here instead to decide just whom we should send? Of course we need to send people with the requisite skills and knowledge they have requested, but I will also need someone in the team who can take a look around while there.'

'I don't want an incident through some clumsy spook of yours plodding around in his size 14s.' Though this was apparently said light-heartedly, those who knew the Foreign Secretary could recognise the warning signs of the rising level of her anger in her steady and quietly delivered tone.

Clearly Sir Joseph was not well enough versed. 'It's much too good an opportunity to miss.'

'Listen to me carefully. We have been invited to send a scientific advisor, invited at the very highest level. They have already identified some of our people who they feel might be best placed to assist. They have indicated that this could become a real issue for the global environment. I want us to send the best person possible to handle this matter and I do not want any meddling to sustain your personal belief that Russia is still the Evil Empire.'

The Admiral surprisingly, given their earlier fencing, seemed to come to the assistance of Sir Joseph by insisting, 'Their teams will all be military at the site and you will need someone who understands their methods and their thinking in order to liaise and to facilitate.'

'Fine, then find someone with those skills. But I do not want any James Bond character injected into the equation.'

The Professor had bided his time through this exchange but was determined to finish his earlier thought, 'It's nothing short of a disgrace what they have done to this environment. And, it would serve them right if Mother Nature has finally decided to bite back.'

# Chapter 12 - *Similian Islands, Thailand*

Tom was shattered yet still had this deep-down warm feeling. He realised it was an all-pervading sense of deep contentment, real satisfaction derived directly from the exhausting work.

He couldn't remember the last time that he had worked so physically hard, he was not even sure that he ever had. The first week had been hell when almost everything ached, but as the second week started there was a flip-flop in his mind and condition. Suddenly new chemicals were flowing through his body and mind bringing a vicarious pleasure to the extreme exercise.

He had volunteered to assist with the post-tsunami effort in Thailand, this was for the 2004 event which still needed lots of support. He had contacted someone he knew in the UNDP, United Nations Development Programme, for they were running the Reef Recovery and Rehabilitation Project in Thailand.

The UNDP had arranged for him to meet up with someone from the Department of Marine and Coastal Resource at Phuket where he had learned that the early efforts to clear the debris, washed from the land on to the delicate coral ecosystem, were still under way. His offer of assistance found him allocated to the Similian Islands.

Fortunately the early reports that the local coral reefs had sustained 75% damage proved a huge exaggeration. It was nearer 15% but even this needed to be resolved before the next monsoon which would add further destruction to the weakened corals.

Their particular project was to try to save some amazing fan corals, many were over a metre in diameter. There were a dozen divers on Tom's boat and a three-man crew, one of whom doubled as their cook. The divers were mostly volunteer recreational divers. Teams of four each dived four times a day, resting, eating and sleeping as best they could. The teams stayed aboard for two weeks at a time.

No one had ever tried to do what they were attempting, to rehabilitate so damaged a coral reef. Tom loved the fact that it was therefore all about using their ingenuity to come up with solutions. Earlier teams had disposed of the debris – corrugated iron sheets, beach parasols, restaurant menus and utensils, identity cards, clothes, shoes, bottles and crates of unopened beers and soft drinks, even kitchen sinks...

They were now able to concentrate on the coral colonies themselves; they found many of the corals that had been knocked over and partially covered with silt.

Initially they had simply righted some of the corals and used local rocks and debris to try to anchor them, but the various teams were trying all sorts of novel approaches. One approach Tom had come up with was to insert nails into the bases of the coral and then fix these to rocks. Tom had recalled that in his childhood he had done something similar with a Lugger falcon that he had been training. It had been committed and was therefore too late in pulling out of a stoop after a very speedy leveret. It had therefore crashed into the top of a hedgerow and damaged several of its primary feathers. Tom had reconnected the tips with a small pin and they had been fully restored as the pin rusted in place.

Others had similar ideas and were attaching small colonies to rebar metal netting, there were even corals being lifted from the water and glued to rocks before being reintroduced to the water. Nobody knew whether any of this would work, but it was clear that the monsoons would wreak havoc on the weakened corals if they didn't harness them in some manner.

It was hard physical work, fortunately not at very great depths, but constant. So as he came ashore he planned not to be too long at the bar with his team wanting instead to make his way back to the small tented area they were using and to crash out.

As he stood to leave a stranger approached him and asked, 'Can you spare me a moment, Mr Carter?'

Though it was phrased politely enough, Tom recognised that this man was issuing an order and was someone clearly used to being obeyed. British, initially he had appeared pretty nondescript, but on further assessment there was something quite menacing about him, he looked useful, committed, a man of action. There was a quite jagged scar at his throat that looked as if it might have been earned in a knife fight; assessing him, Tom assumed the other person would have sustained worse injuries.

He led the way to a table away from the throng at the bar. 'Sorry to disturb you when you are obviously doing good work here, but I am afraid we need your help.'

'I have no idea who you mean by "we", but whoever you are I am very much in need of crashing out. On the boats you can only ever really doze.'

He smiled, 'This won't take long. By we, I mean HMG of course.'

Tom was exasperated by this comment. 'Are you from the embassy? Isn't there some pressing cocktail party you should be getting to?'

'No, not the embassy. I trust we do not need to remind you that you are still a reservist, or that you're still bound by the Official Secrets Act?'

'Look, of course I know both of those things, but neither of them allows you to interfere with my well-earned rest.'

'The sooner I can get to the point the sooner you can get to your bivvy.'

'Just who the hell are you?'

'All in good time, all in good time. I need you to sign this document confirming that you are aware of these two facts and that you still recognise and acknowledge your obligation to the State and to Her Majesty the Queen.'

'Will I hell as like! Until you tell me what this is all about I am signing nothing, acknowledging nothing.'

'Very well.' The man reached into a small knapsack and from his demeanour and tone Tom, irrationally, fully expected his hand to come out holding a gun. Instead he pulled out what Tom recognised as an official navy file. He could also see from the spine that it was his official navy file.

'Look, just what is this? Who are you? If you have access to that file then I figure you must be some sort of spook. Just what is it that you want?'

The man did not respond but merely lifted and opened the file, flicking through what appeared to Tom to be a surprisingly thick sheaf of papers. He stopped at something and raised his eyes over the file to stare at Tom, then dropped his eyes and read on. Clearly he found something else to make him reappraise Tom.

'Tell me about the Tripoli incident.'

Tom was damned if he was going to play games with this guy. 'I assume you are not talking of the place in Libya. Presumably you mean the US ship that hit a mine in the Gulf War?'

'Yes, there appears to be no satisfactory explanation for your actions aboard that day. Friends in high places arranged for the authorities to turn a blind eye by the looks of this. It's so easy to tidy away things that happen during a war situation of course.'

'That's a damned lie and I'm not spending another second here for you to get your jollies making false accusations.'

'Sit down, Mister Carter .' There was steel in the order and the way he stressed the 'Mister' implied that he still saw him as a military person and not a civilian. 'We need a chat about how you can assist your country, perhaps clean up this file for any future reader.'

'There's nothing I am ashamed of, nothing in that file, nothing I need to repair. If you have some accusation to level then go ahead and see how you stand up against my lawyers. Be assured that I can afford the very best!' Tom slumped back into his chair too tired to march off to his tent. 'Look what the hell is going on?'

'It will go much quicker if you stop threatening me.'

'Me, threatening you!'

'We've set off on the wrong foot here. Perhaps it's something about my style, my approach? Perhaps it's down to the way I look?'

Tom cursed himself as he found he adopted an apologetic tone, 'No, it's nothing about you. It's being confronted at the end of two exhausting weeks and being made to talk about a time I would prefer to forget. War is ugly.'

He said this while internally he cursed himself because he recognised it as a typical British failing that he could not just say, 'Yes, you offend me. What you are saying offends me.' It was some deep-rooted part of his upbringing that would not allow him to be quite so personal. It was a result of the same damned thing that made Brits less likely to complain about bad service. Worse he recognised that this guy had known this and played him like some sort of quiescent fish.

'Let's just get this over with. I don't know what you're driving at and I've absolutely nothing to answer for, as my file will clearly have indicated.'

'I can appreciate fully why you don't want to be reminded of that day, so indeed let's move on.' He reached into the bag again and brought out a map. 'This is the Severnaya Zemlya, a group of islands in the Arctic Ocean. Obviously as you will have already realised it is an island group that sits within the borders of Russia. Boris has had some sort of accident there and they need our help. They want some bright boys like you to go and sort it out.'

'Thanks, but no thanks. I've a very busy diary ahead and besides my specialism is the Earth sciences. I've absolutely no interest in the many ways in which mankind manages to screw up the Earth.'

'This is not a request.' He produced a buff envelope. 'In this you will find the necessary papers to invoke your reservist status. You've been called-up, Lieutenant-Commander Carter. If you play your cards right you might even get a promotion out of this.'

Tom refused to acknowledge the envelope or open it. 'This is a charade, I have more important matters thank you very much.'

'No, you need to start appreciating that you cannot just walk away from this. My job is to ensure that you do appreciate that fact. Your celebrity and wealth count for naught, you are still a member of Her Majesty's Forces. When She needs your help you have to realise that your duty is to put your life on hold until She says you can move on.'

'This is nonsense, perhaps it's true of Thailand but back home there is no police state. You can't dragoon a private individual to just park his life and go off on some nefarious state business.'

'That is just precisely what we can do. You took the Queen's shilling and when She says leap, there's no looking first, you have to jump!'

'I'll have my lawyers look this over and while they're at it I'll ask them to see if your attitude and approach is actionable too.'

'Do you know who I am?' he grinned at Tom who shook his head. 'Then the best of British, mate! Just make sure that you present yourself at this location next week at the date and time shown.' He handed Tom a small index card with a typed address, a date and a time. Then without another word he rose, slung the bag across his shoulder and walked off down the beach.

# Chapter 13 - *Russia*

Paul was not particularly comfortable in the aircraft seat, but managed a smile as Ellise shifted her position. She was asleep, perfectly at peace lying across his chest. He realised that he still enjoyed her company after what was probably his longest relationship in many years. She challenged him intellectually, she more than matched and satisfied his sexual drive and she was just plain good fun to be around.

Fortunately too, he thought, the 'M' word, marriage, appeared to be nowhere in her vocabulary; she had made it clear that while it remained fun they could stay together, if it faded she was gone. He was surprised to find that for the first time in his life he was working hard to ensure that it did not fade.

He looked out of the aircraft to see that there was still nothing to see apart from the railway carving through the otherwise featureless landscape. It was as if the pilot was relying on the railway for his navigation. This was something of a sobering thought. Russian-built and managed aircraft did not get a very good press and this apparent lack of sophistication was unnerving.

Paul smiled as he thought of something rather more pro-Russian; though as it was disparaging to the Yanks he would never dare mention it to Ellise. Americans had apparently spent many years and millions of dollars developing a ball-point pen that could work in space, where the concept of up and down was meaningless and therefore a standard ball-point pen would not work. The Russians had solved the same problem by issuing their cosmonauts with pencils thereby proving effectiveness and not sophistication was often the best approach. So sophistication was not always best?

What they were following was the famous Trans-Siberian Railway that was leading them directly to the city located at the centre of Russia. The city existed only because it had been the place at which the railway's planners had decided to cross the mighty River Ob. At the selected crossing point there had been an insignificant village on the left bank called Krivoshschekovo. The coming of the railway turned this sleepy village into one of the largest cities east of Moscow, the administrative centre of West Siberia, the city of Novosibirsk.

He had expected snow, particularly at this time of the year, and had been surprised to learn that this 'Sleeping Land', the literal translation of Siberia from its original Tatar, was notable in fact for long, yet snowless winters. Yet another of his beliefs about Russia had to bite the dust.

Since entering Russia Paul was constantly reminded that most of what he knew of this vast country was stilted, out-of-date or deliberately misleading. He realised the Cold War had been nothing less than a long-term investment in disinformation, that demonised these Russian peoples.

Paul during this long journey had therefore been reviewing his beliefs. The Russians' desperate defence against Hitler's forces had depleted the population by many more millions than the more-often movie and book-featured Jewish Holocaust. But then the reported bestiality of Russia's entry into Berlin at the end of WWII had wiped away any sympathy for this earlier, literally last-ditch, battle to sustain their nation. This impression was of course not at all improved by Russia's later subjugation and separation of much of Eastern Europe from the West.

Paul, like most of his peers, had grown up on a diet of cold war spy novels, full of gloomy dead-of-night prisoner exchanges on stark, lonely border posts. George Smiley, sitting single-handedly in a lonely office, infested with moles, using just his intellect to fight the East's insidious infiltration of the vital institutions of the West.

Even more risible were those caricature Russians who always seemed to have a desire for global domination, their intriguing ideas constantly thwarted by 'Bond, James Bond'. Surely such individuals could never survive, never exist? Then there was the tall blond Lundgren character who pushed Rocky to the very last inch of the third-reel of that movie. But he'd now met numbers of Russians and they seemed strangely normal, not one with a glint in the eye for global conquest. Though he had to admit a few had shown an extremely naked ambition for his foreign currency.

Much of his visual imagery of Russia he realised was derived from black and white images and films, with extremely black and white portrayals of the two sides.

Though he had known instinctively that this was most probably a false stereotyping he had still been a little surprised that the Russian women he saw at the airport had not been all short and dumpy sitting astride a tractor. Actually a number he had seen had been rather glamorous, tall, thin, blonde and somehow extremely open-faced, seemingly very keen to be approached. This would normally have been the first real test of this 'thing', whatever it was, that he had going with Ellise, though he felt confident that he could manage to resist their temptation; but they'd only been at Moscow Airport for three or four hours!

He realised that he was beginning to feel some sympathy for the Russian 'mis-casting'. The most appalling false impression he realised was the way in which the American military-industrial vested interests had consistently overstated the might of the Russian industrial, technical and military strengths. Only months after the fall of the Berlin Wall the truth had emerged of overstated outputs, wasted materials, rampant pollution, crippling alcoholism… Where was that slick military nation with its finger poised on the nuclear button now? Where were its legions of tanks, like some motorised Cossack horde ready to sweep through Germany right into the unprotected heart of Europe? Now he saw that this was clearly propaganda.

During his time in the navy the Russians were presented as the 'Red Menace', he had been trained to kill or thwart them, never to trust them. But now he could see them as misjudged, after all they were fellow human beings, simply striving to make some sense of the world, wanting the right to a quality of life, the same quality of life that the West promoted so passionately. It was the constant stream of output from Hollywood, Detroit, Nashville and Seattle that had instilled a desire for US brands and beliefs, leisure pursuits and lifestyles. It was these ideas, these icons, and not politics and military might that had hastened the lifting of the Iron Curtain. Further proof to Paul that Russians were just the same, with the same goals once the politicians could be thrust aside.

He was therefore keen to reach their destination, a satellite town to Novosibirsk, situated just a little to the south and called Akademgorodok. This meant the 'academic city' and had been proposed by Brezhnev as early as 1979. It was widely accredited as the very birthplace of *perestroika. Perestroika,* or 'restructuring'. This developed momentum when Gorbachev galvanised it by linking it with *glasnost,* or 'openness'. These internal ideas had prepared the ground for Western ideas to take seed. Paul wondered if any of these changes had brought them any joy. 'God knows,' he smiled, 'whoever or whatever, He or She might be.'

There was a change in the tone of the aircraft's engines and Ellise stirred and stretched herself awake. Paul watched her feline movements as she rubbed the backs of her hands across her eyes, straightened out each of her limbs and finally extended her arms into the air. She turned and smiled at him sleepily. He'd fight the whole Russian military to keep that look all for himself.

'I wish I could just shut down like you. You've been out for hours.'

'It's a trick I picked up from my grandfather.' Ellise sat up straight and lowered the armrest between them as if, in recalling her grandfather, she needed to re-establish a boundary between them. 'He was in the army, took part in the D-Day landings and marched all the way to Berlin. Have I mentioned that he always did exaggerate? He said you need to take every opportunity you can to get to sleep because you never know when the next chance will come.'

'We appear to be losing speed. I think that's what woke you.'

'Yes, look, I can see the Ob stretching away up to the north.'

'Confident it's not the Yenisey? You've been asleep long enough to have missed the Ob.'

Ellise seemed to take him literally and turned to fill the window with her tousled hair, staring down at the river meandering through the flat countryside, 'Which is the larger?'

'The Yenisey I think, but they're both right up there in the world's largest league table. Both stretch from the mountains off to the south of here all the way up to the Kara Sea. Neither of them seems to have any sense of urgency about doing it. The Yenisey drops by around 150 metres along its entire 2000 kilometres of length, so it's officially the most languid river in the world.'

'That plain out there seems to be so marshy.'

'The river's slowness means that there's very poor drainage here, so you end up with either marshes or swamps and the permafrost stretches for thousands of square kilometres to the north. And you're not just looking at any old plain, that's the West Siberian Plain.' Paul shaped his hand in a rapper's gesture, 'Respect – it's the largest bit of flat land you can find anywhere in the world.'

'OK, so you're a few pages ahead of me in the guidebook.'

'Not guilty. It's just that at college I did a lot of work on the geology of the Central Asian Plateau, that's a ways south and east of here, but I picked up stuff about here as well to aid me in my research. It's a great oxymoron, a really interesting flat bit!

'It was created when the Indian sub-continent crashed up into Asia's belly about 55 million years ago. It gave Asia one hell of an initial thwack too, and it's still moving north pushing under and thrusting up the Himalayas to the skies and that's what is building up these plains behind that range.'

'Save me! What is it about geologists that they have to trot out nauseating detail about how something's made, not just look at it and say "Wow, that's awesome".' Bickering was still a key part of their relationship. 'I thought I'd be safe from that as we're just about as far as we can be from any ocean, but no, now you can bore me about the land too!'

It was clear that the landing gear had been lowered and they were coming in for a touchdown.

'That's just great, where's the announcement?' Ellise parodied, 'Welcome to New Siberia. Please fasten your seatbelts, stow your trays and put your seats in the upright position. Doors to manual and cross-check.'

They both had a fit of the giggles because this small aircraft had no lights for 'No smoking' or 'Fasten seat belts' in any language. There had been no in-flight service, no flight attendants and the seats had just one position, uncomfortable.

They had been met and greeted at Moscow's Sheremetyevo airport although they were surprised that this happened well before they'd passed through any sort of customs control or immigration. A surly looking individual held up their names on a board. When they approached him he spoke good English and was perfectly welcoming in his words. None of this reflected in his eyes or body language, he had so thoroughly fitted their preconceptions that they were not at all fazed by this.

When he had asked them for their passports they tried to hide the briefest of nervous pauses with a quick glance at each other. He strode off into the airport complex disappearing for a worrisome twenty minutes. When he finally returned their smiles were strained, but he passed back their passports duly stamped and to their amazement he had someone in trail with their luggage neatly stowed on a trolley.

He bade his farewell as he ushered them on to a small bus from which they watched as their luggage was loaded. From here the various people who processed them showed no interest in exhibiting any skill with English, and perhaps more disturbingly absolutely no curiosity. They were whisked across to a smaller facility that had looked rather more military than civil.

Paul had been surprised that they were simply shown on to this aircraft without anyone accompanying them. Yet another myth exploded, which was somewhat disappointing. His preconceptions had expected the pretty Intourist guide, cum spy, cum honey-trap and he had looked forward to having to fight her off, proclaiming his prior commitment to Ellise.

They had undergone a State Department briefing before setting off for Russia and it was clear that the official there had read far too many poor novels too. Almost everything he had told them appeared to be out of date and his most important piece of advice, that he had repeated precisely three times, had been to be sure to check in at the embassy in Moscow as soon as they arrived. They of course had not been allowed anywhere near the city and were not even sure if their arrival had been officially recognised.

So it was with no expectations that they now left the plane, beckoned to do so by what looked like some sort of lowly ground-handling person, rather than any formal welcoming committee from the Akademgorodok facility.

# Chapter 14 - *London*

As evening drew on, the office tended to grow mellow, little pools of light illuminated the Foreign Secretary's desk and fell upon selected pictures of her predecessors.

Professor Groves was pacing the room, clearly deep into his lecture mode. 'If what Sir Joseph's intelligence sources are saying is true, and there is some threat to water supplies, then you need to understand that this is actually a very serious matter. The amount of available water on the Earth is a closed system – what water we have on this planet is what we've got and all that we're getting.

'Only a tiny 2.5% of the world's water is not salty and some two-thirds of that 2.5% is in fact semi-permanently frozen at the poles and in glaciers. Of the meagre amount remaining you have to factor out the quantity that is usually falling or lying in the wrong place, either in remote areas or coming too unhelpfully as monsoons and floods, these are of course not particularly available or at all useable.'

The Foreign Secretary was obviously willing to let Groves have free rein and nodded for him to continue.

He added, 'One in three people across the world have no access to safe drinking water and one in two have no safe sanitation with the resulting disease and other implications. So we are already at a critical state in many parts of the world - before there's any new threat to contend with.

'Then factor in that over two-thirds of the useable water that we do have is required for essential agriculture. The World Water Council has reported that by 2020, just to meet the global agricultural requirements, we will need 17% more water than there is in fact available. Agriculture takes 70% of water, industry 20% and domestic use 10%. So that's an interesting challenge for us that sits just around the corner. If we cannot resolve it then our supermarkets will begin to be less bountiful and much more expensive too. That's before we begin to look at any of our domestic and industrial water requirements.'

She asked, 'Is this shortage mostly about the growth in world population?'

'That doesn't help of course, but if you take a worldwide staple like wheat as an example, in production it takes a massive 1,200 litres of water to create just a single kilo of wheat. Rice needs more than twice that volume. And this is boldly assuming that there is efficient production, when of course many places will be much, much more wasteful than this.

'Worse still, it takes sixteen times the water to produce a kilo of meat than it does a kilo of wheat. Just imagine if all those Asian vegetarians espoused our Western red meat culture. We seem to be trying to sell them our way of life yet each "convenient" McDonald's hamburger, or anyone else's for that matter, uses up a stunning 2,400 litres of water. So for the future we really do have to begin to question how we might be able to run agriculture more water-efficiently.'

The Foreign Secretary stood up and started pacing too. 'And of course the global warming trend can't be helping that?'

'No, that's true, but everything I am describing existed as an issue before anyone started talking of global warming. You see that small cup of coffee each of you is drinking, well, in growing the beans for that 140 litres of water were expended. Even that single sheet of A4 paper that Sir Joseph has been doodling upon used up 10 litres of water when you factor in the tree's growth and the paper's manufacture. And just as another example, Admiral, your smart pair of leather shoes swallowed up a massive 8,000 litres of water to be created.'

She persisted, 'And we then have to add in the effects of global warming too?'

The Professor pondered this and sat down to flick through some papers. 'Global warming and the Kyoto thing prompted lots of column-inches about our "carbon footprints" but no one is talking about water footprints. We all have them. Carbon footprints are a measure of wasted energy and pollution, but it's your water footprint that will creep up behind you and kill you!'

'I've never heard the expression before, is it in general use?'

'Clearly not. The USA's water footprint of course is huge.'

The Admiral offered, 'They wouldn't want to have it any other way!'

'Now let's see,' the Professor flicked through some papers. 'The UN Human Development Report of 2008 shows that in the USA the average consumer uses 575 litres every day, the UK is more modest at 150. That compares with China at just 100 and India at 140 litres per day per capita. Given the huge populations of China and India and their current incredible rates of growth, just what would happen if all of their populations demanded the same water consumption as an American?'

The Foreign Secretary prompted, 'Go on then, answer your own question, what would happen?'

'Well, as one example, to assist with their water footprint some nations might find it much better to start to import water-intensive products rather than waste their own water supplies to produce them locally. Wheat is a classic example. Because its price is more about a political issue than a market-generated calculation, it is usually sold at a very low subsidised rate, well below its true cost of production. So a country short in water might do better to import wheat at these knock-down prices rather than use its own water to produce it locally. That approach is better both economically and for addressing the water footprint!'

'That's OK if they have the foreign currency, but what about the impact on their local labour markets if they do that in too many areas?'

'Agreed that's an issue, but it's a lot like the carbon market that the Kyoto Protocol has created. The fears for global warming have picked up momentum and the simple course of action is to blame it largely on carbon emissions. Well carbon emissions are clearly a global phenomenon. We have only one shared atmosphere, so you can't address it nationally.'

The Foreign Secretary paced, 'Yes, but an idea like this has to start right down at the individual and individual action to control their waste.'

Sir Joseph laughed, 'You mean like someone living in a leafy Surrey suburb changing over to an eco-friendly light bulb and recycling their waste, taking fewer holidays, walking the children to school, planting trees... None of that comes anywhere close to a resolution. How does any of that begin to address just the traffic emissions in downtown Beijing, Mumbai, Bangkok, Jakarta and so many other Asian cities? The air on their streets is almost thick enough to be sliced up, parcelled and used as a pensioner's winter fuel allowance.'

'That's why the Kyoto Protocol has generated the need for organisations and countries to reduce their emissions by treaty. If they don't reduce them or buy offsets, then it will hurt them where it hurts them most – in their pockets. It's assumed that this sort of penalty is the only way to get their attention. What I meant is, the fact that it exists has also started an international trade in emissions and carbon credits. There are as yet no thoughts of a similar approach being adopted for water, or none that I am aware of currently, and it's just as much a truly global issue.'

Sir Joseph broke the ensuing silence, 'All very interesting, dear chap, but the point at issue, that we are here to discuss and avert, the point is this still water event or incident.'

'That's precisely my point. If someone has the means to damage water supplies there is the potential to exacerbate an already awkward situation. You also need to appreciate that there are already a whole series of water disputes that could lead at least to a skirmish if not full-blown war. There are some 250-300 rivers that either cross or define international boundaries.' He consulted his notes, 'Let's see there are around 70 in Europe, 60 each in Africa, Asia and Latin America/the Caribbean and around 20 in North America. The river basins these create cover 50% of the world's land surface, provide 60% of all fresh water, and...'

Sir Joseph shrugged, 'Yes, yes, and your point?'

The Professor frowned at him and addressed his comments instead to the Foreign Secretary who by her expression had also dismissed Sir Joseph's interruption. He continued, 'Those sharing a river are called "riparian" states. They might face each other with the river's course forming their international boundary or perhaps they're located up or downstream from each other. If one country upstream seeks to dam the river or draw too much from it then the downstream riparian neighbour will clearly suffer. About 10% of these river basins have five or more riparian states, the Danube has eighteen of them!'

'No wonder it's called blue,' muttered the Admiral.

The Professor grimaced. 'It's not at all amusing. Despite some two hundred treaties being signed in the last fifty years, there have been over five hundred water conflicts in the same period. And today there is no formal treaty for the vast majority of these river basins.'

The Foreign Secretary added, 'Yes, I'm briefed regularly on the many hot-spots around the Middle East and right across Asia where water is perhaps one of the main points of argument between neighbours.'

The Professor added, 'It's interesting you know that the very word "rival" comes from the Latin word *rivalis* meaning one using the same river as another!'

The Admiral commented, 'But aren't we talking of states that would always find something to argue about and water is just one of their many excuses?'

'There's a tendency to jump to the conclusion that developed nations would not be so silly as to argue over this sort of thing,' the Professor continued, 'but even in the United States they have had heated squabbles. Georgia, Alabama and Florida had what was called, with typical American hyperbole, the "tri-state water war". It was at the end of the last century when Atlanta, having assessed its future water needs, decided to set reservoirs along three rivers so it could withdraw increasing amounts for its own needs. Downstream Alabama and Florida, already annoyed by having to deal with Atlanta's pollution flowing down their shared rivers, saw their water supply was likely to come under further, even greater, threat. They believed it would reduce the potential for agricultural, industrial and population growth. Florida in particular saw a threat to its profitable oyster business. So the issues of sharing water courses are real, and real everywhere.'

Sir Joseph pushed himself out of his chair now. 'But surely water supplies are not only about rivers?'

'True, but groundwater doesn't offer us a solution either because it is already being used at an unsustainable rate by most cities around the world. During the 1990s the water table in northern China was dropping by one and a half metres each year. Places like Libya have taken so much out of their coastal aquifers that they are now too heavily salty to be useful – but luckily for them they've found a source, of all places, under the Sahara. Bangkok and Venice are two other obvious examples where the underground aquifers have been so depleted that the land surface level is subsiding.'

'Didn't I read that Mexico City is actually sinking because of the amount being pumped out from beneath it?' the Foreign Secretary queried.

'Yes, but worse than that, their inadequate plumbing means that they also lose around 40% of their fresh water to leaks. Don't overlook that on occasions we've not been that much more efficient here either! Poor drainage means that sewage is mixing in with any rainwater so that any irrigation has to be carried out using water of pretty dubious quality.'

'So, what about desalination of seawater?' Sir Joseph proposed, nodding towards the Admiral. 'With two-thirds of the world covered in sea water surely that's the way forward?'

'Desalination plants are currently too energy-intensive, so yes, as water prices escalate and the supply gets more critical, then this will become more significant,'

The Foreign Secretary offered, 'Like North Sea Oil, we had to wait for the prices to rise before its extraction was viable,'

The Professor pondered. 'Yes but there are differences, in the case of desalination we need to find a solution for its bi-product, the brine; it would require some ways to use it or dispose of it.'

'There's always bottled water,' chuckled the Admiral.

The Professor looked exasperated. 'That's just another process that is taking water out of the system to pick up dust in warehouses and on retailers' shelves and in people's fridges.'

The Admiral added, 'Not to mention the huge profits restaurants are taking from selling some pretty questionable spring waters!'

The Foreign Secretary decided to move on. 'So let's focus on what we perceive is the threat of this new type of water and how we can best plan to counter it.'

# Chapter 15 - *Kent, UK*

Tom had received confirmation that the documents given to him by the man on the Thai beach were in fact completely legal; somehow they had taken advantage of his reservist status, he was back in the navy!

As he approached the location he had been 'ordered' to visit, he was surprised to find a large country house in the middle of Kent, a good 20 miles or so in from the coast.

A look at his simple road map had shown the Services' Museum at nearby Ashford but nothing else indicated it as a military area, but then what he had was hardly an Ordnance Survey map, just something he had bought for a few pounds in a service station.

On arrival he had seen no sign of any military markings, no sign of any extravagant fencing, guard towers or searchlights. It looked like thousands of other grand homes in the stockbroker belt, smart and desirable but nothing particularly spectacular.

His previous 'protagonist' from the beach had greeted him and introduced himself as Patrick Brain, but Tom was under absolutely no illusion that this was his real name. He sensed a warped sense of humour was at work in this choice of pseudonym, that this individual, whoever he was, certainly did not have a P-Brain.

Brain looked to be only in his early 30s; he had a quality that made it difficult to describe him, apart perhaps for the jagged L-shaped scar under his jawline. Studying it more closely Tom assumed that the old wound suggested something broader than a knife had been inserted back near his left ear and pulled forward.

However it seemed he was merely there for continuity, because after ushering Tom into a room Brain closed the door, remaining himself on the outside. The room was a traditional study and it was empty. Tom felt uncomfortable about sitting down so instead looked at the titles on the large bookcase but they did not really reveal anything about the owner. There were popular novels side-by-side with reference books and other non-fiction. There was no sense of order, not alphabetic by author or title, no logic in the juxtaposing of the books, no sense of a theme in the selection except that they were clearly not assembled by, or for, a woman.

The door opened to a patrician figure who made no attempt to shake hands, he merely introduced himself, quite unnecessarily. 'Hello, I'm Sir Joseph Maudlin.'

It was unnecessary because Tom was, as would be most Britons, fully aware of both his name and his role. He had recently been pictured extensively in a number of newspapers over a case seeking to muzzle an ex-agent from publishing embarrassing details of his exploits in the secret service.

Sir Joseph clasped his hands behind his back and strode up and down the study. 'I'm sorry we have interrupted your busy life, but we really do need your help.'

'So why all the threats from "Mr Brain"? Why didn't you just ask me to assist?'

'If he has overstepped the mark or upset you in any way then let me apologise and assure you that he will be carpeted later.' Sir Joseph said this with such evident insincerity that Tom was confident that Brain, or whatever his name, had clearly followed this man's instructions to the letter.

He beckoned Tom to a chair. 'Look, let me be frank.'

Tom thought the man was probably incapable of ever being frank, but he took the chair to listen anyway.

'We have read your body of work with interest and believe we might be able to help each other in your quest to make some effort to correct many of the things we are doing to destroy our world.'

'Forgive me if I smile, but it's the governments and industries of the world that are destroying our environment, and aren't you managing perhaps the most extreme agency that is charged with protecting those very bodies and their interests?'

Sir Joseph sat down. 'You have to appreciate that we see the same things as you do and there is absolutely no value in us allowing the resources of the world to be wasted and polluted. That's not good business or good politics.'

'So why are you not publishing or legislating any suitable policies, in fact from what I can see you're not doing anything.'

'Well this is precisely the issue. What can we do and what resources can we apply? I have been asked to develop the case with others from the G8 countries for what some pretty uncreative politician has termed the International Environment Defence Corps. It says what it is I guess, a team that is empowered and funded by the major economies of the world to examine, analyse and propose appropriate courses of action so the politicians can prepare policies and actions.'

'If true,' Tom still did not know where this was all leading, 'it would be an interesting first step, but is there a sign of any desire being expressed by the politicians, or more importantly the multi-national businesses that fund and control them, to implement anything that this Corps might propose? Or is it just a commission or committee whose eventual report would be kicked in to the long grass. More a delaying tactic, to tie down people like me in lengthy discussion and report-writing and then to be ignored?'

'There's the rub of course, how to enforce? Where we are with this IEDC currently is we see it in part as the investigating police force, examining events and their causes, providing the data to a judiciary and to policymakers. It will need to cover off the science, the forensics, then it needs some teeth to control a situation, to make arrests. The obvious route is perhaps as an organ of the UN, but there is a view that inside that bureaucracy the IEDC would be hamstrung.'

'If it's not securely within the UN how could it have international validity?'

'The current wisdom is for it to start out as a covert arm of the military. We can conceal the funding from those with commercial interests that may need to be contained. This funding will need to be considerable as the issues are truly global. We can annexe resources that already exist within our military without any questions being asked and where control, peace-keeping and arrest are required we can also draw on those with the appropriate skills.'

'That sounds far too much like the creation of more Guantanamo Bays, or of CIA rendition flights to locations outside the rule of law, where torture and other human-rights abuses can be applied.'

'Not if the right management team is installed to provide the direction, the morality. We are considering that you might be that manager?'

'So what was all this subterfuge to get me here, and just why was it necessary to use my reservist status to call me up?'

'Well we have, let's call it a role play, for you to perform as part of the job interview. And where we are asking you to go to do it, you will be very much safer if you are clearly seen to be part of HM Forces. We wouldn't want any misunderstanding on the part of our red friends while you are there.'

'Called up or not, I certainly have not yet agreed to any sort of trip into Russia.'

'Let me explain. We monitored a great deal of Soviet activity in this area.' He pointed to a map he spread out on his desk. 'We had no idea what it might be, but from the electronic traffic and the weight of equipment they moved into the area, well, let's say they would have been sure to attract our attention. Now they indicate that they have a problem that they suggest has oceanographic dimensions. It's not clear from what they have told us whether this is a natural phenomenon or some sort of accident of their own making.'

'What precisely have they said?'

'It appears that the water up there is behaving strangely. Water is pretty darned strange anyway, given that we accept as perfectly normal that water may naturally appear on this Earth as solid ice, liquid water or gaseous steam. Then there's all that rocketry stuff about heavy water back in WWII, can't say I know what it means precisely chemically but it's apparently yet another form of water.'

'No, that's mostly man-manipulated and not really a naturally occurring form of water at all.'

'See, that's precisely why we need someone with your knowledge and expertise. They seem to be indicating that the water in this area was behaving differently and they don't seem to know if it's a chemical imbalance or a new form of water that they have encountered. Our boffins have suggested that perhaps the polar cap has melted off some of its ice and delivered up some early prehistoric form of water. But they've named it as some sort of new variety. They have coded it as "Still Water".'

'Water has all sorts of forms but you can't change the natural chemistry and physics of it, and that's a fact.'

'It gets worse. It seems that just as they were getting their act together to investigate it, some group operating within their higher echelons popped in, took samples and destroyed the site so that it will be difficult to work out what had happened there.'

'So what's left to investigate?'

'They still have some samples of the water in Novosibirsk. But our ursine friends, and their neighbours, seem suddenly to be having all sorts of problems with their water just lately. You may not have caught this news item from last weekend.' He passed to Tom a single piece of paper showing a transcript of a TV news article.

**CNN Breaking News:**
*News is being received that in the Lake Zaysan area of eastern Kazakhstan there appears to be a new ecological disaster unfolding. The lake which is beside the Chinese border is fed by a river that crosses from China. It appears to have been polluted in some manner and has already been the cause of friction between the two nations. Reports suggest that a state of emergency has been declared following a reported loss of life and widespread damage to local wildlife and flora all around the area. Western aid organisations have been asked to provide advisors and material aid. Reports as to the cause and the type of assistance that would be appropriate are rather sketchy at present.*

'You see what I mean. Either they have been very clumsy with their husbandry of natural resources, perhaps the hitting of all those five-year plans is coming back to haunt them, or as we suspect this official/unofficial group has used some of the still-water as a test or a warning. So, back to the business in hand; we'd like you to pop over there, find out what's going on. Once the job's done you can get back to your life.'

'What do you mean pop over there?'

'Ah but dear boy they've invited you in! They have asked HMG to send in its finest to investigate this still water.'

'I still don't understand why I couldn't just do that as a private individual?'

'Hm, well that's because while you are there we would like to make sure that you are fully aware of what is going on around you. We want to brief you on certain matters so that you can make the most of this little foray.'

'I'm certainly not going to do any spying for you, if that's what you mean?'

'Nothing so melodramatic, my dear boy. Just simple observation of who is there, what they're saying, that sort of thing.'

'And all these threats from Brain, that's how you think you're going to blackmail me to do your bidding?'

'Well most assuredly it would be good to tidy off your file for posterity, don't you think?'

Tom leapt up from his chair. 'There is nothing in my file of which I am ashamed.'

'There's no need to get all hot and bothered. We were just trying to give you something in return. Your family has a good long record in the senior service, shame to let this matter linger on. Perhaps some other motivation might be more interesting? Did you know the Americans were invited to send in a team too? They've sent in Ellise Walker and uh, Paul Wells I believe.'

Tom sank back in his chair, 'He's hardly appropriate.'

'Yes, I gathered there was some "previous" between you two. His great success in the Pacific has given him some celebrity and he and this Ellise Walker appear to be seen as a team by the Yanks. They're already deep inside the Evil Empire, but you can catch them up before they get underway. Interested?'

'What is it precisely that you are asking me to do?'

# Chapter 16 - *Novosibirsk, Russia*

Ellise and Paul's host organisation was the AARI – the Russian Arctic & Antarctic Research Institute – and they were being shepherded around the various faculties and buildings of Akademgorodok by Dmitry Korkin. He was young with a mop of dark hair, implausibly bushy eyebrows and a thick moustache. Ellise didn't feel she could adequately describe his facial features because the hair overwhelmed it with just two big dark brown eyes looking out from behind it all.

He had no real accent to his English. It was clearly American English that he had learned, but there were none of the usual Russian tones and constructions to which they were rapidly becoming accustomed. Paul assumed that he must have spent time in the States and asked him where he had been based, but Dmitry had claimed never to have left Russia in his life.

Akademgorodok means literally the academic model town. It was in the 1950s that Nikita Khrushchev's administration had the notion of a city dedicated to scientific discovery, to become the brain for his modern Russia. By locating it near the country's natural resources they believed this would prove a real advantage over the Western equivalents that were historically located in leafy old cities well away from the business and industrial heartlands.

Post-Khrushchev the pursuit of pure scientific advance became subjugated with much more of a focus on seeking out industrial advances and economies. The fact that the scientists at Akademgorodok initiated the concept of *perestroika* had in fact not helped their cause; if anything it had led to even less interest in the pursuit of any pure science.

At around the same time the Americans too had found funding pure science becoming more difficult. The US Air Force had tried to counter the pressure to reduce its budgets by looking back at the previous ten years of glorious scientific research that it had funded. They planned to show off the many valuable new products, services and of course weapons that had resulted as proof-positive that pure scientific research just had to be funded properly. However they were disturbed to discover that they could find none, so they looked back twenty years and found a few, but not enough to be compelling. It was only when they went back fifty years that they found original research ideas that were only currently being brought to fruition as a result of the required advances in materials and engineering to make them practical.

This was not to suggest that everything had been discovered already as some extremists have suggested from time to time; it is just that today's advances are more evolutionary rather than revolutionary, more engineering than science. Modern man is much more interested in what something can do for him. He has rather a limited interest in how it is achieved. Modern industry today is more about accountants and administrators than scientists and engineers, more about bottom-line numbers than front-line advances.

This new water was a scientific discovery, an advance of sorts. It was appropriate that they brought it to this city of academics to chew over and consider, before politicians, militarists and others could interfere.

So far they had held three or four relatively pointless meetings with senior individuals at the facility, which Ellise had suggested were more about respecting their political status within the Institute than anything else.

Paul was keen to get on with the task in hand and asked Dmitry, 'When do we get to meet your team and learn about the situation we're here to investigate?'

Dmitry smiled, 'Sorry, we forget that the Western attention span is so much shorter than our own.' It was said with enough charm so that it did not seem like a criticism, and yet? Ellise kidney-punched him as Dmitry turned away, showing that she had picked up his restless vibe too. Paul realised that perhaps he needed to be just a little more diplomatic in his comments.

Dmitry responded by making it a whirlwind tour of the next series of facilities. He confirmed this was a response to Paul's comment by looking at his watch and sarcastically adding, 'It's fifteen hundred hours, so it must be the Numerical Software facility.'

Paul expected that they would have Dmitry with them throughout their trip and so accepted all this with good humour but it was clear from the reactions of those they met that Dmitry was not part of this facility at all. The various individuals showed a great deal of respect to him – no, Paul thought it was more like deference than respect. There was certainly more of a reaction than would be expected if he were just a simple translator or guide.

Paul made a mental note to watch him carefully as presumably he was 'connected' in some manner. Dmitry was perhaps late 20s early 30s. He was short yet clearly muscularly well-developed, but these looked to Paul more like muscles that had been honed in a gym rather than by street-fighting. He would probably be more of a follower of the Marquess of Queensberry than some of the security guards they'd seen here.

There was no sign he was military and certainly no feeling that he was from academe. But any sign of menace was well concealed behind his readily-smiling eyes, even if the smile barely reached the rest of his face, well that part that was visible anyway.

Paul asked Ellise as an aside, 'It's the Orientals where you have to worry about the meaning of their smiles, isn't it?'

Finally they reached a lecture theatre where around a dozen people were already gathered. Mark Elliott extracted himself and walked over to greet them with a big grin and hugs.

Ellise said, 'I didn't expect to see anyone I knew. What are you doing here?'

Mark smiled, 'You know my dad, won't let me chill for a second, sent me over to look at this spooky water.'

Ellise was confused. She and Paul represented the official USA presence here so who was Mark's father? Just what was his business here? Dmitry interrupted and ushered them away and showed them where to sit, then went to stand with two other people to one side of the stage. One was a brute of a man, much bigger than Dmitry, with none of his finesse and an annoying sort of grin on his face. The other was late 60s, yet dark-haired with much more presence that the others.

It was this person who walked to the lectern. He flicked the microphone and reassured by the loud twang through the sound system he began, 'My name is General Goncharenko and I have been appointed to look after this team through all its phases. We still await one or two more players for this undertaking of ours, but we must press on. I will be in charge of your security and safety both here and later if we should need to visit the Arctic.'

A quick look around the others satisfied Paul that there were perhaps three or four obvious non-Russians in the group other than he, Ellise and Mark and he assumed that these were the other international advisors assembled for this exercise.

'All of our team can speak English. Sorry to our French comrades but not all can speak French. So the mission will have as its official language, English.'

Paul noted that two of these non-Russians reacted to the General's comment with a pure Gallic shrug that would have stamped out their origins better than the General introducing them personally.

'I believe you have all met with Dmitry Korkin, think of him as your concierge. He is here to take care of all and any needs that you may have, both while you are working here, and also while you are outside the laboratories. Lev Solonik is here in charge of your security and of the security of this project. We are all here to assist in your briefing, so that we can develop a strong understanding, a...' he stumbled for the word.

'Esprit de corps?' offered Valéry Sechet, the senior French delegate, with undisguised heavy sarcasm.

'You will all be keen to get on, wondering what it might be, the thing you have come here to investigate. We don't yet know what it is, but as we have indicated to you we are calling it "Still Water".'

Paul mumbled under his breath to Ellise in comic accents, 'Or, how do you say, l'eau plate? It is ze agua sin gas.'


A day had passed during which the team, after a fairly flimsy briefing, had been housed, assigned their PC work stations and passwords, and finally entertained to a fairly high-alcohol evening. Now at last they were getting to the point of looking at the data to hand which proved to be pretty thin.

The team had not yet settled down into a pecking order and so it was proving difficult to develop any sort of working process or to start to formulate any working hypotheses, let alone to get to terms with testing the material itself.

# Chapter 17 - *Novosibirsk, Russia*

When he arrived Tom found he had walked in on one of these sessions that was seeking, unsuccessfully, to break the previous pattern. The area was big enough that he was not immediately spotted and so he took the opportunity to take a good look around before revealing his presence.

The large room was perhaps 60m along each side, square with a low false ceiling and tiers of pillars that served to break the room into sections. There was an imposing central zone which was clearly a biological containment area with several forms of container placed inside, stored at its centre. Several white-coated technicians were inside an outer wall and using gloves built through the walls to the inner sanctum to decant the contents of one of the containers into a series of small phials. Environmental plant serving the various areas was groaning away to make the ambient noise levels pretty unpleasant.

Across the room, slightly concealed by the containment area, was a long table with some pretty basic projection equipment set at one end. On the screen was what Tom recognised as a representation of a molecule of deuterium oxide. Eight or ten people were around the table in deep conversation and Tom immediately recognised the sort of session that was in progress; too many of them were sat forward, seeking to break in and lead the discussion. Clearly he hadn't missed anything as yet.

He had almost reached the table before the others realised he was there and he was hugely entertained by the impact his entrance had on Paul and then on Ellise. Paul turned to see what the others were looking at and his jaw just dropped open. Ellise, also now aware of his arrival, looked at Paul to see his inevitable reaction and casually used her hand to lift his jaw back into place.

Mark grinned and waved from across the table. Dmitry who had been notionally chairing the session jumped up and shook hands introducing himself. He directed Tom to sit at the table and amusingly the seating arrangement placed Tom directly opposite Ellise and Paul. Tom took further delight from Paul's discomfort as Dmitry trumpeted Tom's credentials and publications. He then went around the table introducing the other team members.

When he reached Paul, instead of the usual nod or grunt Paul said, 'Still making the grand late entrances I see?'

'So long as they continue to have such an impact on you, why would I ever consider changing?' Then Tom quickly turned to Dmitry and asked, 'I read the briefing notes that you very kindly supplied me as I transited Moscow. So where are we?'

Dmitry described at length the technical features of the central facility while Tom looked across at the containment room. 'Is this all the material that we have, just a few hundred litres?'

Tom noted at least three body language 'tells' as Dmitry paused before he replied, 'Yes, unfortunately many of the containers we used were unsuitable and so we lost much of the sample taken.' He seemed to cringe under Tom's scrutiny as he said this, it was clearly not the truth.

'And at the site, is there anything left to harvest?'

'We're not yet entirely sure. The site investigation team was concerned by the malignancy of the material and napalmed the site. No one has yet returned to see if that destroyed the material or not. The winter has come for that area and we may not get reliable test results until the spring.'

'I understand there is also the body of one of the unfortunate sailors?'

Dmitry was edgy again. 'I am afraid that the autopsy has already been performed, so it is more a case of body parts. We have made the major organs available for any tests the group may request.'

Tom persisted, 'And what did the autopsy conclude?'

'There was a complete shutdown of all the organs and a complete blockage of all the vessels. The still water appears to have just seized up every fluid in the body.'

Tom moved on, not wanting to pause or else the meeting would subside back in to the battle of egos that he had witnessed earlier. 'So, tell me, why have we a picture of deuterium oxide on the projector? Is that what you think this still water is, heavy water?'

# Chapter 18 - *Lhasa, Tibet*

Anatoly Goncharenko, known simply to all those present as 'the General', looked around the carefully assembled group then switched off the video that they had been watching of the Arctic site.

'Welcome to a new sort of weapon, and a true 21$^{st}$ century approach to conflict.' The General beamed at his audience, pleased that Kabitsin's sideshow had at least made sure they had assembled some of the biggest hitters from around the globe, all thanks to his Kazakhstan test of the material.

'Water abounds on our Earth, it wouldn't be the Earth we know without water. We humans consist of around two-thirds water. up here in our brains it's nearer 85% water, so it could not be more vital to us. It maintains our temperature, it helps us breathe and digest food and lubricates our moving parts.' He paused and raised a glass. 'We can live without shelter for as long as we care to, we can go for perhaps a month without food,' he took a deep gulp of the water, 'but we would last only three to five days without water.

'Thank you for giving up your time to join me here.' He looked out of the large picture windows to see the glacier spread before them. 'Here we sit at the top of the world, on the outskirts of Lhasa which locally means "the place of the Gods", Today I will show you how we can become the new gods, the bringers of life and death.'

Kabitsin sat ill at ease at the rear of the room looking right down the circular table towards the General. He had appointed one of his own men as head of security for the meeting and he was confident that he had checked everyone, so he was not concerned whether anyone in the room had any weapons or recording equipment. He knew that these individuals had been very comprehensively scrutinised on arrival.

In fact he had heard that they had argued most vehemently to retain, not their weapons, but their cellphones. He fully appreciated how they felt completely cut off from the world without the opportunity to press a phone to their ears. He had not been so completely out of touch with his people in… well in fact, he had never been out of touch like this before.

The root of Kabitsin's unease was that he was not himself leading this vital meeting. He had to let the General appear to be the instigator. He had learned early that the real power lay behind the throne and not sitting upon it. It was also a much safer and more informative location to operate from, because he could watch, listen and assess what was happening more thoroughly.

But this was such an important meeting that he would have much preferred to have cast off this management-by-remote-control role and driven this issue forward personally. His real fear was of course that the General actually believed that he himself was the instigator, the real power in the room, and there lay the real dangers for Kabitsin. If you put a figurehead forward and he points in the wrong direction, how do you then recover from this position? The moment would have passed and to reconstruct this team would be difficult.

These movers and shakers had spared the time to fly to Lhasa, their various contacts making sure that none of them showed on any passenger list. None had required visas or gone anywhere near passport or customs control. If necessary all had been advised to use as a cover story that they were technical advisers to the road construction that implausibly the Chinese had built a few hundred kilometres away from Lhasa, running from Tingri up to Everest's North Face base camp. The camp being over 5,000m above sea level, the road was created so that the Olympic torch could be carried by runners and mountaineers to the summit as part of the opening ceremony at the 2008 Beijing Olympics.

The room where they were all assembled was a pressurised area to ease the altitude sickness that they had each experienced upon arriving rather too promptly up at these giddy heights. In the room the effects were salved, but that was just a palliative until they left.

'You may ask why we have gathered up here on the Tibetan plateau?' The General was clearly relishing this meeting and his role.

Kabitsin knew from other such meetings that the man loved to be presenting, loved the sound of his own voice, and was extremely proud of his use of English. Kabitsin didn't understand why he couldn't just get on with it, but he knew from hard experience that the General would take his own good time.

The General had been a high-profile member of the KGB, *Komityet Gosudarstvennoy Bezopasnosti*, or as they renamed it subsequently, the FSB, *Federalnaya Sluzhba Bezopasnosti*. He had huge international experience that had been mostly in the West.

He had even spent some time living under deep cover at 'Little Odessa', the Brighton Beach area of Brooklyn, where many expatriates had based themselves in the USA after the break-up of the Soviet Union. But he was a patriot and had been there to report on the exiles; as soon as he could he came back to live inside Mother Russia, to build a final career for himself. This made him good news to Kabitsin.

The General was an acceptable face for the *apparatchik,* the Russian government and its officialdom. His notable successes in the intelligence service meant he had broad celebrity too. Kabitsin had seen the value of this and had used it to project him as the apparent leader of this loose arrangement of Russian *mafiya* and other criminal groups. The General's image was completely clean. He could be seen to be appointed to official committees, to run projects like the work now being carried out in Novosibirsk

Kabitsin tried to relax, after all Moscow was not erected overnight, and he had developed huge respect for the man's capabilities in terms of motivating very senior people like these, people with such power. They had so much power that they had become world-weary, jaundiced, virtually impossible to convince of anything that they had not already bought into for themselves. The General's key skill seemed to be the ability to make them think this was their idea, what they wanted.

'The glaciers from this area create seven major rivers including the Yangtze, the Mekong, the Indus and the Brahmaputra. They all start out from here and go on to supply almost half of the world's population with their basic water needs. Just ponder that for a moment, if you can. This remote outpost of mankind controls the water supplies for billions of people, their agriculture, their industry, their health.'

Kabitsin understood the background to why the General was seeking to show that there was profit in interfering with these rivers. The General never ceased to amaze him with his thinking. He thought that in another life he would have been a chess grandmaster, always several steps ahead of the rest in terms of strategic thinking. But he was not a hands-on person and had next to no practical skills, so was completely unlike Kabitsin himself. The General never got down and dirty, never rolled up his sleeves, always leaving that for others to do. He was the strategist, a thinker. Kabitsin was proud that this was something in which Russia had always led the world. Its thinkers were the World's best and the General was right up there with the very best.

The greatest thought in the world still needed someone to execute it. That's what he was for, to admire, appreciate and implement the General's plan. He believed that their different skills would be able to be merged into the perfect partnership; it had worked in several previous ventures, but for this particular undertaking he was not that sure that the General had quite got it right.

Kabitsin had the beginnings of his agenda already in play but needed to see how he might be able to use this group. Frankly he was a little afraid of operating outside Russia. In Russia he knew how everything worked and how to grease the wheels to make it work. OK, he had occasionally to deal with foreigners on some projects but he was always within his own comfort zone, on his patch. What he hoped these individuals around the table would do was to extend his reach.

The General pressed on. 'Most rivers in India and Bangladesh are named after females but the one in which we are interested, the Brahmaputra, is appropriately named for a male, the son of Brahma in fact. Appropriate, for as our local colleague can confirm this river has been a source for manly antagonism in this area for many years.'

As he said this he pointedly looked across the table at the attendee from Irkutsk, a place perhaps most famous as the birthplace of Rudolf Nureyev, but there was absolutely no sign of anything remotely balletic in the short, squat and heavily-muscled Vasily Cheriktei. The General thought he looked almost square in appearance, with shoulders that appeared to be as wide as he was tall.

Clearly a Yakut, he had been named Vasily after Vasily Manchary, the Yakut Robin Hood, who in the mid-19th century had developed the habit of escaping from gaol. But this Vasily had not been nearly as successful in terms of escape, in fact serving several harsh and formative prison terms in his early years. And he had certainly never developed any concept of robbing from the rich to give to the poor.

In fact there hadn't been any rich around him in his youth spent in his Siberian region, but through his control of the grey and black trade across the border into Mongolia and China he had become very, very rich, and with brutal effectiveness he fully intended to stay that way. He was an essential and key player for this group. Because of his strong Chinese connections he was accepted as the one 'responsible' for a large chunk of the eastern globe.

Kabitsin wasn't quite sure where he stood on the Yakuts, having never previously spent any time with one. Those in the north of their region sounded like good simple folk, hunting, fishing and herding reindeer. He was not so sure about those further south like Vasily. Here they had tried in the early 1990s to declare themselves as an independent republic. 'We soon put a stop to all that nonsense,' he thought.

Vasily belatedly realised that he was being asked to participate, so offered gruffly, 'The Brahmaputra runs for thousands of kilometres up at this height in Xizang Zizhiqu, what you are incorrectly calling Tibet. Then it turns into India and runs on down through Bangladesh. What the General means is that where it actually enters India has been the source of much argument. My Chinese friends stress that Arunāchal Pradesh is still in fact part of China!'

Across the table another attendee laconically responded. The speaker was Asil Chahbaz, a suave, nattily-dressed Turk who even here looked the epitome of the corporate financial man. Operating out of Dubai, he was the Middle East and Indian representative for the group. 'But that was surely way back in the 1960s when your friends seized the area. They pretty soon withdrew back to the McMahon Line, the line the British had set way back at the time of the Great Patriotic Revolution.'

Kabitsin inwardly smiled at this comment. These non-Russians always seemed to try to show understanding and sympathy towards Russian history. He felt it was very patronising. It irked him that the rest of the world saw Russians only as gangsters or peasants, factory workers or Cossacks, and had little respect or appreciation for the true culture or the national resolve. In fact Asil was referring to World War II which Russians call the Great Patriotic War, not Revolution. The only revolution had been in 1917 and this was known by Russians as the October Revolution. He didn't understand why, but these sorts of characters tried so hard and yet always managed to get it wrong.

Russia and Turkey have never really been great allies in their pasts but in recent years there seemed to be a much better understanding. Kabitsin fully accepted that Turkey was now a key conduit for Russian gas to be sold and delivered into Europe, and that today Russia was the second largest trading partner in the Turkish economy. But he could never quite understand someone who lived as an expatriate away from his roots, as this Turk was doing in Dubai, completely disconnected from his own culture. Did he not cherish what made him what he was?

Asil continued sardonically, 'Supposedly, the sides have agreed calming measures including no-fly areas, pre-notification of any troop movements, exchange of maps and so on to resolve these matters.'

Kabitsin knew not to judge from Asil's appearance. Although he looked and dressed like someone whose worst weapon might be a barbed comment across a meeting-room table, yet this was a man who had brutally maintained his position throughout the Middle East. He had also achieved control or interest in much of the Afghanistan trade in opiates. Anyone who could command respect of that bunch of bloodthirsty savages clearly demanded Kabitsin's respect too.

Vasily replied, 'In theory that's true. But soon China will begin to build its planned dams on the Brahmaputra and will divert the waters for use in its agriculture, to supply the dryer northern regions.'

Asil frowned. 'Surely they must know that if they do that it can only lead to a war. It would decimate the water reaching India and Bangladesh.'

'China has always been much closer to Pakistan than these countries, particularly since the Indian's started "buddying" up to the Americans.' Vasily smiled at his use of the Americanism.

The General interrupted, 'Isn't this just China trying to learn from the Arabs? – You know, their saying "a neighbour is an enemy, a neighbour's neighbour is a friend".'

Asil promptly disagreed, shaking his head, still playing it as Mr Cool. 'It was in fact an Indian who said that. Kautilya, sometimes called Chanakaya, in his great work "*Arthasastra*" he set out his advice on statesmanship and what he actually said was "your neighbour is your natural enemy and the neighbour's neighbour is your friend". But that's more of a common sense comment about realities rather than any strategic advice. I personally always believed much more in Sun-Tzu's practical advice in his "Art of War" where he suggests more usefully to "keep your friends close and your enemies closer". The Chinese appear not to be taking notice of their own great man's thoughts!'

Vasily pondered this. 'To some extent that's true, but here's where the dog is buried. You asked me to look at water supply in China, and it's very simple. The Chinese have to find a way to resolve that while they have well in excess of 20% of the world's population, they have only 8% of the world's fresh water with which to support them. Then there's a hugely unequal distribution of population and water to make it even worse. In the north they have two-fifths of their population but only one-fifth of their water.'

Kabitsin was relieved to see the General wanted to move the thought process forward as he said, 'Neither China nor India is particularly good at looking after the fresh water that they have. I understand that China has the dubious privilege to be the home of eight of the world's top ten most polluted rivers. In India, Delhi and Mumbai's air quality generates acid rain that is spoiling its groundwater reserves too.'

Asil sought to explain, 'You asked me to look at the water situation in India. You have to start by recognising that the Indian economy is growing almost exponentially year-on-year. It has a very water-intensive irrigated form of farming for starters. It seems to consume ever more water to support its economic growth. Then there's also the industrial growth, again mostly in water-intensive industries like paper, steel and so on.

'The population continues to grow and in particular there is a large and expanding middle class. They're now demanding the comforts of washing machines and dishwashers, putting even more strain on water resources. And as if this isn't enough, it has the opposite problem to China and needs to siphon off some of its northern water to assist its drier southern areas. It just feels like something really has to give.'

Asil punctuated his point by using his arms to describe the shape of India before him and then his hands to point out the places as he mentioned them. 'That's precisely why India has water disputes with almost every one of its neighbours. It's not just with China, but with Pakistan over the Indus basin, with Nepal which is at least fortunate to be upstream from it and then with sorry little Bangladesh, which being downstream at the very best gets its water arriving polluted, but often the flow is slowed and occasionally even stopped from inside India. Water is needed by all these neighbours, not just water for agriculture, for industry and for people, but in some locations for hydro-electric power too.'

Kabitsin was thinking that his own plan just kept looking ever better and better.

The General stood back up as a clear sign he was ready to lead the conversation forward. He let the murmurs subside and moved back to a more formal presentation. 'This specific region that we're visiting and discussing has another real concern as a result of the current global warming. As I said earlier, the glaciers up here on the Tibetan plateau feed seven major rivers that serve almost half of the world's population. These glaciers are receding year-on-year. As they melt they deliver unhelpful floods, but how long before their erosion leads to droughts?'

He paused. 'So India today sees this Brahmaputra issue as therefore being two-fold. First, it has to fear the glaciers altering and eventually reducing the volumes of water that reach the river, then there's the fear of the Chinese diverting what is there to their own ends. In fact some of their researchers say that global warming alone could reduce India's per-capita water availability by as much as a third. Anything China might do would just serve to worsen this statistic. Of course any decline in water availability has drastic impacts on health but it would also pretty effectively bring India's industrial growth to a shuddering halt.

'So that's the situation as it was yesterday. Two of the most powerful emerging nations, with great geological resources still to exploit, both populated by hard-working people creating an unprecedented industrial growth for their nation, squabbling over a declining water resource that is essential to their well-being.'

The General paused. 'Then today, along comes our still water, and with it we can catapult one or both of these proud nations back into the Stone Age!

'Now just consider that quietly for a few minutes. Just what do you think they might be prepared to pay? We're not just talking of money, what other sorts of deals might they do to avoid that possibility?'

# Chapter 19 - *Brighton, UK*

The Foreign Secretary had broken off from her final preparations for a major conference speech the next day to hold this meeting in her hotel suite. Any excuse would have done, but Sir Joseph and the Professor had jointly asked for a meeting and she was eager for news.

They stood by large windows that opened on to a precarious-looking little veranda that none of them trusted enough to step outside. The windows provided a bird's-eye view out over the promenade looking down at the cold pebbled beach and the steely grey English Channel. Two piers could be seen, one all garish with neon and multi-coloured buildings, the other a gnarled wreck with rusting framework that no one appeared to want to resurrect.

Sir Joseph kicked off. 'We now have our man installed within the Novosibirsk group and we are getting regular reports from him. There's nothing of note so far, but it does seem most likely to have been some chemical spill that has created some pretty noxious form of water. However something rather more serious has come to our attention. We have received reliable reports that there is another sort of game in action around the use of this material. It's coming from a fairly disparate, though largely Russian, group of troublemakers and rabble-rousers.'

The Foreign Secretary was reluctant to stop looking out at the Channel. She always felt something reassuring and calm about even the roughest of seas and this grey calm version was almost soporific. 'What do you mean? Military? Criminal?'

'A little of both it seems. Not quite gipsies, tramps and thieves but the sort of dross that, when the Soviet system collapsed, rapidly rose from under their rocks to fill the vacuum. Powerful, ruthless individuals, they've built up private fiefdoms, created private armies. In Russia they are still connected into the old frameworks and networks, able to work very effectively in the shadows of government, military, industry and crime. Overseas their access to their domestic wealth and their apparent state support gives them piratical status.'

The Professor smiled. 'They sound just like your sort of people.'

'Very droll. At least I can understand them, what they want, what they're capable of; I prefer them to these suicide bombers who are completely unpredictable, beyond reason. These people though have sprung up all over the globe with the resources and the lack of scruples to take on any opportunity that they might uncover. This still water is perhaps just their latest opportunity.'

The Foreign Secretary broke from her reverie, closed the large windows and walked back to the lounge area of the suite. 'So how are they connected to this still water?'

'We believe they've gained access to some of the material and our intelligence says they have already used it. You will have seen reports of that incident in eastern Kazakhstan; well we are fairly reliably informed it was still water that had been deliberately used. We had initially thought that there had been some sort of spillage or pollution. It devastated a local water system killing all the plant life, all the fish and a dozen or two unfortunates who had in some manner come into contact with it.' Sir Joseph went to the brandy decanter and nodded. Getting assent he started to pour into the first balloon, tipping it on to its side to ensure that he achieved just the right level.

'Perhaps rather more interesting is that it effectively knocked out a major hydro-electric plant and major metal works along the course of a river. But only for several days, mark you. There was no lasting damage after they'd been swilled through with fresh water. As a weapon it could be even more effective than a neutron bomb.'

He was passing out the brandy balloons and added for the Professor, 'You may recall that the neutron bomb was designed to minimise any material damage while killing the humans on the battlefield. This water seems to manage all of that, together with the effective seizing up of any industrial plant without apparently damaging it.' Having completed the distribution of the drinks, he raised his glass. 'Let's toast, the perfect weapon.'

The Foreign Secretary took a deep draught. 'Boys and their toys! Let's stop admiring it and work out how we can counter it please.'

Sir Joseph replied, 'While there's no real progress on international water dispute mechanisms, something like this is a real risk. As the Professor advised us, the vast majority of the world's river basins have no treaties in place between the neighbouring states. In Asia it's estimated that more than a fifth of the population has no easy access to water and there are some sixty potential flashpoint river basins. It's not just Kazakhstan, it's all the other "stans" too, Uzbekistan, Kyrgyzstan, Tajikistan... Then there's the River Jordan with Israel, Syria and Jordan squabbling over it. Also the Mekong area where it's China, Myanmar, Laos, Thailand, Cambodia and Vietnam that are all at odds.'

The Professor added, 'None of this is news. The UN has long forecast that competition for fresh water will become a source of conflict and wars. The USA's National Intelligence Council said that interstate conflict will increase during coming years as countries press up against the limits of available supplies.'

Sir Joseph countered, 'I believe that the last recorded actual water war was over 4,500 years ago, in Mesopotamia. Appropriate as the very name means "land between waters". In more recent times there has generally been common sense and cooperation in creating treaties.'

'Yes but in just the last fifty years the world population has grown from 2.5 billion to some 7 billion – just that fact means mathematically that the renewable water supply per person has fallen by almost 65%! At least oil, gas and coal do have some substitutes but water does not! Within ten years, some 40% of the world population will live in locations where it is at least difficult, and in some cases impossible, to mobilise enough water to satisfy the food, industrial and health needs of that region. So what will they do? Sit back and let that happen to them?'

This last comment had them all nursing their brandy balloons, trying to add warmth to the spirit. 'But is there any useful data from this Kazakh event? Do we know how much of the water they added to the river? Do they have a process that changes the water? What made it stop? Do they have some sort of antidote?'

# Chapter 20 - *Novosibirsk, Russia*

Deep inside the Akademgorodok Dmitry tried again to call one of the assembled scientific team's interminable meetings to order. 'The General has made clear to me that we have three prime objectives.'

He checked them off on his fingers. 'First to understand fully what this still water is and where it came from; we do not seem to be getting any closer to knowing that. Second, to understand if there is an antidote or some way we can stop any water that it touches from converting into still water. Third, is for us to establish if there are any positive uses for this new material. Valéry, you are leading the team in trying to understand it, so what is being done here?'

Valéry had proven clearly to be first a politician and only second a scientist. Medium-height, dark haired, dark-eyed, Paul thought that he must have brought a hairdresser with him or maybe he got up very early each morning to get his hair to be so perfectly coiffed. Perhaps it was something to do with a bloke living his life with a girl's name?

'We have split this investigation into two teams,' Valéry mirrored Dmitry's finger counting. 'A research team that is trying to investigate anything we know of the location where it was found, what might have made it appear there. Then we have a technical team that is investigating the material itself though we are having a great deal of trouble with compatibility of the various equipment you have provided.'

Dmitry countered, 'I understand about the scientific equipment but surely the PCs we've supplied have a normal qwerty keyboard, Microsoft Office and all that you might need?'

'We French of course use the "azerty" keyboard and your pirated version of the Microsoft software has a number of flaws; for one it keeps defaulting to Cyrillic. It's the combination of these problems that is slowing us up. The scientific equipment is all labelled in Cyrillic too and so we have to try to explain to the technicians what we want and then try to understand what they are saying that the equipment is showing. Are there technicians with better English, or better still French?'

'I'll put your request to the General.'

Ellise was a tad surprised by this criticism. She had also experienced a few minor difficulties with the computers but in general had been pleasantly surprised by the competence of the local technology. She had expected far worse, but there really was nothing worthy of this complaint.

Valéry continued, 'Then there is the matter of Monsieur Solonik and his team.' He looked across at the 'guard' at the door. 'Please tell me, must they follow us everywhere? We can find nowhere that is private, for us to discuss our thinking. Can we have some privacy?'

Paul agreed that Lev and his goons were taking things too far. They seemed particularly dogged in following Ellise. He virtually had to stand guard at the toilet door for her to be sure she was undisturbed, but he believed that the Frenchman was really trying just to hide the fact that the technical team that he was heading had made next to no progress.

Paul and Ellise had been placed within the research team, which suited him as he hoped this would mean they would get the chance to go up to the Arctic to investigate the site. The two other members of this team were a Russian, who nodded enthusiastically as if he understood everything Paul said to him but in truth was perhaps getting less than half of it, and a Pole, who appeared to have been based in Russia long-term and so might best be now considered a native. Though the Pole's English was better he didn't seem to have any more luck in getting information through to the Russian.

Paul had therefore relegated the two to fetching and carrying for him and Ellise. They appeared to be content with this approach but did seem to lead them off on tangents. Paul's request for maps and any data on the area led them into producing a whole world of data that was of dubious value.

The general location from which the still water had been taken proved to be a veritable potpourri of fact and fable, all wrapped up in confusion that was either deliberately secretive or dementedly semantic. It felt to Paul just like that local tourist staple, a Russian doll. It was necessary to peel off layer after layer to establish whether the requests were just not being properly understood or whether they were asking about something that the Russians considered secret and were deliberately deflecting them.

It reminded Paul of Winston Churchill's 'bodyguard of lies'. He had said in WWII that the truth, perhaps specifically of the Allies' cracking of the Enigma code, was so important that it needed to be surrounded by a bodyguard of lies. That's just how this felt. Far from trying to help, the locals were more interested in hiding anything useful deep inside that Russian doll.

From the facts that they could establish it could be seen that the small island group, where the still water was found, formed a virtual north-eastern boundary to the Kara Sea. The sea was bordered to the north-west by another large island, Novaya Zemlya, leaving a wide northern route out to the Arctic Ocean. At the southern edge of the Kara Sea was mainland Russia, the long coastline passing through two autonomous regions, Yamalo-Nenetskiy to the west and Taymyrskiy to the east.

Taymyrskiy proved to have had a rich ancient past. It had been part of Earth's supercontinent, Pangea, that Paul knew had once reached from the South Pole to the North Pole, the rest of Earth being covered by one large single ocean.

His hosts had, irrelevantly yet joyfully, mentioned there of course had been an earlier supercontinent called Rodinia from the Russian *Rodinya* meaning motherland. This existed around 900 million years ago and their suggestion was that somehow, because of this, Russia was in fact the mother of all lands! They also pointed out that the name for the early super-ocean was Mirovia also from the Russian *mir*, meaning globe. Paul made a mental note to investigate why these words, that he had been fully aware of before, but had failed to see any Russian connection, were not more traditionally based on the Greek or the Latin.

What Paul had found was that it was also this very region where an extremely hot plume of mantle rock had exploded through Pangea some 250 million years ago. Of course he knew all about this event, it was what had brought to an end the Permian period, the end of the whole Palaeozoic era, Palaeozoic literally meaning 'ancient life'. This was the geological period when early plant and animal life that had first flourished on the Earth had a mass extinction – thanks to this plume.

His hosts provided data to show that outside the city of Noril'sk, the northernmost city of Taymyrskiy, in fact the most northerly city in the world, there was an area of well over two million square kilometres of volcanic debris in places up to three kilometres deep, providing a lasting memorial to that important incident in our pre-history. The explosion had erupted huge quantities of dust, water vapour, carbon dioxide and sulphur dioxide high up into the atmosphere where it effectively blocked out all the sunlight. The water vapour and sulphur dioxide then combined to become sulphuric acid and bathed the Earth in an acid rain.

Paul knew that while this event was by far and away the largest there were also coincident eruptions in China. As a result over 90% of the relatively-recent emerging onshore life had been extinguished. This included small tetrapods, early reptiles and many species of insect; marine life that had taken over 300 million years to evolve to its then current state was simply wiped out too. Corals, sea-lilies, lampshells, ammonoids were all devastated. It was also to prove the end for the trilobites, today one of the more popular fossils for amateur and professional collectors alike. Paul knew that geologists' investigations had concluded that this was perhaps the single most catastrophic event in the Earth's history.

Sea levels declined at around this period too. It had been surmised that perhaps the one-sea, one-continent format had interfered with ocean currents making the seas stagnate. If true then ocean floors would have sunk, the receding tides would have exposed huge coal deposits around Pangea and these would in turn have released vast quantities of carbon dioxide. This greenhouse gas would then have heated up the atmosphere and paved the way for the dinosaurs and mammals to emerge and to inherit the Earth. The dinosaurs did just that for somewhat less than 200 million years before another mass extinction some 65 million years ago saw most of them off too.

So was the proximity of this event related? Was this still water some ancient form of water? Perhaps something created by these catastrophic times and only now being released as modern man-made greenhouse gases were melting this area of permafrost and ice?

The steadily reducing weight of ice up at these northern regions had allowed the land mass to move slowly back to its 'natural' state. Paul knew that Scandinavia had risen well over a hundred metres in the last 7,000 years and was calculated to need to rise by another two hundred metres to return to its naturally stable state. Could this steady rise have brought something new, or rather very old, to the surface?

Paul concluded that they could not know without going to see for themselves.

Tom was not part of either of Valéry's teams; he had managed to arrange to be working independently with the sample itself, not worrying where it came from, just trying to understand what it was. The technicians were doing all the grunt for him, taking samples of the material and applying the tests that he and others of the team requested.

It did not seem to have any radioactivity but then deuterium should not have shown any. Tom would only have expected there to be radioactivity with $^3$H or T, tritium, or any of the unstable $^4$H to $^7$H varieties that are only really able to be synthesised in laboratories and not naturally occurring. The basic form of hydrogen is protium, or $^1$H, named because there is just one proton in its nucleus.

Tom had researched deuterium, the other relatively stable form of hydrogen with one proton and one neutron. He learned that it occurs naturally, though insignificantly, in water, is not at all toxic in small quantities and can be used in experiments and medicines as a 'label'. It was used in WWII as heavy water rocket fuel and is expected in the future to become a suitable fuel for nuclear fusion.

Tritium, with one neutron and two protons, can exist naturally in the atmosphere and is one of the by-products detected in nuclear weapons testing, though it tends to decay into a form of helium with a half-life of around twelve years.

The other forms of hydrogen – tetranium, pentium, hexium, septium, muonium – do not appear naturally and when fabricated disappear many times faster than the blink of an eye and so were highly unlikely to be found, but still they tested the samples for any presence.

Overall their efforts showed the presence of only the simpler hydrogen isotopes of protium and deuterium.

Having pondered these old events at length, Paul decided to spend his time initially seeking out some more modern cause for the still water. The Kara Sea, is the outlet for both the Ob and the Yenisey Rivers. These two rivers cross the flat ground of the West Siberian Plain.

He talked his thinking through with Ellise, 'Geologically Siberia has always proved pretty stoic. It was originally a part of the Arctica continent some 2.5 billion years ago, then later moved away to join up during the formation of Rodinia.'

'The super-continent?'

'Yes, but then Rodinia broke up, Siberia slipped in to a few other combinations. It even went its own way as an island for a while, but later coalesced again with the creation of Pangea.'

'Another super-continent?'

'Yes but it happened much later. Then when Pangea broke up Serbia went through various other groupings later to become part of Laurasia. This grouping subsequently fractured to become North America and Eurasia. As part of Eurasia, Siberia had to take the brunt of the impact from the Indian subcontinent as it abruptly joined up with Asia.'

'An awful lot of shuffling around.'

'Yes, but remember we are talking of millions of years.'

'So it wasn't like continental dodgems?'

'Siberia's determined patience appears set to be rewarded as it is currently assumed that it will become a subtropical region perhaps 250 million years into the future.'

On their flight here they had both seen that the plain today has a vast system of marshes covered with glacial deposits. Paul was aware that through this area modern Russia had managed to pour almost every known pollutant that all of mankind's ingenuity has managed to create.

Logically Paul assumed that therefore there must have been some chemical or more likely nuclear change to the water to create this still water. But then water does not change its chemical structure through any of its phases; it dissolves and carries almost anything you care to mix with it, so to make changes at the molecular level would imply must have been a nuclear issue, surely?

There lay the rub; these guys were never going to admit to a nuclear spillage or an accident. Again Paul concluded the only way was for them to go there and see for themselves.


Tom loved the 'weird' sciences and over the years had written reams about them. Straight science is dull; add a bit of strangeness and he found he could eat out for weeks on the articles he wrote. He particularly liked those ideas that almost appeared counter-intuitive and he very definitely appreciated those where they seemed to have emerged from an individual's dogged nagging and niggling at the facts, working against all the odds, finally coming up with something significant at the end.

In this latter category he placed dendrochronology, a means of dating wood by its tree-ring growth. Just imagine the research, the mind-numbing amount of analysis, then setting up the database to allow it all to work.

In a similar vein there was hydrogeology, a way of tracing the geographic origin of the earth's waters by comparing the given sample of interest against an established series of water standards. By measuring any small detected variations in the abundance of deuterium and the heavy oxygen isotopes $^{17}O$ and $^{18}O$ you could conclude from where the water had originated.

He thought that this technique might be unknown to the technicians here and was therefore surprised that they were not only able to understand but had already run the investigation for him.

This came back with disturbing results. They did not relate to any of the recorded results within the database which was pretty much a comprehensive list of all the world's waters. So where had it come from? If didn't match any in the extensive databases then might it be extra-terrestrial?

Ellise had been supplied with reams of data of an incident from the more recent past that had occurred at the Podkamennaya Tunguska River, a tributary of the Yenisey.

It happened 600 kilometres south of Noril'sk, itself being around 900 kilometres south of where the still water had come from. Ellise felt that this might be something of a stretch being so far away, but there was that Yenisey connection again so she collated the data for Paul.

In June 1908 there had been a tremendous explosion said to have devastated some 80 million trees across an area of 2,000 square kilometres. Yet its impact on the Richter Scale, which was developed a generation or so later, would only have shown it as a 5.0, a quite moderate range event that happens around 800 times in the world every single year. So at first sight it was not a particularly significant occurrence, but the more she read she realised that given its other features this was very much a one-off event.

The associated explosion in the air was perhaps a thousand times greater than Hiroshima. Although most of the documents talked of it as an impact, many of the subsequent investigations had concluded that in fact it was a meteor or comet that had burst in the air before it had a chance to reach the surface to in fact make an impact. Supporting this approach were reports of a bluish light seen in the sky and then a whole series of small impacts being heard. Windows were blown out hundreds of kilometres away and a shock wave was said to have knocked people to the ground.

Any initial investigations were either cursory or, more likely, lost. This was a remote region with little real inherent interest and a very small and powerless population. Europe at that time had other things on its mind as it was fermenting towards WWI. More locally the Russian Revolution, followed by the civil war, created a series of much more pressing matters at that time. So the first real accounts supplied to Ellise were not dated before 1927 and they seemed largely to show that the investigation team had been disappointed not to find a crater but instead a fifty kilometre trail of devastation through the heavily forested land.

The notion of an impact was pretty tenaciously retained in their thinking, with subsequent investigators even draining a bog to try to prove it was the site of an impact crater. Quite recently some Italian scientists suggested that Lake Cheko was the impact site but silt in the lake and pre-dated records of the lake's existence indicated it had been around long before the event.

When Ellise showed her findings to Paul he felt they really needed to go to the area and see it and figuratively to touch it before he could really appreciate what was going on.

Tom had asked for a full chemical analysis of any traces in the water expecting to find something there as a significant solute that would explain some of its properties.

The first printout he received started at the simple level, looking almost as if the technician was performing more as a pool guy or perhaps an aquarium keeper. It gave the pH levels, the temperature and conductivity, then commented on the chlorine levels and the hardness. It looked at the salinity and alkalinity, investigated what ammonia, nitrites and nitrates existed. Tome felt that all of this was perfect if you were checking whether you could trust it enough for your valuable koi carp!

There was nothing in this report that reached to the heart of the matter. Were there any biological traces? What about metallic solutes? What was the mix of $D^2O$ to $H^2O$? He tried again setting out his thoughts as to what he was wanting to see or to eliminate.

Hoping that this time he would get what he needed, he turned his mind to the subject of still water and normal water and how they might interact or affect each other.

Mark was allocated to a team that was looking at the potential for an antidote, how to combat the still water. As a team they were initially short on experimental evidence and were therefore keeping the technicians busy with a whole host of tests. But Mark had some inside data. He alone among the team members knew the details of the Kazakhstan incident and had some qualitative information about what had happened there.

His father was certainly in government but not the political wing of it as he tended to suggest. 'Father' was his word and his alibi for the Company. As an experienced CIA hum-int operative he found the Okie persona and the story of a high-powered father worked every time. The CIA did rely for much of its data on electronic and satellite intelligence but the human intelligence variety, or hum-int, had not quite been squeezed out of the equation yet.

Every Western organisation was fully familiar with rich-kids or spoilt kids, who despite privileges never really did much with their education, then after college never settled to anything, probably because they really didn't need to. They were all familiar with fathers who had the power to pull strings, of nepotism putting incompetents and wasters into roles that they just had not earned.

A folksy kid, who was fun and likeable, one who wasn't challenging your role or taking a management role above you, proved to be a winner every time. Particularly if this person appeared to be ready to take on any chore without complaint. He had found this simple approach in any team would ensure he was able to move around a facility with ease, gain access to all and any files, physical or electronic.

Fortunately he looked eight to ten years younger than he was, but he thought that perhaps he should already be working up a new approach for three or four years' time when he would cease to have the look that he had developed as his key asset.

His people had monitored everything at the original site. They'd even had a submarine in the area when the research ship had been scuttled, though it had been ordered not to interfere and not to get in too close.

He had been down in the Galápagos both to collect geological data but also to acquire DNA samples of the more unusual animals found there including the extremely long-lived giant tortoises, but with the whole world looking at the islands as some sort of almost religious site, they had to go gently.

When this new Russian 'away-team' was being recruited, his previous contact with Ellise, Paul and Tom had brought his file to the top and the Company had no trouble getting him invited. He assumed they must have someone deeply located within the Russian group. Though Ellise and Paul were completely unaware of it, the locals believed he was part of their NOAA team.

He had also seen some data and pictures on the Kazakhstan incident; interesting, but there was not enough real information. The photos offered no insight other than the floating bloated fish at the surface but he had seen some detailed shots of the moment that the still water was being added to the lake. It could not be completely confirmed but he was pretty sure one of the three at that lakeside was none other than the large head of security who often stood at the main entrance to the labs.

It was clear that the amount of water added could not have been more than a hundred litres so just how had it expanded? Then why had the still water not kept on spreading? Did it just run out of steam at Semipalatinsk, or was there an effective antidote that it encountered and it was this that had stopped it?

Vital questions if they were to be able to mount a credible defence for it for Homeland Security. He reflected, 'Just imagine somebody putting still water in to the water supply for Washington, New York, Los Angeles,' he smiled, 'or even Oklahoma?'

Ellise was reading through some rather more scientific appraisals from the 1950s and 1960s and commented, 'This impact investigation team looking into the 1908 event at ground zero had recorded that they found lots of tiny glass-like spheres that proved to be largely nickel and iridium.'

Paul quoted from a report that he was reading, also from the late 1950s, 'Apparently lots of the local people were covered with boils after the explosion. Whole families dying as a result. Initially it was dismissed as perhaps a smallpox epidemic. Later investigators with more modern mindsets had tested but found no significant increase in radioactivity in the area. But that's clearly what they had expected.'

Ellise cited yet another report, 'There were reports of very bright nights for several weeks after. It was bright enough to read at night.'

Paul was then enthralled to find a whole report, punctuated with photos, of an experiment from the 1960s where a model of the area was recreated with matches to represent the trees and a series of charges were slid down a wire and exploded to try to replicate the butterfly-shaped damage that had been noted. This Heath Robinson approach did manage to conclude and prove that the body must have come in at an angle of $30°$ and at $115°$ east of north. Investigators also concluded from this that the 'meteor' must have exploded between perhaps six and ten kilometres above the surface of the Earth.

From the Internet they worked their way through a whole raft of papers and theories on the subject; some were clearly from crackpots, but some championed the theory that this must have been a small comet which explained the blue light. Also it was suggested that as it would have been made up of mostly ice and other debris, it would have largely been dissipated on entry and that would explain why there was no impact site. A comet called Encke, discovered next after Halley's, does deliver meteor storms called the Taurids at several times through the year, June being one of them, so this was quite a credible suggestion.

Paul was bemused when following up on that proposal. He'd found a referenced document that described an interesting Han Dynasty comet-atlas. It had been produced in around 168 BC, on silk, and it used special symbols attributed to particular comets, none too surprising given the Chinese calligraphic approach to communication. Encke, or perhaps it was in fact an even earlier larger comet of which it had once been part, arrived at an odd angle to the Earth and probably had gas coming from it at an odd angle too. This gave it a Catherine wheel appearance and the symbol used for it in the atlas was perhaps one of the earliest recorded drawings of a swastika!

Other reports had asked if it had been a comet then why had it gone on to cause such damage if it had in fact disintegrated? Others preferred to think it was part of an asteroid as one piece of research showed it appeared to have come from the asteroid belt. Still others had postulated that this might in fact have been a black hole, though this did not seem to be well considered in the scientific 'hierarchy'.

Perhaps the most chilling document in the pack was one from the late 1980s. Ellise said, 'Look at this, this team considered whether the incident may have been a natural hydrogen bomb. They suggested that if the comet had contained high levels of, wait for it, deuterium!, then on entry to the atmosphere it could well have created a natural nuclear fusion reaction. They go on to say that it would have spread carbon-14 but any radiation would have been negligible, so that works too. Perhaps there was still enough to cause boils?

Paul asked, 'Where's that report you had about the glass beads?' As she looked for it he sought out an earlier reference he had seen to the mass extinction of the dinosaurs. Comparing the two, he added, 'There I thought I was right. It says here that they discovered a clay that was very rich in iridium in the Gulf of Mexico. It had been deposited 65m years ago, which is precisely where and when it's generally accepted the massive asteroid or comet impact had landed to kill the dinosaurs off.'

'Isn't the area affected just too far away from our site to be of any interest?'

'What's a mere 1,000 kilometres when we're talking of astronomic events? I read somewhere in amongst all of this that someone calculated that if whatever it was had been less than five hours later in arriving, then it would have wiped out St Petersburg. I bet you we'd have had a much more detailed and prompt investigation of that one!'

'So what are you thinking? That somehow this comet deposited stuff in the Yenisey and somehow now a century later it decided to pop up?'

Paul went very quiet, then pulled her close, spread out a map and said quietly, 'What if the Kara Sea was the impact site? All that we've read of here may be just a sideshow, a fragment that broke off the main solid core of the comet. And then it travelled on 1,000 kilometres.' He turned around a map, 'Just look at that island, Novaya Zemlya, doesn't that look like the debris pushed up by an impact to you?'

'Surely this would have been noticed?'

'They didn't even get to the North Pole until, what, 1908 or 1909 so who would have been around there at that time? Where's that article on Noril'sk? Here you are. The settlement didn't start until around 1920 when they mined for nickel, copper and palladium, most of that formed by the magma plume.'

Ellise skimmed the article, 'Noril'sk sounds like a great place, it manages single-handedly to emit an amazing 1% of all the sulphur dioxide emissions in the entire world! They say here that its pollution of heavy metals is such that its soil is actually economically worth mining!'

Paul said, 'I'm not quite so sure that I do want to go there!'

# Chapter 21 - *Lhasa, Tibet*

Still deep in session up in their Himalayan eyrie, the General brought them back to the table following a brief coffee break.

'So I think that we are all agreed then that the "best game in town" for us will be to exploit this China versus India opportunity, two huge markets threatened by just one attack. Yes there is much to do, both to establish the means by which we will present the proposition to them and we need to create a foolproof series of cut-outs back to us so that our security is assured. We can assume that both countries will use all of their national resources to seek us out and to stop us if they can.

'While it was a little helpful for us to understand the sort of effects the water can have, the lack of any documentary material from the Kazakhstan event means that we need to find the site for another demonstration or a series of them as a means of convincing our potential clients of our proposition. Twenty-six dead and some floating wildlife is not really going to be very compelling to our clients.'

Kabitsin had never been any good at taking criticism and this was how he saw the General's comments. This was really why he hated taking the back seat. Here was this clown who wouldn't have the first clue of how to handle the real world, pouring him a bitter drink and he just had to sit there and put it behind his collar and swallow it. He decided to relax and while this idiot prattled he would take his own thinking forward.

The General looked around the room. 'I can run through some alternatives, of course, but I thought this was a good opportunity for each of you, now you have had chance to ponder, to make your own pitch for handling the next demo site.'

Asil was first up, 'I have one for you, right in my own backyard. My country has our South-Eastern Anatolia Project or GAP, which is a whole series of dams and hydroelectric plants along both the Tigris and the Euphrates. My vote for the demonstration would be that we use it on the Tigris where it flows into the Kurdish part of northern Iraq, from the Taurus Mountain area down to Mosul. That would be my proposal.'

The General smiled. 'I am fully aware of your issues with the Kurds but surely this would then enrage and engage the Americans and their allies. It would appear to be an attack on their fragile control of Iraq? We don't want to put our fingers in their mouth.'

Asil smiled back, 'Personally, I saw anything that might also annoy the Americans as just another major benefit of the scheme.'

The General queried, 'But just how are they meant to notice? The number of bodies they have been pulling out of the Tigris in Iraq is incredible. In the last year alone there have been many hundreds of them, most of them seeming to have been tortured before being dumped in the river. The others are those who were trying to re-establish fishing on the river. They seem to persevere despite the huge amount of both industrial and military pollution. They either get shot by the military, as it is currently illegal to fish, or get in the way of the insurgent freedom fighters who are trying to set traps for the military that use the river. So please appreciate that we've done our homework. Who else has a proposal?'

Kabitsin's geography was pretty weak but he did know enough to be aware that most of the oil was in the south of Iraq not up in the more lightly populated north, so how could this be interesting to them? He didn't really care too much about this as a target, the Kurds were a bunch of losers anyway, the numbers involved would just not be interesting enough for him.

Another contributor who looked more of a city-type was their western and Central European representative, Pavel Borovik, a Russian based out of Frankfurt. 'My vote goes for the Danube. I mean specifically the stretch that forms the border between Romania and Bulgaria. I don't begin to understand how this still water works but don't both Sofia and Bucharest have tributaries running through them that then join up with the Danube?'

The General flipped open a large atlas, 'Yes, you're right. It's the Iskûr from Sofia and the Arges from Bucharest. They join the Danube only about 150km apart. But why there?'

'Throughout the major western Europe cities most of our real problem in maintaining our grip on prostitution and drugs is being faced with strong opponents from among those two countries' nationals. They need to be taught a lesson or two, learn their place in the scheme of things. At the moment they are greedily and ruthlessly hurting our operations.'

'To be honest this sounds a little too much of a straight piece of revenge. But I can appreciate that removing or preoccupying an enemy of our enterprises has some value.'

Borovik countered, 'Surely for our demonstration, we just need it to be effective. It doesn't need to have any direct return?'

'I don't think that the Chinese or the Indians will be too concerned about those two nations. We've had centuries of troubles in the Balkans but does anyone ever really care?'

Kabitsin felt warmer towards this plan than the Iraqi Kurdish one. The Balkans and Yugoslavia had always been a big disappointment for him. Other than the Romanians they were largely fellow Slavs, weren't they? But after all that Russia had done for them down the years, all of this was completely ignored until the Serbs run into trouble and then who did they run to for support? Mother Russia of course.

'There are quite a few options in my area.' The speaker was not someone you would lose in a crowd. Kabitsin thought he must be pretty close to 2m tall and big with it, perhaps 120 kilos, yet fit and capable of carrying off all that bulk. If he'd been an American he would have been signed up instantly as a line backer or for a basketball team, but as a South African he'd been recruited for the heart of a rugby scrum. His face showed he'd not spent much time in the relative safety of that position. It was not just the broken nose but the fact that all the other features appeared to have been sand-blasted smooth. His ears were just solid lumps of meat that had little obvious sign of a remaining hole to hear through.

Wim Brockenhorst was based out of Cairo and, so far as this group was concerned, controlled the whole of Africa from there. 'The Congo River is a hot spot, but I guess again it's a question of who really cares? Then there's the Zambezi but while Mugabe clings to power in Zimbabwe, because he's such a *schmo*, who would care? So I guess the Nile might just be my favourite. I'm talking of course of the Ethiopia and Sudan stretches of the Blue Nile from Addis Ababa to Khartoum, well away from Dharfur and all those pop star photo-opportunities.'

The General was placatory, 'Hm, it's interesting, not sure where our angle would be? And again would the Chinese or the Indians care?'

Kabitsin had no interest in Africa. He had never been there, couldn't see the point. It seemed to be run by a whole bunch of degenerates who starved their people to make themselves and their cronies rich. They couldn't seem to control themselves on any level, as evidenced by the HIV and AIDS epidemics spreading across that continent. It served them right so far as he was concerned.

Wim had grown up believing in apartheid and had felt that his country had been completely ruined by its recent history. He believed the African was generally lazy, ungrateful and definitely inferior. But he was a modern person and had moderated what he said and did in this subject area. He knew that most people he met would assume his beliefs were as they actually were, but he found there was little benefit in confirming this view. But if he and Kabitsin were to be tested according to the extent of their racism then Wim was a mere B-minus to Kabitsin coming top of the class.

Wim countered, 'The Chinese would certainly care in the Congo. They're virtually grabbing everything that they can in the area for their own needs. Congo, Ghana, Tanzania, and Uganda – you can't move for the Chinese. They suggest that they're helping these Third World countries as some sort of genuine and humanitarian initiative. You only have to look at their record at home to see that this isn't the motivation. They promise all sorts of infrastructure projects in return for keeping the Chinese home economy served with oil and the other natural resources it needs. Rest assured that anything we did in Africa would be sure to get all of the Chinese attention.'

'So that's one for our shortlist. Others?'

# Chapter 22 - *Novosibirsk, Russia*

The days at the Akademgorodok started to institutionalise them, their routine taking on a programme of working sessions, group meetings and regular breaks for refreshments and meals. Paul had agreed with Ellise to keep his theory to themselves for now, but they did share it with Mark over drinks later that evening in what served as a mess hall for the team.

Mark was at his Okie best, 'That's brilliant, worthy of Sherlock Holmes himself. Did I mention I went to see 221B Baker Street when I was in London? What a huge disappointment!'

His wanderings would not dampen Ellise's pride in Paul's discovery. 'Don't you see this comet could have deposited a huge supply of deuterium deep in the Kara Sea. The deuterium would have frozen at higher temperatures than the surrounding water, as we've seen here, so even in June it could have solidified. And, because of its density it would have sunk to the bottom, again as we've seen the still water does in our experiments.'

Mark asked, 'But what blew up then to cause the 1908 event?'

'Part of the comet blew up, but a lumpy piece could somehow have ploughed on and sunk into the sea just as Paul described.'

Paul said, 'We must be able to prove it before making an announcement. I've downloaded all that I could find on these Novaya Zemlya Islands. Disappointingly I learned that they've been recorded in history since the 11th century and the general wisdom is that it's assumed to be the northern edge of the Urals. It is very mountainous; the northern island is covered in glaciers. Given its location in the frozen north, perhaps the actual shape and mapping is all so vague that a 1908 reconfiguration might well have gone unnoticed.'

Ellise pressed close, 'When did they start living on it?'

'Various explorers called there including Barents himself in the late 16th century. The west coast wasn't mapped until the 1820s, can't find any reference to the east coast. Seems that there were some people living there from 1870, but there's only around two thousand souls who live out there even today.'

Mark queried, 'What, are they fishermen?'

'Yes, there do seem to be some who fish, trap and apparently they also hunt polar bears and seals. But it's really been used as a military base for some time. It has an airbase, Rogachevo, where they ran intercept missions early on in the Cold War. When aircraft ranges were much shorter, it was a useful staging base. It's also been a nuclear test site for both underground and atmospheric tests. Most of this appears to be around the middle portion where there's a narrow strait between the two main islands.

'I found a reference to an underground test in 1973 that registered at Richter 6.9. It apparently set off a huge avalanche that stopped several run-off streams from the glaciers and created a new lake. So it doesn't sound like they treasure this bit of real estate too much.'

'When did they stop testing there?'

'Formally, from what I can see it was around 1990 after *glasnost* revealed it was there and as a result there had been some Greenpeace protests to focus attention on it. They were the last tests Russia did apparently. But then it seems that this refers only to nuclear test explosions and they still run tests called "subcritical hydronuclear experiments" there each autumn, whatever that means. Seems these are based on small quantities, around 100 grammes a time, of weapons-grade plutonium. They're carried out on the most northerly part of the southern island.'

Ellise was still enthusiastic, 'So there it is. We have our comet core sitting off, against or perhaps even on the island. Then, we have these subcritical nuclear whatsits every autumn somehow wakening it up. The timing's right and just look at the map, the flow into the Kara Sea must be almost directly north, out from the estuaries of the rivers. These must then get swept around eastward with this island group acting as a baffle. So where else would you expect anything to end up? Right here in the location that the still water did in fact show up.'

Mark let down his guard a tad. 'But I don't envy you trying to get them to admit to any of that!'

Tom had managed to stay late; perhaps the security was relaxing a little, for they had left him in the labs alone. He was still keen to look at how the still water and normal water interacted. He wanted to understand why it appeared that they did interact in some conditions and not in others.

He had managed a process where he could get two small samples not to interact but because the materials to all intents and purposes looked very similar this was a tough situation to monitor. He had the idea to add an inert dye to the normal water so that he was able to see the meniscus that formed across the area of contact between the two materials.

The normal water had done as it did normally, pushing out a convex meniscus due to its surface tension, the water molecules inside the water being in a sort of stasis with their fellows, but those at the surface being pulled back by the fluid.

It is this surface tension that allows insects to walk on water. The same effect makes water bead on a freshly polished car, the small quantities of water naturally curving into a sphere as this provides the smallest surface area for a given volume of water.

Tom knew that surface tension could be altered by temperature and pressure, and that a solute in the water could change the surface tension too. He therefore committed himself to a whole raft of tests at various temperatures and pressures, and he then performed the same tests with a series of solutes.

He settled down to the sort of dogged 'gnawing at a bone' that he so appreciated in others. It was a pleasantly mindless repetitive task that he hoped would expand their understanding of this new water. Apply a defined series of conditions, record the result, keep modifying the conditions until a change occurs, and then start with a new sample.

It was quite late when he heard approaching voices. Like some sort of guilty child he found himself hiding from whoever it was who was coming.

From his hiding place he eventually realised that it was Mark who was currently talking. It took a while because Mark's tone and delivery were different somehow. He sounded much more assertive, more decisive, still with his distinctive accent but none of the folksy 'Oh gee' stuff.

'Look I cannot deal with someone sight unseen. If this guy wants to talk with me directly then I'm happy to look at his proposition.'

Tom strained to hear the more quietly spoken companion who had entered with Mark. A Russian, but it was not immediately obvious who it might be.

'Clearly he knows of your affiliation because he specifically asked me to talk with you and with no one else.'

'So just precisely what is it that he is proposing?'

'I have been placed here by him. My only reason for being here is the still water. He wants me to feed him with all the conclusions reached by the team. I can of course report anything that is concluded within my role here. But he wants to be a little ahead of that point, to hear of the theories nice and early. What he asks is that he has any useful thoughts or lines of enquiry confirmed with him early enough that we, you and I, can ensure that they never do become part of any published conclusions from this team.'

'Just what does he need this information for?'

'I am afraid that he will have to tell you himself. He has not told me what his objectives might be. But as confirmation of his credentials he has asked me to tell you that the Kazakhstan event, that your people will have monitored, was something he did as a demonstration. That there will be another.'

Tom was crawling behind the bench to seek a position to identify the Russian.

'Is he after the samples?'

'No, he already has enough of the material. But he is interested to know if there is any way we can manufacture the material for him to expand his supplies.'

'So what, other than manufacture, does he want to hear about?'

'Well, clearly any antidote would be of a high priority, and he has asked me specifically for details of any new applications that the team members might have considered, no matter how outlandish the thought might be.'

'You say he knows of my Company connections.'

'You were identified pretty early in the process of agreeing the Western attendees. We looked at everyone. There were bound to be at least promises of support from the national intelligence organisations in each group, and just what were you here for unless you were Company?'

Tom risked a slow and cautious manoeuvre to peer around the bench at floor level as the shadows of the high walls of the containment chamber made this a particularly gloomy part of the labs. He withdrew back behind the counter having confirmed that the Russian was Dmitry.

'So when do I get to meet this Kabitsin?'

'He's tangled in a conference out of the country at the moment, but in the next few days.' Dmitry opened the door for Mark to leave, neither considering that the lights should be extinguished.

Tom was stunned. He had to get all this information back to Sir Joseph but first he needed to finish his sequence of tests. Returning to the chamber and his interrupted test, he jumped at a noise across the room but when he concluded it was just one of those odd creaks that signified nothing, he turned back to his investigation. It was then that he noted something pretty unusual.

He collected all his observations together, on paper, not on the networked PC that could be monitored, and concluded that these results could not be turned in to the team.

# Chapter 23 - *Lhasa, Tibet*

The time they had asked the attendees to set aside for this meeting in Tibet was drawing to a close; if these high-ranking individuals did not resume their lives then their absence would be noticed, their lieutenants would become restless, their hold on their power bases weakened.

'So thank you all for your contributions. But let me outline the key proposal that we have developed for our main demonstration.' The General felt he had allowed the democracy to run long enough, allowed them in some cases to talk themselves out of their own proposals. Now he was ready to tell them where Kabitsin had always intended this next event to be.

Kabitsin looked around to see those who looked quiescent at the General's comment and those who showed a reaction. He was delighted to see that they presented in the way that he had predicted, just the two he had forecast would be concerned by this dictatorial approach. But the General had given them their chance, hadn't he?

'What, you thought we came here unprepared?' Kabitsin smiled to relax the moment.

The General began, 'It's the Mekong that caught our attention, the mother of all rivers. No I'm not using some crude Americanism, that's what it means in the original Tai. The river runs through six countries, China, Myanmar, Thailand, Laos, Cambodia and Vietnam.

'The last four countries work together to manage the river within a body they have established called the Mekong River Commission, but neither China nor Myanmar are members. The river runs for around 5,000kms, it's said to be the world's tenth largest river. It's calculated that around 90 million people rely upon it, both for their lives and their livelihoods. Kabitsin assisted in the research for this project, so he can tell us all some of the background.'

Kabitsin gathered up some notes, relieved that he could now participate in the presentation. 'I guess the real issue in the area that we are talking about is that the countryside has some pretty difficult terrain, too many falls, lots of rapids, so it's not a particularly useful or navigable river. There is also a difficult local populace. They are hard people up there, most of them rebelling against their countries. But there is a sort of awkward truce that permits them to carry on their illegal trade in return for allowing their country to negotiate internationally on exploring and obtaining the natural resources that are also located there.'

The General added, 'It also has the same concerns that we talked of earlier. Along the Mekong those that are downstream naturally fear China, both in terms of their potential damming and their current pollution of the river.'

The General seemed reluctant to give up the floor. 'This is particularly feared by Cambodia, because it depends almost entirely on the river for food as well as water, and particularly because they believe it has all happened to them before. They point to the ruins of their Khmer empire at Angkor, especially Angkor Wat. To many Cambodians it stands as a testament to another time when a civilisation was brought to its knees by the lack of water.'

Kabitsin almost snorted at the reference to a religious monument, and then added, 'It's a pretty fruitful river. Further upstream they say they have more giant fish that any other river in the world. Not to mention the Mekong Dragons.' He smiled, 'Relax, it's just that on the Laos-Thai border there are often sightings of balls of light rising from the water. They're called locally *Phaya Naga* or Mekong Dragons.'

The General took back the presentation again. 'Let's make it clear that we are specifically interested in the Shan State of Myanmar that nestles between China, Thailand and Laos, with the Mekong forming a large section of the border up there in this heavily forested and mountainous region. Here in Lhasa, we're less than 1,500kms from there as the crow flies, though he would have to be one tough crow to get there.'

He paused for effect. 'This area is the original Golden Triangle. Not what Thai tourism is trying to use the term for today, but the original usage, the centre for opium production. Grown in Shan, it's taken by horse and donkey up to the Thai border for refining and export.'

Kabitsin said, 'They also specialise in *Yaa baa*, orange and green tablets packed with methamphetamine and caffeine. *Yaa baa* means "crazy medicine" in Thai and they actually used to sell it in gas stations. Truckers used it to help them stay awake – you can imagine the sorts of accidents that this led to! Now it's more often used as a party drug, apparently a useful substitute for ecstasy.'

The General returned to his background material. 'As Burma, this country was once the largest exporter of rice, it used to provide three-quarters of the world's teak, had good oil and other resources, a good workforce. A shocking military regime turned it into a Third-World state. It became a global pariah because of the house arrest of the opposition leader, Aung San Suu Kyi, and a host of other human rights abuses. All this from the country that once supplied one of the great Secretaries General to the UN, U Thant. But they are awaking from that period.

'Why are we interested? Remember, God loves the trinity. One, we can interfere with this drug-trafficking,' he looked around their faces to see some degree of confusion, 'so that our investments in the Afghanistan trade can increase its prices. And, once we've shaken it all up and the still water has gone, then perhaps we can set out to gain some control of this market too.

'Two. By ensuring we use the still water only in this area we do not interfere with the main parts of Myanmar. We will keep well away from the rivers Irrawaddy and Sittang for example as these act as the main thoroughfares for local business. Let me make clear that this is because Mother Russia is now perhaps the biggest trading partner with this country, that's on the legal side of their trade of course. It means we do not need visas for example. There are even student exchange programmes.'

Kabitsin added, 'We have an MOU, a memorandum of understanding, between the two countries' business organisations. We're even building them a nuclear reactor. We've sold them MIGs and other weapons. We have oil interests in Pinlebu, north of Yangon, but our area of operations will not be anywhere close to this. Russia also has exploration rights for offshore oil and gas which of course will not in any way be bothered by our event. The one thing that worried us is a Russian government-owned initiative to build a cast iron plant in the Shan State where of course we will be, but it's early days for that project so we shouldn't harm it, and of course it provides us with good cover when we need to go in to the area!'

The General stood to make his third point. 'Three. With this demonstration we can interfere with the strategic relationships that China and India are developing with Myanmar, at the same time making sure we get their attention for our main proposition that will follow.

Kabitsin quoted from his notes, 'China is selling them weapons and has a major new pipeline project that would see Middle East oil land on the Bay of Bengal, run right across Myanmar and into its Yunnan province. India has agreed a gas pipeline too and is working with the Burmese government to stamp out some insurgency along their common border. We, Russia, have actually worked with China at the UN to veto condemnation of Myanmar, both of us of course seeking to protect our interests there.'

The General said, 'For all these reasons an action here will be sure to get both those countries to take notice. Then once we have their attention we can explain what it is that we want from them.'

Kabitsin looked around the faces for a reaction to the proposal and received little real clarity as to what they were thinking. The General was also gauging their reactions and looked disturbed that they were not applauding or at least appreciative.

Before Kabitsin could do anything the General obviously sought to gain approval by adding, 'Now for some good news. We are happy to support all of your earlier objectives too. We have enough of the still water for you each to pursue your own pet project. But we ask just a few things of each of you.'

Kabitsin was shocked at this news, this had not been agreed with him; he did not believe that this gesture was at all necessary. He had wanted to be sure to keep personal control of the still water.

The General carried on, believing that his unilateral decision would be seen as common sense, the way forward. Completely unaware of the impact he pressed on. 'First, if you run after two hares, you will catch neither! So let's coordinate the timing of what we are planning for maximum impact and let's not let the material fall into the wrong hands. Most importantly we urge you to look at your projects and see how you can use the material to maximum impact, not just to create a few days of panic and paralysis, or to achieve a number of vindictive deaths.'

Kabitsin positively wriggled in his chair, thankfully unnoticed because they were now watching intently and listening to the General's every word. He must be crazy, looking all wet-eyed to some dreamed-of future perhaps? But Kabitsin was not going to cede control of the still water to anyone.

The General continued, 'Work loves fools, so before acting please first think how you can use the still water to show what is possible, then use the threat of further action to create a major business opportunity.'

He pressed on. 'We are not political, we merely use politicians to achieve our own ends, maintain our markets. We do not care about regime change. Let governments have the pain of governing while we build our own structures ever stronger across the globe. We exist outside the rule of law. These laws are what make us strong, make us what we are, for they create markets that politicians and governments are too squeamish to satisfy, too worried that if they permit them, legalise them, then their ability to govern will be weakened.

'It is the peoples of the world who are our consumers. For every demand we will create a supply. We are here to develop their needs and satisfy their ever-expanding tastes, their desires, their dreams. We do not question desires, do not seek to be the arbiters of taste, we do not seek to legislate or control, we just empower the people. We are a global brotherhood and we deliver!'

Managing enough of a positive display not to stand out, Kabitsin watched as they all clapped and cheered the General but he was furious. What was this brotherhood the General had just outlined? Where had it come from? Yes, they as a group had come together because they had each exploited the loopholes in the various national and international laws, ignored international boundaries and made huge profits in doing so. What Kabitsin needed them for was the breadth, the muscle, the control to achieve what he wanted. He had no plans for a club, no plans for others to share his powerful new weapon.

And he had absolutely no interest in empowering the people. His business interests were no noble defence of the individual's rights against laws and governments. If he was honest, he could only just about accept mankind when it formed up in groups to become his markets. He much preferred them when they acted en masse, like cattle or sheep, then they were predictable, never questioning the way that they were prodded along. He could forecast what they were likely to do and therefore could stay well ahead of the pack. He could stomach only a very few of the individuals that he was forced to deal with, for they were unpredictable, ungrateful, always challenging the status quo. If he was completely honest with himself then he had to accept that he did not much like people at all. If still water could be used to reduce the number of people in the world then he could see that as a truly noble endeavour.

If what the General and others said about the shortage of water and other resources becoming critical was true, then he thought he had the simple solution.

Use this still water to reduce the people problem and the world's resources would then have far fewer to supply. There would be much more to go around this reduced population.

There were too many pointless people, too many lesser races using too many resources. Still water would allow him to establish a new world order, where Rodinya would be assured to take its rightful place at the centre, in control, safe.

# BOOK THREE

**Mikhail Gorbachev a**s President of Green Cross International:

*'Water, like religion and ideology, has the power to move millions of people. Since the very birth of human civilisation, people have moved to settle close to it. People move when there is too little of it. People move when there is too much of it. People journey down it. People write, sing and dance about it. People fight over it. And all people, everywhere and every day, need it.'*

**World Commission on Dams**, November 2000:

*'The number of people displaced by dams is estimated at between 40m and 80m, most of them in China and India. The costs of dams were on average 50% above their original estimate. Some designed to reduce flooding made it worse, and there were many unexpected environmental disadvantages, including the extinction of fish and bird species. Half the world's wetlands had been lost because of dams.'*

**3rd World Water Forum** held in March 2003:

*'Water demand is increasing three times as fast as the world's population growth rate... Some 1.2 billion people lack a safe water supply and 2.4 billion live without secure sanitation. At least five million people die yearly from water related diseases, including 2.2 million children under the age of five. An estimated one half of people in developing countries are suffering from diseases caused either directly by infection through the consumption of contaminated water or food, or indirectly by disease carrying organisms, such as mosquitoes, that breed in water.'*

# Chapter 24 - *Novosibirsk, Russia*

Time spent in Novosibirsk was now becoming dull for Paul, the work schedule repetitive, the days seemingly unending. He recognised that he yearned for the sea, even the flat and boring old Pacific that he had railed against would be preferable to this unvarying and featureless place. At one low point he had even worked out, very depressingly, that the distance to the nearest sea would best be expressed in 1000s of kilometres.

Yet this still water was not the sort of water that he craved. He wanted to be next to a refreshing, surging, splashing, ever colour-changing, ever mood-changing sea that was life-giving, not this murderous stuff. What neither of them realised was that, back in the apparent safety of his room with Ellise where he regularly expressed his thoughts on the matter, they were being monitored.

As part of Valéry's team, their focus to define the make-up of this still water, he and Ellise had decided not to share their theory with the others, and so they had to do lots of make-work tasks to satisfy Valéry that they were in fact still contributing. This meant that there was little time to spare for pursuing their own theory, though in reality what could they do from here to prove or disprove it?

Their notion was now in motion elsewhere.

Mark had reported his conversation with them on the subject of their comet idea back to the Company's HQ in Langley. They had considered landing some expedition there themselves but after much internal wrangling, plus a detailed review of the security on the islands, it was decided that it would be better if the theory was passed on by Mark to the Russians with a request that the Brits and he be invited along to assist in the search.

He approached Dmitry who in turn had communicated this back to Kabitsin, who was anyway getting the highlights from the tapes of any 'private' conversations. Kabitsin had deliberated on the theory with the General and they decided the best approach would be to corral the two of them, Paul and Ellise, into a separate facility where they could set out their thoughts as to the original event, particularly this idea of a natural nuclear fusion explosion. He could then find out how they might set about permitting Paul out to the islands to seek out this comet fragment, as they concluded this was the only approach that could prove or disprove the theory. Kabitsin ordered Dmitry to ensure that anything relating to Paul's theory and this proposed mission to the Arctic should only be reported directly to him and should not be circulated to anyone else in the team.

Dmitry chose to approach Ellise first and caught her alone over breakfast. He had planned his approach so that he engineered their conversation in a direction that appeared to be questioning Paul's value to the team's effort, whether he wasn't more suited to something more sea-related, less science, more action. He simply echoed Paul's recorded comments to her in the assumed privacy of their room. He basically goaded her until she eventually volunteered the information of their thinking about the comet as her defence of Paul. From there it was easy as it became almost as if it was Ellise and Paul who had proposed their extraction and northward trip.

Tom was working at the containment area but noticed when Paul was fetched away, presumably to a meeting elsewhere. Then several of the security team had come to gather up Paul and Ellise's materials and take these away too. The rumour mill was rife for the rest of the morning until Dmitry called them all together to advise that regrettably Paul and Ellise had needed to head back to the States because of other demands on their time. He was pursued from the room by an aggravated Mark who also failed to return, the same goons coming to collect his material later.

Valéry commented to his French colleague, in English to ensure that Tom and the others would hear, 'I could never understand why the Americans were invited in the first place. They should comprehend that it is La France that has always been the naturelle colleague of Russia!'

Tom thought about this as he worked on. His recollections of the relationship between the two countries was Napoleon's march on Moscow in 1812 that had inspired Tchaikovsky so magnificently, but the reality was less uplifting. He'd been taught at Britannia Royal Naval College in Dartmouth that this had been one of the most disastrous military campaigns. The Russian burnt-earth policy of tactical withdrawal, Napoleon's extended supply lines and his troops being delayed until winter, had between them reduced the half-a-million force that set off on the campaign to a mere ten thousand who made it back. Hitler's campaign had essentially been almost a carbon-copy, with the same waste of manpower and resource.

So where were the positives in the relationship? He knew that the French had stayed aloof from joining NATO and had maintained a relationship directly with Russia. They had both very vocally opposed the Americans and British on the Iraq war too.

He smiled as he worked, for the only other thing he recalled that the countries shared was their SECAM television system. They had not gone the American NTSC route or with the rest of Europe's PAL system, developing their own SECAM. Technicians on one of his ships had told him this stood for System Essentially Contrary to the American Method but as the same guy's explanation of NTSC was Never Twice the Same Colour, perhaps they were not being contrary, just more efficient?

Paul and Ellise found they were placed unaccompanied on a series of dubious flights, their progression of aircraft getting progressively smaller. First they arrived at somewhere with the unlikely Russian name of Perm, but they were greeted on arrival by a garrulous ground crew member who explained that this was one of the largest cities in Russia and that it had given its name to the Permian geological period. It was the very period that they had been studying, the period that had been halted by the plume 250 million years ago that had wiped out most of life on earth. Paul wondered once again just what it was that had implausibly made so many geological names derive from the Russian language.

On arrival at Perm they were simply walked across the airport to a smaller plane that took them on to Novvy Urengoy, an even smaller aircraft brought them finally, and exhausted, to Nadym. Met by a greeter they were far too tired to be polite, each unable to paste on the appreciative smile that they had managed at the earlier arrival points.

This only served to encourage the greeter to even more bizarre and pointless claims for his town. 'In 2004 Nadym was named the best town, of the Russian Federation, in the Ural Federal District,' that Paul thought sounded a lot like another book he had enjoyed in the past, David Nobbs' "Second from Last in the Sack Race".

**Nadym, Russia**
They had been whisked from this last airport to a small guest house where they soon realised that they would be the only guests. They were politely shown their rooms by the landlady or housekeeper who showed no knowledge of English. The tour finished with a large meeting room area where there were desks, PCs, printers, a large table and chairs plus a fax/copier that had a protruding note from Dmitry.

'Guys, make yourselves at home. Relax tonight and by the morning all your disks, files and notes will be with you. I will arrive late tomorrow afternoon.'

Paul commented, 'Well I guess at least we're closer to the sea here. From the maps I tried to read, you know I think I might be getting the knack of this Cyrillic stuff, it seems that we are pretty close to where the Ob forms a long gulf that runs out to the Kara Sea. This place is on a small river with the same name, Nadym; I think we're only about a hundred kilometres from the gulf.'

'You see you should be careful what you wish for. You wanted some sea action, next time make sure you ask for somewhere warm too!'

Ellise wasn't entirely joking, the guest house was pretty stark. And although they appeared to have communication with the outside world from this office space they were ostensibly lost out here in the boonies, all she needed was a kid on a stoop playing a banjo! She was certainly not planning to accept any canoe rides down to this gulf of Paul's under any circumstances!

She had to assume that they'd not seen many black people around here because of the way she had been the centre of almost gormless attention throughout the journey. She knew she was good-looking but this much attention was just plain ridiculous! Besides she was so wrapped up no one could see more than part of her face with any sort of clarity.

She also assumed that many of the people here would have pretty poor English skills. She was not sure she was doing as well as Paul on the Cyrillic, having to laboriously look at a sheet of A4 that depicted the transliteration of the two sets of characters which she took everywhere with her. It still looked like a code even once she felt she'd gotten the letters down pat, because she had no idea of the Russian structures or grammar. She was great at machine code, could see a hexadecimal character for what it was without any trouble at all, but here she might as well have been on the moon.

And to tell the truth it was a pretty wild idea of Paul's that had brought them here. In the comfort of the labs with a team thrashing around trying to understand what was happening it had seemed as credible as some of the other notions, but here? All they had ever heard of the area when researching it back at the labs was uniformly bad – abused ethnic groups, poor working conditions, pollution, poverty, poor weather. This was no resort location.

What was coming next? If they were to travel out on to the Novaya Zemlya islands she would want a Geiger counter with her. It sounded like the Russians had irradiated the place to hell and beyond. Who in their right mind wanted to choose to go there?

# Chapter 25 - *Novosibirsk, Russia*

Mark had managed one last conversation with Tom before he was reported as being packed off back to the States as no longer required, surplus to requirements.

They had met in the refectory. 'Well I shall be glad to get back to the good old US of A, catch a bit of quality time with my father.'

'Why are you going? And what happened to Paul Wells and Ellise Walker?'

'Can I level with you?'

'I wish you would. All this Tom Sawyer stuff is beginning to wear a little thin with me.'

'Well, none of us are quite who we appear to be, are we? You aren't just here as the celebrity scientist either! Your government accreditation looked pretty rushed from where I'm sitting.'

'OK, so we are each here with our country's interest at heart, what of it?'

'Have it your way. Look, this still water is worrisome stuff and we are aware that there're some people in the shadows out there who are seeing this as a real opportunity for mischief.'

'You're referring to Kazakhstan.'

'Precisely. For some reason they got off lightly across there from what we can see, and we don't really understand quite how they did.'

Tom decided to be frank. 'From what we have, there doesn't appear to be any good record of what in fact happened. It's all second and third-hand stuff, and all captured well after the event itself. All that's clear is that it must have been still water from the things that it did manage to achieve. But do your people think that there is an antidote and that this event tested that too?'

Mark said, 'Why would Dmitry be pressing everyone so hard to come up with one if they did?'

'I think that makes it worse. If they had no antidote and yet were prepared to release it, how stupid are they? Don't they know that water is all part of a global cycle? That it could have entered into the cycle and carried on multiplying until we were all goners?'

'It appears to have naturally run its course and then reverted to normal water, doesn't it?' Mark caught the reaction as Tom wriggled a bit at his comment. 'You're leading the team to see how that could be, any theories?'

Tom had tried, but failed to hold good eye contact as he said, 'There's nothing conclusive currently.'

Mark persisted 'Heh, I don't need it gift-wrapped, any old theory will do.'

'Nothing worthwhile.' Tom put perhaps a little too much determination in the response and sought to move off the subject, 'What do you know of Paul and Ellise?'

'They seem to have come up with some theory as to how the still water came about. They've decided it's a deuterium comet that struck up in the north back at the beginning of the last century. Their theory is that a lump of it didn't break up or explode and it's the source of this stuff.'

'Sounds like a Paul concept! He would always prefer something heroic, superhero, out-of-this-world. That's why he's chasing tsunamis, can't stand the normal or the micro worlds, it all has to be bold, big and brassy for him.'

'Not how I would describe Ellise at all!' He smiled. 'It does have some precedent. There have been others who conjectured that this was what happened. Look it up, it was 1908 in Siberia. Tell me what you think when you've looked through the material.'

'How?'

Mark passed him a scrap of paper with three email addresses; none of them were for Mark Elliott, each appeared to use the nick-name 'elzo' and a string of numbers.

'So what's really happening to you?'

'Dmitry is going to set you and me up to meet with a guy called Kabitsin, and he's one bad mother. Gangsta, blackmailer, racketeer, general all-round bad guy but he also seems to be able to move in pretty exalted circles here in the Land of the Freeze. He seems to be at back of all this. General Goncharenko who was introduced as running this project seems to be looking to his retirement portfolio and is only notionally heading it up. That's both this overt investigation and the black side too, where they seem to be looking for buyers for the still water. And, from what we hear, they seem to be offering it to some of the world's baddest SOBs.'

'Sounds like we would be walking into the lion's den if we agree to meet him. No, worse than that, into the bear's cave while it's awake! What will he want?'

Mark smiled. 'For me it's simple, they want to get through me to my father. He's a big player in the US military-industrial-congressional complex. They know he knows how to get Congress, the Pentagon and the big defence contractors to get together for a good old song and dance. I think they're going to offer us the still water franchise for North America!'

'But they're criminals.'

'What, and your government hasn't ever dealt with criminals? C'mon it's what they're best at, that's what your colonies were all about, you old-world rapers and pillagers. You sought out the malleable leaders or supported the up-and-coming bad boys and bent them to your cause by giving them what they wanted for as long as you could get away with it. Sell 'em your religion, your weapons, your goods, your way of life, while you grab all their resources, abuse all their cheap labour. And, when they step out of line, which they surely always do, then they get UN sanctions sicced on them, or they get pilloried and denigrated as a dictatorship, accused of planning to build WMDs, of sponsoring terrorism, whatever, and if that doesn't bring about a regime change, then just zap the bastards off the planet!'

'That's not how I would interpret our history, personally.'

'Heh, we colonials are just following your example! Imitation is the sincerest form of flattery I was told! We just have bigger and better toys than your old gunboats that we can apply to the principle.'

'I think I preferred the Tom Sawyer impressions! But why would this Kabitsin want to see me?'

'That's where I am a little unclear, unless you are more than you seem to be. Have you any connections into British Intelligence?'

'Would you believe me if I said that I do not?'

'So I'll take that as a yes then! Heh, nothing's lost by listening. As a minimum we get to see this animal, look him in the eye, see where he's thinking of going with this. Work out what their strengths are, where they're based. A meeting could give us some data to work with.'

## Chapter 26 - *Nadym, Russia*

Isolated here in this cold and remote northern location, Paul was trying to emulate the model he had seen in the pictures. He'd arranged for Dmitry to supply some modelling clay and other materials so that he could recreate the experiment from decades earlier. Ellise accused him of a 'Close Encounters of the Third Kind' fixation, and said she fully expected him to start modelling his food like the Richard Dreyfuss character.

In fact Paul thought she was on the money. He loved that film. The 'first kind' was defined as a sighting; well there had been enough of those for this UFO. The 'second kind' was evidence which had been the disappointing bit to those that had gone before him. They had the explosions and the devastated forestry but no evidence of an impact site or any residual material. What he was indeed seeking was the 'third kind', contact!

Paul finally completed his model. Of course he had realised early on that this had been make-work while Dmitry arranged for them to go to the islands, while he assembled the necessary approvals, gathered together a suitable team and the required equipment.

Having completed his model forest-scape he needed to think through his next step. In principle what he was trying to achieve was first to establish for himself the direction and angle of the descent of the comet, for he was now firmly convinced that a comet it was. This was achieved in a day of playing with minor explosive charges when he confirmed the original experiment as to the angle and direction that the exploding portion of the comet had taken.

Now he had this, he wanted to find a way of modelling various sizes for the comet that might work both to achieve the explosion and yet to leave a sizeable chunk that impacted in the Kara Sea. Neither he nor Ellise had the requisite skills to do this and so it was back to Dmitry who had found someone, somewhere back at the Akademgorodok, to try to run some models for him. They had come back saying there were too many variables to make a start.

So it was either back to waiting or applying some guesswork. He didn't have the experience to do the modelling but what if he turned the question on its head? Assume that the other part landed where he had projected, then assume the atmospheric point of entry was where the two parts had separated, one part to become the portion that caused the explosion. Surely then a model could be constructed to show what size the second portion must have been not to have broken up and yet to end up where he presumed it did.

Ellise was bored. There was little she could do from here other than browse the Net. She didn't think that there had ever been a time when she had gone beyond the third page of a Google search, but here she was working through all 6.6m references to the 1908 Siberian explosion! Weren't there people who sought out searches for which Google came up empty, a Googlewhack, why did hers have to go and find 6.6m? And Paul had asked her to check out the other search engines too!

Then he asked her to switch her search on to comets. The brief joy of a new project was short-lived when she googled 'comet' and registered 3.3 million results for this! But she butterflied her way through some of the early pages to get her bearings first.

She summarised her findings. Many of our long-period comets, those with orbits that are best measured in thousands of years, are believed to come from the Oort cloud, two zones located about a light year away from our sun formed from the debris of our star's nebulae. These objects are largely made from ice and are spread too far apart to coalesce into planets. She learned that there is said to be a conveyor line of comets that emerge from the inner and outer Oort clouds, and that the mass of material out there is the equivalent of three earths, so it doesn't appear that these will run out any time soon.

She read of one theory that our sun has a gaseous giant companion planet called eerily 'Nemesis' that passes through the Oort cloud every 26 million years creating a huge shower of comets that would whizz through the solar system perhaps colliding with planets or being lost into the sun. But it seemed this theory had very few followers.

Periodic comets, those with an orbit of under 200 years, are said to come from a closer point, the Edgeworth-Kuiper belt, about a 1,000 times nearer than the Oort. This belt is similar to the even closer asteroid belt but being further out it is much more ice than rock-based.

Pluto is in fact in the Kuiper belt and many now dispute that it deserves the description planet, which would screw up Ellise's memory jogger for the planets – 'My Very Elegant Mother Just Sat Under Norah's Porsche'. She thought about this for a few minutes and came up with a revision – 'My Very Excruciating Mother Just Speaks Utter Nonsense', based more on last night's phone call to her mother which had not gone well.

She gave up on committing this to memory when later she read that it was perhaps the objects in the Kuiper belt that had so wobbled the outer planets that Uranus and Neptune had changed places at some stage! She'd always thought the solar system to be an immutable fact not some astral game of pool!

Apparently it is the planet Neptune that upsets objects in the inner reaches of the Kuiper belt sending them down into the solar system or out into the chilly wastes of interplanetary space. There seems to be one major exception and this is the satellite Triton that appears to have been captured by Neptune from the Kuiper belt and somewhat bizarrely rotates around Neptune in the opposite direction to the planet's rotation.

She read that both sorts of comets appear to consist mostly of ice, both ammonia and water ice, but there is also evidence of other materials like hydrocarbons present too. The astronomers' court is still out on whether these other detected materials were always an original part of the comet or were formed by impacts with other bodies.

The lore of comets was plentiful, perhaps overwhelming the facts. Comets had always been considered an ill omen, so when in 1910 the earth passed through Halley's tail, or coma, there were, fortunately ill-founded, fears of a mass poisoning. As recently as 1997 the Hale-Bopp comet triggered thirty-eight members of one cult to suicide in the belief that they would then join a UFO that was shadowing the comet. In reading a pretty scathing report, Ellise thought, 'Who knows? They may just have been the sane ones, and we idiots are those left behind on the Mother Earth ship with all its problems.'

She really had to get a grip she thought. By googling 'deuterium comets' she cut the results at a stroke to 67,000. Hale-Bopp came up again on the first page as it turned out to have been one of the best investigated comets, perhaps because the return of Halley's a decade earlier had been something of a non-event. By comparison so many were able to see Hale-Bopp that it had captured world attention and interest.

Analysis of it showed that the deuterium present in it was at a level about twice that present in our oceans. And the various compounds detected in the comet also had a high incidence of deuterium rather than straight hydrogen.

That's where these investigations seemed to part company with her interests, they instead went into the fact that the presence of deuterium suggested that the ice in comets came from interstellar clouds. But Ellise figured, 'Who cares where it came from, it's where it is now that we need to know!'

She found a reference to water on Mars and was surprised to learn that the water on Mars has 5.5 times the deuterium-based water than is the case on Earth, and that this was therefore more than double the substance's presence in comets. She had to conclude that the level of deuterium oxide in water could vary quite widely out there in the cosmos, so perhaps Paul's idea was not so very outlandish.

On one of the pages she pulled up, she found out that there appears to be a small number of meteorites, some 34 out of the 24,000 discovered to date, that have been identified as clearly coming from Mars. She heard the Jeff Wayne song in her head, "The chances of anything coming from Mars is a million-to-one - but still they come!" This sample suggested it was only a thousand to one!

She thought it best to move on from meteors as Paul was pretty clear that he did not want anyone raining on his comet theory! What was it about guys, the way they hung on to their theories, would even fight you for them, whatever the evidence showed?

# Chapter 27 - *Novosibirsk, Russia*

Still in the Russian scientific facility, Tom found he had more time to think now that the team had thinned out, but still no one in whom he could confide in, no one with whom to chew over his thinking. But then he consoled himself that he had never proven much of a team player.

The Russians appeared to have lost interest in the team. The General had not been seen since the first day. Dmitry, who had notionally managed the team, had been gone for many days. Valéry who ran one of the project groups also seemed to have become side-tracked and appeared to be showing up less often in the labs.

The conversation with Mark had been the most unsettling factor. If this Kabitsin character was trying to abuse the material then just what might be done to stop him?

So, now free of supervision, or any particular overt interest, Tom was able to work systematically through his own findings. The technicians seemed to have no particular desire to be occupied and so had no problem with him doing his own experimentation.

Arriving late back to his room with piles of notes and a laptop cradled in his arms he had been in no position to resist when someone stepped out of his bathroom and pinioned him back against the wall with a hand pressed over his mouth. The intruder allowed him the few seconds before recognition dawned in his eyes then he released him but with a warning finger to his mouth.

It was Brain, or whatever his name was, dressed just like one of the technicians, at first almost unrecognisable except for that scar. Brain motioned for him to put down what he was carrying and follow him outside. Neither spoke until Brain turned and said, 'We won't be monitored out here.'

'What are you doing here?'

'I've been here almost as long as you have. Food's awful but I find that the vodka more than makes up for it!'

'So why are we meeting, here, now? I've been sending reports as you requested.'

'Yes we have them. But the agenda is changing. This operation here will be closed shortly and you will be sent home.'

'How do you know this? And why close it, we haven't reached any conclusions as yet?

'Ah, it seems the Russians have lost interest in the project. We're not even sure that this was ever truly official. It now appears more likely that it was a group calling itself the Brotherhood or some such nonsense that was actually behind it all. They seem to be able to move in pretty exalted circles, not really part of the administration, but to an outsider they certainly look like they are.'

'Is this being run by the General and this Kabitsin character?'

'We received your report on the conversation with Mark Elliott. It seems that the real power is this Kabitsin, who is a very cheeky chappy. We're trying to find out more about him, his whereabouts and what he's up to currently. You definitely need to meet up with him.'

'You could have delivered that message to me without turning up here, what do you want from me?'

'Some still water old chap, unless of course you have solved the riddle of how to manufacture it yourself?'

'As I reported I begin to understand the process of how to replicate it, but we would need the source material to achieve that.'

'How much would you need?'

'For research the need would be quite small, but the real question is what you might want it for, what purposes you might have in mind.'

'I agree. I guess we need enough to continue your research and then perhaps hold some in reserve against any future requirements.'

'I'm not going to even ask what they might be. You do fully appreciate how potent this stuff is? How vital it is to make sure it does not get in to the water cycle?'

'I leave all that to you boffins. They suggest that we will need at least a hundred litres?'

'They'll notice that much disappearing.'

'We thought of that. We just replace a container with normal water; who'll know if it has been miraculously changed back by one of the experiments? Simple, eh?'

'When?'

'No time like the present!'

'You do appreciate that 100 litres plus the container will weigh about 120 kilos.'

'That's why we,' he pointed to a guy dressed in drab greens, with camo face paint who had been lying just twelve paces from them in the garden and only became apparent to Tom when he waved. 'We each have a special 50 litre Bergen, we can yomp anywhere with a 60 kilo pack. Those wimps in the Marines still go on about the Falklands, they carried less than 40 kilos for three days across 90kms, bloody bootnecks don't begin to know what hardship is!'

Tom went back into the labs with Brain, and his colleague, whom Tom had immediately decided to nickname 'Brawn' for his evident physique. Brawn was posted to watch the two doors into the facility. They had the lights turned down low so that anyone coming into the area would not have any great clarity as to what was happening, who was there.

Tom passed the two containers through into the containment room and was in the process of transferring the still water into them. He had not yet worked out how he would replace the still water with $H^2O$, but first he wanted the difficult part done safely.

One rucksack, or Bergen, completed, he fixed the plug and screwed it as hard as he could using the remote arms. Then, though he had been careful and had seen no drips miss the target, he used cloths to dry the whole of the container, lifted it and wiped the base and where it had rested on the bench. Setting it down elsewhere, he then lifted and dried it off one more time, just to be sure.

He was opening the second Bergen container when the door swung open suddenly. Tom looked around and couldn't see Brain or Brawn anywhere. The security man did not hit the lights but instead came over to where Tom was working.

Tom recognised the guard as one who had no, or very limited, English. At least previously he had never appeared to want to speak with the foreigners. He was a big guy. Weren't they all? He didn't look too bright or particularly fast, where the hell were the others?

Tom just had to carry on, assuming to stop or look nervously around would be the wrong thing to do. The guard was staring at the Bergen container; clearly it looked out of place, somehow it was clearly 'other'. Tom ignored his stare and carried on filling it. When would they strike?

The guard grabbed Tom's arm and pointed at the container. Tom gabbled, 'It's a new field experiment that Dmitry has asked me to perform. We need the water in one of these containers to take it outside and run the test.'

The security man clearly did not understand a word but seemed to smell Tom's fear, becoming ever more suspicious. Where were they? Surely they should have leapt across the room and despatched him with a deadly blow by now? Wasn't that what they did for a living? Why were they leaving him to deal with this?

The guard was getting quite agitated and it was clear his next step was to attract the attention of one of his team who could understand this bloody foreigner.

Tom decided to act himself and carried on blabbering as he waved the guy towards the containment chamber. Reassuring him with a smile as he led him through the two doors to the inner sanctum and still gabbling about anything, he wasn't sure that he understood any more of what he said than the security guy. The guy was like a nervous animal at the watering hole, looking around, considering whether to follow, but surely this foreign scientist would not have entered if there was any danger?

Tom led him right up to the Bergen and started pointing at features on it, still talking. There was an odd-looking clasp on the side so he pointed at this very particularly and touched the guard's back willing him to look at it more closely.

Tom reached for a petrie glass that he had been working with earlier in the day. As the guard turned with a confused look on his face, Tom tossed the petrie dish contents directly into his face. leaping backwards to ensure there was no splash of the material that could reach him.

The guy's confused look turned to an angry one, then an expression of panic, for he must have known enough about the stuff to fear it. That's how he died, with a look of fear still on his features as he crumpled to the floor.

Tom stared at the man he had killed, his mind in a turmoil. Brain was looking through the glass. 'Great, there's your alibi. We can set it up to look like he was part of a team that took the still water.'

Tom was still in shock, 'I just killed someone!'

'Good stuff, isn't it? Felt sure he'd thrash about a bit before he tossed off his mortal whatnot.'

Almost to himself, Tom explained, 'The still water went straight into his eyes and from there it would have taken milliseconds to reach his brain.'

'Come on then, snap out of it. Fill that second Bergen, then you can tip over the empty container and splash the dregs around a bit. You can barely see him from out here, but when someone does, the splashes should stop anyone rushing in to investigate too quickly. We can be well on our way by then.'

Tom was coming through the doors, 'I trust that "we" is inclusive, that you'll get me out of here too?'

'No can do. You have to walk out the front door as an innocent man or else you can say goodbye to your celebrity lifestyle. Don't forget you came here proudly being you. We'll stage the whole thing, then you need to get back to your room unseen and come in tomorrow at the normal time and do everything as you would have done.'

'But I killed him!'

Brain smiled at him, 'You did well! From my viewpoint, you should just think of it as making a good start! There're many more we're going to have to deal with before this matter will be closed.'

# Chapter 28 - *London, UK*

A large meeting room in the Foreign & Commonwealth Office had been arranged for the Professor to summarise the situation to a much larger group. The Foreign Secretary judged that this could no longer be an in-camera subject reserved only for her closest advisors; it needed others to provide insight, to investigate and to prepare for any required counter-measures.

The Professor chose to start with the real issue, water. 'You will have already received a pretty thorough briefing on the situation but I thought perhaps we all need some scene-setting and perhaps we should get some of the scientific stuff out of the way. First you must appreciate that there is pretty much a fixed quantity of water that is available to us here on our little planet. It's estimated in fact to be a little less than 1.5 billion cubic kilometres that exists out there and we all, and by that I mean folk, flora and fauna, all of us, depend on it for our lives!'

The Foreign Secretary interjected, 'Personally, I find it a bit sobering that someone can actually quantify the volume of water quite so readily.'

The Professor nodded, 'And let me be clear that this is a closed system. There is currently no factory line making top-up replacements! Although we have detected some sort of water on Mars I don't think we can wait for that to be sourced, tested and brought back.'

'Why can't we make it?'

'To get the two hydrogen and one oxygen atoms to combine isn't just a matter of putting the two substances in to a jar and shaking it up, you need to carefully apply a burst of energy. Don't forget how inflammable these substances are, without care you could just have a big explosion. The Hindenburg airship was filled with hydrogen and hit by lightning, some say by saboteurs, but the energy with the two substances only had one outcome.'

The Foreign Secretary wasn't easily convinced, 'Can't you just evaporate it from the sir?'

'Of course, but that is part of the closed volume of water, you aren't making new water.'

He projected an image on to a large plasma screen, and talked through the chart displayed upon it.

'This water we have is forever working through the cycle that I am showing here. Think of this as a short Year 6 geography refresher lesson, to be sure that we all know what I mean by this cycle. As you can see, essentially it starts with the sea evaporating some of its water, this then condenses into clouds and later falls as precipitation. Some gets stored as snow and ice on mountains, in glaciers, at the poles. Some of this sublimates which means the solid ice turns directly into water vapour, without ever really being liquid water, and sits in the atmosphere later to condense and precipitate again.

'From the land the water runs as streams, and rivers, and then this water can get deposited in lakes, held up by dams, led off into reservoirs or it simply passes back into the sea. Alternatively, as it crosses the land it infiltrates into the soil where it is stored as groundwater in aquifers for example, or it is sucked up into plants and trees. This big word here, evapotranspiration, is just the term for water coming from soil and plants back into the atmosphere.

'It's only at certain points of that cycle of course that the water is at all useable or available to us as a fresh water resource.' He changed the slide. 'The bulk, some 94%, sits out there bobbing along in our seas as salt water and though it appears to be pretty constant, it in fact cycles and replenishes itself every 2,600 years. Of this huge reservoir somewhat less than 500,000 cubic kilometres will have evaporated out of the sea at any given time, and quite a proportion of this of course falls straight back into the sea.'

He looked around the room to be sure he still had his audience, 'So precipitation on to the land should be readily available to us, but even that is not that easy to assume in that it has to drop to the land in places where we can collect it. And, if it comes as monsoons or floods for example a lot of that just cannot be gathered or become useable.'

A new slide appeared, 'Now, here comes the awkward piece of arithmetic. Of the 6% not in the sea just over two-thirds of this meagre available total is located underground in aquifers etc and, as I told several of you before, we are using these far too fast. It takes 5,000 years for the aquifers to replenish themselves. It's a very, very slow process and we are taking it at a rate that makes it completely unsustainable. Some aquifers have already been damaged beyond repair, some have become very salty and so on.

'So this leaves us with rather less than 2% in other forms and the vast majority, 85% of this small percentage, is found as snow and ice at the poles and in glaciers. I know that all of you will have read that global warming is melting both of these but sadly it's not in such a manner that it turns this ice into useable fresh water for us.

'So it is just a minuscule part of Earth's water system that is in our most common useable form – the lakes hold 0.02% or 0.23 billion cubic kilometres and the rivers ho;d just 0.0001% or 0.001 billion cubic kilometres. The lakes usually have a ten-year replenishment cycle and rivers take just twelve days, by the way. And, what are we doing with these invaluable lakes and rivers? Polluting them of course!

'The note takers with a mathematical bent will have realised that we haven't quite hit 100%. That's because there's water as atmospheric vapour cycling every ten days – water in the soil, water in plants and trees, water in animals, and for the avoidance of doubt I include us in this.

'The wags amongst you will want to know about the water stored in our cisterns, or our mineral water bottles,' and he waved one he'd picked up from the table. 'Amd, I won't get side-tracked into the profligate waste that the water companies manage to achieve through leaks, spills and other matters. But the sum of all of these does not add up to a row of beans in the scheme of things.'

The Foreign Secretary made clear she wanted to take up the story so the Professor sat down. 'What the Professor has so elegantly explained is that water is a very precious and yet perilous resource. This "still water" looks to be a threat to the world's water supplies. At best these unscrupulous people are seeking to blackmail us with the material, at worst this is perhaps one of the biggest threats that we face today. Forget the war against terror, this will be the war against thirst.'

This gathering had followed directly after the Foreign Secretary's final meeting on the forthcoming budget. She was in a bad mood; some of her treasured objectives had been agreed to be sacrificed to fund her colleagues' departmental goals. If she could be dispassionate she would see that she and her team had loaded their plan with many items that they had, in truth, expected to lose and actually she had not lost them all. But who could be dispassionate about losing?

She was vehemently opposed to that cornerstone of Englishness of being a good loser. Losers she believed were, well, losers, and there was absolutely nothing good about that status that she could acknowledge. OK, she could magnanimously lose a board game or a game of cards because these were just pastimes, literally played just to pass time with friends and family. But in her business and political life there was no time for losers. In her high-profile role the losers had to leave the field of combat and seldom lived to fight another day.

'We have intelligence that suggests this group, calling itself the Brotherhood, has already struck. Sir Joseph?'

He looked around the room cautiously. He had learned by hard experience that the bigger the audience the more there was a chance of a leak. 'Can I start by reminding everyone here that this meeting has to remain confidential, not because of some secret-squirrel nonsense, but any whiff of this could spark panic on a global scale!'

The Foreign Secretary underlined his point. 'You really do have to take Sir Joseph's comment very seriously. I will hunt anyone down who even whispers it on the pillow to a loved one. I will make sure that individual's life in government is over and then do all I can to ensure that there will be no prosperity in any other walk of life either. Is this completely clear?'

Sir Joseph and the Foreign Secretary scanned all those present, one-by-one, for a very clear sign of acknowledgement before he proceeded.

'What we know is that not all the still water that was taken from the original site in the Arctic arrived at Novosibirsk for investigation. The Cousins had satellite coverage and a submarine at the site and estimate that less than 40% of it was delivered to the laboratories.'

The Foreign Secretary interrupted. 'Of course we have no idea if the napalming of the research vessel and the surrounding sea destroyed all the still water at the site.'

'Ah, but the Cousins come in handy again here. Their team came up with some cock-and-bull story about comets and convinced Ivan that they should be permitted to go to the site. One of our nationals is in tow and now that spring is advancing it looks as though they could be on their way up there any time now.'

One of the people at the table asked, 'So where is the other 60%?'

'We believe that some was used in Kazakhstan, presumably as some sort of test of the material.'

The Foreign Secretary asked with some venom, 'So earlier the Professor was able to give us chapter and verse that included an absolute quantity for every drop of water on Earth, and you talk of "some"?'

'Apologies, Foreign Secretary, I'll try to be a little more specific. The satellite imagery showed that a rented Toyota Hilux, that would clearly have failed a British MoT, offloaded a container that was probably consistent with a 100 litre barrel. Three of the protagonists dropped it into the lake, presumably fearing the contents, and it was subsequently opened at a distance with what we believe to have been a hand-gun. But as to whether said container was full, we have no data.' He looked her full in the eyes and smiled.

The pompous bastard – she had to get him, somehow, and soon!

The Professor stepped in before she said anything. 'So deducting the assumed 100 litres from the missing 60%, how much do they have?'

'We would estimate it at a little under 1,000 litres.'

The Foreign Secretary had gained the time to recover from her anger a little as she asked, 'And have the Cousins indicated to you where it might be?'

'As you know, Foreign Secretary, on the meagre budgets that you allocate to us, we need to use all the friends we have.'

She had to pace the room before replying, 'Stop playing games! Do we have any idea where the still water might be?'

'Not at the moment, Foreign Secretary. Though we have managed to acquire some litres of our own, recently spirited away from Ivan's labs.'

'I want your word that every single drop of it gets to Culham. I will not accept any stories of spills or evaporation.' She looked him squarely in the eyes. 'They must receive every drop!'

'May I ask why we are to take it to that particular location?'

'The UKAEA is managing our fusion research. It already works with this deuterium and heavy water so the Professor and I judged that it would be the most appropriate agency.'

Sir Joseph looked across at the Professor. He recognised that she had assumed the other major benefit of this location would be that his access would prove a lot more difficult inside a nuclear facility with a high level of security, particularly with the 'War on Terror' having placed the world at an elevated level of threat.

He was not about to disabuse her of this so looked suitably glum as he said, 'Would that we had the resources to have taken it all from their labs.'

# Chapter 29 - *Odessa, Ukraine*

They were staying in a house that Kabitsin owned in the Black Sea port of Odessa. No trace of his ownership would ever be found by even the most determined investigator. He had killed not only the owner, who had made the mistake of crossing him, but also every single member of his family. Russia recently having taken control of the Crimean Peninsula, Kabitsin was one of those urging for Putin to take the other key parts of Ukraine back under Russian control, including this sea port of Odessa.

The General was as yet unaware that some of the still water was missing, unaware that the administration was becoming restless. Kabitsin had created a barrier around the General and only what he wanted him to hear could pass through to reach the old man.

It was not just straightforward control-freakery. Kabitsin recognised he still needed the use of the General's mind with his grand master-esque gambits to help him finalise the way forward, but he could not allow him to set any policy or make any decisions. The remote and secret location also helped further to control the communications to and from the old man without it appearing to be a deliberate policy.

It was also a good operational location from which to disappear – by land it was less than a hundred kilometres to enter Moldavia; by fast boat he could sweep across the sea to Romania, Bulgaria, Turkey, Georgia or even back into Mother Russia; by air there were a score of airlines to whisk him to an abundance of direct locations.

The General was thinking aloud. 'So we are agreed that we can't just walk in to a meeting with either the Chinese or the Indians and make our demands. Of course we could, but I do not believe our freedom, or our life expectancy, would be improved by such a move.'

It was late evening and they had just completed a meal of *borshch* and *varenniki* and were finishing off a second bottle of Cabernet Magarach. The General asked, 'Where are we with the antidote?'

Kabitsin held his eyes as he lied, 'We are confident of this being resolved in the next week or so.'

'And the manufacture of more of the material?'

'That seems less straightforward but of course when we put it in a river it does reproduce so perhaps we just need to find some safe way of collecting that.'

The General moved the subject forward to why they were there. 'Of course what we need is an intermediary or some other means of dealing with these governments remotely. But we don't want to lose any impact by that very remoteness.'

'First we need to mount our next demonstration and this has to be handled to be much more effective than Kazakhstan!' Kabitsin, as if reminded of Lev by his comment, went to the door and shouted for him to come and clear away their plates.

Lev entered with one of his team and they set about clearing while their two leaders topped up their glasses. 'Is everything in order downstairs?' Kabitsin asked and received confirmation.

The very old and substantial house sat on top of a section of the city's maze-like series of catacombs, a section that had been sealed off from the rest of the tunnels. These had been originally mined for limestone and later were expanded by smugglers for their nefarious purposes. The previous owner had boasted that his antecedents had been among the biggest smugglers in town. Now his and his family's bodies were eternal residents, unceremoniously piled deep inside one of the thick walls that had been built at the various outlets that had originally connected the rest of the catacombs to those below.

They had sealed off an area of perhaps four times the floor space of the house itself down in these passages and this was being used as their current operational centre for pursuing their plan. It was where they were keeping their still water. Dmitry, with several technicians, was currently busy arranging for the water to be decanted from its original containers and sealed into suitable 100 litre containers for future use in the field.

Lev had cleared everything away and left them with some fruit, to be washed down with a Magarach fortified white wine.

Kabitsin asked, 'Can we make our contact with them be just some form of electronic message? Perhaps send them a DVD or an email that can't possibly be traced?'

The General was from an age where there had been no need to learn of these technologies but he certainly had no regrets about this. All he saw of this modern gadgetry was that it took people over and they spent inordinate hours achieving precisely nothing.

He had long since personally concluded that it was the facsimile machine that had heralded the first step towards this decline. Prior to it, you had time to ponder a difficult decision or agreement but as soon as a fax arrived it was expected that you would respond. First there was the assumption that you were always available and not engaged on other matters that might have similar or greater importance to you. Then there was the expectation that on receipt of the fax you would make an immediate response or confirmation. He often regaled youngsters on how many times he had found that after sleeping overnight on a subject he was able to improve the drafting, the thinking, the plan, the outcome.

Just look at Kabitsin, always with a mobile to his ear, sending texts, receiving emails, satellite phones when out in the field, who could possibly need to be so constantly in touch and contactable? Then there were the GPS devices to make sure you could get lost even more profoundly, for when they misdirected you the lack of paper maps or prior route-planning meant you had absolutely no idea where you were or even the general direction of your destination.

Maps, letters, orders, reports, what had Dmitry called them? Dead-tree technology! And letters he called snail-mail! Were people any smarter for all their technology? Well they certainly rushed around a great deal. From what he heard of Kabitsin's phone conversations they seemed mostly inane, pointless, simply confirming where people were, repeatedly asking whether they'd done as they had been asked. In his day you gave your subordinates an order, having ensured by training them properly that they would go off and get it done. Once they had been instructed you left them alone to focus on the task, and didn't constantly interrupt them by mobile, text and email.

'No. The problem with your technologies is that they leave forensic evidence, how the communication was initiated, perhaps what sort of equipment was used. I think this in fact calls for the delivery of a simple printed note. And not the sort of melodramatic note loved by fiction writers, made from cut-out letters and words from newspapers and magazines!'

Kabitsin accepted the idea because he was actually no more comfortable than the General with technology. He always feared that there were those out there who knew more than he could ever achieve. The young guys all talked as if they knew it all, but who was to be trusted to be secure? 'What would the note say?'

'We could set out the evidence from our latest example. By then the others in the Brotherhood will have managed their own events too, so we can perhaps draw on some of their results. We need to make it very clear what we are capable of doing, how pointless it would be for them to try to defend against it. But this all has to be kept very general and certainly we do not mention our likely target location or locations.'

He gathered momentum to his thoughts, 'I see it as a considered presentation of what this would mean to them, with forecast damage reports, likely fatalities, industrial and agricultural damage and so on. Make it clear that we can and will keep on doing it, with new targets and ever-more damaging outcomes.'

Kabitsin found himself relishing the thought of these outcomes as the old man continued.

'Then we will need to outline our demands clearly. Finally we need to advise them how they must respond. I think they should also use what your young man calls "dead-tree" technology – a specified advertisement to be placed by them in a newspaper perhaps? Dead-tree indeed; seems to me as if all your computers have only served to increase the need for paper and as yet show absolutely no signs of ever eliminating it!'

Kabitsin snapped out of his reverie. 'There's quite a lot of work to do then, and we'll need to prepare the outline and then update it with the data as the events happen.'

'Precisely, but the thing that will make this really credible will be if you can ensure the document is delivered directly to the Chinese General Secretary and the Indian Prime Minister so that they receive it personally. There are to be no intermediaries or flunkeys able to control the time and the way in which it is to be presented. Do you think that you can do this? Perhaps through Vasily's and Asil's contacts?'

'I'm confident that we can and it will definitely add to the effect. Perhaps we can make it look like an internal briefing, even suggesting it's coming from dissidents within their own country. That would have them thrashing around on witch-hunts too.'

The General was not yet finished with his thought process. 'I believe it's very important. If it can be delivered in a personal environment or at a personal time then this will bring some different pressures to reach the correct decision. I know how cocooned these people can be and the fact that we can reach straight into their personal space would be very compelling.'

Kabitsin loved this terrorising tactic and this approach was now settled in his mind as the one they would use. 'So next, let's discuss what our demands might look like. What do you think we can ask for and receive? Don't forget there's a whole new and different dimension to maintaining our security as we take delivery of our demands. That's perhaps where we are even more vulnerable to a counter-attack by that country's forces. We don't want something delivered with polonium or any form of tracker.'

'Ah, there's perhaps where your virtual world of electronics comes into play and where, regrettably, this old Cold War warrior isn't really well equipped to assist you. But the really vital thing is that we must make these people realise that we can strike globally, that we cannot be easily eliminated. That's where the Brotherhood assists us greatly..'

The meeting over, the two men went down to the catacomb to see what had been achieved. Lev and three of his men had been lounging around but immediately became alert. Dmitry glanced away from his work to see what had caused this sudden movement and smiled at the General. He much admired and respected the old warhorse; he was a true national hero to Dmitry. He had been at the forefront of their country's defence, had presided over a generation that had seen so many changes in Russia.

It was only the General's involvement that had brought Dmitry into the team. He would not have been here to help these gangsters and racketeers. Just by being there the old world patriot connected their endeavours back to an earlier, more pleasant, cleaner time in the history of their country. An earlier time when rights and wrongs were set out more clearly. Somehow back in the General's prime it had seemed that it had all been much more straightforward.

Dmitry was an idealist, in fact just as committed as Kabitsin to see Russia resume its rightful leadership role in the world. However he wanted this so that the Russian people might develop, recapture their more intellectual roots, shake off the oligarchs and gangsters and create more equality, more opportunity, more justice.

Lev tried to explain where they had reached in the process but realised he really didn't know, so instead gruffly asked Dmitry to report.

Dmitry focused on the General and explained that they had in total some 1200 litres of the still water and had so far distilled this into eight completed 100 litre packages. He pointed to them.

They were marked to suggest that there were biochemicals contained in them, which of course there were, and yet the labelling had been chosen to suggest there was nothing too toxic, too esoteric and especially none too valuable. The containers bore a red symbol signifying that there was a biohazard. The General glanced at this and thought the international symbol looked like three crescent moons superimposed over a ring – appropriate symbols for a hazard given all the problems that Islam's ever-rising crescent moon had brought across the world in recent years.

The labels said 'Live Hepatitis E. coli – Laboratory Material' in a series of different languages and scripts. The ownership was attributed to the well-known USA-based global pharmaceutical Pfizer; their research had shown this was a company operating in more than a hundred countries. Pfizer boasted on its website that it was responsible for six of the top twenty-five medicines and Kabitsin had joked that it could now claim to have its brand on the new number one anti-medicine too.

They had judged that this description would not lead to any interest that might prompt the containers to be stolen in transit; hopefully it was dull enough that there would be no big demands for any *baksheesh* at borders, yet still scary enough for there to be no interest in opening the container to check its contents. There had been some discussion that perhaps they should have chosen a Swiss company for the labels in order to avoid any potential for any anti-American feelings to hold up their progress, but it was concluded that Pfizer appeared to be a global brand and the name was not immediately recognised as being American anyway.

The General asked Kabitsin, 'How much are you planning to send to each of our colleagues for their own use?'

'We judged that 100 litres was enough. That much spread far enough in Kazakhstan to make its point. The purpose is for them to demonstrate the material and threaten further attacks, not actually carry those through. Anyway, our major demonstration will give further evidence that can be used in their local markets.'

What Kabitsin had not explained was that the price for each 100 litres had been set by him at $10million so this too would limit the demands for more. However as each colleague should be able to recoup many times the investment there had been few complaints. Of course if they were really smart they might consider capturing some of the still water that their events would generate and setting up their own market in the material. But Kabitsin already had plans in place that would make this possibility very unlikely indeed. The material would never leave his control!

The first $10million had already been deposited into his account by Wim Brockenhorst. Kabitsin thought of Wim as merely some form of mercenary, a stateless person, nowhere on any priority list in Kabitsin's personal estimation. He did however accept the General's view that they needed to show global reach and so on his own terms would allow this to proceed.

Kabitsin considered Africa a complete wasteland, unworthy of interest or attention. He felt that the black regimes had proven to be much more oppressive than the old colonial administrations had ever been. The leaders who had emerged were corrupt, lining their own pockets and never caring if the populace prospered or died. They starved, tortured and killed their own people, still squabbling along old tribal divisions. Then their peoples were too lazy in work terms and yet so uncontrollably sexually active that they were killing themselves with their AIDS epidemic. On so many levels they just did not deserve his interest or attention.

The General asked, 'Where is our first shipment going?'

'It's going to Africa for Wim's planned Congo event.'

'Ah yes, I read his briefing paper earlier and he does appear to have thought it all through.'

'I'd prefer that we used this supply on our own black-arses. Who cares about a bunch of bloody natives in the middle of a pointless continent? I've looked and there are plenty of lakes and rivers we might use. We should go for multiple sites in the Pamir and Amu Darya Rivers. They run all the way from the Afghanistan-Tajikistan border and then through Turkmenistan and Uzbekistan. And there's the Vakhsh that starts in Kyrgyzstan, crosses Tajikistan and ends up joining up with the Amu Darya. The Vakhsh provides 90% of the Tajiks power. We could switch them all off at a stroke.'

The General was surprised by this. 'We've always agreed that our true purpose is to weaken this meteoric rise of India and China and to assure our leading role in the world. This isn't about revenge, or worse murder, without purpose.'

'It would be a direct strike at five rebel states that need to be reminded who they should be serving, shown who really owns their resources and energies. If we don't, that region will end up just like the Middle East where fat lazy locals become rich from their resources, too rich to know what to do with their money, with the rest of the world having to fawn over them, pay their ridiculous prices. Or worse they could end up as pointless and ruthless as the African nations!'

Dmitry had never liked the man but now this. It was just too much to bear. Dmitry could pass almost anywhere as Russian and he usually did, but in fact his mother was pure Tajik so he might be considered as one of Kabitsin's 'black-arses'. He kept quiet, head down at his work, but listened very carefully to their conversation.

Kabitsin wasn't finished. 'I just think that while we have limited supplies we should be sure that we have the right strategy in place.'

The General was insistent. 'But the meeting in Lhasa was the venue for these discussions. It was quite clear that we agreed with the Brotherhood the targets that we would hit.' He counted them off on his fingers, 'First there's Wim's and the Congo River, where it passes between Kinshasha and Brazzaville. Asil's and the Tigris close to the border within Turkey, yet striking down on to the Kurds, perhaps reaching all the way to Mosul. Pavel's is perhaps the most difficult but we will hit the Danube as it passes between Romania and Bulgaria.

'All of those are just the hors d'oeuvres before our own demonstration that will make the Chinese and Indians fully appreciate our threat. This must be a demonstration that strikes directly at their interests. We need it to hurt but show that it is clearly just a precursor to our eventual threatened target of the Brahmaputra. They will not take long to work out that we have the ability to poison the rivers running from the Tibetan plateau, all seven of them streaming death and industrial disruption to their half of mankind.'

Kabitsin was angry with himself for having revealed his thoughts too freely to this old dinosaur. The Brotherhood! The General was old world, *perdoon stary*, an old fart. Yes, back in his days of espionage all of them made very clear that they thought it was mostly some sort of game, an academic exercise, an intellectual challenge pitting their wits against each other, and if all else failed there was always a night-time exchange across a border to sort it all out.

Kabitsin knew that the world was no longer like that. Today it was full of those trying to threaten and to take away what was rightfully yours, and the way to stop that was to stand up to them, to fight for what was right, to kill to keep it whenever necessary. In Kabitsin's world there was no banter, no polite prisoner exchanges. You killed them so it was an end of the matter, killed their family so there was no one left to come back at you for revenge. It worked at the family level, so why not at the national level too? There was clarity in this for others too. They would know what you were capable of, what you could and would do, and that was the way forward.

The General could feel the emotions that were churning within Kabitsin's brooding silence but down the years he had become used to being obeyed. 'Let's hear no more about changing our plans. You must appreciate that proper leadership is about maintaining your plan, what the Americans call stickability.

Once you have a plan, you see it through.' With this parting shot he left the catacombs and went back up to the house.

Kabitsin waited until he was out of earshot and called out '*Deirymo*!' Shit! Then he slammed his fist into the side of a filing cabinet leaving a deep impression. Belatedly realising that he was losing face in front of Lev and the team, he followed the old man upstairs.

In his anger he had not realised that the old man had listed their targets in front of Lev and his team, but more significantly Dmitry had heard them too!

# Chapter 30 - *Novosibirsk, Russia*

Still at the Russian facility, Tom thought that almost anywhere he had worked in the West there would have been some camera or access system that would have made clear what had happened. Perhaps there were some here too? Weren't the Russians supposed to tape every foreigner's conversation? How difficult would it be for them to have listening devices in the electronically active laboratory? Surely it was more unlikely that they did not have them? In fact the Russians had found that the hum of the plant and equipment in the laboratories made this completely impractical. He feared Brain had left him hanging out here as the patsy.

Brain had been right. The Russians did not consider for a second that their celebrity scientist had been involved in the theft and death. They had not even mentioned that anything was amiss. The laboratories had been closed for the whole of the next day, the team having been told that there were some fears for the integrity of the containment chamber.

He had spent that long day waiting for a knock on his door, to be carried off to the Lubyanka prison in Dzerzhinsky Square. In all the books he had read of the Cold War this was the ultimate fear, to be brought, tortured and then forgotten inside the KGB's Lubyanka headquarters. He was already in Siberia, so what other threat could they have?

The following day he threw himself into his work on the still water, quashing any concerns he still had by pressing on, recovering that earlier feeling of him against the world, seeking the solution through both perspiration and inspiration.

What he'd noticed days before was that the still water was susceptible to perturbations. In his field this term usually meant geological perturbations, alterations in the alluvial deposits brought about by climatic changes or by the nature of the materials deposited. But here he was thinking more of biological perturbations brought about by temperature or pressure or, in the case that he was interested in, by some form of osmotic shock.

He couldn't stop himself from doing his normal knee-jerk response to any unusual scientific term. He automatically sought out a way in which he might try to describe osmotic shock to a layman, for example in a television interview.

He felt that the general term osmosis was probably recognised by most laymen, more as a matter of some piece of general knowledge than any real understanding of the process. It would be described as some manner in which plants 'suck' water from the ground in order to feed themselves. Osmosis is not a sucking up as if through a straw-like hollowed stem, it is more a controlled passage of water through a series of membranes.

He felt that those same laymen would recognise the term 'learning by osmosis' as it is used quite widely to mean that a student can learn just by being put into the learning environment and assimilate knowledge almost unconsciously.

He knew that osmosis is in fact vital to many biological systems. What the semi-permeable membranes in those plants do is to stop the larger molecules in the soil from passing, but allow oxygen, carbon-dioxide or water, to pass through.

He stopped worrying about his word-smithing, he needed to concentrate on how osmosis might be operating with the still water. If he put an animal cell or plant cell into a liquid consisting largely of normal water, then the membrane surrounding that cell would do one of three things. If the liquid had a higher concentration of water than the cell, then the cell would gain water by osmosis. If the liquid and the cell had the same water concentration then there would be no net movement of water through the membrane. If the cell had the greater water concentration then some of the water would leave the cell. Was this latter case what happened with still water? Did it mean that because plain old $H^2O$ was relatively low within the still water that it would drain out the water present in the cell by osmosis? Was this how it extinguished life?

If this was the case and there was some form of membrane formed between the water and the still water – what they had until now been assuming was a meniscus – wouldn't this membrane then function to allow the normal water to enter and dilute the still water solution by the same osmosis? It did explain why the still water did not pass the membrane to the other side, but there was no evidence that the still water was being diluted. Just what was going on at this membrane?

If normal water was passing through the membrane this meant that his many unsuccessful tests for detecting solutes in the still water had missed something. With osmosis the direction of travel is always towards the heavier concentration, so this meant that the normal water had to have a weaker solution of whatever it was that was unable to penetrate the membrane. His assumption had been that the normal water should be more of an active material packed with many more solutes than the still water. Clearly this still water must contain a very particular solute that was driving the process. What had he missed?

Tom decided for now just to make the leap of faith and assume that the meniscus was some form of membrane. Once formed it would create a barrier between the normal water and this new variety. The membrane would let through $H^2O$ but stop $D^2O$.

But then what was happening in the Kazakhstan event that broke this membrane down? And why was the membrane not forming all around the $D^2O$? It certainly appeared to have mixed with and changed the normal water on some occasions. So, on the downstream section, was it that some sort of perturbation was causing osmotic shock, where the membrane would try to form but then rupture and allow the two waters to mix?

There were just too many questions that required careful experimentation, but with the political situation that was going on all around him he had little interest in being seen to either define or solve them here.

Theorising was good. The Russians could not tape or video his thoughts.

# Chapter 31 - *Istanbul, Turkey*

The team had been disbanded and the various members were scattering homewards. They had been advised that the remaining still water would be held securely at Novosibirsk, awaiting any conclusions the team members might reach subsequent to returning to their own lives, careers and facilities.

Tom had been approached, as Mark had advised he would, and invited to meet with Kabitsin. He had been provided with travel documents to Istanbul and then on home to London. He had never been to Istanbul. His work had never taken him there and he had little time for holidays, always feeling his work was much more interesting than leisure time anyway.

He had been instructed to check in to his hotel, take in the sights, relax and he would be invited to the meeting at some stage. He chose to take a guided tour, always preferring to get the background from a local. His guide showed how Constantine had built the city on seven hills as some sort of replication, the creation of an eastern Rome. He was taken to the Golden Horn and shown how the city was the crossroads of two continents. He was shown the Galeta Bridge, the Topkapi Palace, the 6th century Hagia Sophia, the Blue Mosque. From here on the sights began to merge into one so he looked instead around at the people on the streets who were a glorious mix of cultures.

The tour ended, or rather he escaped, when they showed him the Sunken Cistern, underground water tunnels, also 6th century. Supported by hundreds of Corinthian columns, he learned it covered an area of almost 10,000 square metres holding 80,000 cubic metres of water. He was sure he'd seen an action thriller use this as a location and the guide later mentioned that one of the early Bond movies 'From Russia With Love' had indeed featured it in one of its sequences.

Tom was bemused that this earlier Turkish civilisation had been so powerful and innovative, yet today its status in the world did not put it at the front in most modern measures of significance. How and when did it lose its way?

The guide explained at length the importance in Islamic tradition of making an offering of water, the scarce yet vital resource in so many of the Islamic countries. He stressed that despite losing many of the old facilities the city still boasted some five hundred fountains and more than seventy other water resources similar to, though not as large as, this Basilica Cistern.

Given his current focus Tom began to find the proximity to so much water and the talk of spies, even fictional ones, to be quite forbidding especially since the man who controlled the still water was to meet him in this very city. He left the tour to wander the streets back towards his hotel.

When he got back to his hotel there was a note in reception advising him of the meeting point. It came with a small brochure and a map. It was to be held in the *Kapalıçarşı*, the Grand Bazaar. Tom read the brochure and saw that this vast covered bazaar was home to around 4,000 shops and had a confusion of some sixty streets that criss-crossed each other in a bewildering pattern.

Some of the buildings dated back to the 15th century and the whole was like a huge labyrinth that, according to the brochure, would be packed full of in-your-face traders in gold, jewellery, carpets, pottery, leather goods… Boy was he going to enjoy that! Not!

He later followed the map to the location that had been marked and immediately recognised Lev, the huge security head from Novosibirsk. Even here he still had that annoying smirk that he had used particularly towards Ellise. It was the sort of smirk you would like to slap until it left his face, but that was if it had been pasted on to a lesser mortal than this powerful guy.

Lev grunted a, 'Follow me.' He walked through the crowds and Tom noted that none of the traders seemed to bother the big man, preferring to turn away, make way for him through the otherwise bustling walkways. They turned suddenly into some awful toilets; the smell was cloying. Normally Tom would have rather wet himself than go into one of these places, but Lev had stepped in there just to frisk him, which he did quickly and thoroughly and they were back out in seconds.

They were off at his fast walking pace once more, he led Tom to a small café with the patrons at the front sharing deep draughts on their *nargiles* or hookah pipes, again not somewhere he would have ever dared enter alone. They passed on through to a stall right at the back where Kabitsin was clearly the person on the nearside with another individual inside him on the bench seat. Neither deigned to rise to greet him, just motioned him to sit opposite. Lev chose to sit at a table across a small aisle rather than overwhelm the fourth position at the stall.

Kabitsin beckoned and a thick strong Turkish coffee was set before Tom who used the time to try to assess the man sitting opposite. There was an elusive something that clearly stamped him out as being Russian. He had clearly come through a 'hard school', bearing some of the experiences very clearly on his face. He was probably only early 40s, definitely not younger, but he might have been anything up to fifteen years older.

His very short dark hair had not been shorn to conceal baldness; it was clearly the right style for his selected image. He had a big, round face with high cheekbones and there was just a hint of Asia in the shape of his eyes. His nose was not the crushed lump of a boxer although it had clearly taken some knocks, but not too many.

He was dressed very formally in a suit jacket with collar and tie, but the tailor's skills did nothing to hide the girth of his shoulders, the thick neck and the strength in his arms. He was not a giant like Lev but he looked just as hard and unyielding.

At the centre of this whole threatening impression was a pair of very lively, striking blue eyes that failed to fit with the rest of his image. Someone intelligent and bright appeared to be trapped inside this Hollywood gangster façade.

Preliminaries over, Kabitsin spoke in Russian and the guy inside him translated into good English. 'So you have been in Mother Russia, you have been working with our still water, you comprehend its power?'

'It's terrifying stuff. If it ever managed to penetrate the water cycle we would all be finished, not just us, all of life.' Tom watched as the interpreter appeared to struggle to describe the term 'water cycle' in a small interchange with Kabitsin. Tom was unsure the translator really understood the term and cautioned himself to simplify anything he might say from hereon in.

'So you will understand that something of this significance needs to be carefully managed. It needs to be in the right hands?'

'My thoughts are that it just needs to be contained, or preferably expunged, umm, I mean stopped, killed.' Tom struggled to find the right word that might be translated fairly.

Kabitsin listened to the translation and looked puzzled, but pressed on. The translator paused, then said, 'Nothing in life is free, except the air we breathe and the water we drink. Until now. What this new water allows is that now it will only be air that will be free, peoples must pay for the water.'

Tom had been struggling to read between the lines until now. He could see where this was heading. It was clearly Mark's franchise arrangement. How best to proceed? He assumed if he showed his horror at the thought then the conversation would be over. He had to string this guy along.

'It's almost that way already. We pay for bottled water, we pay for water supply from the utility companies. What precisely do you propose?'

Kabitsin asked through the interpreter, 'First, we are on neutral ground here, so you have nothing to fear from me. I need you to confirm that you are in touch with British Intelligence?'

'I am not in any way a member of the intelligence community, but I guess that I can pass on a message to the right people.'

'Good, it will all go more quickly if we are frank with each other. Do you know Sir Joseph Maudlin?'

Tom was a little shocked by this and did not immediately know how to respond.

Kabitsin scowled unhappy that he had to explain himself. 'The leader of our group is a long-term Russian intelligence man and he says that he has met and respects this man.'

'I know of him. He's actually quite famous at home and I suppose I could reach him if this is what you want.'

'It is to him we wish to address a proposition. We need to be convinced that you can reach him with our message?'

'I can.'

'Then we have a package you need to take back to London with you. It describes how a small group of the right sort of people can manage this still water to gain control of a new market opportunity. We need the right people who can understand that still water can be used to recover from the problems of the modern world and regain each of our national prides, win back control of our own countries from the threat of the displaced minorities, from the threat of Islam.'

The slow translation of this long diatribe gave Tom a chance to reassess his man. The darting eyes were telling him a different story now. This man had the stamp of madness deep within those eyes; he was even more dangerous than his physique had indicated. His madness and his still water were a monstrous combination. Tom felt a chill in this hot, sweatiest of places. This guy needed to be stopped.

# Chapter 32 - *London, UK*

When Tom finally returned to his London apartment he was still profoundly worried about Kabitsin and his plans. As yet he was not sure he was too keen to pass the proposition on to Sir Joseph, unsure if he could be trusted with what it contained.

In the end he just crashed out. He had not realised how tense he had been feeling since the incident with Brain, until he reached home and collapsed on to his bed. There was nothing that felt quite like his own bed, safe within his own space and with that combination he just shut down.

He had never slept for ten hours before, ever. When the ringing of his doorbell penetrated his sleep he was shocked to see that this had been the case that night.

It was Mark and he had brought Starbucks coffees and muffins with him.

'Glad to see you made it back from the Evil Empire.' He twirled. 'And as you can see I escaped the clutches of Ernst Blofeld unscathed.'

Tom was still half asleep.

'C'mon get out of your jammies. We need to talk!'

'My mouth's like the bottom of a parrot's cage. Let me freshen up first, but give me that coffee, I need caffeine!'

He returned to find Mark with a mouthful of blueberry muffin flicking through news channels on his television. 'So what is it we need to discuss?'

'I've had some progress on this whole still water thing, but I need you to introduce me to your connections within your intelligence service.'

'Why is it that everyone thinks I'm involved in intelligence work all of a sudden?'

'You wouldn't have been allowed to go to Novosibirsk without their sanction at least. It's more probable you would have had a very detailed briefing by them of what they wanted you to look for and full instructions of how to feed them your reports.'

'OK, so let's assume I know how to contact them.'

'I'm not trying to embarrass you. It's just that I want what I have to get on to the right desk.'

'You met with Kabitsin then?'

'Yes and now I need to talk it over with your folks.'

'Surely you spooks stick together, go to the same cocktail parties?'

'I certainly do not, honest. I really do work for my father. Yes, he is part of the US intelligence community, but on this matter we find we don't know who to trust.'

'So just what is it that has spooked the spook?'

'It's this Kabitsin character. He approached me with a very generous offer, the franchise for still water for North and Central America. Apparently he has the rest of the world covered already and didn't want to lose out on the lucrative market that he thought we could control. Hasn't he contacted you?'

'Not yet. You told me you thought it was what he wanted you to meet him to discuss. What would the franchise be for?'

'Put simply, the opportunity to extort. We could threaten the governments, corporates and others with death and mayhem if they don't give us what we ask.'

'How would you expect to get away with that? Surely you'd be hunted down by everything that those governments could mobilise.'

'There's the frightening bit. The Brotherhood – it's a sort of global mutual-support organisation. Take one of the parties out and the others are pledged to deliver on the party's promises. So if I threatened to pour the stuff into the Mississippi, then I would lodge the plan and all its details with the Brotherhood and if I was 'disappeared' then they would make good on my threat. All the branches of this organisation need to be taken out simultaneously or, like the Hydra, one of the other heads will get you!'

'I'm not sure what I can say to you, but I will make some enquiries. I really am what I appear to be, a jobbing scientist with my agent and publisher screaming at me for my next book!'

Tom had forwarded the Russian's package to Sir Joseph with the forlorn hope that he could sidestep its consequences and get back to his life. But in truth he was relieved when he was also invited to attend the meeting that he had requested for Mark. It seemed they were not going to let him walk away from this matter just yet.

They met in the Army & Navy Club in Pall Mall and were shown to a comfortable private room with a series of deep armchairs drawn up around a large fireplace. They were greeted by Sir Joseph and Brain, though no introductions were offered or given by any side.

Mark had made some effort to look the part of the Englishman in a gentleman's club but somehow he still looked scruffy and out of place.

Sir Joseph said, 'Welcome to the "Rag".' Initially Tom flinched as he thought Sir Joseph was being rude about Mark's fashion statement, but realised that this must be some sort of nickname for the club.

'First time?' Tom had been there before for a dinner but Mark said it was his debut. They settled deeply into the chairs as Brain officiated with tea all around. Brain caught Mark's eye, expecting him to ask for coffee, for which he probably had some smart response, but was disappointed as Mark happily accepted the proffered tea.

'Well, dear chap, how can we be of assistance?'

Mark looked at Brain and Tom pointedly, 'Well I had hoped that we could keep this to a limited number of ears.'

'Nonsense, nonsense, both of these gentlemen have my utmost confidence. Besides they have both become heavily involved in this monstrous stuff and as you can see I'm well past practising any form of fieldcraft myself, don't you know.'

Mark breathed in deeply and captured their attention quickly, 'My father's real fears are that many in our branch of government would find the Brotherhood's offer too tempting. The hawks abound in Washington. They are all too ready to apply something like this still water to forward their foreign policy objectives. They're sniffing around. They know something of interest is happening and we don't want to give it to them. I assume you guys have established quite what a weapon this stuff could become?'

'Yes, of course, and I appreciate your dilemma. But where do we come in?'

'First, you appear to have some of the material.'

Sir Joseph couldn't help glancing at Tom who gently shook his head once, 'I'm afraid I have absolutely no idea where you might have received that idea.'

'Let's just assume for the moment that you have or could get hold of some, then the question is how you might use it.'

'We would probably destroy it, too damnably dangerous to have lying around.'

'True, but wouldn't you want to try and find an antidote first?'

'Well, hypothetically of course, if we did ever get hold of any, then that would indeed be a sensible approach.'

'And if you were to do such tests, would you like to have all of our assembled data too, so that your investigation could have more chance of success?'

'Well, that would seem a jolly good idea.'

'So you have some?'

Sir Joseph smiled. 'What I would be interested to hear is where you met with this Kabitsin and something of the meeting.'

'Sure, I have no problem bringing you to the same page on that one. He looks and is a cheap hood, a throwback to our 1930s Chicago mobsters. Physically he's quite commanding, he's arrogant of his status, clearly ruthless and apparently well-connected. It would appear he's a hood who had a plan, did everyone's dirty work and kept the evidence. Whether he was just fortunate that he had backed some winners or whether his services were what let them rise to the top is unclear.'

Sir Joseph was enjoying the young man's concise report, having sat through too many convoluted debriefings, 'That accords with the intelligence we have on the man. Started out being muscle and then muscled in on to the top table itself.'

'Cool, so I needn't waste too much time on history. Today he has some pretty big hitters supporting him. He walks in and out of the Kremlin more frequently than a tour guide, can stroll in and out of the Duma where he seems to have a large number of the members in his pocket. He has established General Goncharenko as a figurehead for this Brotherhood. The General's a distinguished and long-serving KGB-cum-FSB man, something of a thorn in our side in his time. But it's not like him to be part of this sort of criminal crowd. He must have become disenchanted, pension not good enough or something.'

'No respect anywhere in the world now for age and experience. I dare say I too shall be cast off to some dreadful seaside resort to see out my days on a pittance.'

'You wouldn't turn to crime to supplement it, would you?'

'Perhaps then it's the other thing that bothers you as you get older. Legacy. He's served his nation with distinction for a lifetime. But what's left of the dreams of his youth? What point did those decades of agonising, plotting, planning and executing achieve? Does he have children?'

'Not according to our research.'

'There you are, no grandson to dandle on the knee and regale with tales of his youth, no son for him to offer guidance and support. All he has is his past glories and no one to share them with. He probably wants one last real adventure that can warm his evenings, put a smile back on his face despite all the aches and pains, smell the success long after his olfactory senses have left him, hear the applause despite his deafness. Legacy!'

'He and Kabitsin do appear to be strong-suited in patriotism.'

'So he should be pleased with President Vladimir Putin turning back the clocks to the glorious Soviet past.'

Mark smiled as he acknowledged that Sir Joseph had quite deliberately pronounced the name as *Putain*, the French slang expression for whore.

'Yes, but perhaps it's all going too slowly for them? They want to chivvy it along a little.'

Tom had stayed quiet through this exchange, but now asked, 'Is it your assessment that they are just threatening to use the "still water" or do you believe that they actually plan to go ahead?'

Mark stood up and walked. 'Oh, they will use it. Kabitsin is clearly disappointed that the Kazakhstan event was rushed, not properly monitored, not enough evidence, not enough fatalities for it to be taken very seriously. He made it clear that they have a planned "spectacular" to make their case compelling to the governments and peoples that they've targeted. He even suggested that we should stage a demonstration in our own "territory" so that there could be no doubt of our willingness and ability to deliver.'

Sir Joseph asked, 'You, of course, agreed that you would take up his offered franchise?'

'Sure, we need to keep close to him and his plans. But he's not asking much, just $25million for us to join up and this includes two 100 litre barrels of the material delivered to our intended site. The General or Kabitsin seem to have swallowed a McDonalds' franchise contract and manual in the terminology they have used in their proposal.'

Tom almost commented on this but saw the warning glance from Sir Joseph.

'So you have a printed proposal?'

'Yep, but not one I was allowed to take away. I had the impression I would not get it even when I paid them my $25million. They seem to be planning to be a very hands-on franchiser.'

'The money...'

Mark interrupted, 'Yes, we're setting up to follow the money all the way back to them. We have our very best folk on it, diverted all sorts of electronic wizardry to be sure to stay with it. But I'm told if their people are good we've only a 50-50 chance of success. They have to make an error somewhere for us to be able to follow it all the way.'

'Oh and where precisely did you meet with this Kabitsin?'

'Oh, didn't I say, in a café in the Grand Bazaar, Istanbul, Turkey. It was perfect for his purposes. We had no chance to prepare, no surveillance potential, too much background noise and just too many ways in and out. The restaurant was busy and presumably stacked with his men if we'd gone for a take-down. Our followers did well but lost him when he went into a nearby shop specialising in counterfeit brand labels for the fashion trade. He must have ducked under the counter and out the back, but when our guys followed suit there was no trace of him'

'Points of egress?'

'Of course we pulled all the strings we had with MIT.' He explained for Tom, 'The Turkish intelligence service. The only thing they came up with for sure is that he did not leave by aircraft. Have you ever seen the waters down there? All sorts of craft milling around in apparent confusion, not a hope of sorting your way through those.'

'So when do you transfer the money?'

'That's not the difficult bit. First I have to finish my assignment, do my homework as you say here. We have to submit our plan, the demo that we propose, the main threat that will be used for the extortion, how we plan to deliver our threat, how we would ensure we stay clear of capture. It's like writing a blockbuster novel.'

Sir Joseph said, 'And, of course, hoping it always remains a work of fiction!'

# Chapter 33 - *Oxfordshire, UK*

Tom had been invited to work out of Culham Laboratories as he followed through on his thinking. On arrival there he was also given access to the American material and thought processes that Mark had diligently supplied.

This UKAEA (UK Atomic Energy Authority) site houses one of the world's foremost centres seeking to develop nuclear fusion as a new and sustainable energy source. Tom learned that it was also home to a flourishing Innovation Centre that had attracted a broad group of technology-based companies that could draw upon the resources of the labs.

He had been briefed that the UKAEA projects handled there are expressed as a plethora of UK and European acronyms and initialisms. JET, the Joint European Torus, which had achieved the world's first fusion-power production back in the early 1980s. START and MAST were successive technologies for something Tom had to look up, a 'tokamak'. He found that this was another acronym but from a set of Russian words meaning a toroidal, or doughnut-shaped, chamber set inside magnetic coils that could contain a plasma. Given the Russian derivation, he wondered if any of this work had first been formulated at the Akademgorodok, where he'd so recently been based, but could find no suggestion that it had.

He was allocated a secure laboratory in Building F4 and shown the facilities available to him which impressively included a conference facility, business travel office, post office, cash-point, a crèche and several catering outlets – what more could he need?

He read up on the stuff that they were involved with at Culham. From what he could establish this fusion was all about slamming hydrogen isotopes together, those same isotopes that seemed suddenly to haunt his every waking moment. By colliding deuterium, D or $^2H$, and tritium, T or $^3H$, nuclei into each other they briefly combined as an unstable Helium-5 nucleus; which then rapidly decayed to give up one of the neutrons. That freed-neutron and the leftover Helium 4 parted company in a very marked manner, and it was this parting of the ways that was assumed would generate the desired high energies.

Tom was drawn into further reading because it was not long ago that he had never even heard of deuterium, now here he was reading about it being present in fusion reactions – the very stuff that powers the stars. It seemed the trick that they were still seeking to resolve was somehow to flick the fusion on and off. If the reaction was sustained for too long then the outcome would be a thermonuclear explosion but from a constricted reaction they hoped to harvest real energy.

He called a halt on this side issue but marked it down on his smartphone as something he should investigate further for a potential future publication. He decided to codename it 'Steam to Stardust – a review of the sources of power down the ages'.

Now, back to this still water; he had been allocated a very bright young assistant, Stevie Tasker. Stevie was a pretty blonde, probably an early 30-something and a little strange on first meeting.

At such a first meeting, one might have been forgiven for accusing her of displaying the attributes that her hair colour automatically suggested. But given some days of working together Tom realised that it wasn't the case; there was no limitation between her ears, it was more as if there seemed to be rather too much going on in there on occasion. When she had one of those moments it was evident that everything was all happening at such a pace in her mind that she was almost unable, or more likely uninterested, in holding a conversation while she strove to marshal her thoughts.

Her eye movements on these occasions were quite disturbing too. Even the most practised practitioner of neuro-linguistic programming would have been unable to establish what was going on. Was she in visual, auditory or kinaesthetic mode, was she creating a new thought or drawing on past ones that she had filed away?

Another oddity was that Stevie seemed to have no concept of personal space and tended to stand just that little bit too close when she was prepared to join you in conversation. Though of course proximity to this pretty woman was not all that bad a proposition, it was unusual, unsettling. Early on Tom had moved the furniture around so that he could escape behind a desk when necessary.

Yet sitting at that desk he was feeling relieved; for the first time he was able to discuss his thoughts with someone whom he could trust, well whom he assumed that he could trust. The fact that Stevie appeared to be a good listener suited Tom too. All he currently wanted was to be able to voice his theories and thoughts and he could always assume that Stevie's silence was agreement.

So he was surprised when Stevie suddenly strung together perhaps the longest sentence he'd heard her utter. 'What you are postulating is that, on contact with $H^2O$, your new material creates a sort of membrane, but you don't know why it doesn't form completely around the material, in particular down-stream. Could it be that there's a separate process going on, a simple hydrogen-deuterium exchange? We can make this happen in proteins quite readily, why not here?'

'The million-dollar question is – can we stop it happening?'

Stevie was making up for all those silences. 'It's a chemical reaction to change the hydrogen atom into a deuterium atom. All we need is to stop that reaction.'

Well, as might be expected it was not quite as simple as that. It took time to dig it out of her but Stevie explained that a chemical reaction in this case, as in many, was not the simple issue of the colour changes they could both recall from childhood use of potassium permanganate or litmus paper. It was not the spluttering, smoking and exploding of materials that she admitted had retained most of her attention back then. It was about a movement of electrons, the exchange of single electrons or pairs of them. 'What we're after here is to chemically decompose the still water, strip the $D^2O$ to $H^2O$.'

'Yes, that's what we want to achieve. And we need to understand how it seems to have done that naturally.'

Stevie considered this for a while and replied. 'The natural thing? All I can say is that the natural order of a hydrogen-oxygen mix on earth is normal water, so perhaps it is just nature re-establishing its norms. But for us to achieve it, all we have to do is add oxygen.'

'What do you mean add oxygen?'

She went to a white board and scribbled, 'What we have is $D^2O$ or $2H^2O$ and, if we double up on the oxygen, we end up with $2H^2O^2$. You can bet your bottom dollar that these would separate out into two lots of $H^2O$.'

So Tom and Stevie set about the apparently simple task of injecting oxygen into still water to try to change it. It was something that Tom believed had been tried in Novosibirsk but perhaps it was not done that diligently. The politics there seemed more important than the science.

This proved not to be as straightforward as it sounded for when they bubbled oxygen through it the bubbles stayed stubbornly, well, bubbles until they broke the surface of the still water and passed on.

They looked at mixing oxygenated or super-oxygenated water, pressurising the water and the still water, each atmosphere of oxygen adding five times the original oxygen content into the straight water. The theory was the extra oxygen in it might be grabbed by the still water, but it didn't happen.

Days passed with each coming up with more and more esoteric approaches, pressure, temperatures, different materials and new apparatus to mix, shake or spin the material. There was some minor progress with several of their approaches, but nothing worked to the extent of significantly converting the still water to water. It was such a simple notion, it sounded elegant chemically, but the stubborn stuff refused to budge. In Tom's mind it began to take on an animate recalcitrance, a pig-headedness that was wittingly countering their every move, making sure all their efforts were in vain.

As is often the case it was by accident that Tom broke the deadlock. Or more accurately it was by a piece of serendipity, or lateral thinking, call it what you will. He had been pondering their dilemma while boiling an egg, watching the bubbles on the surface of the water, and was reminded of the failure of their simply bubbling oxygen through the still water.

Still water! He knew the origins of the name – someone had said it was different and yet it was still water. But perhaps whoever said it had been even more perspicacious than they had imagined. Perhaps it needed some reasonable degree of stillness to be what it was.

This simple thought led to a very new approach. They created a sort of Mississippi River boat paddle that would churn through the material and now all they needed to add was a material that would exchange oxygen atoms with the still water.

It was Stevie, whose knowledge on occasions seemed encyclopaedic, who opted for zinc hydroxide. Her notion was to somehow reverse-engineer a zinc-air fuel cell where the zinc was oxidised by taking oxygen from the air. She explained that these cells were in general use for hearing aids and were being considered too as the best approach for electric vehicles. The issue they needed to address, if it worked, was that the chemical operation of this cell was an ongoing process, and it would mean that the zinc fuel had to be replenished and the resultant zinc oxide cleared for it to be sustained.

The paddle-steamer wheel approach was retained but the blades became more complex. Stevie called in some favours with a nearby workshop and the blades became hollow with a hydraulic system able to smoothly eject a constant film of zinc hydroxide along their leading edges. The whole structure had a low current applied to it, and, to the surprise of both of them, it worked.

The effects of the turbulence cleaned off the used material, the combination of an electrical charge and the zinc exchanged oxygen with the still water and it became simple water again. Eureka!

They were making all sorts of engineering modifications in an attempt to understand the process better when, without any prior notice, Brain arrived with a message from Sir Joseph.

Brain first sent Stevie off to the Costa coffee shop. To Tom she looked hurt as if somehow he was demeaning her with this domestic chore, for usually she and Tom took turns to fetch their cappuccinos.

Brain watched her go and said, 'You have to stop now. You've used 20 litres of our supply and we can't exhaust it all on your follow-up tests.'

'We need to understand how and why it's working. Plus, we have to create this zinc hydroxide as it doesn't appear to be something you can buy off the shelf. Perhaps there's a simpler alternative material.'

Brain smiled. 'We don't really care to understand it. We just need to stop it! Sir Joseph asks if you have a functioning system that we could use in the field.'

'Well, it's cumbersome and pretty complicated, takes two of us to use it even in these laboratory conditions. If you were by a river in the field, and the water flowing by was still water, it would add many new dimensions to the difficulties. You need to generate the zinc hydroxide, prime the blade array, then the current electric motor could be improved, but I guess it is already quite a sturdy device.'

'Could you show me how to use it?'

'Hm, it's a tough ask right now. How long have you got? I could run through it with you if you have say a half-day and then practise with it for another half-day?'

'That's just too long. You're both to pack it all up and you'll just have to come with us. You have four hours before we'll come and collect you.'

Stevie arrived back with the coffees just as Brain was leaving. He called back to her, 'Hope your passport is all up to date? Make sure you travel light, just a small rucksack at most. There will be little time for relaxation, so leave the make-up behind. Oh, and it will be very hot where we're going. Think equator and you won't be very far out!'

# Chapter 34 - *Democratic Republic of the Congo*

The Congo River rises in the East African Rift, taking water in part from Lake Tanganyika. Then, after pooling the resources of a number of tributaries, it gets down to business with some nine thousand kilometres of navigable waterway. Its river basin includes the second largest rain forest, second only to the Amazon.

It travels an area of amazing biodiversity that has been raped and pillaged by wars, by the taking of large mammals for the bushmeat trade and by illegal logging. For around 1,750km of its length it runs completely undisturbed by any rapids or falls. Sadly it is this very ease of navigability that is the reason that the poachers and forest-strippers can operate so readily.

Its equatorial location and huge network of tributaries mean that it has a constant flow that maintains an impressive girth, ranging between 6km and 16km through its central stretch. It's so wide and constant that the animal species on the two banks have developed very differently. The constancy of the Congo has been a physical barrier since way back to the time when the river was even bigger, spanning both Africa and South America when they were joined as Gondwanaland, the southern supercontinent some 500 million years ago.

The Congo turns southward and narrows for a section, down to just two kilometres wide. This was the target location that Wim had originally considered for release of the still water. Below this point the river broadens out again to form Pool Malebo where, on opposite banks, the two Congo national capitals of Kinshasha and Brazzaville are situated, with a combined population of more than nine million. It was these cities that he wished to target.

After this brief pause at the lake, the river then cascades down the Livingstone Falls, a series of more than thirty rapids, to the port of Matadi. It empties into the Gulf of Guinea and from there out into the Atlantic.

Wherever there are non-navigable sections a series of railways have been created to 'join up the dots' and form an economic 'highway' reaching right through the heart of Central Africa, it brings its minerals, cotton, coffee, sugar and palm-oil kernels down to the ocean port.

Much of its length is contained within the Democratic Republic of the Congo, the old Belgian colony that should of course never be confused with the old French colony, the Republic of the Congo. This other Congo is just one of ten neighbours that have made the history of the D R of the Congo a very frantic one. After living its life for twenty years as Zaire, in its current guise it was shaken to its core by the Second Congo War, sometimes referred to as "Africa's World War" because at its height it involved eight separate African nations and their supporters. More than twenty different armed groups marauded through the area. Though never quite meeting in a formal battle, they were responsible for almost four million deaths and well over three million more being displaced.

Wim's background notes to his plan identified that the country had always been defined in blood. King Léopold II had run a tight and brutal colony. $20^{th}$ century Belgium, while much gentler, still prised away the mineral wealth while giving little in return to the inhabitants. The CIA had meddled to bring about regime change in the 1960s and even Che Guevara had travelled there to train revolutionaries at one stage.

After the USA, other western countries and particularly any foreign investors lost direct interest in the country it was effectively left to the local militias to wreak their havoc, literally raping and pillaging the region into its current state. Kabitsin nodded knowingly as he read through this background detail.

The Democratic Republic of the Congo's capital city, Kinshasa, is a large city that is expected to become the biggest French-speaking city in the world, overtaking Paris. Kinshasa and Brazzaville, the other Congo's capital, have a unique claim to fame. They are the only two national capital cities that can actually see each other, just a few kilometres apart across the Pool Malebo.

Wim's report first considered the smaller city, Brazzaville, as his base of operations but he had learned that upriver from there on the west bank was quite difficult terrain that rapidly became swampland. Therefore his report had concluded that the city looked perhaps more interesting as one of the possible escape routes via its Maya-Maya airport. He had decided that movement around the larger city, Kinshasa, would be easier with him and his team being much less obvious among its seven million plus population.

In reviewing Wim's plans, Kabitsin was unsurprised to learn that the first-ever recorded AIDS victim in the world was a man in Kinshasa! His comment to Lev on learning this was that he believed this was because of sexual interference with a chimpanzee.

Wim's report went on to say that the conventional wisdom however was that having been first identified in primates, it was either passed by a bite or scratch from a wild chimpanzee or perhaps someone caught it while butchering an infected chimp. He did also mention that there were some who suggest it came about from researchers who had been looking for polio vaccines in the region. Kabitsin however was perfectly content with his own explanation, just further proof that this continent did not deserve his attention.

The four teams travelled to the Congo from different directions and by different routes, but all arrived within twenty-four hours of each other.

Wim and his team had flown into Luanda in Angola, where they collected weapons and other equipment. They had come this way so that there could be no record of their arrival. They had then driven non-stop for much of two days and right through the night to get to Kinshasa. They set up a camp well outside the city so they were not on record as having entered the capital.

Lev and his crew arrived directly at Ndjili, the Kinshasa International Airport, on a chartered cargo flight together with two of their 100-litre packages. Kabitsin, of course, was not deigning to accompany them to this 'corrupt' continent. The South African and Russian teams met up at the campsite.

Brain was joined by Brawn, who Tom learned was actually called James though whether this was his first name or surname was never made clear. They had also brought another guy, whom they did nothing to introduce either. They had brought Tom and Stevie in by what was clearly the most uncomfortable route. They had flown reasonably agreeably to Lagos in Nigeria, then across to the east of that country in a not so pleasant military plane, but it was the three legs by oil company helicopter that had finished them off. They had refuelled first at São Tomé, the small island that with Principe forms one of the smallest African states. Nigeria and São Tomé were jointly exploiting some offshore oil fields which gave them their cover there. Then again they had used oil exploration as their reason to refuel at Tchibanga in Gabon. They eventually landed at a virtually abandoned Tshimpi airport near the ocean port of Matadi and subsequently took a train upriver to the city. Tom had complained of the journey but stopped when Brain pointed out that this way he was never there, that his celebrity reputation would remain intact.

Valéry had arrived before all of them. The Operations Directorate of the French Intelligence Service, the DGSE, or Direction Générale de la Sécurité Extérieure, had fairly significant 'resources' in both cities. As a senior member of that organisation he had seconded the local teams to monitor and follow all of the arrivals from the moment that they arrived. Though they only in fact located Wim's team by following Lev from the airport to the rendezvous.

It was Mark who arrived last of all, simply flying in on a scheduled flight with a passport and other documents that identified him as Mark Scott. He was collected at the airport by a DGSE operative who drove him directly to the offices being used by Valéry's team. It was Mark who had asked for their support in this patch, and therefore he was to be considered one of their team for this operation.

All were aware that the insertion point had been chosen to be near Mikala though few had seen Wim's detailed reasoning. He had considered whether they could have travelled on further north up beyond Maluku to where the Congo first broadens to form the Pool but as this area was a sparse savannah he was concerned about being too exposed there. There might also have been travel difficulties to and from that point.

Mikala is a quarter-million population city linked with Kinshasa by the A1 motorway, but no one could establish how advanced they were with the road construction until they saw it for themselves. Mikala is to the east of Kinshasa, sitting beside the Pool Malebo on the southern side facing the large island that is at the heart of the lake. The southern leg of the Congo flows from there straight on to Kinshasa.

What Wim could not establish was whether the flow downstream would sweep the still water down towards the rapids so that it would not reach out across to Brazzaville. He had left this as an open question in his report, asking the General to establish from the work that was still being done in Novosibirsk what might occur, but the only answer appeared to be to suck it and see – though none would take that advice too literally with this deadly stuff!

Wim's report then went on to spend a lot of time on working out the location, detailing how it could be seen as a direct strike at the Chinese, and identifying several other African targets as his next steps. The still water would do its stuff but the General and Kabitsin had asked where was the profit?

Wim explained that it was his choice of an insertion point that was much more likely to damage Kinshasha and the Democratic Republic of the Congo, and would probably spare the Republic of the Congo, that created the opportunity that he had identified. It was the far bank that the water would probably not reach, the Republic of the Congo, where the Chinese were most active and involved. So while they would be sure to understand the threat to them, their interests there would be relatively unharmed.

While the Chinese were seeking relationships with both the Congos, the frequent coups, armed militias and refugee movements in the Democratic Republic of the Congo had tended to interfere with any business-like progress. They had therefore had much more success with the Brazzaville side.

The president of the calmer Republic of the Congo had been the leader of the country when it had earlier experimented with Marxism and then had come back to power with almost ninety per cent of the vote following a civil war. These were clearly exceptionally good credentials for trading with China.

The president had welcomed the much more practical approach of the Chinese and so they had become very deep-rooted there. He argued that the West tended to set unreasonable goals in return for their investment. For example they had once sought from him a commitment to 'better government'. The president thought this was a lot like being asked to 'stop beating your wife' when you in fact were not beating her. He felt they already practised good government, how could they show or measure 'better'? And the people would not prosper, or get fed and watered, on better government alone.

The Chinese on the other hand offered them low-cost finance for their infrastructure projects – roads, power and hydroelectric projects, construction schemes like new radio and television headquarters, interspersed of course with the essential palaces and ministry buildings that they required to exercise this 'better government'. These were built by Chinese companies and very largely financed directly by the Chinese administration.

This was no charitable act, no altruism. In return China was ceded half of the oil production and was free to plunder the timber with no constraints about the sustainability of what they were doing. China's economic growth at home was so voracious for these resources that its trade with Africa had been expanding exponentially in recent years on similar arrangements agreed all across that continent.

Wim explained that something threatening the Chinese in this region was therefore able to be used to full advantage both in Africa and directly against the 'Central Kingdom' as the Chinese referred to themselves.

He explained and developed his approach as making his profit directly from the government of the Republic of the Congo. They would be shown the damage wrought upon Kinshasha and be required to pay him a regular 'tithe' to ensure that it would not happen to Brazzaville. They would see that they had much more to lose than their under-developed neighbour.

The joy was that all of this would be sure to be reported to the Chinese, so that Kabitsin might use this demonstration in his later approach to them.

On the savannah from a safe distance Valéry and his DGSE team were covertly watching the encampment which the South Africans and their Russian cohorts had located just a little north of Mikala. Between their 4 x 4 vehicles Wim and Lev and their respective teams had set up a sprawl of scruffy tents and canopies within a heavily wooded area. Savannahs are not as most imagine them to be, they are not sparsely wooded areas. The term savannah indicates that the canopy above the trees does not form intensely enough to close off the light from reaching through it to the ground. In a savannah tall grasses survive beneath the many trees.

The bad guys had posted a guard overnight, as a result the French watchers could not get close enough to mount an attempt to eavesdrop. They had not been so cautious with their campfires and it was only luck that their lack of attention had not started a bushfire.

Mark, who had positioned himself a little apart from the French team, took the binoculars and saw signs that the 'bandits' were all striking camp. This had also been noted by Valéry and his men who were quietly preparing to follow them. It was not going to be easy in this terrain but they had located themselves between the Russian's camp and the river so that it should not be necessary to use their own 4x4s. This decision had placed them upwind but they didn't think there was much bush-tracking expertise on show at the camp and Valéry's locals were very adept at concealment.

As the 'enemy' vehicles crawled past their observation point it was clear the gamble that their location would not be spotted had paid off. The Russians were headed to the river where their maps showed a channel or creek, formed by a series of three large and a number of small islands that hugged the shoreline. The observers could reach there promptly on foot without the need for their vehicles, but it would probably take ten to fifteen minutes to do it completely stealthily.

The other vehicles drew up in an array along the shoreline Lev's vehicle manoeuvred past them and reversed so that its rear approached a small inlet that branched back upstream. He had chosen this point for his convenience because he could see that there was a gradual slope down to the riverside. But Wim leapt from his vehicle and ran across to disagree.

Lev's men drew their weapons at the sight of the sudden and unexpected movement and Wim's men, also on a hair-wire, reciprocated. There had not been a great deal of mutual trust formed between the two groups despite their overnighting together.

Wim stopped in his tracks, held his arms wide to make clear he was no threat, and called out, 'Look at the water flow. This is just a recess in the river; look you can see for yourself that the main flow is bypassing this inlet. Just look at the weed growth here. If you do pour it in here then there's no guarantee it won't just sit there for ever.'

The two groups relaxed.

Lev had his driver move downstream to a location that had a clearer and evident flow that was running back from the shore and out into the main thrust of the river.

The "argument" had given the French team the chance to get closer and they were now on the ground snaking silently through the grass, but this sudden last-minute change of location had placed them wrongly for their planned crossfire to work. As a group they had previously agreed their individual positions which would provide both mutual support but most importantly mutual safety. The team was experienced and given the changed circumstances they set about reworking the geometry but now it was down to individuals who could not see each other. Their well-rehearsed hand signals were of no use here.

Lev's driver applied the brakes, placed the gear stick in neutral, left the engine running and jumped out. The other members of Lev's team moved to join him at the rear of the vehicle, promptly pulled up the flap and started to unload the two cylindrical containers.

Mark had reached a new observation point and noted with some surprise the confidence with which the Russians handled the containers. They did not seem to have any fears in rolling them off the bed of the vehicle; they were allowing them to drop the metre or so to the ground. He wasn't sure that he would have been quite so trusting. They rolled the two containers to the riverside and stood them on end.

Lev smiled at Wim. 'There you are. All delivered as promised. It's your party so you can have the pleasure of pouring it into the river.'

He and his men stepped back from the river to form a semi-circle perhaps a dozen paces back from the containers. Wim and his team were clearly suspicious of the slick manoeuvre, reluctant to enter into the hemisphere that the Russians had formed. But then they were partners in this plan, weren't they? He'd been invited to be part of the Brotherhood, so they should work as a team. Then he'd never been that comfortable with these guys. He felt his hackles rising. Why did everything tell him to run for cover?

Lev with that annoying grin, waved an exaggerated "after you" sign towards the containers waiting at the riverside.

Wim nodded almost imperceptibly to two of his team to step forward, taking the opportunity himself to use their movement to sidestep a little further away from the Russian arc. He was now looking at one of the four Russians from behind, and another from the side. When they did not change their position he began to relax a little.

Where were the others? They were leaving this all very late. He was an experienced bushman and had been aware that they were under observation all the time they'd been here, but why were they not taking action as agreed?

Wim's two guys opened the top of the containers and kicked them on to their sides, keeping well away from the open ends. The two containers initially gulped their contents into the river, until the level in the containers dropped to allow it to flow more smoothly. Everyone at the riverside was watching the flow and that was the moment when the British team stood up. They had been securely in position well before the others had arrived, closer than the French and perfectly located in crossfire terms.

The Brits, with surprise on their side, had their weapons fully at the ready. The Russians and South Africans had been caught in their mutual reassurance game and so were completely unprepared. James and his colleague, Lewis, had an AK-7, the Indian Ordnance Board's clone of the Kalashnikov AK-47. Lev calmly assessed that one had a 75-round drum magazine and the other a 40-round box.

Brain had the British Army L86 light support weapon, only 30 rounds in the magazine, but there were just eight 'bandits'! He ordered the two 'Yarpees' to set the containers upright, which they both did very cautiously, as he walked across to the riverside.

As Brain passed behind one of the South Africans, one of the Russian team thought he glimpsed an opportunity and went for his pistol, only to be felled with a short burst from James. Brain could not get a clear shot away as the other two Russians dropped to the floor and made for the grass, but Lewis followed them making clear he would fire unless they stopped. One did stop but the other made it into the grass.

Lev used this as his moment to leap the few paces to his vehicle that still had its engine idling.

Wim had been the first to react to Lev, raising his pistol and aiming at the vehicle, but a single shot rang out and Wim fell to the floor, his head having virtually exploded. The Brits immediately dropped to the ground, trying to see where the shot had come from, crawling away from their initial location to confuse the shooter.

In the melée Lev managed to reach the vehicle, slammed it into gear, not bothering to release the handbrake until much later, not that this appeared to slow his pace in any significant manner. He raced the vehicle directly away from the scene, every moment expecting the burst of automatic to strike the vehicle – and him!

The South Africans, confused by this development, also dropped but stayed put, fearing the Brits were double-crossing them. Hadn't Wim told them that the Brits were coming there to assist?

There was a sudden noise in the grass followed by a bloodcurdling cry which added further to the confusion. Lev had made it away from the 'arena' by the time that Mark started shouting, 'Don't shoot we are friends, friends! Hold your fire! You are surrounded by French DGSE specialists. Lay down your weapons and raise your hands. You have nothing to fear!'

Brain shouted, 'You bloody idiots you took down a friendly!' He put down his weapon and broke the impasse by slowly rising with his arms outstretched. James followed, but Lewis called out, 'I can't. I'm holding this Russkie here and there's another out there somewhere.'

'Not any more,' said one of the French guys rising carefully holding a wicked looking knife still dripping with the last Russian's blood.'

Brain said, 'What about that last bastard? Shouldn't one of us be chasing him down?'

Valéry shrugged, waving a radio, 'It is not a *problème*. He will be apprehended at the road. What of the water? Isn't that our main concern? Quite a lot was poured into the river.'

'Hopefully our man has it covered.'


Brain led Valéry downstream 100 metres or more and then called out to Tom. He and Stevie emerged from behind a large clump of trees and moved swiftly back to the riverbank. They made busy with their jury-rigged device that was set in the river, hopefully doing its stuff. Tom only briefly registered surprise at Valéry being there, his focus being to ensure the equipment was working effectively.

Brain asked, 'How is it going?'

'Tough to tell just yet. How much was spilled?'

'No idea, perhaps 50 or 60 litres at most?'

'That would be good news. Thank God for my scrum-half days, I think I managed a some sort of pass that delivered the device so that the paddles were out in the centre of the point where the surface current suggested that it would pass us. The problem is I have no idea what currents are going on below the surface and that's where the still water will be.'

Stevie added, 'The counterweights are holding the device pretty well in the flow as far as we can see though.'

Tom remarked, 'It was only your convincing Wim to use this particular location that made it all possible. It's shallow here. If we'd been out in the middle we'd have needed an actual Mississippi paddle steamer to make it work.'

Stevie commented, 'Not that bad an idea, actually!'

Valéry asked, 'But can we make tests to see if the water has passed your *truc,* um, thing?'

'About another 50 metres down this channel we've positioned a device that's collecting samples every few minutes, but I am afraid we need to take them to a laboratory to do the testing. I've no other means of checking it.'

Brain suggested, 'We could toss in a fish into it to see if it dies.'

Tom smiled, 'Did you bring any?'

Stevie who had not enjoyed the journey or Brain's indifferent attitude of superiority said, 'You could go for a paddle yourself and give us a shout.' Then striking her stupid blonde pose, 'Oh, of course you wouldn't have time to, would you?'

Brain chose to ignore her, 'I'm not seeing any dead fish coming to the surface. Is that a good sign?'

Valéry looked at the amateur-looking equipment and questioned, 'But if your equipment is not working, this could mean that Kinshasa needs to be warned, even evacuated. We have no time before it will reach the city.'

Brain replied, 'That's your call. Leave us to do what we can here to at least minimise it. You have to think through what you need to do about the city. And what about that Russian that got away?'

'No news of him as yet. But I must let the city know, we can't let thousands die through delay on our part.'

Just then Mark arrived with Lewis, who was guarding the remaining Russian. 'Relax guys, it was a double-cross. Kabitsin wasn't prepared to waste his water here, said he wouldn't pee on an African if he was on fire. The drums were filled with normal water.'

'What makes you so sure he's telling the truth?'

'When I got hold of your man here and threatened to toss him into the river, he said there was no need, just reached down and waved his arm in the water. I'd thought earlier that they seemed to be handling the containers just a little too freely when they offloaded them.'

Tom started to reel in his equipment and commented, 'So Wim was right, he couldn't trust them.'

Mark looked at Brain. 'I see, that's what you meant earlier by a friendly being down? If we'd known what you were planning we'd have let Wim take down that Russian. We couldn't be sure it wasn't aimed at one of you guys!'

Brain answered, 'Yeah, well he was still a bad boy. He only reached out to us because he felt he wasn't properly accepted into the Brotherhood by Kabitsin, felt there seemed to be more to what was being planned, probably recognised he was getting in out of his depth.'

Mark was the only one who appeared to have recognised the humour of the comment so he let it pass. 'Well, he was a non-Russian, and all that we hear of Kabitsin is that he is a very rampant patriot, gagging for what Putin appears now to be giving them, but yet he seems still to be impatient.'

Brain said, 'Wim would have understood him pretty well then from what we saw. He was another one who was almost blind in his patriotism, though in his case it was for a country that doesn't exist any longer, and never will again.'

Valéry was confused. 'I now comprehend. This is how you knew precisely where to be! But if he's a South African patriot shouldn't that make him anti-British too?'

'No, he was against majority rule. He thought that this was what destroyed his country. Perhaps we Brits reminded him of happier times. Or more likely he just couldn't think of anyone else to go to.'

Tom had stowed away everything. 'I can't begin to appreciate what that must be like. I'm pretty patriotic too. Not the tattoos or flags outside the house sort, but I do care, follow our national teams, worry about our place in the world. OK, so it's a bit of a moving target because our country keeps on changing, but I can't imagine a world without Britain in it.'

Valéry smiled pleasantly to take away any venom from his comment, '*On espère!* As you say, "we can always live in hope"!'

Brain was quiet for a few moments and Valéry became concerned that maybe he had offended him, but when he spoke it was in an entirely different direction. 'OK, so we all know how we came to be here, but what of you guys, how did you know about this?'

In his worst cockney accent, Mark said, 'It's a fair cop, guv'nor! OK. So, you guessed it, we do have someone on the inside.'

# Chapter 35 - *Kinshasa, D R of the Congo*

They could now all go safely into Kinshasa, finally to see it as a real living place, no longer a target, no longer a sitting duck seemingly waiting for the still water to scour through its population.

Tom and Stevie enjoyed walking alongside the river, passing the vibrant mass of people. It was perhaps one of the few times that Tom had not been annoyed by the clamour of street vendors. He enjoyed their banter and relished their very vitality. These small traders had not been aware how close they had come to disaster, nor would they ever know. For them life went on.

They walked past quays full of boats and barges that would spend their whole lives plying their way on the river, to and from distant Kisangani, never to escape, land-locked by the rapids down-river and the falls and rapids upstream beyond Kisangani. Others had even less ambition, seemingly content with criss-crossing back and forth to Brazzaville. Tom wondered just how they all got there in the first place.

They just walked, content without conversation, taking in the noise, the buzz and bustle of mankind, each thinking of just how fragile it could have been. Just take away their water and this would all have been gone in less than a week. But behind their relief and joy for these people, they couldn't fail to notice the obvious signs of the country's recent past. Many of the buildings were run down, some looked as if they were not in use, the streets were a mess, a good deal of them unpaved, but it didn't matter, it was still life!

They meandered and found their way to a large market with foodstuffs and African art. Just strolling, they were no longer being bothered by any of the vendors. Stevie wondered if perhaps it was because their clothes were so clearly grubby and a bad hair day wasn't in it. But clearly no one seemed to care here, personal daintiness not that high a priority in this country struggling to shake off its history. It was evident that they must be giving off an aura that showed they were not really interested, just passing through. It was as if they had formed their own membrane from which they were looking out and into which no one here cared to enter.

Much earlier that day he and Stevie had been installed in their location downriver from the expected insertion site. It had felt like the middle of the night and they had absolutely no idea of what might ensue. The three guys with them had seemed matter-of-fact, exuding a confident competence, but they all knew that this could rapidly become a combat situation. They had no idea how many Russians would be there, no idea how trustworthy the South Africans might turn out to be. They just had to sit in the dark straining at every sound. Despite their vigilance they were concerned that they had heard nothing when Lewis suddenly appeared, quietly advised them to get their equipment set up, that it was "game on".

Their laboratory-built device had to be lavished with care following its multi-stage journey. The packaging they had used had just about kept it intact, the moving parts still true. They had first to produce the zinc hydroxide and then prime this into the blades and then the real trick was to set the whole thing up in the water.

It was immediately clear that they were being pretty naïve to assume this thing was going to work, it was proving mighty impractical in the field. Dropping it into a living, fast-flowing river had not been part of their prototype's design criteria. It had been conceived as a controlled lab-based device and they had not yet had time to consider the design needs for the field. They had just wished to prove to themselves that the water could be converted. Now they had seen it in situ they were both already evaluating how to make something rather more practical.

That morning they just had to make it work, nothing else was there that could provide anything of a solution. Of course they had no idea if the water that was flowing past as they set up was good water or was already converted to its lethal 'cousin'. They'd weighed up several approaches until Tom just improvised his rugby pass out to the centre of the flow. They both grimaced at the noise he made, fearful someone would come running towards them to investigate.

Nothing happened and the device appeared to be holding its position, working to the best of its ability, but would that prove adequate? Just one large piece of driftwood striking it and all would have been over. Even a large dead fish hitting their rotor might spell disaster. They had been full of doubts that were cascading through their minds at a pace much faster than the river flow. But it seemed to function!

Unless Brain and his team could stop the insertion, they had feared the worst. Brain had been keen to reassure them that there was a high likelihood that the still water could be captured and added to their stock. More material would mean they could expand their tests. But the impression he gave was more as if he was trying to convince himself.

Then they had heard the gunfire and later a terrifying scream; they had no idea what had happened, no concept of who might come back down the path. Given their inability to hear Lewis earlier they strained every sinew for any approach. Tom thought at the time that he had absolutely no idea how they would get home, they had entered the country covertly, had no passports with them. Without Brain he had no idea who to speak to, they were here completely unofficially, illegally, deniably!

No surprise then that when they sought cover, first they had simply huddled closely together for mutual support. On hearing that awful scream Tom had hugged Stevie who was shaking with fear. Without words they were both staring out through the brush upriver. Listening intently for the next noise, they heard someone approaching and his speech was clearly not that of an Englishman. So there was huge relief when Brain called out, and then some embarrassment as they unclasped each other and hid the awkwardness between them by rushing to check their equipment.

There was relief again when Mark announced there had been no still water insertion. Valéry had then taken charge of proceedings. They were advised later that the South Africans would be put on a plane with their passports marked in some manner that Valéry assured them would curtail their future international activities. The remaining Russian was being interrogated to find out what he knew of Kabitsin's plans and whereabouts. Tom had shuddered at the thought of what the word interrogation in a country like this might mean.

The British team was being permitted to fly home late the following day on an Air France scheduled flight to Paris. Even in the cattle-class seats that had been provided, they anticipated this would be a dream compared to their inward journeys. But for now, the three British guys were heading for the DGSE offices to compare notes and, in particular, getting Mark to fill them in on his "inside source". They made it obvious that this was not for the ears of Tom and Stevie, clearly they were mere pawns in these global political games – games that these others seemed to enjoy playing just a little too much.

They had been given rooms in a guest house for their last night but neither of them felt inclined to do other than bathe themselves in the life of this city – life that had so recently been wrested from the jaws of a disaster. The mixture of the heavily accented French and the local Lingala sounded very lyrical, charming. The heat of the day was slowly dissipating, the humidity becoming bearable. They didn't need any alcohol to become drunk, it was intoxicating just walking here and feeling the lively pulse of the city all around them.

They came across an Italian restaurant and suddenly realised just how hungry they were. The food was good, the ambience relaxed and they ate and drank in companionable silence. What was there to say? Work colleagues for less than a month, suddenly whisked to another continent, put into harm's way by their own government. Now the crisis had been diverted they were just abandoned here to wander this alien city.

After they had eaten, they suddenly found plenty to talk about, though later neither would have been able to summarise the topics or content. They had just been getting to know each other in the afterglow of the action and a good relaxed meal.

They arrived back at the guest house in great spirits. He walked her to her room and there was an awkward moment as neither of them wanted to part, not wishing to break the spell of the evening.

Tom was considering his next step, when he heard a noise behind him. Before he could turn he felt the most excruciating pain in his kidney, so painful that he could not identify whether it was from a punch, a knife or a bullet. He sank to his knees, managing to complete his turn to see the big Russian thrust past to grab Stevie and slam her against the door of her room. He then pulled her back against him with a knife held to her throat.

'Where is your equipment?' Lev demanded, then impatiently, 'You should believe that I will slit her throat, where is it?'

Tom, recovering a little from the punch, quickly complied, 'It's in my room, over there.'

'Get it for me. Now!'

Tom really didn't want to leave Stevie so defenceless, but realised he had no choice and went to his room. If only he'd had a gun, but all he could do was grab their two carrying cases and take them out to the Russian. He wondered if perhaps he could strike out with one of the bags, but Lev was standing behind Stevie with his knife still at her throat.

'Put them over there.' He pointed down the corridor near to an emergency exit.

Tom did as requested and then turned, trying to see a way to help them survive this encounter. His attention was caught by a large fire extinguisher. Could he get across to it and use it in some way?

The big Russian had been looking at the two cases, and obviously assessed their evident weight and awkwardness. He revised his plan. 'Pick them up and go through the door.'

He pushed Stevie forward with the knife still firmly held to her neck, where Tom could see he had already drawn a little blood.

Tom pushed through what served as an emergency exit and it set off a distant bell. There must have been an alarm connected to the door.

'Down the stairs, across to the car park. Now!'

Tom descended the metal staircase and crossed to the cars parked there, not knowing for which one he should be heading

Lev indicated a 4x4 towards the front of the building and Tom dutifully toted the bags towards it, turning to watch Lev and glaring at him with impotent venom and intent. The Russian smiled back at him, taunting him, fumbling one of Stevie's breasts with his free hand to make clear just who was in charge of the situation.

'Put them in the back.'

Tom lifted the flap and threw in the two cases, hoping to damage them with his ferocity.

'Now back off over there,' he pointed to a location perhaps twenty paces away.

Tom stared at him. If only looks could kill.

The Russian stared intently into his eyes and pointedly drew the knife across Stevie's neck, though mercifully without any contact achieved. Holding the eye contact, he grinned to show he could just as easily have slit her throat – and that it would have made absolutely no difference to him either way. Then he shoved her violently towards Tom so that her momentum made him stagger backwards. At the same time Lev turned, leapt into the vehicle, started it and pulled away, in one smooth movement driving off in to the night.

# Chapter 36 - *Novaya Zemlya, Russia*

Paul and Ellise had finally received the necessary approvals and were accompanied by Dmitry across the Kara Sea to the islands. To their surprise the islands turned out to look so unexpectedly normal. It was of course the thought of atomic tests and comet strikes that had created their imaginary place, which was something more like a hyper version of the landscapes in the Lord of the Rings movies than anything that was likely to exist in reality.

Ellise had insisted on a radiation badge for she feared the island's main activity of the recent past; she found she did not have any faith in Russian science, or rather believed only too readily in their lack of care for their citizens. Look at how they had ordered those people to go and clear up at Chernobyl without any special clothing or consideration for their life expectancy. Surely they would be just as cavalier here?

Ellise had researched the subject thoroughly whilst stuck in Nadym and had established that the acceptable radiation dose for an adult, as set out by the US FDA, was 3,000 mrems when measured across the whole body at any one time. Repeated dosages were to be no more than 5,000 mrems across any one year or, she was amused to read, it could be set a little higher if looking just at an individual organ. As she didn't plan to exist separately from any of her organs she would work on the lower level and then still insert some wiggle-room below that.

The millirem she now knew stood for one thousandth of a roentgen equivalent in man. Bloody typical she thought, what about woman? Surely with the female physiology, the child-bearing role, this would require a lower permitted dosage? So she downgraded the level a tad again for her comfort.

Paul had scoffed that the general limits were set very low already. 'If you'd been born and lived in Aberdeen in Scotland you would have many times that dosage in you and still be perfectly OK. We call it 'granite city', because that's what it sits on, granite containing a notional amount of uranium and therefore naturally it is radioactive. So just living in a building built out of granite you can get a whole body dose of around 200 mrems each year!'

She was not interested in his dismissive attitude. This was dangerous stuff and much of its danger lay in it being invisible, while remaining so very invasive.

Dmitry, under some pressure, had come up with some luminescent badges. He had shown her that by shining a green light that he had provided on to the crystal within her badge, she should beware of any blue response from it. The bluer it was, then the higher the exposure to radiation. On several notable previous occasions she recalled she had found it necessary to use a different device for which blue meant bad news, but this time at least she didn't have to pee on it.

She decided that she would shine her light on to the badge at least once an hour, even waking in the night to test it. Any glimmer of blue and she would be back at the airstrip demanding the next flight out.

They had flown in from Naryan Mar airport on the mainland, which had for many years acted as the staging post for the islands' Rogachevo airport, on the south-eastern part of the southern island. Their approach gave them a great view of both it and the northern island stretching away far off into the distance. Many of the nearer slopes on the northern island were covered in snow and further north it looked much more ice-covered with glaciers reaching down into the sea. Quite a lot of the north island was shrouded in clouds and there were large patches of fog lurking around both of the islands. The sea around them was littered with ice floes, but this was not the total ice-pack that they had expected.

Paul suggested to Ellise that it looked like the location of Superman's ice palace, but she was still one-tracked, commenting that what was buried here was not an instruction manual from Krypton, but materials that were much more deadly than Kryptonite was to Clark Kent, irradiated matter that could weaken and kill any human, probably any superheroes too.

Ellise noticed a dark-blue mountain that seemed to glow in the thin sunlight. When she mentioned it to Paul all he could say was, 'It must be frozen alumina, aluminium oxide, probably contains a lot of pyrites-crystals too.' He went on about the material's resistance to weathering and its thermal and electrical insulation properties, but she programmed him out, preferring to look with her eyes, rather than see with her mind. Her mind was on the colour blue. Blue mountains, blue glaciers, blue seas, just so long as her badge showed no blue then she could still appreciate the beauty of the various tones.

Of course the person Paul should have been talking with was Tom. Alumina is not just naturally occurring but is also a by-product in the industrial process to prepare hydrogen. Pellets of aluminium and gallium are added to water to generate the fuel. Perhaps a reverse-engineering of this might have proven more useful than the zinc approach that Tom and Stevie had come up with at Culham? But of course Paul would not have been interested in helping Tom by telling him, even if he had known of their efforts.

As Paul and Ellise were transported by land from the airport to Belushya Guba they looked out on a scene that made clear to both of them that the original thought that the islands were formed from the spoil of a comet strike was patent nonsense. These islands looked so substantive that Paul thought it would have taken something nearer the size of the moon than some fragment of a comet to have been responsible for them. It was not at all surprising that the northern island alone ranked as one of the world's largest islands.

Belushya Guba was the main settlement on the islands and they were surprised by how neat and tidy the place was; somehow it looked very purposeful. Dmitry explained that there was a plan to make the island the first

Arctic national park, to make it appeal to tourists who would come to see the flora and fauna. Ellise had noticed during the ride that there were quite a few large seabirds there. Dmitry was happy to identify them, but as they mostly proved to be various sorts of cormorants, terns or gulls, she stopped asking.

When they pulled into the town itself, Paul glimpsed a sudden movement down one of the side streets. When he pointed it out and tried to describe what he'd seen, Dmitry said it was probably a lemming or maybe an Arctic fox. They did tend to hang around for scraps and liked to attack any garbage, but were otherwise pretty harmless. Only the polar bears had to be avoided at all costs he explained.

Now they were here, they found it felt a lot like queuing at Disneyland. They moved but only to arrive at another point in the line, their destination never seeming to come closer. Dmitry explained that things of necessity had to move slowly and securely in these climes.

After they had both experienced a few excursions around the town they could fully attest to this. With the very bulky clothing they had been supplied, they moved like some Sumo wrestler; swinging their legs in an awkward waddle that simulated walking.

They had to wait here for the availability of a mini submarine to be arranged. But these, they learned from Dmitry, were all currently committed to Putin's plans to seize control of the Arctic gas and oil reserves.

Many estimated that these reserves represented a quarter of all the oil and gas that existed anywhere in the world. Russia of course already had the world's largest reserves of natural gas, and in oil reserve terms ranked second only to Saudi Arabia, but that didn't seem to be leading to any sort of complacency on Russia's or rather Putin's part.

Western Europe was heading into a period of a very uncomfortable dependence upon Russian pipelines, so uncomfortable that the previously dismissed and unpopular subject of nuclear power was now securely back on the agenda for many countries. This was particularly uncomfortable given that all the effort going into alternative energy sources still seemed to offer only a noise-level contribution to the ever-growing energy demands of the people.

The word 'Arctic' comes from the Greek, *arktos*, which means bear, chosen because the Great Bear, Ursa Major, appears to sit over the region. Now a new acquisitive 'bear' wanted to watch over it and more importantly over its trillions of dollars in oil and gas, a figure based on today's prices that would only increase with time. Not to mention that geologists had suggested that reserves of diamonds, gold, nickel, platinum and tin were there aplenty too.

Russia was engaged in trying to prove that, because significant parts of the Arctic land mass were contiguous with Siberia, it should control more of it than any previous treaties had agreed. No one country owns the Arctic, though Canada, Denmark (as the owners of Greenland), Norway, Russia and the USA's Alaska all have lands inside the Arctic Circle. Russia however was pressing its case that the Lomonosov Ridge was an integral and connected part of Siberia and the mini submarines were being used to seek out the geology that would prove his case.

Some of the current global warming effects were only just now being fully understood. Canada had established that the retreating ice had finally opened up the long sought-after North West Passage. It's an ill-wind that blows nobody any good; suddenly Canada found it might have a valuable new direct link between the Pacific and Atlantic. Consideration of how the geological resources in the Arctic might be transported in the future was already prompting not just submarine, but ice-breaking supertanker technologies.

The Arctic would be the next frontier and things were set to really heat up by the middle of the 21st century. Green protestors and local inhabitants were also preparing their response to the impact on this wilderness.

Oblivious to all of this background, Paul and Ellise were delighted when the news came that their project had been awarded a whole month's use of a mini submarine, not now but perhaps very soon.

In the meantime Paul had not just been sitting around. He had worked through each and every map and chart to be found that detailed the islands and their surrounds. He was looking for any obvious cratering on the island or the seabed but had so far found nothing convincing.

The maps did clearly show three distinct areas on the islands where 130 nuclear tests had taken place. Zone A was at Chernaya Bay, way below them at the southern tip of the southern island. There the Soviets had carried out atmospheric, surface and three underwater tests between 1955 and 1962 and later there had been a handful of underground ones. Any craters down at this end of the island or in the offshore area were therefore more likely to be man-made.

Zone C was north of Matochkin Shar, the channel that separated the two main islands. Located on a peninsula, it had had been the site of atmospheric tests from 1957 to 1962. In retrospect, to Paul these appeared to be the most horrendous events for anyone to ever have instigated. It was so irresponsible to have exploded lethal materials like these out in the open air, the very air that we all depended upon for life. It was particularly crazy to have done them when the long-term effects were not at all properly understood at the time. On the other hand, he realised that this still water could prove to be even more lethal, so he pressed on with his search with renewed vigour.

It was in Zone B on the Gulf of Matochkin Shar that the bulk of the underground tests had been undertaken from 1964 right through to 1990. Paul presumed that this was where the current 'sub-critical' tests also took place and so did not plan to go anywhere near there if he could help it. Besides, if his comet fragment had fallen in any of the three test sites the Russians would have achieved more 'roar for their rouble' than they had counted upon, and there had been no such reports.

He had then spent a great deal of time cajoling Dmitry for details of the dump locations used by the Russians for their waste material from the earlier tests. Waste disposal had not been necessary in the later underground tests. The miners, drawn from all over the USSR, had spent days of toil hollowing out a site; the technicians had placed their devices and sensors, and the collapse of the entrance of the site had been part of the test itself, hopefully managing to seal in its deadly materials as a useful by-product.

His enquiries also uncovered further marked sites. On asking he was advised these were the locations of six nuclear submarine reactors and ten other nuclear reactors that had been dumped in the Kara Sea. Apparently the International Atomic Energy Authority was content that these had minimal radiation and any they had identified was very localized to the sites. He decided it would be best not to mention this discovery to Ellise.

He had also read of a small rebellion on the island. The armed unit that was charged with maintaining the safety of the nuclear test site had at that time some five members who came from Dagestan, the tiny republic tucked between Georgia and Azerbaijan on the shores of the Caspian Sea.

While on the island they heard of an explosion back in their capital city, Makhachkala, and one of them had grown fearful for his relatives. The five of them killed a guard and with his weapon took a school's headmaster, several teachers and forty children as hostages, demanding a plane to fly them home. The FSB stormed their position and they were captured and charged with murder and terrorism, although at no time had they gained any access to the nuclear material.

This was something that Paul was finding he had to learn. Even in the current smaller Russia, following the demise of the USSR, there was not just one people. There were in fact many quite different indigenous groups. On this island, ignoring those who were either posted there or visiting, there were two indigenous groups, the Nenets and the Avars.

The Nenets had once been called the Samodi, a name they gave to the distinctive Samoyed dog that they had bred to assist them with their reindeer herding. As of today there are only around 40,000 Nenets left in the world. In fact they are more often disrespectfully just lumped in with Enets, Selkups and Nganasans and called the 'Samoyedic peoples'. This group term is then usually described as a mere sub-branch of the larger Finno-Urgian language family.

The effect of this grouping is like being an item of stock, taken in and progressively moved further and further back into a warehouse until no one can quite remember where to find it. This has already happened to the Kamasins, Koibals and Mators who had once belonged to the same grouping but have either died out or been assimilated. Whatever the case, they are deemed no longer to exist as a distinct ethnic group. Paul assumed that this was probably the eventual outcome for these Nenets and Avars too; once you got pigeonholed away in this manner, it was a pretty slippery slope towards oblivion. Of the remaining 40,000 Nenets, just three-quarters of them can still speak the Nenet language, perhaps another reason for despair of their managing to remain distinct or of any ongoing interest.

There were only around a hundred Nenets on the island but Paul decided he should seek them out. Dmitry arranged for someone who could interpret their very complex mixture of spoken Nenet and the Russian language.

Paul pondered whether he should test the urban myth that people in these northern climes had hundreds of words for snow. But having spent some time in the region he realised that even in English we have around forty words for water in its solid state – berg, glacier, ice, slush, frost, sleet and so on – so the basic premise starts out being pretty much flawed. But the other flaw he had realised was that there were so many indigenous groups up here, whether you called them Eskimos, Inuit, Aleut or Samoyedic peoples, that if each of this multitude had a similar forty expressions for frozen water, then the total across all of these many peoples, their many languages, had to be, by definition, huge.

What he really wanted to hear from them was whether there was any 'tribal' history, any verbal inheritance of a story that featured a big explosion. Or was there any family tradition mentioning a past big splash? He persevered in his questioning and his meeting with the third family group was rewarded.

The patriarch of the family was said to be 52 but in view of his heavily-lined appearance he could quite easily have passed for 82. He was proud of his status as one of those individuals who was keen to maintain the tradition and language of his people. Paul and the interpreter had to listen patiently, showing enthusiasm for a lot of pretty dull stuff about past life on the island, of hunting stories, some discussing great kills but as many about the ones that got away. They tried to steer him from the subject but then he spent quite a lot of time complaining of the nuclear tests and the subsequent devastation of local animal life and massive depletion of available fish.

Then finally he moved on to recount a story of a bright blue light that was seen to come from the south and create massive disturbance as it dropped into the sea just a short distance from shore. This had been considered a good luck omen because the next few years had been exceptional for hunting and fishing. His people had not seen anything like it since.

Ellise greeted the news of something blue with a knee-jerk flash of her green light on to her badge. This unusual reaction took them away from the subject for some time while the interpreter had to describe to the old man what Ellise was doing and a good deal of background as to why. Paul glared at her and tried to get them back on track.

'Can you ask him precisely when this was?'

The interpreter eventually came back with a comment of five or six generations ago. Paul, momentarily calculating at 25 years per generation, was disappointed by this answer because this would not match with the Siberian 'impact', but then he realized that people in this harsh environment should of course be calculated at a much lower rate per generation, so with this revised arithmetic it could well work out to be 1908.

Paul asked whether they could indicate a general location, expecting some comment about a cardinal direction, south for example, or at best a vague intercardinal direction like south-east. He was extremely pleasantly surprised when the old man appeared to be able to be quite specific. He had the impression that the traditional compass-rose was not much used up here, that instead the physical characteristics of the coast and the position of mountains were much more used as the means to measure where they were, where they were going.

The patriarch was detailed. It had occurred apparently a little way below the Matochkin Shar, south of where it enters the Kara Sea. The point of entry was translated as perhaps two kilometres off that spot and the old man was confident he could point the direction out to them.

He talked fondly of this narrow channel that connected the Kara and Barents Sea between the two large islands of Severny and Yuzhny. He explained that this 100km long channel was usually covered with ice, meandering between these rocky islands with high steep banks for the length of the channel. The family talked at length of the area which was apparently heavily populated with seals and was once a place where polar bears were guaranteed to be found. Today it was not quite so fruitful, though it remained a favourite spot for them to fish and to hunt.

The decision had been taken, Paul and Ellise and their supporting cast would move and set up camp at Litke. Paul bowed to the inevitable definition and learned that it had been named for the 19th century explorer Fyodor Petrovich Litke who had mapped parts of the island and apparently went on to become an admiral, the president of the Russian Academy of Science and eventually a count. Given the august namesake it was located in a disappointingly small cove, tucked just inside a channel from the Kara Sea end, about a third of the way down the southern island from the strait.

It took a day or so to organize their team's removal across to this tiny hamlet of a place. The old Nenet had agreed to come with them by helicopter so that he could point out the direction.

The Nenets have a sort of animistic belief structure giving a spirit or soul to many island features and the old man described some of these to Ellise through the interpreter as they crossed the island. He also explained a little of their tradition of taking spiritual journeys through time and space. Ellise thought it sounded a lot like the Australian aboriginal 'walkabout', only much colder.

When they arrived at their new quarters it was as if the previous occupants had just stepped out, maybe gone on one of those spiritual journeys. There were slippers by the door, magazines and the other paraphernalia of life dotted around the simple rooms. Ellise was concerned that they had caused a family to be forcibly removed, worried what might have become of them. Dmitry pacified her explaining that they had probably just moved to another township, something the locals did all the time, but Ellise wasn't particularly convinced.

The old man had advised them that he had to be on the water to be able to show them the direction, so the next morning they set off early, rounding the small bay into the channel just before 'dawn', even though the sun dipped below the horizon for just a few hours at this time of year.

Paul and Ellise were stunned when straight ahead of them they saw the sun first break the horizon. It was not the expected globe that appeared but a long thin bar of light. Anticipating that this was a reflection of the sun, itself still yet to rise, they watched it carefully as it rose further as a bizarrely rectangular sun. It looked alien, weird, and challenged all that they held as real.

The old man had watched them closely, letting them react to the phenomenon before revealing to them that this was a fairly regular polar mirage. Refraction through the atmospheric thermoclines was projecting the sun so that it dawned much earlier than it would have done without this light bending trick. Dmitry, who had heard of the mirage, explained that it was first reported by a crew member from one of the unsuccessful voyages by the Dutch navigator Willem Barents, who had set off to seek out the rather less credible North-East passage back in the 16th century.

A new shorter route in either direction between the two great oceans would have represented a major trading step-function back then. No one was particularly concerned if it were to be the North-West or North-East route. So many lives including Barents' own had been the price of these quests. Now merely through the popularity of CFCs in aerosol cans and our industrial and automotive emissions the ice was melting and heralding a time in the near future when the quest might finally be realized – in the North-West direction at least. However the overall global impact of this melting might of course heavily outweigh the convenience of this route.

They picked their way through the broken ice floes out into the centre of the channel. The old man took his bearings, looking back at both shores, at the visible mountains and eventually pointed out a direction. The interpreter asked him to look at a chart but this proved meaningless to him. He could not appreciate that the map was a representation of his islands, but where he had pointed they were able to conclude was an ENE direction.

Discussion of the distance was pretty futile too. His appreciation of distance was about as good as his ability to understand a two-dimensional map. They tried to express this as a matter of lapsed time, as in how long would it take a man to row out to it. But time too was a mystery to him, he had never lived his life by a clock or watch, nor could he understand radio or television so had no reference to time from these. They just had to conclude it was somewhere between two and five kilometres offshore.

Now all they needed was the submarine.

News of the mini-submarine's arrival seemed to keep changing. It was always promised to arrive in two days' time. It reminded Paul of taxi companies, they always gave the arrival time as ten minutes away, just as a takeaway delivery would always be in fifteen minutes.

Then, without any warning, it was there. Paul immediately spent long days in the craft with its pilot criss-crossing the area, seeking to maximize each of the meagre twenty-eight days that they had been promised.

This left Ellise at a loose end with no connection to the outside world, nothing to do. She strolled the area but it rapidly became pretty dull and repetitive, same terrain, same flora and fauna, same annoying insects. But as she was returning from one such foray and she heard and then saw an incoming helicopter. Flight comings and goings always added interest to the day so she scrambled back to the pad just in case there was any chance that she could climb aboard for the return trip.

As she was arriving back at what they were now calling the 'hamlet' she stopped to observe a strange series of events. Three guys had descended from the helicopter and two of them had gone into their building. Dragging out Dmitry they threw him at the feet of the other who lashed out with his foot, placing three or four carefully aimed blows to the head and body.

Dmitry was only discernible because they had dragged him out in his indoor clothes. She was too far away to hear anything that was said and would not have understood it if she could. She did not recognize any of the newcomers, though the larger one appeared somehow familiar. There was something reminiscent about the way he stood, balanced, coiled for action. It was this that made her think that perhaps he had been the head of the security team with them at Novosibirsk, the one who had seemed to have been stalking her.

They tugged Dmitry from the floor and frog-marched him to the helicopter, his feet not getting any purchase on the ground but trailing behind him. He was hoisted into the helicopter and it took off, thwacking away out over the water and ice. She watched its progress and a few kilometres off shore it climbed up to a greater height, then it paused hovering, the fuselage lazily describing a circle.

She saw the side flap open and was frozen to the spot as she observed what could only be Dmitry's body pitched out of the helicopter. She knew that if he was fortunate enough to survive the fall by avoiding the ice, then he would die in an instant out in that cold sea. Of course if by chance he had survived she assumed he would rapidly fall prey to the local polar bears. She had to accept that he was effectively a goner.

What could it mean? What would this mean for them out here on this remote outpost of mankind? For the first time she forgot her regular time slot for checking her badge. Her fears were now directed elsewhere; how could she contact Tom to tell him what had happened?

# Chapter 37 - *Iraq*

The previous target, the Congo, had its source very close to the earliest finds of human life; it was the currently accepted ground-zero for all of mankind. In an unseen and unintended progression, Asil's selection of the second site was to be aimed securely at the birthplace of that next step in human history, the very earliest of human civilisations.

His proposal set out by discussing the site of ancient Mesopotamia, so named for its two rivers, the Euphrates and Tigris, the name meaning literally 'between rivers'.

The Sumerians founded the very first civilisations here. These were created and funded by their ability to manage river waters through the creation of systems of canals, dykes and reservoirs. These facilitated the creation of the first forms of an irrigation-based agriculture. It was this wealth from this that allowed the area to attract, accumulate and support a large population.

In turn, the challenges and pressures of large numbers of people coming together to cohabit, had forced the creation of the first structures and rules to enable and sustain these early civilisations. For instance the development of a religious framework clearly became essential in order to define and manage the necessary social structure.

Asil went on to explain that his actual target was planned to be some way north of Mesopotamia proper, at a spot where the Tigris briefly formed the Turkey-Syria border, then entered Iraq, flowing down towards Mosul. This target area ran right through the heart of the region that had fought for years to gain recognition for a stand-alone state of Kurdistan. Asil was aware that the fact that this was another something-stan would be more than enough to get Kabitsin's vote for his approach.

Then Asil was just teasing with all this background; he had left something juicy up his sleeve to make them want this strike to go ahead.

**Odessa, Ukraine**
Kabitsin and the General had had a blazing row about the unilateral decision that the Mafiya leader had made in not supplying still water to Wim and his Congo team.

'You lost us some key men at the site. And worse, there was no example created that could be useful in making our subsequent case. There is no experience, no data that we can use to build towards our main thrust.'

Kabitsin almost didn't care to answer the old man's complaints but something told him that he needed him for the real event yet to come. He countered, 'But these sideshows are just wasting our time, using up our resources and diverting us from our main objectives.'

The General responded, 'The whole principle of having these other players is a central and essential part of my plan, their events are intended precisely to be just that, a distraction. We want to show the target countries that we can mount a simultaneous series of global events. They need to see that we have a broad and deadly reach. It will also help us to develop the mystery as to who we are and just where we are capable of striking, and might strike, next. These will send out clear signals that we cannot be beaten, cannot be out-thought or stopped.'

Kabitsin snapped, 'The intelligence community already knows of us. Wim Brockenhorst called in the British, and we had both the French and American intelligence services involved at Kinshasa. The moment for mystery has already passed.'

'But I now have the other Brotherhood members asking me what went wrong. Just what do I tell them? You have to understand that they can still help us to confuse and spread those intelligence services energies all across the globe as they chase our shadows. Then, while they are busy watching the Brotherhood we can mount the main event, when and where they least expect it.'

'I can't be held responsible for the South African betraying us. It's probably just as well that we didn't risk any of the still water there. And don't forget that it was while he was there that Lev learned of another leak, the person who had advised the Americans of the Congo event.'

Kabitsin was not going to mention that Lev also managed to capture this British guy's device too. It was said to be able to neutralise the still water, but so far his people hadn't been able to work out how they should use it. Physically it was described as being like some old American river-boat mechanism which was fairly simple to understand. There were traces of various chemicals in and on it and they were trying to reverse engineer it to see how this was supposed to work as an 'antidote'.

A second case had also been captured but this seemed to contain samples and a device that could take specimens from the water at timed intervals. How did that fit in with the first? For now he would keep these facts to himself until he knew precisely what it was capable of achieving. He feared if he told him, then the old man would blurt it out to the Brotherhood to pacify them, and Kabitsin certainly did not want that just yet.

The General queried, 'I'm actually very confused about that. If Mark Elliott is the man you are talking to about taking the franchise for North America, then what was he doing in the Congo?'

Kabitsin knew all about Elliott's true affiliations and had never really expected to do more than feed false information through the "boy". However if, as seemed likely, his people were stupid enough to pay the entry fee, then all to the good. But he chose not to put the General in the loop on this matter either.

'He advised me he wanted to see the water in action before they bought into it. He has told us that he was there when the French and the British burst in upon our team, but he claims to have played no direct part himself. We have to accept that he was no spectator, no passer-by. He'd worked closely with the French team and it was his intelligence that allowed them to follow the South Africans to discover our men at the site, so we have to remain very suspicious of him. Let's just wait to see what he does next about our proposition.'

'You can never trust Americans. Drop him. What is our next step?'

'We can resolve the Brotherhood's fears by making this Tigris event work. We need it to work so that everyone learns to fear our capabilities. Therefore I plan to be there personally, assisting the team for this next one.'

# Chapter 38 - *Kurdistan, Turkey*

Asil's target was pure and simple – the Kurds. It was pure and simple because he just plain hated them. The modern father of the Turks, Atatürk, had made clear that there should be no sub-groups in Turkey; spoken-Kurdish was declared illegal and any suggestion of a Kurdistan was violently and speedily suppressed as separatism.

Asil believed that they had forgotten the lessons from their great leader. They had even allowed a Kurdish woman to be elected to the Turkish parliament in the 1990s but, as they should have expected, she couldn't help herself and later made a separatist speech. She was imprisoned for fifteen years. But what his country had to learn was that the Kurds would never stop looking to create their own country!

Kurds described themselves as cousins to the Iranians. Both were derived from ancient Indo-European Aryans; a nomadic early people, they had once controlled large areas of Russia and Siberia. Their religions, Zoroastrianism and Manichaeism, were quite clearly major influences in the much later formation of Judeo-Christian beliefs.

Asil recognised that their threat was highlighted by their very longevity, their ability to survive. Down the centuries as a race they had managed to see off Alexander the Great, the Mughals and the Mongols and in the north they had also dealt with a heap of trouble from various Slavic peoples. More recently Saddam Hussein had tried and failed to deal with them. Clearly they were not a people easily consigned to the past.

Yet somewhere down the years the Kurds had become marginalised, almost literally, as they always appeared right on the edge of everyone else's map. What they called Kurdistan is actually spread across what everyone else in the world accept and recognise as Iran, Iraq, Syria and Turkey. As a result, in most of these places they had been committed to a long cycle of oppression, rebellion and subjugation. Nonetheless they tenaciously seek their independence and their own country.

The total Kurdish population was difficult to estimate, given the reluctance of host nations to be clear on the subject and its huge diaspora distributed around the world, but most estimates are somewhere between 30 and 40 million. Kurds made up around 20% of the Iraqi and Turkish populations, 8% of those in Iran and 7% in Syria, so their presence is significant.

And now the status quo had just changed, because the accursed Americans and British had needed the Kurds to open a second front on Saddam to serve their own purposes. In gratitude now these two states were virtually granting the Kurds autonomy in Iraq. How long would it be before they demanded self-government from Turkey too?

However Asil's proposal held little of this background. He provided only material that demonised the Kurds, showing their unrest as terrorism, their claims as unfounded. Frustratingly, in his native Turkey the Kurdish areas had proven to be very fruitful with good oil and mineral resources, and these selfish people sought to hinder the Turks access to these supplies, disrupting their pipelines, stealing this vital asset from those who had sustained them.

Asil explained he would be satisfied for now with a direct assault on the Kurds, but he saw this event as one that the rest of the Brotherhood would then be able to use for their own ends. For his reward he explained he was content to assist with the delivery of the proposal to the Indian authorities in return for a promised share in the fruits of the payments that India would be required to make to keep its water safe. He also proposed some side targets that he might like to take on later.

First and foremost he made clear he was offering a very significant event, one that would reverberate throughout the world. It captured Kabitsin's interest and vote when Asil went on to show how his target would be able to send a clear signal to all Jews, Christians and Muslims!

Asil now built his case up to what he saw as his crescendo. He had developed it across a number of carefully prepared pages and he knew the reason he would get their agreement was this final item.

The appeal of his case was based upon an ancient craft that was said to have been launched from Al Küfah, on the Euphrates, quite close to the location of ancient Babylon. It had sailed from there in a great inundation, reaching the holy city of Mecca where it had circled the sacred Kaaba. Then, according to the Qu'ran, it struck north and eventually came to rest on Mount Kudi.

This craft and its voyage were mentioned in the Bible and the Qu'ran, yet both were vague as to its final destination. The Bible suggested that it finished up in the region of the mountains of Ararat, though many down the years had come to misread this and presumed incorrectly that it was on Mount Ararat itself. The Qu'ran also used a term that many saw as more referring to a region, rather than naming a specific place or mountain.

At a place within this general area that both mentioned, following the effects of several earthquakes and heavy rains back in 1948, the remains of a boat-like structure were indeed unearthed. The actual location was subsequently named as Durupinar after its discoverer's name, but after investigations made in the 1960s it had been dismissed as of no importance. However interest was resurrected in the 1970s and 1980s when a team equipped with ground-penetration radar confirmed that the structure was entirely compatible with the 300 cubit length that was referred to in the Bible.

It was of course Noah's Ark that had ridden its way into the pages of these great books and had come to rest in Asil's target area! And it was in these mountains, in the south-east of Turkey from which the Tigris took its sustenance that they would plan their attack.

Asil's pitch stressed how iconic this location was; three major religions revered the story of Noah and the Great Flood, and now their own deadly flood would emerge directly from its resting place to engulf humanity again, or at least the Kurdish branch of it!

He challenged them to try to name one other global event in human history where water played a more significant role.

# Chapter 39 - *Cizre, Turkey*

Kabitsin accompanied Lev and a reconstituted team. They flew into Turkey, this time with three of their containers, for they had selected three distinct planned insertion points to ensure this time they would maximise the effect, the death, the data, the deterrent value...

There were no problems whatsoever for the Russian team to fly in or out of this country. The Republic of Turkey is the most easterly of the NATO members, was currently seeking to join the EU and had always acted as a unique crossroads between Europe and Asia.

In recent times Turkey had been forced to rethink its approach to Russia. Since the USSR had been dissolved it meant that it no longer shared a border with Turkey, and the latter's fears were now redirected instead to the instability of the new republics that surrounded it. However Turkey could not quite forgive its old enemy, feeling that the definitions of these republics' borders might have been drawn up deliberately by the USSR to ensure that there would be constant ongoing trouble, a sort of divide-and-conquer by mapping.

Turkey was the birthplace of both the Byzantine and the Ottoman Empires. But, in a manner not too dissimilar to the Kurds, it had rather lost its way through much of the 20th century. It was the Mongols who had drained Byzantium out of existence and WWI that broke up and dismembered the Ottoman Empire. However echoes of the Ottoman Empire were still felt in hot spots all around Eastern Europe and the Middle East and clearly many of the current problems along the old Ottoman Empire extremities harked back to those past deep divides.

In fact Turkey appeared to have a strange love-hate relationship with Russia. On the one hand they had arguments, Turkey accused of giving succour to Russia's Chechen terrorists and Russia counter-accused of doing the same for Turkey's Kurdish separatists. Both countries were challenging each other all across their region on energy, for example seeking to dominate oil exploration and production in the Caspian Sea.

On the other hand Russia was now second only to Germany, based on its large Turkish diaspora, in terms of trade with Turkey. Russia was supplying arms and there was significant cooperation on energy too. Russia had bought into a number of Turkish energy businesses and there were joint ventures for distribution pipelines. So they worked on within this unholy and holey alliance, and perhaps the one overt sign of peace between them had become tourism. Of the 15 million tourists a year to Turkey, around a quarter of them came from Russia.

Kabitsin had been appalled, when he had visited Istanbul previously to meet up with Carter and Elliott, to find there was a very high incidence of north and trans-Caucasians living in Turkey, most coming from his hated republics.

But for this current trip they had flown directly to Siirt and driven down through the Şirnak province in the south-east of Turkey, passing a series of fertile plateaus in an otherwise very mountainous area. They headed on to the Silopi district and all along their route they could see that the vast majority of the people here were very distinctly Kurdish.

Silopi depended almost entirely on its control of the only major crossing between Iraq and Turkey; its Habur frontier gate was host to many kilometres of queuing trucks patiently awaiting clearance to pass the border. It was also the location of Iraq's major crude-oil pipeline, carrying up to one million barrels per day through the border, though regular sabotage by Kurdish groups meant it seldom achieved anything like that rate.

But they managed to avoid the queues and travelled on to nearby Cizre, sited alongside the Tigris and right on the Syrian border. Asil had marked up a map to show that Cizre and the city of Şirnak virtually created an equilateral triangle with Mount Cudi, the supposed final resting place of Noah's Ark.

He had added some brief notes about the South Anatolia Project, *Güneydogu Anadolu Projesi* or GAP in Turkish, with its plans for a score or more dams and around the same number of hydro-electric power stations on the Euphrates and Tigris in this part of Turkey. This project of course had its critics in Iraq and Syria, who saw water supplies being reduced, but the Kurds too were rejecting many of these vital provisions for Turkey to continue its rapid growth and influence. Already part of the G-20, Turkey had greater ambitions and securing these resources from the troublesome Kurds was therefore key.

Asil had also described how the Kurdish Human Rights Project, backed by all sorts of Western 'do-gooder' organisations, had brought his attention to arguments about the major dams here. Perhaps if they had not made such a fuss then he would have focused elsewhere.

Asil could not believe the convolutions of the Kurdish mind. How was it that they saw the whole project as an undermining of the Kurdish separatist movement, when in fact it was likely to make them economically better off? Then, perhaps belatedly realising the flaw in their thinking, they argued that ecosystems were being threatened because the previous fast-flowing rivers would suffer from a reduction of the oxygenation of the water when it gathered into lakes and reservoirs. Well he planned to show them a much better trick than de-oxygenation of the water!

As a result of this background material they had agreed the principle but then argued he should change his original plan so that now they would have three distinct insertion points. This was in part because the General had stressed that they needed to maximise their impact. They didn't want the still water penned up above dams, they wanted it free, for while it was on the move it was able to do the most damage.

The first entry point was to be near where the Khabur River met the Tigris and where Turkey bordered both Syria and Iraq. There were in fact two River

Khaburs, one that flowed from Turkey to join the Euphrates and the one they were targeting that began in Şirnak and joined the Tigris.

Asil's homework had been wrong but this first error had gone unnoticed. In trying to add to his religious justifications he had suggested that their target river was the equivalent of the Greeks' River Styx within the Sumerian mythology, but actually this was the wrong Khabur. He had been seduced by the other river's myth that it had been used by the ferryman in transporting lost souls from earth to the underworld. In his proposal he had claimed that if there was such a thing as a soul, then what they planned would transport quite a few on to the afterlife.

This first insertion point was chosen so that the water could flow down the Iraq-Syria border and on into northern Iraq, saving them the need to find a way to enter Iraq themselves. They planned to travel back upstream for the second and third insertion points.

**Van, Turkey**
Mark had learned from Dmitry that this general area was to be the next target but, but contrary to the case for the Congo, his information on this one proved rather vague. Dmitry had overheard the xenophobic exchange between Kabitsin and the General and, while he had sought out more information, he had never managed to reach the inner sanctum, never caught sight of the detailed proposals, not before he had seen the ice come racing up towards him as he was thrown from the helicopter.

In the Congo Brain had the additional information supplied to him by Wim, and in fact had even been able to steer the South African team to select a more containable release point. Then of course, Mark had ridden on Valéry's coattails to identify and follow the bandits once they had arrived in the Congo.

Here they were operating completely blindly. They knew only that the still water was to be used in the Tigris and that it was the Kurds across the Turkey-Iraq border who would be the target. They had gained some idea of the dates from the meagre delivery data that Dmitry had been able to access. Brain had called on every favour that they had in the region to have the locals watch all ports, airports and borders, but as yet they were getting no hits.

Brain had been able to arrange to have a special forces platoon diverted to the general area. This team had crossed over from Iraq and was located within the area to act as a rapid-response unit. He had placed them outside Diyarbakir, further upriver and close to one of the two main sources of the Tigris, Lake Hazer. This turned out to be almost 150 kilometres from the first planned insertion point.

Brain and his team, with Tom and his equipment in tow, were flown into Van which would place them a tad closer to the action, but separated by some 250 kilometres from their 'rent-a-thugs', as Brain referred to his colleagues from Hereford. He had hoped that this disposition gave them the maximum flexibility to reach any point along the likely stretch of the Tigris in Turkey. First they had to take a circuitous journey to pass around Van Lake as it appeared on their map, so that they were stationed at the other main source of the Tigris.

The team had expressed some amusement at the name of the city implausibly called Batman, situated somewhere out there between them and the Hereford squad. Then to add to their amusement one of the places they transited was Tatvan. This caused much banter as their local contacts had supplied them with perhaps the tattiest camper van they'd ever seen. Its appearance suggested it had previously been home to generations of hippies. But it did seem to be mechanically sound and thankfully it caused no undue attention on the road, which was all that was of importance to them for this mission.

Both teams had been equipped with Tom's new device to combat the still water. With Stevie's help, and lots of midnight oil, he had come up with something much more resilient, more fitting for the field application. While he was keen to see it prove itself in action, he would also be perfectly happy if it never came to that.

To Brain the new device had resembled a series of battery-operated food mixers fixed onto a floating structure. In fact they were precisely that, though these were heavy-duty professional catering mixers. The "float", which was around 1.5 metres on each side, also contained the chemical that was to be squirted directly into the centre of each set of rotating blades. Simplification of the construction and maintenance meant that if the blades sustained any damage they could be simply pulled out and replaced. The use of multiple blades allowed for a degree of redundancy in case of any flotsam strikes.

The floats also came equipped with four powerful radio-controlled motors fixed at each side's mid-point. These allowed the operator to drive the construction out to the middle of a river, though the remaining fear was that if and when the water was converted into still water then the motors might have somewhat less success in manoeuvring the float. The teams had practised with the device and made sure that they could each drive it reasonably simply with the two-joystick controller.

With the help of a small engineering operation close to Culham, Tom had produced four of these devices that could either be tethered from the shoreline or even allowed to travel down the river to seek out the forbidding water. Each team had been equipped with two of the devices, each set to a different frequency. They were much better prepared than they had been in the Congo, now they just had to sit and wait for news.

# Chapter 40 - *Cizre, Turkey*

Kabitsin stayed in the vehicle while Lev and his team offloaded the first container. They had travelled out of Cizre passing over a large bridge and they continued on until they could see no signs of life or agriculture, the fertile green areas they had been passing through having given way to dusty ochres and reds.

They pulled up a track to the side of the road, drove as close as they could get to the banks of the Tigris and came to a halt. Two of the team immediately jumped out and took up defensive positions along the track. Lev had two others open the rear of the Toyota Land Cruiser and carefully remove the container using a sort of stretcher device that they had decided added to their safety during the insertion. Kabitsin, still in the vehicle, had laid an AK-47 across his lap just in case.

The whole thing proved to be something of an anti-climax for Kabitsin. He had agreed that he should come all this way to ensure that everything went smoothly, and it had. But he realised now that this was not what in fact he had come for. He had relished the thought of opposition, of some sort of exchange of fire, anything other than this gentle gurgling of the still water into the river.

Of course this time they were using the real stuff. Lev had warned him to expect no great chemical reaction as the water was added, but he had assumed he would see something, feel something. Instead everything appeared completely unchanged.

He ordered the team to dump the empty container into the river and drive back into Cizre so they could look for some signs that the water was working its magic.

They had gone a few hundred metres and only then did they start to see dead fish on the surface but as they progressed further they were surprised at the vast numbers that were floating on this uninspiring stretch of river.

Had they been at all interested they could have learned that there were over eighty separate species of fish to be found in the Tigris. In Iraq the *masquof*, a sort of grilled carp, had always been a firm Friday night favourite. However, because these bottom-feeders would definitely have dined on the huge numbers of rotting corpses to be found in the river today, not to mention the vast array of other pollutants, the local imams had issued a *fatwa*, a religious edict, against eating the river fish. Upriver here in Turkey they were still plentiful and still very much on the menu.

They reached the bridge and could see that the impact on Cizre was already unfolding.

The first human victims had been noticed by the locals as individuals suddenly fell over and died for no apparent physical reason. This had perhaps a unique effect on this population, because deep in the psyche of all Kurds was etched the event in the late 1980s at Halabja in Iraq. This was Saddam's gas attack, when eight MIG-23s had dropped their deadly bombs on that city of around eighty thousand population. People in the area had become inured to bombings at that stage of the Iran-Iraq conflict, but those bombs had sounded different.

They had subsequently been reported to have contained a cocktail of mustard gas, sarin, tabun and VX. VX is a long-lasting nerve agent that looks and feels like heavy-duty motor oil and so persisted at the scene. Many had died or been badly affected subsequent to the bombing through their curiosity in going to see the effects of these new-sounding bombs.

This 'race-memory' had expunged all signs of curiosity and the populace of Cizre just fled, on foot, with animals, in vehicles, few wasting the time to grab up any possessions, just hurrying from the scene. The Russians could see the mass exodus gather momentum from their eyrie up on the bridge but suddenly found that they had themselves become engulfed by it. They could see the look of wild panic in the eyes of those passing them, there was something almost primeval in the clarity and depth of their fear. Now at last Kabitsin felt something, finally he was appreciating the value of his coming here to view all this for himself.

Inevitably they were being observed too. It was not just that they were facing against the flow but they were in a car with plates showing the 34 for Istanbul, and the plates were the blue on white that was reserved for members of international organisations.

This people's fear of a gas attack extended to a deep mistrust of foreign influence too. The aftermath of the Halabja bombings was confusing, the Iran-Iraq war initially making it unclear who had carried out the bombings. There was some joy and then later mistrust of the German help with the wounded as it appeared that they were as interested in evaluating the damage as much as remedying it, as keen to see and measure the impact of the chemicals as caring for those who were affected. It did not help their xenophobia that it was the British at their Porton Down facility who had 'invented' the VX nerve agent in the first place.

The complete story as to what foreign interests had been involved was never satisfactorily established. But now here was another unexplained event, and there were these obvious outsiders sitting on a bridge, not apparently appearing at all concerned to make their escape. Clearly they knew more than the locals for, if anything, they were dispassionately watching the panic and deaths, like technicians recording laboratory results.

The reaction against them built slowly. Initially there were just suspicious looks in their direction, no more than this because the early waves of people still had their prime motivation to flee the feared gas attack. But the later waves were gaining confidence, coming to appreciate that they were still alive after some time had passed. Given there were no signs of those behind them dying either, they now had more of their minds available for other thoughts. Perhaps they should fight and not flee.

The looks were becoming more hostile; one old man passing the car banged his flat palm against the door. Others followed his example. A group of braver individuals stopped adjacent to the vehicle. They were assessing it and its occupants, working each other up with their comments and shouts and clearly beginning to contemplate challenging the outsiders.

Lev decided it was time to act. He wound down his window and presented his AK-47, then fired a short burst in the air. The impact was immediate, some people in the crowd hit the floor, others scampered in conflicting directions, tripping over those on the ground, causing the panic that had been settling down to flare up all over again. The driver started the vehicle and drove directly at the crowds. All the windows were now open with a weapon displayed threateningly at each.

The sea of people separated like some biblical Red Sea crossing, and the Russians drove from the bridge picking up momentum, and were forced into taking the Şirnak road, now blending in with the branch of the exodus that was heading off in this direction.

As they passed through the centre of Cizre, Kabitsin at the rear of the vehicle was able to see a reassuringly high body count along the banks together with the mounting numbers of dead fish flowing down the river. He took out his map and imagined the water flowing towards Syria and Iraq and sat back in the seat smiling. At last they would have their first good example of the power of still water.

**Siirt, Turkey**
Reports of the event reached Brain within twenty minutes of the fracas on the bridge. Details of deaths and dead fish in the river were described to him initially as a feared gas attack, but the contacts whom he had primed were able to recognise it for what it was.

They set off with some haste from Siirt in the direction of Şirnak. Another twenty minutes later and they received by radio the first reports of a group of foreigners and a description of the vehicle last seen headed their way, towards Şirnak. There were so few useable roads in the area that the chances of coming upon it were considered to be reasonably high.

**Cizre, Turkey**
Kabitsin realised he had to reassess their plan. They had expected to leave Cizre on the road towards Batman for the next point of insertion. The name's origin was really a contraction based upon the nearby Bati Raman Mountain and had nothing whatsoever to do with the DC Comics hero. However the province's coat of arms does have a device on it that could be considered vaguely bat-like!

They had planned initially to take some poor roads out of Cizre, in the opposite direction to the one that they had through circumstance been forced to follow; their planned destination had been the Hasankeyf district just outside Batman city.

Asil had briefed them that Hasankeyf had been an important capital in the 12th century and would be one of the places where the water should be used. In ancient times it had commanded a key crossroads on two ancient routes – the Silk Road, linking China's highly desirable silk production with the west and the King's Road that linked many significant points such as the Arabian Gulf to the Black Sea, Iraq through Afghanistan and on through the Khyber Pass. This he suggested would lend some weight, hold more value for use in their presentation of the outcome. Kabitsin thought that Asil was rather too keen on his history, probably because his nation's recent past and present were nothing that anyone could get very excited about.

Instead they now found themselves heading towards the third planned insertion point, Siirt. This had also been where they intended to leave Turkey, via its airport.

The Bühtan River passed through Siirt to later join up with the Tigris. Asil explained that the city was renowned for its blankets and kilims, and that it was also a famous spa town. This seemed to have appealed to Asil's sense of humour when he had selected the site. The Biloris springs, on the Eruh highway out of Siirt, delivered its waters at 35°C. They were not fit for drinking, but were said to be good for healing rheumatism and skin diseases. His presentation had suggested that this new water would be much more effective, it would cure all known diseases and all of their hosts too!

Kabitsin was not quite so amused now. It was all well and good for Asil to propose these locations and provide the background but it was evident that he had not planned to be with them when this was all to be done. Given Wim's death during his insertion this was perhaps unsurprising. Asil had claimed some difficulty in leaving Dubai, Kabitsin saw it as some nonsense excuse but Asil had instead offered additional funding to make up for his lack of personal attendance.

Kabitsin thought about the scuffle on the bridge, judged that they should take in just this final site and pass on the one up beyond Batman. They would dump both containers at Siirt and then leave straight afterwards. Anyway the Cizre 'hit' looked as if it would be good enough for their purposes. Hopefully this other location would be enough to satisfy Asil that he had been presented with a good return on his investment.

**Siirt to Cizre road, Turkey**
The British team rounded yet another bend in the road, pushing hard up behind one of the many trucks that was presumably crawling and spluttering its way to

the border. Brain flipped out to look around the lumbering beast and had to flip straight back in again rapidly when he saw an oncoming vehicle.

However he had enough time to identify it as their target, a white Toyota, a Land Cruiser with a blue and white registration. He slammed on the brakes and handbrake turned with great skill, though the camper van being a wee bit top-heavy for the manoeuvre threatened to reward the skill with an ignominious roll. Brain used the steering wheel, hand-brake and cadence-braking to remedy that tendency and was already pressing the accelerator to the floor as he came around on to the new direction.

James was first to get his window open and point his weapon generally in the right direction. He had been supplied with a Minimi, the original inspiration for the USA's M249, the weapon was called the L110A1 by the Brits. Assessing the state of this mini machine gun initially he thought it might have been one that was purchased back at the first Gulf War when the M249 had been in short supply. Brits used this weapon in Iraq and Afghanistan so it was just as likely that its beaten-up condition was due to it having lived a short yet tough life there.

It was fitted with an optical sight, with a range of 800 metres, it could fire 725 rounds-per-minute, but none of these figures were likely to be achieved while leaning out of a careening vehicle on a poor road surface with the target vehicle bouncing all over the countryside too. Fortunately the stretch of road was clear of traffic so he decided to point and pray, trying desperately to aim and fire in short bursts whenever he thought he was generally pointing in the right direction.

His first shots having gone wide, he was "rewarded" by two of the bandits leaning out of the Toyota and returning the compliment; fortunately they exhibited the same lack of accuracy. The road was twisting and turning and the Toyota was around the next bend.

They raced to close the gap and turned the corner to find a lumbering truck at the centre of the road following its avoidance of the Toyota. There was a heart-stopping moment as they looked sure to leave the road but Brain's driving skills used every centimetre of grip to keep them there.

Up ahead they spotted the Toyota and James loosed off another burst with the same outcome; this time there was no returning fire as both vehicles entered the next chicane.

In the Russian vehicle it took Kabitsin no time at all to recognise that the real threat was the two containers of still water sat behind them in the back of the vehicle, right there in the direct line of fire. Whoever it was back there only had to have one lucky burst that hit the containers and they would be dead from the effects of the water. It wouldn't matter what else the shots hit, the thought of that water sloshing around the inside of the vehicle was what concentrated his mind.

He quickly despatched two of the team to climb over into the rear, where they kicked the doors open while clinging to the rear seat. As the vehicles emerged from the next complex of turns there was a few hundred metres of straight. Kabitsin instructed them to kick out each of the containers.

The Russians watched as the chasing vehicle managed to avoid the first container but were delighted to see it brake to a stop to avoid the second that bounced right down the centre of the road towards them.

Kabitsin urged the team to direct their fire on the containers in an effort to get the better of their pursuers, but they all too soon turned yet another bend and the containers and their chasers were out of sight.

No one could take any credit from the exchange. The rough road and the winding terrain conspired to ensure that not a single shot had reached an intended target. The camper had come to a halt slewed across the road with the second container just centimetres from its side and very effectively blocking its route.

Brain got out with Tom to check the two containers. They recognised precisely what they were, as they bore precisely the same markings as they had seen in the Congo. They were relieved to see that there had been no spillage from either. The first container was off at the side of the road in a deep and dusty side gulley. They stood well back from it and sprayed it with automatic fire, allowing the water to drain off into the arid stretch of countryside, judging reasonably that its chances of entering the local water system from there were minimal. It would evaporate and hopefully nature would take it back to the more acceptable form of water. The second container they placed in the rear of the camper for Tom.

Brain was on his radio calling ahead and arranging first for an airport-watch and then trying to reach his contacts to arrange a roadblock. Leaving the pursuit of the Russians to those they had alerted further down the road, they turned back to Cizre and the border. The SAS team too was racing to the site of the first insertion point to see what could be done to stop the progress of the still water.

Asil's second error had been not to read thoroughly about the GAP scheme, but then he had expected there would be three insertion points to spread the impact. What he'd missed was that directly below Cizre on the river's course there was a new hydroelectric plant with a dam that had created a large lake behind it.

The British team was able to establish this quite promptly and ensured that the plant was shut down so the still water would all be contained within the lake.

Once both teams arrived at the plant they inserted all four of Tom's devices and drove them around for hours, taking it in turn to criss-cross the lake until the batteries had died on the mixers. They then hauled them back to shore to consider how to recharge them.

Their other concern was how to establish when the risk was averted, how to check that the water was, well, water. Tom had defined some tests to resolve this matter and they called a local team for assistance.

Given the locale it was easy for the authorities to ensure that the concept of a gas attack was publicised to any media showing an interest. Sir Joseph also seeded some articles about insurgents crossing the border from Iraq and loosing off some plundered Iraqi chemical munitions.

The story never made it to any international papers or electronic media; the area had so much misery and such regular loss of life that it was no longer particularly interesting. The fact that some internationally known 'it-girl' had received community service for a misdemeanour was clearly much more deserving of the world's media attention.

# Chapter 41 - *London, UK*

'Not apparently the sharpest tools in the box,' said Sir Joseph as he reported to the Foreign Secretary on the recent events in Turkey.

They were meeting in a committee room at No 10, not the famous COBRA that was constantly in the press when there was a national crisis. This rather dramatic name derived simply from the rather dull initials of Cabinet Office Briefing Room A, COBRA seemed much more emotive and far better suited to the era of political spin.

'And thank heavens for that,' commented the Foreign Secretary. 'Let's not test providence but count our blessings, it's just that they're not proving to be that smart – yet.'

'I think it was the IRA who said, you have to be lucky all the time and we only have to get lucky once!' commented the Professor.

'I don't suppose the families of the 238 Kurds who died in Turkey will see that there was much luck on our side. Of course they are politically using these deaths to mount further pressure for being granted their own state.'

Sir Joseph countered with an aphorism of his own. 'Look I've always found that the harder I work the luckier I seem to get! The teams we deployed managed to foil any further deaths, first by capturing two of the canisters before they were used and then by using our man's device to convert the still water back. I would say there wasn't a lot of luck involved in any of that – intelligence, commitment and execution more like.'

'Let's not rest on past glories. How are we going to stop any further use of this material? Are you any closer to finding these people? I assume they escaped from you in Turkey?'

Sir Joseph was thinking how infuriating this habit of hers was. She would often clock up a series of questions like this without allowing any opportunity to answer them in any organised manner. 'They proved to be quite smart on that one point. The senior guys were dropped off at Kurtalan and travelled down by train to Istanbul where they disappeared into that morass of mankind. Their non-essential crew took the vehicle back into Siirt and to the airport where they were taken into custody. They didn't put up too much of a fight as they were caught inside the terminal building and they had, of course, left their weapons behind in the vehicle.

'It doesn't appear that any of them knew anything useful, just freelance, expendable, low-level Neanderthals who had been hired for this one task. They still had enough nous, or more likely fear of the principals, to hold back the news of their diversion to Kurtalan until it was of no use to us. They don't even appear to know who they were working for or much about still water, we'll press on with them for now. Fortunately the Turkish police force doesn't have the human rights or PC constraints that we have to work with here, so if there is anything more I feel sure they will get it.'

The Foreign Secretary was due to join a cabinet meeting so wanted to press forward. 'But we understand there are still two more targeted strikes?'

Sir Joseph considered going back to answer her original question but saw no merit in his likely answer. The only joy might have been to highlight her habit, but he went with the new question. 'We've only the general information of some intended strike on the Danube, with Romania and Bulgaria as the targeted countries.'

'That's something of a relief in itself,' the Professor commented. 'That river runs directly through ten different countries and its twenty plus tributaries take water into it from another ten countries! It would have taken you an army to watch the length of it! In fact the Roman army had to do just that when it used to form one of their longest standing frontiers. However, if we are confident of just those two countries then we are limiting it to just 400 kilometres or so, of the full 2,850 kilometres of its entire course!'

'We have intelligence that this is just another paid-for spectacular for another Brotherhood member. I'm not sure they still have the taste for this and may just press on with their real intention which we understand is something aimed directly at the Indians and the Chinese.'

The Professor flicked through his folder. 'If you talk of those two countries then the choices can be quantified quite easily. Nepal and Bhutan sit right between them for much of their natural border, the Himalayas. They only come cheek-by-jowl within Arunāchal Pradesh. That province has had many years of disputes, it's no secret that they're arguing over the Brahmaputra River right there!'

Sir Joseph said, 'We have gained the impression that this river system might be the eventual threatened target rather than the planned demonstration. It would kill too many for them ever to be forgiven. We believe that the demonstration is to illustrate to the Indians and Chinese what would happen if they did put still water into the Brahmaputra. Wim Brockenhorst had either been uninformed or was quite selective in what he told us on this subject; regrettably the bloody Frogs killed him at the Congo site, so we can't ask him to elucidate.'

A minion knocked and entered and whispered in the Foreign Secretary's ear, she replied and he left. 'Professor, you were looking at some background on these target nations?'

'Yes, I think we need to start by understanding that these two great nations are simply reasserting the natural order of things, re-establishing their rightful places as major world powers. The whole colonial thing and their late industrial revolutions clouded matters and it's only now that they are finally catching up; they're back to claim their rightful status based on their massive growth today.'

Sir Joseph spluttered, 'But 80% of the Indian population lives on less than 20 rupees per day, that's around 20p! A third of their people are illiterate, half their infants are malnourished and they proudly profess that they have more than 100 million mobile phones in use! And, don't even get me started on the Chinese!'

The Professor pressed his point, 'You misunderstand me, what I am trying to say is that these were established rich civilisations while we were still painting our faces blue. The great European cities were nothing compared to theirs. The reason we despatched explorers and established colonies was because these were the fabled ancient civilisations with their untold riches. Our plunder of their riches and then our head-start in industrialisation and even later in commercial and IT implementation is what has made the West dominate in more recent history. Now we're aging, lazy and have no resources of our own, they still hold the geological balance of power. They're annexing their hungry, virile peoples to get back to where they were before we confused the issues.'

'You make it sound like we were playing the role of pirates.'

'I'm not one to seek to rewrite history but I do like to think that I can learn from it. In 1600 as the East India Company was founded, Britain, or rather England as it wasn't until three years later that the crowns became unified under James, and another hundred years for the two parliaments to become one...'

Sir Joseph threw his hands up in despair. 'Do please stay on message.'

'Well, my point was that in the year 1600, Britain,' he used his hands to make inverted commas, 'was creating just 2% of the global GDP compared with Moghul India's 22.5%. By 1870, at the very peak of the Victorian period and the Raj, we were ourselves by then just short of 10% of global GDP and India had been reduced to poverty and famine. So you make your own judgment on those facts.'

The Foreign Secretary asked, 'But if only one in five of their people is gaining from India's growth and the underclass is being left literally by the side of the street, then surely that's not sustainable?'

'Clearly not. But would you bet against their ability to drive the economy to a point where that percentage will begin to improve? We mustn't ignore China either. If anything the Chinese are a tad ahead of India in regaining their true status in the world. Theirs is the civilisation that invented the compass, gunpowder, paper and printing, silk, kites, wheelbarrows, umbrellas...'

Sir Joseph smiled. 'Ah the glorious WanChai Burberrys.' When he saw the Professor's confusion, he added, 'It's what we called the local girls' paper umbrellas in Hong Kong.'

The Foreign Secretary grimaced at Sir Joseph, as she said to the Professor, 'I always enjoy your way of placing things into such sharp perspective. History can always teach us much. But today we're facing a threat that might damage these proud countries' ability to re-establish themselves in the way you outline. What I need to understand is how we can assist them to avoid this barrier being set in their way.'

Sir Joseph pondered aloud, 'Or perhaps we should pause and consider whether in fact it is in our national interest for us to step aside and not remove this barrier?'

The Foreign Secretary leapt from her chair, placed both hands on the meeting table and leaned towards Sir Joseph. 'You are seriously counselling me that we allow death and destruction loose on these peoples? Thousands, maybe millions, could die!'

'Of course not. All I am suggesting is that perhaps we are marauding around the world meddling in things that are not directly affecting our nation, or our specific interests. Perhaps we should pass the information to those directly affected and not become so directly involved. I am unaware as yet of any open threat to the UK.'

'If you let men like these wander the world with this "perfect weapon" of yours, leave aside the moral corruption of such an act of neglect for the moment, just how long would it be before they came knocking on our door, pouring their noxious stuff into our rivers and reservoirs?'

The Professor added, 'I mentioned earlier the sheer impracticality of policing the Danube, but I can't even begin to calculate the way in which we could secure our own water supplies. The sort of "police" force that we'd need to assemble, the technology to cover all of our waters – it's just an impossibility.'

# Chapter 42 - *Oxfordshire, UK*

Securing UK water supplies was just the task that Tom had set for his freshly expanded team at Culham. His field device had worked well in Turkey, now he was looking at how it could be turned in to something that could be used by the water companies to safeguard the supply to domestic and commercial users.

If you had a reservoir contaminated by still water, how could you efficiently ensure that what entered the supply chain would be safely converted back to potable water? And by this he meant both technically and financially.

He and Stevie had been moulded and pushed together in a unique way by their field experience. They had been forced to rely upon each other under fire, something very new to them both. Since they had come back this had led to a close understanding that allowed them to form a great working duo. Almost inevitably they discovered this profound respect in each other's abilities was, all too evidently, leading towards affection.

They had little time to explore this development. First and foremost they knew they had to find a way to defeat this still water. It was clearly still out there, ready to strike again and they knew that there had been a huge degree of luck to date. They had really not been at all ready in the Congo; if the Russian group had in fact deployed still water they were pretty sure they would have failed.

As for Turkey, Tom had decided not to tell her of the fire-fight that he had been involved in on the road while there. He had told her of the Kurdish response to flee from an assumed gas attack that this was what had kept the death rates down, and then the proximity of the dam had fortunately enabled them to contain the spread. They could not rely on this luck holding, they needed a business-like and tenable solution.

As a team they were not currently receiving any intelligence, no inside information as to what was being done to find this Brotherhood. Tom assumed they failed the need-to-know requirement and he was secretly quite content with that as a conclusion. They had received a sincere thank you from Sir Joseph via Brain, but then he appeared to have crawled back under his rock in Whitehall or wherever he lurked.

However they were scientists and there was a back door route available for them. Fellow scientists worked for their respective governments but had their own agenda too, the advancement of their discipline. This led to a regular and unofficial dissemination of their progress among the scientific community despite their respective countries often believing that these matters were national secrets.

This was where they decided to go for information. They called all the people Tom had worked with in Novosibirsk, or at least all those who appeared to be real scientists rather than the many intelligence staff who had been posing as scientists.

The first surprise was that Paul and Ellise appeared to have dropped completely off the radar; no one seemed to know where they were, even the NOAA had been vague when he called them too. Tom assumed that they were still off pursuing Paul's daydreams. And besides, Ellise was really just a cute code-cruncher and Paul very much the loose cannon, so Tom's not being able to reach them was no particular loss. He was slightly more concerned to learn that their erstwhile supervisor Dmitry also seemed to have disappeared over everyone's horizon too.

Where he hit lucky was when he called Professor Groves whom he had met in the past many times. They had regularly shared conference platforms and both had been invited on to various TV 'punditry' panels. From the press he was also aware of the man's close connections into the current government; so he was a natural to call. He had no idea that this had perhaps effectively opened a second front on to Sir Joseph.

The Professor had not been aware of the name of the person who was working for Sir Joseph, need-to-know again, so was delighted to learn it was Tom. He advised the Foreign Secretary that they now had this new asset in the battle against still water, and perhaps if required against Sir Joseph too.

# Chapter 43 - *Novaya Zemlya, Russia*

Paul thought that Ellise had leapt to the wrong conclusions and could not possibly have seen someone thrown from a helicopter. Their hosts were being extremely hospitable to the limit of the resources that they had to hand. He certainly was not going to start accusing anyone based upon what she believed she might have seen. He had always thought Dmitry something of a cold fish and assumed it more likely that his absence was because he had needed to return to his base, get new instructions. He would wash up sooner or later.

In fact Ellise was becoming a real pain. First there was her constant fear of being exposed to radiation, even though this had so far proven to be completely groundless. She seemed to mope around on the infrequent occasions when he was ashore, now this. She had even committed the cardinal sin and mentioned the 'T' word, suggesting that they should try to contact Tom Carter. He had barely been able to talk and stomped away from her in anger.

It was a source of irritation for this to happen, particularly today of all days, when towards the end of their dive they thought that they had spotted something, something they'd marked so that they would be sure to get straight back on to it tomorrow.

If it was the comet fragment then the old man had been pretty accurate as to direction but perhaps the mistake Paul had made was to assume that the splash site would be the final resting place. Of course the angle being so shallow it had to make sense that it would have ended up much nearer the island than the reported splash. He speculated that it might even have bounced like a pebble to its final resting place and that if he was right it was much closer to the shore and thus would be discovered and investigated during tomorrow's dive.

Ellise was not able to be involved in this phase, she had nothing to contribute. She therefore arranged, while he was playing in his mini-submarine, to be delivered back to Belushya Guba on the pretext of needing to collect additional materials.

Once there she headed straight for a PC with an Internet connection and slammed in an email to Tom and copied in Mark. She had found plenty of time during her wanderings to prepare this message and was able to make it resemble some sort of interim report and request for data.

She thought there would be no difficulty in openly advising them of her location in her message and she knew from their conversations in Novosibirsk that Mark would understand what it was that had brought them there.

How could she explain the news about Dmitry? She concluded that she should try to do this covertly and after much deliberation decided to use an apparent reference to music. She had established that Shostakovich's first name was Dmitry too and, as they had never discussed music while together, she hoped that Mark or Tom would be confused by a musical reference and alerted to seek an alternative explanation for her mentioning this.

She looked Shostakovich up and concluded that the most evocative reference would be his opera 'Lady Macbeth'. So she crashed in a postscript to Tom: 'BTW – I have pondered further our conversation of Shostakovich's Scottish play. His subsequent fall from grace at the hands of the Russian government was fatal for him, and this Lady cannot wash her hands of it. Would love to talk it over again with you, any chance that you could get agreement to join us here?'

She looked over the note several times, tweaking and worrying at it. In the end she thought the plea for him to come would be sufficient to get his attention. Perhaps he would mention it to others, or perhaps between them he and Mark could work out something of what she meant.

# Chapter 44 - *Virginia, USA*

Deep inside the CIA Langley headquarters, Mark received Ellise's note but was preoccupied with another matter. He looked at it for a few seconds and of course realised that she was trying to pass him some sort of message. Why were those who brushed up against the intelligence community inspired to become so melodramatic? It must be all the spy books and movies he assumed.

His concern was that Dmitry had supplied him with three vague targets and an ultimate goal but frustratingly not enough data on anything to be particularly useful. Dmitry had identified the three contracts they were supplying as for the Congo, Tigris and Danube, and had been able to come up with some pretty solid dates for when these were to be actioned.

He had also informed Mark that the ultimate threat to China and India appeared to be a threatened attack on the Brahmaputra River, but insisted that there would be a prior demo of what they could achieve elsewhere first. On this, all he could add was that the demo was planned as a direct assault to damage the two countries' interests. Mark concluded this must imply it would be somewhere outside their territories, but where?

He had learnt that one of the individuals who had escaped capture in Turkey was Kabitsin himself; annoying to have lost him a second time, and again it had happened in Istanbul. Did this mean that he was based there, or near there? There was enough of a Russian presence that he could hide himself inside the diaspora, in a city that he was coming to realise had more twists and turns than the Cresta Run.

The USA teams in Turkey were well connected. They had to be to keep this as a forward base for their operations in the Middle East. They had tugged on every contact, run all sorts of enquiries, pulled in every informant they could reach. No chance.

None of those captured out in the Congo or Turkey could provide anything either. They had been stretched and squeezed to the limit, by experts at their trade, but the conclusion just had to be that they really did not know anything. Nada.

As they had no idea where the central team was located they had no opportunity to either infiltrate someone or get hold of one of them to pump or to turn them. Zip.

He had instituted background checks on all those who had been in Novosibirsk to see if they could back-track him towards anyone of interest. The only useful stuff was on the General who had been a career intelligence officer with extensive experience and presence, but he too was managing to achieve a low profile at the moment. There was no trace of him having left Russia. Mark knew a man of his background would have no trouble beating the border controls and his databases. Dmitry had been their best hope. He had wanted to be taken out and protected, but they had sent him back in to see what else he could learn, and they had not heard from him. Zilch!

Back in Langley they had assembled a team with inputs from all sorts of – ologists who studied the materials they had on the Brotherhood, the known targets and so on. The papers these guys had generated on every aspect of this matter would have filled a library. There were profiles of the main protagonists, not just the data on origins and 'careers', but papers on attitudes, motivations, personal dispositions, temperaments, task attitudes, interpersonal skills, team playing abilities and so on. But this was just presumption built on presumption and all based upon too little data in the first place. It all added up to a great big round number. Zero.

So whichever way he looked at it, or expressed it, it was clear that they had no leads.

The only approach open to them was to submit their franchise proposal to Kabitsin and hope that during the process they might be able to get some purchase or some angle or new facts about what was planned. They had worked up some IT wizardry too. They would submit their plan containing a photo, but embedded in the code for the photo would be a subroutine.

When any PC opened this file, the subroutine would immediately leap into the 'Normal' template in the Microsoft Office Word file and would create a macro in the Microsoft Excel template, then erase any trace of itself. Langley had ensured that this subroutine was enabled by all the leading virus software packages, AVG, Norton, MacAfee and a host of others, without anything amiss being reported to the user. On opening either a Word or Excel file while connected to the Internet, the PC would send a message to Langley, faithfully recording its route home so that the PC would be traceable in the virtual world. Other techniques could then translate that back to the real world.

The tough thing in preparing the proposal was to come up with a credible location for insertion of the still water that would confirm their bona fides as being just as crazy as the Brotherhood. Yet the location of course had to be defendable in case they decided to attack with or without Mark's commitment. This meant the expense of tying up personnel to be on site until the end of this matter.

Mark had another consideration. He needed somehow to ensure his pitch would generate an exchange of notes or even a conversation with Kabitsin that might along the way provide insight into the Brotherhood's intentions. He needed the emailed proposal to have some element that would guarantee there had to be a follow-up conversation. What would make them call? An attack into another Brotherhood member's patch perhaps might do it.

Best of all would be if they could somehow double-guess them and select one of the targets already in process. Surely the Brotherhood would have been pretty analytical in picking their target originally, so perhaps all he had to do was to try to replicate the very same analysis.

Thus a whole team was set to create a review that plotted river basins, first by their 'publicity' value, then by the political, economic and racial characteristics that the rivers flowed through, and also by any history of riparian dispute. They then arranged to cross-cast this data against the known Brotherhood leaders' and members' interests, hatreds and desires. The General's past postings, as he was the most travelled of the crew, were plotted against these factors too.

In the list of the top twelve world rivers they immediately dismissed the Ob-Irtysh and Yenisey in Russia as the Brotherhood was primarily a very patriotic Russian group. The Amur and the Lena in Siberia were assessed a little longer as being possible but they too were eventually discounted as being ostensibly Russian. This left in size order the Nile, the Amazon, the Mississippi-Missouri, the Yangtze and Yellow Rivers of China, the Congo, the Mackenzie in Canada, the Mekong and the Niger.

They assumed that the Congo attack meant that the Nile and Niger were alternatives that had already been dismissed. Wim had certainly indicated to the Brits that they were all considered as his patch and he had of course selected the Congo. There were no immediately obvious Chinese or Indian interests along the Nile or Niger valleys, so these were marked down as unlikely.

Given the belief that the threat to China would be the Brahmaputra River it was also decided to downgrade the Yellow and Yangtze Rivers. They could not imagine any way that the Amazon would disturb the two targeted Asian superpowers, so it was downgraded too. For the same reason the Mackenzie seemed pretty implausible as a valid target.

The Jefferson-Mississippi-Missouri would form their own ultimate North American threat, so unless the Russians planned to slip into the States and do this for themselves the analysis was able to reduce the Big-12 down to just one – the Mekong.

Just in case, they extended their thinking to the second division of river basins. The analysis assumed they should disregard any in China, India, Russia, Africa and North America and discounted too those that did not have any multiple riparian states. The Danube they knew was to be the next paid-for target, the Euphrates was dismissed based upon the neighbouring Tigris event having pre-empted it.

Research also deleted the Orinoco, Paraná and Tietê in South America on the same basis as the Amazon, because they assumed these all had limited Asian interest. The Sava flowed through Slavic countries which they assumed would not be a target for the Russians and also it joined up with the Danube, an existing target. So the research into the second tier threw up just the Amu Darya in central Asia, the Dneister and Sava in Eastern Europe and the Jordan.

In this way they ended up with just four prime targets: the Mekong, the Jordan, the Amu Darya and the Dniester. Each had a good fit with the Brotherhood's 'enemies' but they concluded that only one would impact heavily on the Chinese and Indians, and further it was the biggest of the four – the Mekong!

# Chapter 45 - *Oxfordshire, UK*

Still at Culham, Tom was surprised to receive Ellise's note and pleased with the confirmation that she and Paul were still in Russia and that they were indeed seeking out Paul's comet, though he wondered if it might also be cover for a means of locating more of the still water.

He forwarded a copy of the note to Brain suggesting that this might be some attempt on the part of the Russians or, given Ellise's presence perhaps the Americans, to acquire further supplies of this dreaded material that had come along and seemed to have completely hi-jacked his life.

He had not spent a second on any of his promised papers and books and his agent was harassing him daily. Worse he had made no public appearances and he knew how ephemeral the whole celebrity-expert thing was. If he was not out there on the circuit soon he would drop off of every production assistant's contact list.

He re-read Ellise's note. He had no idea that she and Mark were into classical music, he had never heard either of them discussing it. He assumed that this was something for Mark and not himself. He had no interest in music and would certainly have had no idea of Shostakovich's first name.

There was something about the note that was just not Ellise, her natural confidence and almost aggressive tone was completely missing. He knew that Paul had the tendency to suck everyone else's enthusiasm dry; he would bend them to serve just his own narrow world, his ambitions. Surely she was much stronger than that and would not have become cowed in this way so quickly.

With nothing back from Brain, he felt he needed to respond to what he felt was a *cri de coeur* from Ellise, something was clearly rattling her, and something was odd about the content.

He also felt constrained. He and Stevie were becoming closer by the day, now here was Ellise with whom he had that moment on the islands, would he be betraying Stevie by replying? Recalling that moment rekindled his memory of Ellise, she was instinctive, living for the moment, right on top of her game, confident, sexy – it was just not the same person who had written the email!

He decided he must reply. He tried to show her that he was worried while not sounding like someone trying to rekindle an old flame. He showed interest in what they were up to, but ensured she knew that he had realised there was more to her note by enthusiastically asking after Paul as if they were firm friends. She was fully aware of the reality of his relationship with Paul and would realise that here was a note from someone trying to understand what her problem might be. He pressed 'Send' with a CC to Mark and a BCC to Brain.

# Chapter 46 - *London, UK*

In his excuse for an office Brain knew all about Paul and Ellise's quest in the Arctic. His room was set deep in the bowels of the building, surrounded by heating pipes, conduits and cable trays. From here Brain very much appreciated the trend in modern architecture that placed all this paraphernalia on the outside of a building.

Sir Joseph had advised him that the Americans had a submarine in the area monitoring precisely what was happening off the coast of Novaya Zemlya. The special relationship between the USA and the UK was alive and well.

The last report that Mark had forwarded to them showed that their submarine, stealthily resting on or near the bottom, had reported some excitement on the mini-submarine's radio frequency. They believed Paul had found something of interest. They had marked the radio beacon he had dropped at the site of interest and had been contemplating a look-see of their own while the mini-submarine was out of the water. As it was far too close to the island they sent a dive team but had found nothing significant. It would appear that the mini-sub's crew had become excited about an unusual area of ice on the floor.

This was the only flow of information that Sir Joseph was permitting. He stressed to Brain that his focus must be the Danube. He told Brain they could not draw upon any local intelligence sources within this next target area. Sir Joseph considered them flaky, too prone to penetration from elsewhere. Both countries, Romania and Bulgaria, were less than a generation free from their prior Soviet rule, so the Russians would still have sources deep within their organisations.

They were to leave both the monitoring in the Arctic and the mid-term task of searching for the Brotherhood's base to the Cousins for now; after all they had the better hardware and software to address this. Brain was to concentrate instead upon the planned events. If Dmitry's timetable was right, there were two rapidly upcoming insertions.

Known to be in the Danube, the first one had to be the focus for now, though heaven knew where they might strike along the 1,000+ kms that formed the border between the two target countries, the countries that Sir Joseph had called flaky.

They had to narrow this down somehow and assuming that the insertion point would be before where the Iskür joined the Danube from Sofia and the Arges joined it from Bucharest they were able to reduce their focus to 150km. However the Tigris episode had shown that the Russkies had been prepared to use multiple insertion points. Perhaps this time they might use multiple teams too, so how did they cover off the Danube and these two tributaries as well? What resource could he draw upon in terms of personnel?

Brain had to set his plans in motion. The only real outcome of the two received emails was that they served to remind him of Tom Carter . He would like to have taken Tom and his glamorous assistant to this next site, in part because he felt he needed everyone who was inside the loop available to him, available to discuss what they were seeing and hearing, available to respond to whatever might occur. He accepted that it was as much because deep down he would enjoy making clear to Tom that he could intrude upon his life so routinely and decisively on a whim. He felt that there was something glib about the man; perhaps it was an inflated view of his own importance. Whatever it was, Brain felt he would enjoy deflating it.

He disagreed with Sir Joseph's strategy and felt he should also be spending some time thinking of the main Brotherhood team and the major planned event after these paid-for incidents, yet on this they had no information whatsoever, even the Yanks were drawing a blank on this one. So he would, more by default, do as Sir Joseph requested and concentrate on what was on the table right now – the Danube.

# Chapter 47 - *Odessa, Ukraine*

Kabitsin, now safely back in his Odessa house, had decided he would not join the field team this time. He remembered all too clearly the lottery his life had depended upon in Turkey; just one shot from that fire-fight breaching those canisters, or worse directly hitting him, and all he had worked for would have been destroyed. More importantly, he had absolutely no plans to die anywhere other than in Russia. He wanted to be sure his DNA would return to his beloved soil, not be left halfway up some mountain with its only claim to fame some fable of a floating farmyard.

He planned to stay here in Odessa, it was clear that the Americans and Brits were having no luck with their efforts to discover him. The General did not seem to realise he was under virtual house arrest, still thought he was running the show, and in truth there were more things that Kabitsin felt he needed from him before he was ready to cast him off.

They had already agreed the plans for the Danube and were making the final arrangements. It was intended to be the most significant event yet, a definitive action that they could use for their purposes.

Pavel Borovik's pitch had none of the flowery bits with which the other two had infested their proposals. There were no history lessons, no geography lessons, but given the issue of the dam below Cizre spoiling the effect, they had made him have someone drive the length of the river to photograph every twist and turn, every feature so that there would be no mistake this time.

Pavel's objective was clear, he would regain control of his markets from the Bulgarians and Romanians by threatening further insertions until their homelands were dead and empty. Gangsters from the two countries had brutally taken control of extortion, people-trafficking, prostitution and drugs in most western European cities, achieving supremacy by being more brutal and driven, by being hungrier and more needy. He, himself, had found it was always a lot easier to take something than to hold on to it.

Pavel would continue to attack them anyway in the more traditional manner, where they all lived, down on the streets, but what he needed the still water to do was to 'up the ante'. He planned to terrorise their families, their heritage, their culture – their countries could be completely wiped out. He was aware that they were fiercely patriotic, for instance they followed their football teams with a terrifying passion. Any threat to their countries would be sure to capture all of their attention.

Kabitsin admired the thought process, though it came as no surprise because Pavel was a true Russian, not one of the mongrels they had been dealing with before. Wim, a displaced Dutchman, had not been sure if South Africa or the Netherlands was home and was unable to live in either. Asil was a disenchanted Turk, growing fat and lazy, sating himself in that glorified building site on the Gulf, a skin-deep place. The Arabs thought they could buy their way to a style and a culture, when all they managed was to become ever more like the worst of all hybrids, building American malls beside Caribbean resort hotels.

When he received Mark Elliott's proposal it was somewhat unexpected and pulled Kabitsin away from putting the final touches to the Danube plan. He had assumed that the franchise proposal would come to nothing, that Mark was stringing him along just as a loyal intelligence guy should, or maybe he was not connected into the right people in the States. Either way he had not expected the proposal.

What he had hoped, or rather the General had suggested, was that Mark's 'father' was connected to the powers behind the throne. Was he one of those people who really ran the USA, the ones who created, supported and perhaps on occasion had been known to even assassinate its presidents?

The proposal appeared to suggest that they had judged him and his father correctly for here was a plan outlining in detail the threat they would use against their own government.

It was an attack on the Potomac, not as he had expected on the Mississippi-Missouri. There was a great deal of detail as to whom they would approach and the content of that threat. It was all good stuff, and it looked well thought through in terms of how they would be able to stay clear of any recriminations or attack. He re-read it carefully; he thought there were points in this planning document that he could use himself with the Chinese and the Indians.

The proposal talked through likely insertion points and had satellite pictures of the two best locations. The report went on to discuss likely casualty counts, wildlife impact and so on. He had to admit that these Americans were good at the detail. What was it the Arabs call the Americans? The Great Satan, wasn't it? Perhaps the saying that the 'devil is in the detail' was right.

He was surprised that there was nothing in the report about the British 'antidote' device. Kabitsin's intelligence from Turkey was that they had some new means of combating the still water. But this was sketchy; certainly the contraption that Lev had brought back from the Congo did not appear to be at all effective. They had been reverse-engineering it to try to have a working solution of their own but no real progress had been made.

He had reports that the British had cleaned up the lake below Cizre in some way. Surely if they had such a device then the American would know all about it, would have included some material on how they would circumvent it. But there was no mention of this at all, perhaps the British device was not as effective as he had imagined.

He turned the page to receive a complete shock. The American spent several pages developing a case for why the group wanted to use the still water as payback upon the Vietnamese and Cambodians. The vitriol was extreme, they railed at the Vietnamese withdrawal having set back American global interests for decades. Even today its domestic and international policy was plagued and shaped by liberal cries of 'we don't want another Vietnam'. Kabitsin had not realised how damaged the Americans felt by this piece of reasonably recent history.

At the centre of the section was a large photo, the iconic picture of their withdrawal as the helicopters pulled off the roof of the Saigon embassy leaving behind locals who had helped the Americans, pressed up against the railings, pleading for their passage out. He remembered the picture and could appreciate the shame that was summed up in that historic image.

There was a section explaining that it was the Vietnamese shaming of the American war machine that had encouraged all the ensuing problems they faced. Even Saddam had assumed he could manipulate the American public and energise a general Arab counter-resistance when he launched his rocket attacks on Israel. The ensuing insurgency in Iraq and Afghanistan was clearly modelled on the way in which Vietnam had successfully sapped and ultimately defeated the Americans.

Kabitsin understood their hate, their anger. Here was this nothing little state, their fighters giving the impression that they wouldn't even be able to stand up in a strong wind, yet they had defeated the United States of America. At least the Russian debacles had been at the hands of Chechens and Afghans, both blood-thirsty fighting men, street-hardened, mountain-hardened, with a long martial history of note. You could point at these enemies and show that you had been fighting real men, not frail lady-boys dressed in their pyjamas. It was no small wonder that they still bore a grudge!

The shock was not just that he had expected a planned North American demonstration, but that what he had in front of him was a proposal for the Mekong – his own planned target! Of course this plan was for much further downriver than his own but it was still the same river that they were putting forward for their 'spectacular'.

He needed to talk this through with the General and decide what they might say to the Americans; perhaps they might suggest they share the target? But for now he needed to get back to finalising the Danube plan.

The Danube insertion would be greatly assisted by their strong relationship with Serbia, their fellow Slavs. Kabitsin had, through the General, recruited some strong local personnel who would assist them. They need not know anything of what they were involved in, and would not have expected to anyway. They would just lend their support and vital local knowledge. This was now a test of strength. A good clean demonstration of the power of their new weapon was needed.

Kabitsin had his team expand his stocks of the water by taking over an old, rundown and closed facility in Odessa. They had mixed in some still water and converted a whole 50 metre long, eight-lane-wide swimming pool's worth of water. As much as they needed for their two remaining events had been pumped out and a small team was trying to work with the stolen British device to clean up the residue. He didn't really care if they succeeded or not. There were no plans to drain the pool prior to their departure from Odessa so it was safe where it was, they might even need it later.

They would attack the Danube in two different ways and the trick with this insertion was to be all about the timing of three separate releases to gain the maximum impact.

They wanted to ensure that the Serbs did not inadvertently get damaged, for the Sava River flowed from Belgrade to join the Danube near to the *Porţile de Fier*, or Iron Gates, Europe's deepest gorge, gouged between the Balkan Mountains and the Carpathians.

This gorge had been unhelpful in the past, breaking up the Danube at its constricted point. There were a series of cataracts and other obstacles through the section, so over the years there had been a number of deliberate steps taken to improve navigability.

Early attempts opened up the river from the obstacles but left the Iron Gates with such a strong current that boats had to be towed back upriver by locomotives. It was the creation of a large dam and hydro-electric plant in the 1970s, located south of the Romanian city of Orşova, that finally calmed the river and raised the levels almost all the way back up to Belgrade, the Serbian capital. The dam had not been without critics as it permanently interfered with the spawning route of many types of sturgeon, with the obvious outcome in terms of their numbers. Kabitsin liked his caviar, but did not rate any from outside Russia, so he felt that this would have been no great loss.

He would make sure that the still water was inserted below Orşova and for this he sent two of the original containers to his team in Belgrade. They would travel down the E75 from Belgrade to Paraćin, and then turn along the E761 to Vidin in Bulgaria. There should be no border formalities and they would insert the material right where the new bridge across the Danube between Bulgaria and Romania had recently been opened.

Currently there was only two bridges across the Danube linking the two countries. One that had been built sixty years ago between Giurgiu in Romania and Ruse in Bulgaria. Called the Friendship Bridge, it was almost three kilometres long with a two deck-structure, one used for rail and the other a two-lane road.

The recently completed bridge spanned between Calafat in Romania and Vidin in Bulgaria. After these bridges the Danube ran uninterrupted, forming the long border between Bulgaria and Romania and running as such virtually the whole way to the Black Sea. Other than these bridges all traffic had to be carried by ferry between the two nations.

He wanted to be sure to hit the two capitals and so that other than the Serbian event there would be two further insertion points. This introduced something of a timing issue. The bulk of the still water was to be transported up the river from the Black Sea having crossed from Odessa. It would travel to the port of Giurgiu, where it would then be split into two loads, one to travel north to Bucharest and the other south to Sofia. What they did not need was for the Serbian batch to flow downriver too early so that it caught up with these other teams while they were still on the river. The clever part of the plan, so far as Kabitsin was concerned for he had come up with it, was the very means of delivery.

They had acquired two boats from two different brokers, a 35' Sea Ray 355 Sundancer and a 50' Fairline Phantom 50. The two small cabin cruisers had been converted to hold enough fuel for their short journeys and the whole of the rest of the cabin space was given over to a storage tank full of still water. None of this was visible without boarding the boat. Each tank had a radio-controlled outlet and heavy-duty pump to vent out the still water unseen below the waterline.

The two cabin cruisers were already loaded on to a larger boat which had been selected for its powerful davits that could lift and sling the two cruisers down into the river at Giurgiu. The beauty of it all from Kabitsin's viewpoint was that, after the devastation these two vessels would undoubtedly cause, he could simply arrange for his two assets to be recovered and the investment in the boats would not be lost. Despite this he had already added their cost to Pavel's charges and received his approval and payment, so it was definitely a win-win!

The large boat had set sail and the two containers were well on their way to Belgrade. The balance of still water, other than that remaining in the swimming pool, was also underway on its long journey by sea to the Far East. He now bade his farewell to the General, for while he was not planning to be directly in the field, he was travelling to the area to supervise.

He would be based in Sofia so that he could travel readily to at least two of the insertion points if needs be, and perhaps watch the impact of this their largest planned event right at the heart of the expanding European Union. The same EU that competed with, and would soon be pressing right along the borders of, his beloved Russia.

# Chapter 48 - *Virginia, USA*

Mark's team in Langley received an alert. They had previously captured several containers in the Congo and also brought the one back from Turkey. It had been noted that they were marked up in precisely the same manner, so he had left a watch on all ports for anything of a similar description. They had not expected the Russians to use the same approach, but here suddenly appearing on a manifest from the Ukraine to Serbia by air freight were two containers that matched his bulletin.

### Drobeta, Bulgaria

Mark contacted Brain who was already installed neaar the town of Drobeta-Turnu Severin in Romania, hard up against the Serbian-Romanian border and at the start of the stretch that they judged to be 'of interest'.

The improbably long name commemorated a Roman defeat of the Gauls. The Byzantines in celebration had built a Northern Tower, the literal translation of the two last words, and in Roman times *Drobetae* had been the site where Trajan's bridge had been constructed with twenty arches, suspended between stone pillars, to cross the 1200 metre width of the Danube. It was at that time the largest bridge in the Roman Empire, a proud creation of the Greek architect Apollodorus of Damascus, perhaps the main architect of the Pantheon in Rome.

Just like Apollodorus, Brain and his team came to realise quite what a boundary the Danube could prove to be, and why in fact it had acted so effectively as the border for the Roman Empire for quite so long. Though he was only 200 kms from Belgrade, as measured by that annoyingly peripatetic crow, he now faced the real issue of just where to cross to the other side of the river.

Brain gathered up his 'troops' and they drove their two vehicles like crazy. Initially they set off in completely the wrong direction towards Craiva and then had to tear down the other side of the long isosceles triangle to Calafat. He had seen that there he could get a ferry, he was not yet clear if it was a car ferry. The town of Vidin across the river was likely to be large enough to acquire a vehicle if not, and it did appear to have good road connections. Belatedly he had concluded precisely what Kabitsin's locals had thoroughly appreciated through their local knowledge, that the real nature of the Danube was not a picturesque feature, it was a barrier.

The motivation driving them ever faster was that neither he nor Mark had enough pull in the Serbian capital to be able to ask for local assistance; events to the south of Serbia were still all too fresh, too damaging for both the UK and America. Would they get there in time? But for once they were lucky. It proved to be a car ferry and they managed to get the whole team across to Vidin without a problem.

Tom suggested that freight would take a protracted time to get through the airport and local customs so there was no need to rush unduly. Once across the river they decided to split their resources. James would take the bulk of the team to look for a billet in the town with one of the vehicles.

Brain took just one guy with him, assuming that this would be a follow-the-container exercise rather than a fire-fight. They would have to cross borders, and he foresaw no problems there, but entering the freight facility at the airport might create issues, so they left all the weapons with James and his team. The pair of them hared off down the E79 towards Serbia.

# Chapter 49 - *Belgrade, Serbia*

Lev had been ordered to run the Serbian end of things. Kabitsin had insisted on one of his people staying with the still water at all times. So it was Lev and two recruited locals who turned up at the freight terminal with the correct documentation later that day. The locals had greased a few palms and the delivery was being fast-tracked.

Lev left all the talking to the locals trying, as much as possible for someone of his size, to merge into the background. It was not that Serbians and Russians were not cool with each other, just that he didn't want to be remembered as seen at the pick-up.

Brain's companion, Jonesy, was positioned just outside the warehouse watching, Brain waiting with the vehicle nearby. Jonesy ducked out ahead of the Russians and called Brain giving him a description of the big Mitsubishi that they were to follow.

Brain pulled the vehicle up to collect him and they followed the target out of the airport. Brain's second error of the day was that they now had single-handedly to track it right across Belgrade. To do this and remain unnoticed they would really need at least two vehicles, but it was too late for that now.

In the heavy traffic approaching and crossing Belgrade they could sit behind other vehicles and not be too obtrusive, but as they headed south the traffic became thinner and there was much less of it available for their cover. Jonesy kept an eye on the maps and they dropped back as far as they dared from the target between junctions on the E75, then closed up fast to see if it was preparing to make an exit at the next junction. They were surprised when the turn was eventually made as it was back on to the same road that they had travelled earlier, but they soon realised that of course the Russians must have come to the same conclusions that they had earlier as to the best routes.

On this lesser road they decided they could drop well back from the target vehicle, particularly as it was now getting dark and lights were necessary. The vehicle ahead of them had a small crack in the nearside rear light that was quite distinctive. They just had to hope that their hastily hired car wasn't proving equally as distinctive to those who travelled ahead of them.

They were positioned eight vehicles behind the Mitsubishi at the Serbian border post that would let them back into Bulgaria and were surprised to see that their target stopped at the post, where most had just crawled past it as there was no apparent interest being shown by the guards. Documents were exchanged and then they passed on over the border.

When they themselves arrived at the post they found out why. They were stopped and ordered to step out of the vehicle. Clearly the guards had been bribed or given some story that they were up to no good and they could only watch as their target made its way along the road away from them, to heaven knows where.

They were subjected to a brusque search of the vehicle and of themselves, thanking god that they had not brought any weapons with them. The Serb guards asked why they were in a Romanian car but they simply pleaded that they were working there and had been looking at buying property in Serbia or Bulgaria. They waxed lyrical on how cheap houses were locally until the guards' eyes glazed over and their documents were returned to them. The border guards had only been paid to delay them and had no interest in doing more.

**Serbia/Bulgaria border**

Lev had not been sure the Romanian-registered vehicle had been following them but it had done no harm to delay it at the border just in case. He was surprised at how small the bribe had needed to be to get the guard's commitment. The Serbs may not have been keen on the Americans but clearly the greenback dollar was still a craved-for companion here.

He relaxed now as they came towards Vidin. All he had to do was wait on the word from Kabitsin, his confirmation that the two boats had started up the tributaries to their targets, and he could get this all over and done with. Kabitsin was two hundred kilometres away in Sofia, the boats yet to be offloaded, so they had some time to relax. He looked at his watch; hopefully it would all be over by the morning.

If these Bulgarians were becoming pimps to the world, then with luck they'd left some good stuff for him to enjoy back in their homeland.

**Outside Vidin, Bulgaria**

Brain had called earlier and ordered James to find somewhere along the road to identify and then tail the incoming vehicle. They had assessed that the best place for this was where the E761 joined the E79. The original purpose had been so they could alternate in following the Mitsubishi to its destination but they had just heard that they were now on their own. Though Brain had cleared the border he was perhaps a good ten minutes behind the Mitsubishi.

James found a small track that led to a sprinkling of houses and farm buildings. It was just sixty metres from where the two roads crossed. At the junction there appeared to be no road markings to suggest which of the two was considered the major road. His instinct was that the vehicle would carry on across the junction and go on into Vidin, but he could not take the gamble. It was getting late and the traffic was light. They would be sure to spot the vehicle if and when it arrived, and from their vantage point they could watch to see which route it took at the junction.

The Shogun slowed for the junction and did as James had expected, taking the crossing showing only a little caution through the crossroads it carried straight on. James pulled out with no lights and went through the junction picking a pace that would avoid the need for use of brakes as mysterious red flashes would be a huge 'tell' to the car in front if he did have to dab his foot.

As the road took a right it passed what looked like a large cemetery, Tom couldn't help commenting, 'And on the right you will see the dead centre of Vidin' – a 'tumbleweed' moment in their journey.

As they drove through a residential centre the target took a right down towards the riverbank. Just before taking this turn James flicked on his lights as they were now beginning to pick up a deal of traffic in both directions and he had already been flashed by several oncoming cars and trucks.

Brain had called again. He had made up some time on the empty roads, was just crossing the E-75 behind them and was homing in on them.

**Vidin, Bulgaria**

James followed the Mitsubishi along the riverside right through to the other side of the town, out past the location of the planned new bridge, then after about six or seven kilometres it had turned off into an enclosed area. The Bulgarians had invented the Cyrillic alphabet and were naturally proud of it; on the sign at the entrance the British team could just about recognise the characters for Danube something or other, but no more. They could not follow the Mitsubishi in so made a big show of driving on by, but then turned around further up the road and drifted back without lights, pulling in amongst some scrub on the side of the road.

The fourth member of Brain's team was called 'Face' apparently for some resemblance to the 'A-Team' actor, though Tom had to presume this must have been at some time in the distant past. Face got out and reconnoitred the location. Inside he found a sign in English saying 'Danube Camping' but he saw no tents; there appeared however to be a dozen or more bungalows set right alongside the Danube. The Mitsubishi was pulled up outside what looked to be the main building, its occupants were presumably checking in to one of the bungalows. They called Brain to ask if they should go on in, but as he was so close to their position he asked them to wait until he arrived. ETA was three minutes.

A short time later Brain pulled past them, hung a U-ey and drove up tight behind them among the same bushes at the side of the road. He and Jonesy quickly and gratefully received their weapons as Face reported on his recce. He had been back into the campsite and noted that the vehicle had pulled up in front of one of the two bigger bungalows. Personal stuff had been unloaded, but the containers appeared to still be in the Shogun. Brain despatched him back with orders to alert him if there was any sign of the containers being moved towards the river.

As they were finalising the approach they would adopt, they heard an engine start up. Crouched down behind the vehicles they saw that the Mitsubishi was leaving, heading back towards the town.

Brain and his team hastily boarded their vehicle and followed, again without lights. Face came scampering out to confirm that in the Mitsubishi all three guys were aboard with both containers. He clambered into the second vehicle and James set off after the others back towards Vidin.

Now they had two vehicles they could ring a few changes, but both were on Romanian plates which they feared might be something of a beacon in this Bulgarian town. However as they passed into the busy town a swift look around reassured them that there was a 'broad church' of plates in the town, even some Spanish ones. They thought that this was strange until one of the team remembered seeing a construction site board for the new bridge indicating a Spanish company had won the contract.

The targets pulled up in what passed for the centre of the town, parked their vehicle and entered a cheap-looking restaurant, taking a table that gave them a perfect view of their Mitsubishi. The British team parked further up the same street and their spotter, Face again, approached the restaurant. He was able to see and report back by mobile that the three had ordered beers, though they had not yet appeared to show interest in the menus they had been handed.

Brain worked out their approach. There were five of them against the three targets, but Tom was a non-combatant. He had been told he was there to gain experience and insight into the still water, though Brain suspected he realised that in truth he had made him come along just because he could.

There was a huge opportunity for collateral damage here. Brain realised that the other restaurant users or any innocent passers-by might well get caught in any crossfire so they had to settle for a take-down at the moment the three left the restaurant. With luck they might be well-pissed by then too. He positioned his team where they would not attract attention, then gave each of them each the point to move forward to at the first sign that the three targets were making ready to leave.

Face's next call indicated that they were already on their fourth beers, commenting that they were thirsty bastards for people planning to deny any basic water to others. Then a little later he confirmed that they had ordered food and yet more drinks.

One of Brain's team had a simple objective. James was equipped with the heavier 'artillery' and would make sure that, whatever else happened, the vehicle would not be allowed to leave. But he had to be mindful of the still water containers. The others would take down the three men while trying to minimise any fall-out to the locals. There had been no sign of any local police, so they judged it unlikely that anyone else would choose to get involved.

As soon as they had finished eating the three called for the bill, paid up and headed for the toilets at the rear of the restaurant. But it all started to go wrong in those toilets. The two Serbs finished up and commented that the Russian, still going strong, pissed like a horse. Not being the sort of guys who would hang around urinals watching others about their business, they left the restaurant ahead of Lev. The watching team could not take out just the two of them so had to bide their time

The pair climbed into the front of the Mitsubishi and started the engine; being in playful mood the driver decided to pull a little way up the road to annoy the dour Russian. The watchers were confused as to what action to take, but Brain decided that he must give the signal to proceed. He figured that as the main issue was the water it was time for all four of his team to make a move on the Shogun.

While Brain's team moved on the vehicle Tom acted instinctively, not thinking of the consequences. He had recognised Lev as he entered the restaurant, remembered the big Russian holding and abusing Stevie, passing the knife across her throat, and he was damned if the man was going to be allowed to get away again. He raced through the restaurant, stooped to pick up a fire extinguisher and crashed in through the toilet door.

Lev had finished his mammoth session, zipped up and was just about to pull on the door when two things surprised him. Several gun shots rang out from outside and then before he could respond the door crashed in on him. The very briefest of warnings that the gunfire had provided must have alerted him, so that he was slightly more prepared to respond as the door was forced open inwards on to him.

He jumped back reaching for the gun which was secured at the small of his back. Tom pressed on through the door, first kicking hard at his opponent's shins, then striking out with the extinguisher. Pressing any short-term advantage he might have against the bigger man, he kept his anger focused on maintaining a headlong forward motion driving Lev back against the wall of the urinal.

Lev had finally managed to get his hand on the grip of his weapon and was trying to pull it free; one hand busy he was not able to stop his head crashing hard against the old cistern that served the urinal. It came away from the wall and crashed down on his shoulder cascading water and rust all over him, but he kept working at releasing his gun. It was obvious what he was trying to achieve so Tom smashed the extinguisher at Lev's upper arm several times and then swept it across his face, smashing it against the bridge of his nose.

As Lev's gun came free his hand spasmed from the blow to his nose and he lost purchase on the wet pistol. It clattered down into the gulley of the urinal, sliding down the slope the same way his piss had flowed earlier. Defending himself from another blow to his face he could do nothing to stop the gun skidding out through the ragged hole punched inelegantly in the thin breeze-blocked outer wall.

As his gun was clearly no longer available to him, he reversed the process and charged Tom, using his extra bulk to push him through the stall door of the WC. He had instinctively realised that by forcing Tom into the small cubicle he had also ensured that any freedom of movement for either of them was now very constricted.

Tom could not get any momentum into a swing of the extinguisher at the Russian. The cursed cubicle door on the side made it even more difficult, so he lashed out with his other arm towards the bigger man's face, but Lev parried it with a strong blow that numbed Tom's forearm. It was all coming apart, where were Brain and his team?

Lev grabbed at the extinguisher, but to achieve this he had to lean into the cubicle and Tom didn't hesitate to deliver a 'Glasgow kiss'; all his anger still lending him strength, he nutted him so hard that his own skull rang inside like a bell. Lesser opponents would have at least had the decency to stagger at the direct hit, but Lev just smiled in appreciation of the tactic, surprised this little Brit had the balls for such a blow.

They were both aware that the gunshots outside had stopped and knew one or the other's colleagues would soon be arriving. Perhaps Lev had less confidence in his crew, but he suddenly seemed to grow bored with the struggle, stepped back and using all of his body delivered a punch to the top of Tom's head.

Tom had barely recovered from his own head butt and this additional blow made him stagger, stumble; he was fighting to remain conscious, shaking his head to shrug off the blow. This was all Lev needed to take away the extinguisher. Tom struggled to focus, his mind was waiting for the Russian to step in and finish it for him, there was to be no last minute arrival of the cavalry. All he could hear were some loud bangs, too dull to be shots, and some other noise his addled wits could not immediately recognise.

Staggering out from the stall he was just in time to see Lev who had smashed the extinguisher through the thin outer wall of the room and was kicking out further blocks to make a bigger hole in it. Bending low to crouch under the remaining blocks he made his escape.

Tom's mind knew there was an instant when he should have kicked out at the man's exposed backside and groin, but his body could not process the necessary nerves, muscles and sinews to make the thought become action. He felt a profound weariness, his early anger gone, replaced with a need to slip into unconsciousness, but he must not allow that to happen.

He turned and stumbled out through the restaurant to see what had happened at the front. The restaurant patrons were all out of their seats, standing by the entrance so he had some difficulty pushing through, but they seemed to accept that he was part of the "floor show" and so either respectfully or fearfully let him pass.

He was relieved to see he was on the side of the victors, not that he felt too good personally. Brain quickly explained that they had come up on the vehicle from both sides, James had sprayed a long burst over the top and that had been enough for the driver to keep both hands clearly in view gripping the wheel, particularly when Brain himself smashed the driver's window and pressed his assault rifle against his head.

The other Serb had been a little more resilient and pushing the door open had dropped to the floor, reaching for his weapon. Jonesy had double-tapped and killed him before he could get to it.

Tom was re-gathering his senses as Brain ordered James and Jonesy to move the Shogun before the local authorities arrived. Leaving the dead man in the street, they hurried to their vehicles to get away from the scene as quickly as possible.

The three vehicles met up again outside the town and, with Jonesy keeping a gun on the remaining Serb, they opened the rear door of the Shogun, unloaded the two containers and spilled the contents into a gravel run-off at the side of the road.

They then drove fast for the border, stopping about five kilometres short of it. There they parked up the Mitsubishi and directed the Serb to climb out and position himself against the side of it and face away from them. Terrified he started crying and pleading fully expecting that this was the end of the road for him.

While he had no view of their actions they tossed his set of car keys off into some scrubland and then turned him to face towards them and proceeded to mime what they had done. Keeping a gun trained on him and leaving him stranded, they climbed back into their two vehicles and carried on towards the border. Shortly before reaching it they emptied and dismantled their weapons and took joy in tossing the components off into the surrounding scrubland and subsequently dumping all of their ammunition along the route up to the border crossing. Though Brain made sure he retained one pistol well concealed under a seat, just in case.

Finally they began to relax, they would be able to report their success once they were through the border into Serbia and had switched vehicles. Adrenalin had done its job; they had experienced both fight and flight, heart rates were now down, pupils back to normal, the only fight left in them was to avoid falling asleep.

Tom was unsuccessful in his battle with sleep, his final thought being that it had been a job well done, disaster averted again! Brain however was disturbed that it had appeared to be far too easy. He had a nagging feeling that all was not right, but could not manage to give any substance to the thought.

# Chapter 50 - *Vidin, Bulgaria*

Lev called Kabitsin to explain what had happened. He was convinced that there must be another spy in their midst, perhaps Dmitry had not been the mole, or not the only mole? How had they picked up on them so quickly?

Kabitsin had hard information about Dmitry's betrayal so he was sceptical; since the Dmitry issue he had been very careful as to who knew anything of their plans. He thought about it, but given Lev's belief that he had been followed from Belgrade he concluded that it must have been the airfreighting of the containers, they must have been traced from those. He had considered changing them but decided it was unnecessary in friendly Serbian territory.

Though he reached this conclusion there was still that nagging feeling, a paranoia that someone was out there trying to get them. In this case of course it wasn't paranoia, there really were a number of somebodies out there, very determined to ruin their plans. What should he do next?

He had never believed in any of these side-shows anyway. He couldn't trust anyone to do a simple job, it was hardly brain surgery to go and pour some still water into a river. OK, so Pavel was one of the good guys and he wanted to do his best for him, but they were wasting time and putting themselves at risk with all this running around the world for others.

He ordered Lev to get himself a vehicle and start driving east, then called each of the cabin cruisers. Eventually they had both been offloaded, although apparently the EU paperwork had been like some lengthy ritual dance. Kabitsin assumed that these two new "converts" to the EU party had not yet learned to follow the Italian approach to all EU laws and agreements, which was just to ignore them and carry on as they always had done. But he knew they'd soon learn once they had been fully subsumed into the club.

The first boat was still barrelling its way up the Danube from Giurgiu and was near Nikopol, still a way to go before it could begin to think about turning south down the River Iskür towards Sofia. The other had made much better speed downriver and already turned into the Arges. It was close to Budesti, about a third of the way towards Bucharest.

To hell with it, he thought, why should he care about these little people? Romania and Bulgaria were nowhere on any league table that mattered, not politically, not scientifically, not economically, not culturally. He couldn't even recall, despite their sporting fervour, that either of them had delivered much in the way of football or other sporting glories.

Romania had Nadia Comăneci of course, with her seven maximums at the Montreal Olympics, but she was probably already a grandmother by now. Russia's own Nellie Kim had matched her with three golds; she also achieved a perfect 10, and she was a real woman, not some drug-expanded child. If challenged, Kabitsin would not have known, or accepted as fact, that Kim was born in Tajikistan of a Korean father and a Tatar mother. His racism was very selective when it came to claiming prizes for Mother Russia.

He also recalled that the Romanian football team had briefly flourished in the mid 1990s, but he personally couldn't recall a single famous Bulgarian sportsman. Bulgaria did have one claim to fame of which he was very much aware – somehow they had managed to join the side of the loser in both of the $20^{th}$ century's world wars, surely that must stamp them out as big-time losers!

Today most of their people were spread around the world, almost catching up with Ireland, so that more Bulgarians lived outside their native country than in it!

What did he owe any of them? He packed to leave and called the two boats advising them to find the next sensible place to moor, and then to get ashore and activate the venting of their tanks.

### Nikopol, Bulgaria

The first cabin cruiser was still passing Nikopol on the Bulgarian bank when they received the instruction. Kabitsin ordered Lev to head for the town so he could collect that insertion team, and then move across the bridge to Romania to pick up the others. It would be a long drive but Lev had let him down – again!

Nikopol had always been at the edge of things, which meant perversely that it ended up being at the centre of things. It had been a village at the very north of the region of Moesia in Roman times, part of the Empire's northern border, then much later it was still the northern border of something, this time of the Byzantine Empire.

It had also been the site of the largest and last large-scale crusade of the Middle Ages, the Battle of Nicopolis. A smaller Ottoman force had defeated the assembled might of the Holy Roman Empire, the Knights of St John, and large groups from each of England, France, Hungary, Poland, Scotland, Switzerland, and Wallachia, not to forget those representing the Republics of Genoa and Venice.

The city withstood a siege from perhaps 120,000 crusaders who were supposed to be on their way to relieve Constantinople. These crusaders were then unexpectedly set upon by 60,000 Turks, defeated, and with this the taste for crusades appeared to wither, as many of those states preferred to fight each other in the future rather than combine against the Turks.

The team tied up and paid generously for a long-term mooring to the west of the town on the upriver portion. It took Lev a little over three hours to reach them. As soon as he did they triggered the venting of the tank and set off back away from the river to pick up the E83 cross the bridge to Giurgiu.

### Budesti, Romania

The second boat turned back to Budesti on the east bank of the Argeş. Its only claim to fame would have pleased Kabitsin as it boasted the highest proportion of Romani people, what Kabitsin would immediately have transliterated into gypsies. Such a high number lived there that it became the only place where Romanian and Romani languages were considered equally official; signs and other formal business were expressed in both.

They moored where the Dâmbovita River joined the Argeş and dawn was breaking as Lev reached them and they released their cargo. Job done they then all made their way towards Bucharest airport just 40 kms away, not one of them at all concerned as to what was happening in the wake of their discharges.

**Bulgaria-Romania**

The Danube ran east from Nikopol and the conversion to still water snaked around a series of islands in the river. It passed around both sides of Ostrov Belene, a large island that had been decided at some stage in the past to be part of Bulgaria. Just past Svishtov it reached the Yantra and spread up that tributary as far as Byala before its progress was halted when a membrane formed. It swept under the bridge between Ruse and Giurgiu shortly after Lev had crossed it to reach the second team.

Soon it was joined by the second still water flow that had come down the Argeş. At the second site it had also replicated upriver and along the Dâmbovita tributary right into the very outskirts of Bucharest.

The combined flows pressed on until the river and the international border parted company at Silistra and the Danube turned north into Romania.

Ahead of it lay the Danube Delta that spanned parts of Romania and the Ukraine, a rich wetland area to be despoiled. But for some reason its spread halted near Călărasi. Just as in Kazakhstan it was something present in the waters or some river feature here that made the still water return to its normal refreshing state.

Behind it was devastation, more than 15,000 deaths was the eventual official total. When the news of this reached Tom he wondered how it could be such a round number. This made it sound more a rough estimate. Knowing politicians the world over he assumed they would be understating the actual figures. And no one had even bothered to count the animals, fish and plant life that had flowed dead into the Black Sea.

The news channels and press were very quickly referring to this as a 'modern plague', one that left all the organs of the body dried up and withered. Given the numbers of dead birds, many feared the earlier global concern about bird flu; reports suggested this might have been the cause, triggering off mass culls of poultry and other birds to add to the animal death count.

Experts were then rolled out by the governments on newscasts to gainsay the talk of plague, pointing out that the Black Death had killed 20 million across Europe and as yet this outbreak did not appear to be spreading further.

This was then followed by a brief public witch-hunt for the corporate entity or government body that had dumped something noxious into the river. Al-Qa'ida was tossed around as the organisation to blame, but then dismissed as the usual knee-jerk demonisation.

None of this stopped the mass cancellation of travel plans by fellow Europeans to all parts of Eastern Europe. Most Americans, with their poor grasp of the geography, cancelled all and any trips to anywhere in Europe, as they had during the Gulf Wars.

Inevitably within a week a story about a baby panda born in a zoo, a disreputable corporate financial officer in a major American corporation and, most effectively, an A-list celebrity couple's 'conscious uncoupling' chased any thoughts of the disaster from the pages and screens.

# Chapter 51 - *London, UK*

Deep in several corridors of power they knew precisely what had happened but had judged there was absolutely no benefit in stopping the early and conflicting speculations that were out there in the media. After all there was no point in fuelling the panic by revealing that the reality of the actual threat was worse than any of the speculation.

The acceptance of some unknown effect that appeared to have gone away was judged to be preferable to the likely wholesale panic that would result if the public knew that there might be a need to secure the water supply, particularly as government advisors were not coming up with any simple solutions to the problem that might help to make things sound any better.

The Foreign Secretary called the meeting to order and started the session by asking, 'Professor, when I raised the subject of desalination previously you seemed to dismiss it?'

'The first issue is logistics, not too bad here because we are an island with the sea all around us. Unfortunately places having the greatest need for water are often well away from the coast, then the costs of transportation to the point of need will prove prohibitive. Remember we are talking of water here. We all know what it tries to do to pipelines and containers, so there would be an on-cost of maintenance and replacement and not just the one-time cost of getting such a pipeline laid.'

Sir Joseph commented, 'Surely that's just a question of will, if we need them then the price has to be met?'

'You should understand there are several different processes used for desalination; the most common requires a great deal of heat to be generated, so for this we have to face very high energy costs. That's why around a quarter of the desalination is done in the Middle East where they literally do have the fuel reserves to burn!'

The Foreign Secretary asked, 'You also mentioned before some problems with brine?'

'The process does have a by-product which is the brine, or highly concentrated sea water if you like. If it were just pumped back into the sea then this would harm local ecosystems. Filter-feeders wouldn't be able to survive that intense a salinity. The brine sinks to the bottom, a bit like our still water, so it would attack reefs, plant life and all the bottom-feeders first. So yes there is an issue as to just what we do with this by-product.'

'Needs must, needs must,' muttered Sir Joseph.

'Don't forget the high energy consumption I mentioned that would be required, and this has another by-product, of course – the greenhouses gases that it would emit. Here we are trying to reduce these, desalination would set back all the targets we have here, considerably.'

'You said there were other processes?'

'Well the Russians are trying nuclear-powered desalination.'

Sir Joseph smiled, 'I wonder how they came up with that one, perhaps their habit of dropping nuclear waste and reactors into the salty sea?'

The Professor ignored him. 'Maybe the best hope we have is a new osmosis technology, similar to the thing that led young Carter to his approach to stop still water. A membrane is used to have the salt pass from the less saline water through into the saltier sea water. This approach wouldn't need the energy and greenhouse gas content of the conventional process, and it's quite inexpensive, perhaps 25 pence per cubic metre. But there is still the waste issue and the transportation costs.'

'It's not without hope as an approach?'

'It's going to be a lot like the way we had to wait until we could afford to exploit North Sea oil; we waited until world oil prices made it economically viable. That could well happen here too. But of course that does nothing to remove the fundamental problem of securing this desalinated water from an attack by still water.'

The Foreign Secretary asked, 'Presumably the only approach would be to secure enough of our key water reservoirs, isolate them and distribute this in bottles and bulk containers?'

The Professor smiled. 'Sorry to say, that's unlikely to work. The very idea of containing water in a closed system means you would have to spend energy and chemicals making sure it didn't stagnate. Just think of your garden pond. Leave it untouched for a month and you'd have all sorts of algae and other problems.'

Sir Joseph persisted, 'The suggestion of bottling would work if we can find some way of maintaining the water in motion?'

The Professor paused at the side of the table. 'Currently, we have bottled waters and they are usually from one of four sources – glacial, from springs, from wells or through treated waterworks where we clean it up, perhaps add fluoride and so on. Then of course there are the sparkling waters where carbon dioxide has been added.'

Sir Joseph quipped, 'Didn't Coca-Cola, some years back, draw water directly from our taps, a bit like Del Boy in *Only Fools and Horses*! Though I believe Coca-Cola ran it through a treatment process, and it was this process that added problems rather than improving upon it.'

He smiled at the thought and continued, 'If we look at bottling, the US Pacific Institute calculated that their domestic use of bottled water was pretty damaging. First, the process of making the plastic for the water bottles consumed some 17 million barrels of oil per year and emitted 2.5 million tonnes of $CO^2$. Then, depending on where you stop counting, the process consumes three to five litres of water for each litre bottle produced, the higher number being where you add in the cost of cooling the production plant.'

'They found that 90% of the bottles were then not recycled, so 90% of these factors are lost for all time; here we're even worse, as we recycle only some 8% of our bottles. That same report calculated that one imported litre bottle of water had a true water footprint of 6.74 litres.'

'My god that's an awful set of statistics!' The Foreign Minister was beginning to see that there appeared to be no simple route to resolve this matter.

'This is of course all before we add in any energy costs committed to transporting it to the consumer. To get the more popular waters to London for example means a 930 kilometre journey for Evian which comes from near Geneva and represents the largest market share at around 10%. Even the relatively local Buxton water takes 273 kms to reach here, they have around a 3% market share. Our own figures show our use of bottled water generates 33,000 tonnes of $CO^2$ emissions. Then we ship most of our waste plastic to be recycled in China to add to the $CO^2$ we generate from this penchant for bottled water.'

'That's incredible, I had no idea.'

Sir Joseph added, 'Not to mention that we'd be dependent on acquiring all that oil or gas down pipelines most likely from the Russians!'

The Foreign Secretary was at last beginning to share the spymaster's concerns about the Russians. They did begin to seem rather complicit in the actions of this Brotherhood. She could not believe that they were so inept that they couldn't keep their own people in check, something the tsars and commissars had always managed to achieve in the past. Why did they have to lose the knack on her watch?

'Of course sourcing the water for bottling is not as straightforward as it sounds. Again in the States there was a significant case when Perrier applied to increase the withdrawals from a spring in Florida by six-fold for one of its bottled waters. Fears that Tampa Bay's supply, some sixty kilometres downstream, would be affected saw their request rejected. We're back to riparian strife. How do you draw your proposed bottled water so that those already using that source are not denied supply?'

Sir Joseph added, 'Well, we've privatised our water here, given it away frankly, to the French and other European companies. We would just have to nationalise it, all water would need to be owned and managed by the nation. Pollution or misuse controlled and policed. Hoarding an offence...'

The Foreign Secretary commented, 'I can just see that as my legacy. Margaret Thatcher's later career was haunted by her decision to stop the school milk. They called her "Thatcher, Thatcher, Milk Snatcher" at the time. I can't even imagine what I'd be called.'

Sir Joseph started to say something and she snapped, 'And I don't want any suggestions, thank you very much!'

The Professor returned to an earlier point. 'Hoarding is in fact not an option once you bottle water. The sell-by-date is not the confidence trick that it is with many foodstuffs. Leave your water in its plastic container and it becomes contaminated. The pollutants are phthalates, the stuff that makes the plastic flexible, which can damage lungs, liver and kidneys, or bisphenol A, an anti-oxidant in the plastic which can damage fertility.'

Sir Joseph smiled. 'So we would have to go back to glass bottles!'

The Professor nodded. 'Glass is recyclable. It accounts for, let me see, about 7% of all UK waste. But there are huge energy costs involved in the extreme temperatures that are required in its manufacture. Not only that, but the fuels to reach those temperatures of course give off $CO^2$, 1.8m tonnes are the figures I have seen and that was way back at the beginning of the Oughties. And what we would need is to increase that production many, many times over to replace all those plastic water bottles.'

'Is there any other approach?'

'It's all clutching at straws I am afraid. Just methods to take advantage of the normal cycle for short-term benefits like extracting water from clouds, distributing huge numbers of rain butts, capturing overnight dew and coastal fogs, abandoning high water-content agriculture. Then there's a whole series of water-saving schemes you might propose, like not running the tap when you clean your teeth, bricks in cisterns, sharing a bath. Pretty desperate and ineffective stuff in reality.'

'So what you're saying is that we either have to find some way of destroying all this still water or negotiate?' asked the Foreign Minister.

Sir Joseph smiled. 'Actually we only need to destroy those people who plan to abuse it, not the stuff itself. It is intrinsically what it is; it's just the abuse we need to stop. Who knows what other applications there might be? That's why we're pressing very fiercely for the Russian administration to act against this Brotherhood.'

# Chapter 52 - *Virginia, USA*

Mark's CIA team received a new alarm, not from their port-watch this time, but from their doctored picture of the Saigon embassy. The subroutine that had been hidden inside the code of the picture had migrated into a computer, and this had just come on line somewhere.

The software was like a reverse Internet spider, crawling back through the Web, leaving little threads as it went, like Hansel leaving his trail of white pebbles through the forest. There still needed to be some human insight applied to following this track, particularly as the user had probably taken steps to remain unidentified in the first place.

Mark's team worked at the task and concluded that there was a high degree of probability that the PC was in the Odessa, Ukraine area. There was always the chance there was clever routing from elsewhere through the Black Sea city, but it all stacked up for Mark. Twice Kabitsin had disappeared from nearby Istanbul and the shipment to Belgrade appeared to have come from the Ukraine too. He drove his people on to narrow it down and use all the pressure they could apply on the local internet service provider, and on the local telecom supplier to try to trace back to the source.

Tom was called and brought up to speed with what they had and the two agreed that neither could get there within a half-day, and that might just be too late. It was worth a try to have Sir Joseph call his counterpart in the Ukraine, in the hope that he could assist and maybe ultimately assault the location once it could be identified.

They discussed at length the fact that the Ukraine, still had many direct links at so many levels with Russia and the other member states; the events in Crimea had shown this. Did this connection mean the Brotherhood, being Russian, would be tipped off by sympathetic Ukrainian authorities working directly with the very same Russian departments that the Brotherhood had evidently penetrated?

Sir Joseph had met recently with the head of the SBU, (*Sluzhba Bezpeky Ukrayiny,* the Ukrainian Security Service), and believed him to be sound. The organisation had indeed been formed from ex-KGB individuals originally, but a number of purges and changes of director later, it was now an autonomous operation that could be trusted – to a degree.

# Chapter 53 - *Odessa, Ukraine*

Mark's team had been able to whittle the location down to a small area of the city and the Ukranian SBU was able to take it from there right back to an individual house. Surveillance had seen some minor comings and goings but nothing either to confirm or deny that there was any secret group ensconced inside.

As locals they were fully aware of the catacombs in the area, some 2,500 kms had been estimated as the total for these tunnels, serviced by hundreds of entrances and exits. In WWII the partisans had made fools of the German occupying force, striking from deep within this labyrinth, and much earlier the slave traders had successfully managed to hide women in them before shipping them to the slave markets in what was then Constantinople.

A large squad had been sent into the tunnels to secure any exit from below and they reported back that the tunnels near to the house appeared to have been walled in. They retreated out to a wider perimeter in the hope of capturing anyone emerging from any hidden escape route that may have been prepared.

They had some idea of the likely layout above ground and the assault team went in via two ground floor windows with others going down through the roof. It was a smooth operation and they captured six individuals in various parts of the house and the catacomb laboratory below.

General Goncharenko was the star captive; his patrician appearance and his reaction to capture stamped him out as the only senior person present. The others were clearly either 'heavies' or lab technicians. The assault team also seized several computers and many files which they were now working their way through, having first established that there were no security measures on the PCs to corrupt or encrypt the files. Clearly the Brotherhood had not considered the possibility of being discovered and had taken few precautions.

Mark assumed that the gangsters at the top were not democratic enough to talk with or listen to any IT advisers, and the General was from a past era where computing was still perceived as some religion practised by a high priesthood with a language all of its own.

Mark had flown in for the interrogation of the General, who had proven very good at resisting their direct questions but he was frail and his inquisitors had to keep breaking off to give the old man time to recover. He held out for hours, but started to get tripped up when Mark arrived with his more detailed knowledge of what had been happening.

They made the General confused, and he began to wonder whether Kabitsin too had been arrested. How else would this young American know so much of their plans? Kabitsin had said that he was 'playing' the young man, but had he just been hiding the fact that he had already sold out?

Eventually the General's own replies actually influenced the line of questioning to take, and they were able to nurture and then take advantage of his uncertainties. He clearly believed that Kabitsin was a jumped-up low-life who would sell out his own grandfather. The General started to suspect that maybe that was his own role, the very grandfather who had been sold down the river.

His eventual capitulation was as much based upon his own confusion as to anything that was happening to him. His breakdown, together with the material gleaned from the files, gave them much of the information they needed. They found the abandoned swimming pool and established that it contained still water, and Mark arranged for a device to be brought to Odessa to deal with this material. In addition they were in possession of all the plans from the Brotherhood members, including Mark's own phoney plan for an attack on the Mekong.

This was where the General had become most vague; his exhausted mind and stressed body were confused much of the time by now, but on the subject of the Mekong he was even more muddled. It became clear that there were two planned assaults on this river, one of which was Mark's own fictional approach, but behind the General's woolliness it would appear that Kabitsin already had his own plan for this river. Mark was delighted that their analysis had hit on the correct river basin, but sadly they were in no way any nearer to knowing where along its 5,000 kms length Kabitsin's attack might be.

It was evident from the papers they found that there had been more material created in the pool and it was from these documents that they learned about the use of the cabin cruisers on the Danube. Mark arranged that these boats were found and impounded but there still appeared to be some of the still water unaccounted for. There were small quantities gone astray from the water harvested from the Arctic and Novosibirsk and also a significant amount missing from the new production quantities made in the pool. They had to conclude that these were already on their way to the Mekong or elsewhere.

The SBU team assisted Mark to gain access to all the manifests of boats and planes that had left the Odessa area, but nothing emerged that appeared to relate to the Brotherhood or to Kabitsin. Where was the still water? Where were they planning to insert it into the Mekong? And, just where the hell was Kabitsin?

# BOOK FOUR

**The World Water Council** report on water for the 21$^{st}$ century, March 2000:

*'In the next two decades the use of water by humans will increase by about 40% and 17% more water than is available will be needed to grow the world's food...'*

**John Louma** in 'Water Thieves' published 2004:

*'Multinational companies now run water systems for 7 per cent of the world's population, and analysts say that figure could grow to 17 per cent by 2015. Private water management is estimated to be a $200 billion business, and the World Bank, which has encouraged governments to sell off their utilities to reduce public debt, projects it could be worth $1 trillion by 2021.'*

# Chapter 54 - *Jinghong, China*

Yunnan Province was a place of plenty. The most south-westerly corner of China, it is located right on the Tropic of Cancer. Yunnan, literally means 'south of the cloud mountains' for very obvious reasons as its horizons have undeniably Himalayan proportions.

Its terrain stretches from virtually down at sea level to almost 7,000 metres above it. It is home to an amazing selection of plants; thousands of varieties are arrayed across its four quite distinct temperate zones – rubber, tea, and fruits are there in quantity. Many are ancient varieties, some dating all the way back to the Ice Age, with a large number being used, mixed or developed as medicines.

There is also plentiful wildlife there – tigers, elephants, gaurs, hornbills, peacocks... It is also the site of one of the earliest fossils yet found in China of a homo erectus, the *Yuanmou* Man.

Criss-crossed by the Yangtze, Pearl, Lancang, Salween, Irawaddy and Red Rivers the province enjoys four times the water per head of population than China is able to claim nationally, this also means it has the most tremendous potential for hydro-electric power.

Massive mineral resources are there too, supplying the province with the largest Chinese deposits of lead, tin, zinc and other more esoteric materials.

It is therefore somewhat surprising that the many distinct ethnic groups that manage to co-exist peaceably there are able to be listed among the very poorest in China.

Lev had been ordered to arrive good and early in Xishuangbanna. The lengthy name meant twelve thousand fields in the local Dai dialect, harking right back to the 13th and 14th century Yuan Dynasty, where a *banna* was an administrative division for taxation purposes. Even here in this backwoods, and back in that distant past, the tax man could not be avoided!

He and his team were staying at Jinghong and masquerading as tourists while they set their plans in motion. They had joined an excursion that took them to the summit of Manfeilong Hill to see an impressive series of pagodas, eight of them around a central main pagoda. White and topped with golden pinnacles, they were designed to look like fresh new bamboo shoots pushing out of the earth.

The shrine there was the tour guide's *pièce de resistance*, it was a footprint in the rock that she claimed was that of Sakyamuni. Lev shared Kabitsin's disdain for religion but it was hard here to avoid reference to Sakyamuni Buddha, the living Buddha.

This Buddha had summed up his teachings in one of the earliest 'mission statements' by saying, 'I teach about suffering and the way to end it.' Lev laughed to his team as he suggested that this was their purpose too, to stop suffering.

They drove through a spectacular area of paddy fields punctuated with tropical rainforest to visit a picturesque Dai village. The Dais made up around a third of the population in Xishuangbanna. The guide waxed lyrical about the special regard that the Dai held for water. 'For them it is the symbol of holiness, goodness, purity and brightness. In raising a cup to another, a Dai will call out "Water", if a Dai family moves into a new house, friends and family help them to carry in their belongings calling out "Water, water, water"!'

They had come specifically to see the village well which was indeed an ornate structure with a tower and fence to both cover and secure the water. They were shown how water was drawn using long-handled wooden or bamboo scoops. Their guide explained that the water was kept clean by the structure and no cattle were allowed to use it, there was no washing of clothes permitted, children were not even allowed to play by it.

They had arrived in this region at an appropriate time, for the Dais were holding their major festival of the year. The morning excursion had been scheduled so that they could all get back in time to attend that day's dragon boat races. These were being held on what the locals called the Lancang River, but so far as Lev was concerned it was the Mekong.

Kabitsin had found that the Mekong was extremely mysterious in terms of its source, its course, its length and its huge variety of names. The Chinese indicated they believed its source was at Mount Guozongmucha, where it began life as the *Zayaqu*. Through Tibet it was called the *Dza Chu*, then here in Yunnan it became the *Lancang* or the 'turbulent river'. However the Chinese did have a name they used for the river as a whole that was something close to Mekong, they call it the *Meigong*. In Laos it became the *Maè Nam Khong*; in Cambodia it was either *Mékôgk* or more simply called the big river, *Tonie Thom*. Only in Vietnam did the name for the whole river become more obvious as the *Mé Kông*, but even there its various parts were known as the *Tiền Giang* or Front river, *Hậu Giang* or Back river and *Sông Cửu Long* or the 'river of nine dragons' because where it reached the South China Sea it formed a delta with nine main estuaries.

Kabitsin had decided that they should switch their original Myanmar sites and come here, first and foremost because they feared that the General might have given away the location of the original plan. Another reason for his decision was that it was the closest they could get to where the Mekong left China to form the border between Myanmar and Laos. Finally it was one of the few open borders that China permitted anywhere along its massive frontier.

The team would be able to add the still water here and record its progress travelling from Jinghong along the border area, and then through the infamous Golden Triangle. Once this was done they would then move on to Kyaing Ton in Myanmar where they would exit via Taunggyi, under the guise of being

Tyazhpromexport personnel working for the cast iron plant that was being developed there by the Russian company.

But for the afternoon they were caught up in the swimming races and dragon boat racing. There was a huge fair and the locals were festooned in amazingly colourful costumes. The local girls were attractively dressed in long sheath dresses, with flowers in their hair and each holding a colourful parasol. After a few glasses of the local corn-based liquor served in bamboo tubes, the girls began to look even better to the Russian team.

The river craft were long narrow boats with a raised prow and stern each with at least twenty rowers in bright uniforms. The boats' ornate and colourful designs were intended to make them resemble dragons as they swept through the river waters.

The race was a cacophony of shouting, those in the boats urging each other to greater speeds, those on the shore shouting for their favourites, and all these colours spread out amid rainbows caused by the rising spray in the sunshine.

Lev turned to Vlad, one of his closer team members, to say, 'Can't wait to see them trying to paddle through our still water. Pity we didn't know about all this in time to have some real fun.'

The dragon boat winners were greeted with bowls of rice wine and sweets were thrown from shore to the other boat crews. Each race over, the noise did not abate as those ashore banged on traditional gongs and Dai drums, *xiangjiao gu,* each made to resemble an elephant's foot. They played bamboo flutes, *lusheng,* and still more were firing rockets, *gaosheng,* all around the area. This was not some tired tourist attraction, this was uninhibited fun, an amazingly vibrant display of simple, perhaps even naïve, enthusiasm as the locals unreservedly threw all their energies and joy into their special festival.

Lev was already deep into his cups by mid-afternoon. The corn concoction was stronger than it looked and it had taken its toll on even this hardened vodka drinker.

He and Vlad had come upon a popular and innocent game that was being played by two long lines of young locals. The young men formed up in one line, with the other made up of young girls who faced them and threw miniature bean bags or *Diu Bao.* These colourful cotton bags with two ribbons streaming behind them were called love pouches. Tossed between the lines to a background of giggles and shouts, particular favourites were sought out, messages passed within the pouch and the whole game was carried out as a piece of youthful fun.

Lev found that he was focusing on one girl who seemed to stand out from the crowd. It wasn't that she was any more attractive or better dressed than the others, it was just that she knew how to use what she had, just a little more obviously than the rest. Maybe it was something about the way she moved, gestured and smiled that had caught his attention, but he decided he wanted her.

He lurched through the line of young men, pushing several roughly aside, and strode up to her taking her right off her feet into a big bear hug and then kissing her neck and face. The crowd was horrified by this crass intrusion into their innocent event. It was such an unprecedented shock that they took a little time to react, not quite believing this could happen on today of all days. Two or three of the young lads closest in line rushed up and started to slap ineffectually at the huge Russian. He turned, still holding her with one arm, and struck out at the boys managing to land several heavy blows.

Now more youths joined the fray and the first few working men were beginning to arrive to assist them. They kept a respectful arm's-length away but formed up in a circle around him. The adrenalin rush had sluiced out the effects of the alcohol and he turned to look at each of them, completely confident of his ability to handle the situation.

He goaded them in Russian to step forward and try their luck. When no one seemed ready to do so, he provoked them by ripping the girl's simple dress from neck to waist. When she screamed and tried to cover herself he slapped her with the back of his hand.

As he did so, one man attacked him from behind slamming an elephant drum to the back of his head. There was no real weight in the instrument and it served only to infuriate Lev. He turned and rushed at his assailant but was stopped by another who stepped forward wielding a large wicked-looking machete.

Now more men were arriving hastily gathering up assorted weapons and he realised he had to start reassessing the situation. His concentration having moved on to the crowd, the girl gratefully seized her opportunity and wriggled away from him to run outside the circle of men where she was assisted in covering herself up, led away by her friends.

He looked across at Vlad who was clearly not planning to come to his aid but appeared to be watching to see if Lev could handle the situation. Perhaps he was just watching to see him fail. None of the rest of his team appeared to be anywhere nearby.

Assessing all this in an instant he was back to evaluating his would-be assailants. The streetwise Lev immediately selected the quadrant that appeared to have fewer real weapons and where the individuals looked less likely to know what they were doing. He charged that point with a deep guttural growl.

Some of those in that part of the ring had good self-preservation skills and were quick enough to leap back quickly out of his range. But there was one young lad, perhaps just a little too emboldened by their greater numbers, certainly too reliant upon his belief that the size of his knife would be sufficient of a deterrent. He was seized by Lev before he could even raise the weapon into any useful position to thrust or to stab. He was speedily despatched by one crunching blow to his throat with the side of Lev's hand. He dropped the knife to reach for his damaged neck and it was grabbed by Lev almost before it hit the ground.

Lev wielded the knife in one direction towards the encircling locals, then tossed it nimbly to his left hand without taking his eyes from the nearest Chinese. He slashed out with his left hand at another part of the group and smiled to himself thinking that all he needed now was Jackie Chan or some other kung fu fanatic to turn up, but no one here was shaping up into the characteristic stance.

He was mesmerising them with his skill with the knife, sending out the obvious message that he knew how to use it and, with his stance and look, making it evident that he was about to do so.

The circle had widened. There had been no obvious movement, yet the space around him was perceptibly easing. Individuals in the front row were now trying to implode or to simply disappear themselves, trying to do nothing to make themselves stand out. After all they had managed to get the girl away from him, and that had been their sole purpose, hadn't it?

He suddenly took two large strides to the edge of the ring which just opened up to allow him to exit. He wasn't waiting to see if anyone with backbone might emerge to challenge him. Instead he strode up to Vlad, tossing the knife to him. 'I told you we should have carried our weapons today!' They walked off through the crowds. No one seemed to be raising an alarm.

# Chapter 55 - *Moscow, Russia*

Kabitsin was back home, buried deep inside the comfort of the huge population that made up Moscow, back on the streets where he had earned his reputation, close to the corridors of power that he could bend to his will. He had forgotten the pure simple joy of being among his beloved compatriots. He had not enjoyed a moment of being out there with these lesser mortals, some of them barely human by his reckoning.

The world was becoming too overcrowded, overcrowded with undesirables, overcrowded with those who did not deserve the resources that they were allowed to consume. He needed to breathe in good Russian air, eat good food, drink good vodka, relax with a bad Moscow woman, or perhaps two.

He had learned of the Odessa house being raided, but there was no loss there. He no longer had to placate the old man, listen to his interminable list of past glories and pander to his outdated views of what was right and proper.

He didn't have to waste any more time on this Brotherhood. He had though developed a close working relationship with Vasily and Asil, both of whom he was using for the next stage of his campaign, but he was delighted that he didn't need to waste time on the others.

Wim was dead, no great loss. It was Asil who had messed up, not them. Pavel, a good Russian, had been given enough of an event for him to take his strategy forward in the cities of Western Europe to supplant those east European ingrates in his various business areas.

Now he had no distractions, he could concentrate all his efforts on the Mekong and more specifically on his pitch to the Indians and the Chinese. If he could pull this off he would live like a prince for the rest of his days, no not a prince, a tsar!

The basis for his proposal went right back to his roots, it was based upon the protection racket pure and simple. He was not being greedy, he just wanted to receive a meagre 1% of GDP from each of the countries or he would attack their water supply.

He had concluded that there were to be none of the sophistications the General had proposed, no complicated franchises or complex security safeguards. They would agree an independent reviewer's quarterly statement of the country's economy and then pay just 1% of this into his accounts. Any interference with him, or the accounts, would have dreadful consequences.

His outline of his threat did not just focus on river basins as his targets but instead he described the potential for attacking public water supply systems and industrial plants too. He could not only kill people but his weapon would wipe out agricultural produce, wildlife, water-life and industrial production. 1% was therefore a very small price to pay.

His research had shown him that China's economy was estimated at over 8 trillion dollars, India was some 1.8 trillion dollars. Call it 10 trillion dollars, a mere 1% would not hurt them, they wouldn't even notice it.

That would be a guaranteed, tax-free, $100 million a year he would have rolling in. With that revenue he would be able to protect himself with the best-equipped and motivated team and then take a ringside seat cheering on the two economies to see if they could get back towards the 9% per annum growth rate that they had recently enjoyed. He would applaud them as they strove to improve his investment and return.

He was torn. The proposition had its attractions of course, but he couldn't quite rid himself of the notion that to actually use the water against the nations without warning was the better option. Use it to severely weaken if not destroy all the threats to Russia so that it could take its proper place at the head of all the nations.

It was a close call but the General's warnings had been that too broad a use of still water might lead to a chain reaction that could not be stopped at the Russian borders. This, together with the lack of any success with the British device and no scientific breakthrough on an antidote, tipped the balance towards extortion.

First he needed to use his stored quantities of still water, convert more of it and have it retained in places where he could activate it upon demand. His cabin cruiser idea had been good but he had many more ways of camouflaging the material into everyday objects where they could be installed and sit 'on station', like the General's cold war 'sleepers' hiding out there in the open just waiting on his command. He planned to find some computer geek who could show him the way to send a text or an email that would release the still water as required. He could of course pay him handsomely!

Once he had these two countries under his control, why stop there? He'd be like the oil and gas magnates. No, he'd be the next Microsoft or Apple, but in his case not just controlling the world's software and computers – using still water to control the world itself.

Now there was a very interesting idea that hadn't occurred to him earlier. Of course take each country's money first, but then why not threaten individual businesses too? Weren't a number of them bigger than many of the national economies in their own right anyway? If the corporations didn't pay him his tithe, then their business operations and assets would be selectively attacked until they conceded or crashed and burned. It would be their choice!

# Chapter 56 - *Novaya Zemlya, Russia*

While Ellise was away from their base Paul could just get on with his work, immerse himself in it, spend longer out in the sub, even longer analysing what they had uncovered so far.

He had long accepted the reality of what he saw around him, the islands were indeed part of the Urals, not merely the spoil from a comet. The geology of the Urals and of these islands was remarkable, at any other time he would have loved to have looked at it much more deeply.

The Urals were considered to be nature's marking of the northern boundary between Europe and Asia, and this most northern part of the range had become a World Heritage Site. Heavily forested to the south of the range it represented a very important lumber resource, but more interestingly the mountains themselves were blessed with a huge array and quantity of valuable substances – gold, platinum and silver; emerald, topaz, amethyst and beryl; chrome, nickel, tungsten, palladium, copper, iron, lead and zinc; bauxite and coal. A veritable 'Eldorado', but this Eldorado was not just a legend, it had been waiting to be discovered and plundered as the presence of its treasures and their applications became known.

As one of the oldest mountain ranges, the Urals date back more than 250 million years to when Siberia crashed into Baltica. Although supercontinents came and went thereafter, the mountains had remained stuck to what later became Europe.

He had time to contemplate and review all of this because their work had finally discovered something. They had been quartering the area in the submarine and had come across a feature that was perhaps highly suggestive, at last some evidence to prove his comet theory, but was he guilty of trying to shape reality to fit his beliefs?

In the submersible they had run all sorts of passes across the area and the subsequent studying of the results was painstaking work, although boring might have been a better word to describe it. It would have been easy to miss something and they almost had. There had been a large area to cover and their passes were therefore set fairly wide apart. As a result the feature of interest was at quite an acute angle from their sensors; there had been just enough of an indication for them to query what they were seeing right at the edge of the image. Fortunately although it was at the extremity of their survey they had been travelling in just the right direction to see its length.

Paul convinced himself that it was not just good fortune that they had picked it up. It was the result of his longitudinal thinking. When he had set the direction in which each scan should be run, he decided it should match both the old man's directions and his own calculation of the angle of entry if something did in fact come this way from the 1908 event.

What had appeared on their imagery looked to be a long shallow gouge. When scanned more directly, it proved to be about 8 to 10m deep at one end with a gradual slope for perhaps 100 to 120 metres, pointing in a direction that fitted in with his theories. QED?

The imagery was only showing the echoes of the signals despatched and reflected; when they approached to take a direct look at it, they found that the whole trench was concealed. Not hidden by the expected hundred year build-up of silt, but by ice. Ice hugging the bottom only meant one thing to Paul, still water!

He advised the operator to stay high and up-current from the site. They shouldn't just enter into the direct area as he feared the mini-sub motors would fail in any patch of still water. They had to find a way to remove the ice from what he was convinced was still water and see what lay beneath.

# Chapter 57 - *Moscow, Russia*

Paul's minders immediately passed this information back to Kabitsin who directed his pet scientists to review what approaches could be used to remove the ice at this depth.

However it was Valéry who came up trumps. Valéry who had been on Kabitsin's payroll from the moment he had been selected to go to Novosibirsk. It was Valéry who had said while there, 'La France has always been the naturelle colleague of Russia!'

It was Valéry who, in the Congo, had shot Wim and given Lev his opportunity to escape. Once Mark had contacted him with the information received from Dmitry, he had conferred at length with Kabitsin. His team had not been there to capture the still water as Mark had requested, but to ensure the South Africans did not survive the scene once they realised they had been double-crossed and not supplied with the real stuff.

Lev had assured Kabitsin that he could take care of that insertion, but there needed to be some care in presenting the tableau that they needed Mark to have witnessed. There had to be some sleight of hand to give Mark, and those he reported to, the impression that there was some credible process in play. Kabitsin believed that Lev was more useful as weight of hand than sleight. All this because at that time they had not quite concluded where Mark might fit in to their future plans.

Wim having brought the British to the site could have spelled disaster but Valéry had managed it well and been rewarded commensurately. Kabitsin had established that Valéry was a man of appetites; it was not at all unusual for a Frenchman to have a mistress, but Valéry strove to maintain two and of course he had a wife and family to support as well. As a result he maintained three homes, dressed and entertained three demanding women, all before having the time or resource to pursue his own epicurean interests. His lust for money was therefore nothing short of desperate, at the time it was clear that he had to have new sources of income or he would soon implode.

It was Valéry who sought and acquired from Mark the details of the latest British device to combat the still water. Kabitsin ordered his team to follow the instructions, and their version of the device was despatched to the islands.

While handling this matter Kabitsin had reviewed the backlog of reports from Novosibirsk and had come across a report from a young scientist at the Akademgorodok that had really galvanised his attention. He believed that this was one of his strengths, his ability to sense the potential of situations and of individuals. Some instinct had told him this search up there in the Arctic had future possibilities, that it was worth greasing wheels and keeping the momentum up there, and hadn't this proven to be correct?

He could not afford to be looking at just one opportunity. He arranged that the young scientist, Mikhail, or Misha Nikonov be transported up to the islands. He was to deliver the device and train them up there, but also he had instructions to investigate a number of ideas outlined within his own intriguing report to Kabitsin.

# Chapter 58 - *Novaya Zemlya, Russia*

Paul had mixed feelings when he saw that the next helicopter had brought Ellise back to their base; perhaps he was finally getting over her. But he was delighted when Misha stepped out after her and reintroduced himself. He explained that they had in fact been formally introduced during Paul's whistle-stop tour of the facilities at Novosibirsk but they had not actually worked with each other while there.

He was immediately dragooned into showing Paul what he had brought with him. They completely ignored Ellise as they considered how they might use the device in the target location. Ellise thought they were like a pair of schoolboys on Christmas morning, nothing mattered but this new toy, so she decided to take herself off for a walk. There had been no response from Mark but she had exchanged a few notes with Tom each trying to outdo the other in obscure references to conceal the actual information they wished to convey.

What she had pieced together, hopefully correctly, was that the still water was no longer a laboratory experiment, that it was planned to be applied as a weapon, and that Tom was involved in some countermeasures against it. It was not clear if he had understood her message about Dmitry. It was just so frustrating that all this information wasn't out in the open.

She had to assume all the emails she sent were being monitored and she had not been able to make any phone calls, apparently the lines were down, but then how could the Soviets launch their strikes from this military base if communications were that unreliable?

It was all but over with Paul, so it was the hope that she might assist Tom's countermeasures that had brought her back here, to watch and hopefully establish any useful information. If the Russians were backing Paul's hunch so palpably then Tom needed blow-by-blow accounts of any progress. The provision of the expensive mini-submarine, the very fact of their being allowed on the island, it had to mean something.

Misha had satisfied Paul's need for information and could now unpack his own materials. He had quite another mission in mind, much more within his own area of interest. His declared speciality was cold fusion, which was an odd choice in itself. For almost two decades the notion was considered a pariah in scientific circles, something pretty much adjacent to quackery. Few would own up to even a passing interest let alone declare it an area of specialisation.

Papers on cold fusion had seldom been published or reviewed in scientific journals and as a result those who believed in it tended to become isolated. When two cold fusion aficionados met, it was so rare that there was seldom any effort applied to the usual critical review; instead they wallowed in their subject in too much of a self-congratulatory way.

Paul too was scathing when Misha revealed what he was working on, 'You cannot be serious, cold fusion!'

Misha was well drilled in arguing his corner, 'The urgent global requirement for new energy sources is self-evident. Can we really afford to dismiss anything?'

Paul was too preoccupied with his own project to be polite, 'OK, but surely we need to dismiss anything that's so unlikely?'

Misha felt the need to convince him, 'Back in the 1990s it was acceptable that one-quarter of the world's population was allowed to expend more than two-thirds of the world's energy based purely on the luck of their location. This fortunate minority gave little or no thought to the majority who had to accept access to only one-third of the world's energy purely based upon their geography and history.'

'It's just the way the world is, there's no point in stressing about these things.'

Misha was shocked by this attitude, 'By 2020 that 75% majority because of its higher birth rates will have remorselessly grown to be 85%. It is forecast that they will need 55% of the world's energy. No, not need it, they will demand it! So new sources need to be found, and found soon.'

Paul nodded, 'That's why conventional nuclear fission has been firmly returned to the agenda, a necessary evil in current terms.'

'Even though the whole world is fully aware of its dangers.' He counted these off on his fingers, 'Its ultra-long-term waste products, the high-profile accidents at Chernobyl, Three Mile Island, the leaks at your own Sellafield.'

'It has to be a necessary part of a managed range of energy sources.'

Misha disagreed, 'But can't you see that the notion of cold fusion is so very attractive, a nuclear reaction at or near room temperature and room pressure.'

'Everything I have read is that this is just a contra-indicated notion, completely against the established wisdom. Many suggest it is just plain daft, risible.'

Misha shook his head, 'That's because all the major league labs and scientists have a vested interest in pursuing their high-temperature approaches. They have assembled big teams, large overheads and ever more expensive facilities. Of course they don't welcome anything that might challenge their governments' readiness to invest these big budgets that they currently command. For them the notion that cold fusion could be achieved without any of these facilities and budgets just cannot be allowed the oxygen of publicity.

Paul was now engaged, 'I understand that fusion of either type is the philosopher's stone in energy circles, because the release of energy from fusion is 10 million times greater than from burning a fossil fuel. A one-gigawatt power station using fusion would require a single kilo of fuel each day, whereas the coal-fired alternative needs to consume 10,000 tonnes of coal every day. That's coal that we have to find, mine from a finite and ever-declining resource and then it has to be transported to the power station.'

'All very laudable but is it practical.'

Misha was incensed, 'Don't you understand, the theory of cold fusion is that it could be sustained by a few tens of grammes of lithium, that's about the quantity used in three laptop computer batteries. This would be added to a fuel that could be extracted from five bath-fulls of water, 500 litres; put it another way, that's five days' waste from a leaky tap washer. It could create enough power to supply an average consumer in an industrialised country with an entire lifetime's energy needs!'

'So why is everyone else pursuing hot fusion?'

'Hot fusion needs to be achieved at a temperature ten times hotter than the core of the sun, 100 million degrees Kelvin, a temperature that is between seven and ten times greater than that required for fusion in the stars. Of course there is no container on Earth that can withstand that temperature and they need to prevent it from burning its way through the Earth or getting out of control and exploding.'

'Why are you talking about it here and now?'

'Because at the centre of both fusions' processes is deuterium!'

Kabitsin had been hooked by Misha as soon as he heard that fusion used deuterium!

This substance that he had been completely unaware of just months ago was now springing up wherever he looked. It felt to him that his fate and his very destiny were being pointed out to him. In life you made your own luck; if you acted then things happened and if you were decisive enough then you could take advantage of them at the right time.

Of course, like the substance deuterium, Kibitsin had never heard of the concept of synchronicity and would not have accepted that this was at play in what was happening to him. Instead it underlined to him his feeling that he was stamped out to be someone special. From an early age he had known he was worth much more than he had been born to, that he was put on this earth to do something exceptional.

It was time for him to take his place as a mover and shaker and shrug off his Mr Fix-it role. No longer to be a functionary doing others' bidding. He would have the resources to stride on to the world's stage, like a Colossus.

# Chapter 59 - *Virginia, USA*

Mark had tried to call Kabitsin many times using a prepay disposable mobile that had been discovered during the raid on Odessa. There had been a number stored in its memory shown as 'Kabitsin'! But this proved to be constantly switched off and had not been enabled for taking messages. It had become something of a five-times-a-day knee-jerk for him to try it, so he was stunned when it did actually connect.

Kabitsin too was startled when the phone rang and he pulled over at the edge of Gorky Park to answer. He was fully aware how easily and quickly these calls could be traced, but out here on the side of the road would give away no information. He picked up, curious to know who would be calling.

Mark asked, 'Mr Kabitsin, is that you?'

'Who is that?'

'It's Mark Elliott, Mr Kabitsin. I was waiting on your approval of my proposal? Do we have your agreement?'

Kabitsin smiled at the man's chutzpah; Valéry had made it clear that Mark was just playing him, and had no intention of using the still water. 'Very amusing, young Mr Elliott. Do not worry, we will clean up the US of A's disgrace after you made your hasty departure from Vietnam. I am not sure that even I have the power to help you wash away the rest of your shameful deeds. They call you the Great Satan, for there are so many examples of your meddling around the globe. Perhaps we should clean up the cause rather than the result? I must make sure that I can find time to take care of that, soon. No demonstrations or threats, I will just come from the shadows and take away your water!'

He threw the phone over the railings into the park, not even bothering to close down the line.

Mark's team immediately ran all their traces and an embassy-based car raced to the scene to report back on the location. They found the handset but nothing was gained; the phone had no call history, no programmed numbers and all its surfaces including the battery and SIM had been wiped clean.

Mark felt he had learned something: firstly he knew Kabitsin was or had just been in Moscow, and secondly he had virtually confirmed the next attack would be on the Mekong as they had calculated. Mark focused upon Vietnam for now and planned for this accordingly.

Kabitsin was not at all bothered by what he had told the American. He was content that he had misled him into believing they would strike in Vietnam. Of course Lev and the team had already reported that they had reached Jinghong and were prepared to perform the insertion there; the American would be concentrating on a location thousands of miles downriver.

Thinking of Lev, he was also pleased with himself for he had employed an old Soviet trick. He had appointed a political officer, someone who watched over the person ostensibly in charge of an operation. His responsibility was to report on that person's performance and to ensure that he stayed on mission. He had to be ready to assume command if anything was not progressing as expected.

Vlad had been his immediate choice for the role. He had briefed him separately and assured him he would support any move that he might decide upon if Lev became side-tracked.

So Kabitsin was feeling good, on top of his plans, fully ready to start reaping the rewards for his recent actions. Vasily was right now arranging to handle the delivery of the proposal to the Chinese. Asil would be conveying the same proposition to the Indians.

# Chapter 60 - *Jinghong, China*

The team had gathered back at their Jinghong guest house and Lev decided they should change their plans and make their move that very evening. Who knew what might be coming up the road?

One of his team was ex-Spetznaz and, having spent time training some of the People's Liberation Army in the past, he confirmed there were some pretty useful individuals among their military. Though none of them expected there would be any great force located in this backwoods area, they were not there to attract any official attention. Well not in that way!

They collected together their stuff, loaded it into the large 4x4 and drove across the city without any immediate or clear plan. Vlad was restless. This was the sort of emotional and headstrong action that Kabitsin had said he should be looking out for, but he was not yet ready to intervene.

When they were far enough away by Lev's reckoning from the earlier debacle, he instructed them to pull over at a late night restaurant where they ordered food and rice wine. The customers in the restaurant studiously ignored this rough-looking bunch of foreigners and the owner was smart enough to keep his female staff at the rear and well out of sight; he had dealt with their sort before. The other patrons quickly finished their meals and left the group alone in the small room.

The left-over adrenalin from his encounter and the earlier alcohol combined with his latest intake did not assist Lev's tactical thinking. He was angry at having been challenged, angry that he'd not followed through and shown the locals the havoc he was capable of wreaking. He could still smell her perfume and recall the feel of the girl who had escaped from him.

In particular he was infuriated that Vlad had been prepared to let him take a beating, not at all believing his comment, 'I knew you could handle the situation, didn't want to spoil your fun.'

He'd have to watch him. Clearly he was ambitious and this was not a characteristic he encouraged in his team. His usual response to any real sign of ambition was to expunge, or have expunged, the individual as a potent message to the others that this was not a good direction to take within his organisation.

He felt the need to hit out at someone or something, and decided he should take his revenge upon the whole city of Jinghong. Instead of heading down to the border as Kabitsin had planned he would drive upriver to the west bridge where he would release the still water so that it could flow down through the city. From there it would soon reach the border that had been Kabitsin's target. Recalling the dragon boats he concluded, 'Let's see them race through our water!'

Most Chinese were sensible people. They went to bed as the sun went down and got up when the sun rose. As a result they were up and about much earlier in the morning than their European counterparts. The Russians were surprised, on leaving the bar to walk across a small square to their vehicle, to come across a large group of very old people practising a synchronised t'ai chi. It was eerie walking past these men and women with their exaggerated movements. They almost expected one of them to shout and leap at them, but they continued to patiently follow through their routines. Lev laughed at the slow motion kung fu actions and called out in Russian, 'Where were you when your city needed you last night?'

As they drove the 4x4 across the city, the palm-lined streets were already busy with businesses setting up for the day's trade on this the last day of the festival.

The road passed along beside the river for a short distance beyond the west bridge and they pulled over to where the bank sloped gently down to the river edge. Lev ordered Konstantin to get out his equipment. He was a young guy, computer-literate, a skill that had been lacking among the team. He had been a necessary recent recruit, kitted out with a video camera and laptop to record the results when the still water was added to the river.

This time they had thought in more detail about deployment of the material and had brought along a series of smaller containers with long spouts which could be laid at the water's edge allowing the still water to drain safely into the river. At least, it would be safe as far as they were concerned.

The camcorder filmed the process which was of course initially something of a non-event. There was no fizzing or spluttering of a chemical reaction as the two waters met and there was not even any ice. Here in this sub-tropical heat even the still water would not freeze. There was no real sign that anything untoward had occurred. Konstantin panned and zoomed at the point of insertion and then, realising the river was quite fast flowing, he tracked the camera across where he assumed the still water might have reached, but still he saw nothing through the small screen at the side of the camera.

The still water was indeed already a short distance from them, travelling with the flow. It had been inserted at a gradual turn in the river and the current was carrying it out to the centre. It formed a cone-like shape, with the point of the cone upriver where the original still water was contained inside a membrane formed against the flow. Downstream it was spreading outward as the river water was being steadily converted. Within a few hundred metres the up-down dimensions of the cone had reached from the surface to the river bed, but it took almost another kilometre before the cone extended across the river to either bank.

The last day of the celebrations was the Dai's high point of the year, the Water-Splashing Festival also called the Bathing of the Buddha.

The Buddhist version commemorated the legend of a dragon sprinkling fragrant showers of water on to Buddha at his birth, but to some this was seen to be the later annexing of a pre-existing festival to sit comfortably within the Buddhist religion.

The festival was to honour water as the 'god of life' and to celebrate the coming New Year. This last festival day was *Wanbawanma*, the day the King of Days came. The locals had risen early to carry offerings to the Buddhist temples where they first cleaned all the statues and then asked them for health, harvest and happiness for the New Year.

After this the real festival began, and they got down to the water-splashing proper. There was a degree of decorum maintained towards the elderly, officials, police and suchlike, with them just a trickle of water was poured down the back of their necks. But among themselves the local youths went at it with completely unbridled fervour, throwing containers-full at each other, using water pistols, ambushing passers-by from buildings. Even the traditional parade which included several elephants became soaked within minutes. The theory was simple, the more you were splashed the happier you would become.

Many had prepared early for the battle and so in their cases perfectly safe water had been drawn and was already in containers, bowls and pistols.

The western part of the city had been passed before the still water had extended enough to reach the banks of the river. Further downstream those revellers along the riverside were surprised to see dead fish floating on the surface and being washed to shore. They took this to be some part of the festival. Several therefore assumed them to be artificial and waded out to catch them. They were the first human casualties of this still water.

Parents seeing children collapse in the water dived or waded out to reach them and succumbed themselves. Experience over instinct took some time and many deaths, before those on the shoreline accepted that going into the water was a very bad idea.

Around the next bend of the river people were topping up their basins for more splashing. If they dipped only their hands into the water, they were able to move away from the river unharmed. Provided there were no cuts or grazes the still water would not enter the body. At first it was assumed that those receiving the splashes were falling to the floor in fun, but it did not take long for the awful truth to be recognised.

Still water was everywhere, in puddles on the floor, in sodden decorations and buildings, and in saturated clothing. Those with any sort of cut or graze on lower limbs from the morning's boisterous festival were taken next. Water in the eyes or on the lips meant instant death.

It was a festival so there was a general holiday, but the Chinese work-ethic was powerful and many small businesses that relied upon the river's water were affected. Laundries, fruit-sellers, restaurants all drew on the still water which killed staff and patrons as the cycle progressed.

Inexorably it swept on, leaving many thousands dead or soon to die. The membrane held it in the river flow and swept it onward along the Mekong.

Where it had been taken from the river it left caches and puddles of contaminated water which would claim further victims in the days ahead, but fortunately membranes had formed at the riverside preventing it from returning to the flow to add to the disaster.

The residual puddles of the deadly material on the streets and riverbanks began to evaporate in the heat and, unrecognised by observers, it reverted to a normal water-based steam as it dissipated to form part of the general humidity of the area.

# Chapter 61 - *Beijing, China*

The Chinese had been alerted by the British administration that there was a plot involving an attack on their waters. They had been given details of some of the papers that had been captured from the Brotherhood.

In a pre-emptive broad sweep the Chinese arrested Vasily before he could deliver the proposal, and he was attempting to use the document and his knowledge to arrange his release. He had superb contacts at the very highest level of the Chinese administration and he was calling in every favour he could.

The concept of a 'Chinese wall' in modern times is used to describe an imaginary barrier between members of the same organisation. As an example, investment decisions are kept from those who need not know and might be tempted to act on the knowledge if they did. The origins are vague as to whether this description was inspired by the Great Wall of China or more likely the standing screens that allowed mandarins and courtiers to see but not be seen.

Vasily was familiar with the term and now he became familiar with the reality. His contacts had retreated behind such a wall. They were avoiding him, casting him adrift, probably happy that they could wash their hands of his influence. But it was not going to be that easy for them, like Kabitsin, his files were comprehensive and far-reaching.

He succeeded in bribing a guard to smuggle him in a phone. He informed Kabitsin of events and then he set about remedying his position. His task was to get the document delivered to the right person and to ensure it was taken seriously.

**New Delhi, India**

Asil had an easier ride. Although the Indians too had received similar warnings, their internal systems were slow and ponderous. The decision as to how the threat should be handled had to be made first.

Should it be the responsibility of Ministry of External Affairs as this was clearly a foreign threat, or should it be the Home Ministry, or Defence or perhaps Water Resources?

Even the Intelligence Service, that had received the warning directly, consisted of a large number of agencies – the Intelligence Bureau and Central Bureau of Investigation handled internal security; the Directorate of Military Intelligence and Defence Intelligence Agency might be involved for the foreign threat; then the Economic Intelligence Council might need to consider the potential impact.

The British Raj had caused much damage to India in its time, but perhaps the most damning indictment of its legacy was the way it had prompted the Indian red tape that could tie things up into a complex parcel of inaction.

Asil advised Kabitsin that the ultimatum had been delivered successfully but that they would need to wait upon a reply.

# Chapter 62 - *Moscow, Russia*

'Idiots, incompetents, why is it that I must do everything myself?' Kabitsin was incandescent, 'All they had to do was deliver it as proposed, just deliver it to the right person. Must I be there to hold their hands all of the way?'

He fired off an email to his key contact in each of the two governments. Attaching the original proposal, he underlined that it was a real and immediate threat that they were facing. Any threat or arrest of his people would bring about an instant response that would be deadly.

He demanded a response by the end of the day, and advised them that a demonstration of his intent was already flowing down the Mekong River, dealing out death and destruction.

Back at his home base he felt confident that no one could trace the emails to him, but he still decided to move to another equally secure location, just in case.

His praetorian guard whisked him across Moscow to this new position, not in some sizeable limo but in a convoy of three vehicles that could pass unobtrusively through the general street traffic. Once he had the deal from the two Asian countries he could build an even more secure location, employ an even bigger security team and he would never have to skulk around in cheap cars again. He would demand and receive respect from his countrymen.

# Chapter 63 - *Ho Chi Minh City, Vietnam*

Mark was tangled with the sudden traffic of messages, first getting the warnings out, now responding to requests for more background and advice on what their next action should be.

He was in Ho Chi Minh City though he still thought of it as Saigon. The eleven hour difference was proving awkward, not that Langley wasn't a 24-7 place, but unlike Jack Bauer and the CTU team in '24', the team there did not work around the clock. Key people whom he had come to rely upon were sleeping the sleep of the just, or was it the sleep of the shattered from another long day? He would need them refreshed for the morrow, so let them rest.

He had a team there in Vietnam watching all the local newscasts, waiting for anything that might alert them to an attack location. Valéry was there; given the French colonial past of each of the countries in the region, he was also helping to monitor the French and German broadcasts that covered the area. One of the young guys in Mark's team was trying to write a routine to monitor Internet sites and to come up with any reference to water, or deaths linked with water, on the many news sites.

They had once again decided to use the British group under Brain as one of their teams and Tom was there to run countermeasures for this team. It was decided to locate them at Vientiane, the capital of Laos, nestling right up against the Thai border. Further teams were at Muang Khong in Laos on the Cambodian border and in Phnom Penh in Cambodia.

Experience at the Danube had shown that they needed to be ready to move by river, road or air and not to find themselves stranded for want of a river crossing or a road. In principle they had done what they could but of course the weather, the humidity, the river, the terrain would all work against them. The roads were absolutely nothing like the Central European location that they had found themselves in before.

Tom had convinced Brain to opt for Laos, despite Brain wanting to be at the centre of things in Vietnam. Tom argued that an attack in Vietnam would not score heavily against the Chinese or the Indians. Instinctively he felt that the attack might be in China itself or at least a little more on its doorstep. Brain grudgingly accepted the logic and did not object to being based at the least desired location.

It was a holidaymaker who gave them their break. He had been a late riser. Mark on learning he was a German, suggested he had perhaps bagged his sun loungers the previous night so that he could afford to linger longer. Whatever, when he had woken it was to see carnage outside his window. From his hotel room overlooking the riverside he had used a mobile phone to video short blasts of film which showed dead fish littering the shore line, surrounded by perhaps ten or more human bodies. He had then scanned away from the river across an area on the bank littered with more bodies lying where they had dropped.

At first, terrified that it was something highly contagious, he and his wife had stayed locked in their room trying unsuccessfully to telephone friends at home for news that might explain what had happened. Eventually he decided to call and send the video to CNN, the channel they had been watching on previous days to keep in touch with world news.

CNN Breaking News had carried the footage with a plea for information. The news station had some stock shots of the water-throwing festival in its archives and so ran a voice-over to the two pieces explaining that unconfirmed reports were indicating a massive loss of life in Jinghong, more news as it happened.

At a stroke Tom's hunch was seen to have put them closest to the scene, though there was not too much patting on the back from Brain's team before they all gathered around their maps.

# Chapter 64 - *Novaya Zemlya, Russia*

Paul had applied the modified version of Tom's device down deep on the seabed with only a limited success so they had to test a series of innovations. The succession of requests had Kabitsin complaining as if he was being asked to fund the world's hot fusion budget, especially when advised that they needed a surface boat and some form of powered hose that could be turned on to the ice. Paul explained his requirements were much like the type of things Jacques Cousteau worked with, but no one here seemed to know who Cousteau was.

They delivered him a small naval ship that had been in the general area. It sat just off shore and they used its various pumps and hoses, managing to adapt them so that the mini-submarine could haul a hose to the bottom and by radio get it turned on and off as required.

With one of the sub's arms holding the hose and the other the "still water pacifier", as he had decided to call it, Paul started to make some progress, but of course the hose was stirring up more than just the ice so visibility was shot. They had to be more specific with the hose and so modified its nozzle, though this necessitated going in much closer to gain real progress. The pacifier had better be working!

At last they seemed to be shifting some of the ice and so far the mini-submarine was not encountering any still water to foul its drive mechanisms.

Back from one of these sessions Paul had planned to just crash out but saw Misha was sitting in the lounge working on a laptop; he was so involved in what he was doing that he had not been aware of Paul. On his screen was an English language diagram headed 'Emission of a high-energy charge particle from a polarized $Pd/D-D^2O$ system'.

'What does Pd stand for?' Paul asked.

Misha turned, looking sheepish, but saw no real reason to hide what he was doing. 'It's the symbol for palladium.'

'I just about remember "Sunday Night at the London Palladium" but what's the chemical element palladium? Don't think I've ever come across it.'

'It's a silver-white metal in the platinum group. There is not enough of it to go around. We Russians provide about 50% of the world's supply from the Ural Mountains, close to where we are now. Noril'sk, just out there across the Kara Sea, is the world's largest producer.'

'And one of the world's largest polluters I understand. But, what's it useful for?'

'I know you will appreciate how it was given its name; it was named after the asteroid Pallas by an Englishman back at the beginning of the 19th century. No, there is no direct connection; it was merely that the discovery of the metal and the identification of the asteroid happened around the same time. The main characteristic of palladium is that it loves hydrogen, can absorb up to 900 times its own volume of it.'

'Still rings no particular bells for me.'

'Well, you'll definitely have some in your car's catalytic converter.'

Paul pointed at the laptop screen, 'But why would it be useful with deuterium?'

'That's what everyone is trying to find out! Earlier when I said Noril'sk was the largest producer, I left out the fact that a lot of palladium is made in nuclear fission plants too, but it has to be synthesised out from the spent nuclear fuel. We might in fact be sitting right next to a lot of it on this island, but it's buried deep down in the collapsed tunnels of the nuclear test site.'

'I am aware that deuterium oxide is heavy water and used in nuclear reactors.'

'Yes, but they are fission reactors; as you know my particular interest is in fusion and everyone agrees that the most promising substances to achieve fusion are the two hydrogen isotopes of deuterium and tritium. If we can make them fuse into a heavier helium nucleus it will give off tremendous energy.'

'So where does the palladium come in?'

'It was found by experimentation that if the cathode is a mix of palladium and deuterium then it improves the reaction.'

'So, if my schoolboy physics isn't out of date, there must be an anode too. If it has a palladium and deuterium cathode, what's the anode made from?'

'You're right, there is an anode and it's used to deliver the tritium, and that's obtained by using lithium. Lithium is one of the elements created at the Big Bang, but we have quite a lot of it on earth in clays, brine and other forms. Today most of the batteries in our computers, mobile phones and digital cameras use lithium cells. Currently most of the lithium comes from Chile and Argentina, the Americans have their own extracted from brine pools in Nevada and it's expected that China, and specifically Tibet, will become the big players in the future.'

'So does it work?'

'Lithium deuteride was used very successfully in the hydrogen bomb, but that's not what I am after. I want cold fusion so I can tap into and release energy to change the world in a positive way. I have no interest in trying to destroy it.'

'So what are you hoping for here?'

'I was hoping that your comet particle and your still water might in some way offer me a breakthrough in cold fusion. The materials are very suggestive. If we could make it work we could change the world forever. Wouldn't it be great if we could do it here from deep in the shadow of this island's terrible past?'

# Chapter 65 - *Jinghong, China*

The Russians had toured along the riverbank at Jinghong recording the scene, picking their way around bodies which lay where they had been splashed. They were sweltering in their vehicle with the windows firmly closed, the aircon off and vents all shut, but there was no word of complaint from any of them, they didn't want a drop of that stuff to get into the vehicle.

As they emerged at the eastern side of the city there were fewer casualties in view. They crossed the east bridge and travelled along the opposite bank for a while until Lev called for them to stop. He turned and looked deep into Vlad's eyes as he ordered him out of the vehicle to take some water from the river to take back with them. Lev was looking for any sign of reluctance or rebellion.

Vlad understood why he had been selected. He looked around the rest of the team to see if there was any sympathy to be had, perhaps a sign of support forthcoming, but they were each avoiding his glance. He knew that to front down Lev here, on this matter, would be pointless. He reluctantly took the flask and case and went carefully to the shoreline. To the others he was like a nervous sparrow, jerkily looking around him. All he needed was one of these local idiots to splash him with water and he would have leapt into the air screaming.

He took off his shirt and cautiously, at arm's-length, dipped the mouth of the flask to collect some of the water. Then, using his scrunched up shirt, he screwed the top back on, all the time careful to see that the fluid did not soak through the material to his skin. He carefully set the flask and shirt on the ground and used his boot to roll the flask on the shirt until it was dry. Even after all of this he picked up the flask with a bandana he'd bought at the festival the day before.

Returning to the rear of the 4x4, he placed the flask in the crate which had been used to transport the still water when they first arrived. When he walked back to the car door, Lev was holding a gun on him.

'Lick your fingers,' he ordered.

'What do you mean?'

'Lick each of your fingers, and just to be clear, your thumbs too. Go on do it.'

Vlad looked at him defiantly until Lev pointedly cocked the pistol. He chose the small finger of his left hand first and placed it in his mouth trying not to touch his tongue or teeth.

'Lick it properly!'

He closed his tongue over his finger, his racing mind actively monitoring all parts of his body searching out any sign of a developing symptom. He was immediately imagining all sorts of indications, but once he could find his objectivity each seemed to disappear under careful scrutiny. Seconds took an age to turn into a minute. He was still alive! 'And the rest!'

He grew in confidence as each fearful finger passed the test. By the time he reached the last thumb his tongue was fully extended openly licking along the length of it. He could feel a look of defiance returning to his face but he cautioned himself to suppress it.

Having observed the process, Lev relaxed his grip on the trigger, holstered his pistol and turned his back on Vlad who climbed back into the vehicle and scrambled to find a new shirt. Lev mumbled, not caring too much if they heard or not and annoyed that he had felt the need to justify himself, 'I was just taking care of our security.'

The vehicle pressed on alongside the river, sometimes able to stay with the course, on other occasions having to detour around a feature or an obstacle and work its way back to the riverside as soon as possible. They noted and video-ed the odd body, human or animal, that was swept past them in the flow and they came across a number of isolated incidents along the riverbank.

There was the guy who had clearly been urinating into the river and the still water had followed the flow to invade his body. Another guy who must have stooped to drink from a wooden tub. Encountering still water he had died instantly and fallen headfirst into it with one of his legs pointing skyward. Konstantin recorded all these scenes but they had already become inured to the sights and progressively what they observed raised little comment.

Lev concluded they were to gain nothing more from this and told the driver turn away from the river towards a road that would lead them on to the border via Manglun and Mengla.

When they reached the border at Mohang they found the custom and immigration formalities pretty cursory. Vasily had prepared the ground for them but from what he saw of others passing through Lev thought they really needn't have bothered. But in this he was wrong. Investigation of Vasily since his arrest had resulted in documents being seized and the request for assistance at the border post had been among them. Their passage was reported and confirmed to Mark within forty-five minutes of it happening.

In Laos, the Russian team found the clear and crisp air they had become used to in China was becoming hazy as they travelled on what was a surprisingly good road. The reason for this was of absolutely no interest to the team, but both the mist and the more comfortable ride were due to the forestry in the area.

The Chinese had built the road for the Laotians in return for being granted the timber rights, there being clear self-interest in making the route back to Yunnan as easy as possible, but the Laotians showed their gratitude nonetheless for what they saw as this altruism. The haziness however was not due to the Chinese tree felling, but was the result of the Laotian slash-and-burn method of forestry that they employed to satisfy their own needs.

**Muang Sing, Laos**

The buses and tuk-tuks along the road made the going slow. The Russians had travelled less than ten kilometres into Laos and it was already late into the afternoon so Lev decided to stop for some food when they reached Muang Sing.

This turned out to be a very scruffy village with plastic bags and rubbish strewn all over the street. The buildings themselves however were ornate wooden structures, almost colonial in appearance. The place teemed with a host of different ethnic groups, dressed in bright colours, interspersed with hordes of backpackers from all parts of the world. As soon as they pulled up they were surrounded by a group of young girls offering them opium who became increasingly irritated and intrusive when they showed no interest at all in making a purchase. After all, why else would these foreigners be in the village if it was not to smoke the opium?

They arrived to find that the town had no power, but the locals were quite unconcerned by the electricity outage suggesting they only ever expected to receive a supply in the evenings. While they waited for the power to be restored the Russians wasted time by getting wasted.

Lev was amused by the thought that the still water was probably still working while they relaxed. It would by now have travelled some way downstream. The river ran some fifty kilometres away to their west. He assumed the deadly water would have already described the border between Myanmar and Laos. Then over one hundred kilometres, a tad west of south, he assumed it might already have turned to run along the border between Thailand and Laos. Later still he knew it would swing east to pass down through Laos heading towards Louangphabang.

They were creating two sides of their own triangle at the very heart of the Golden Triangle. The water would wreak havoc among the illegals travelling on the river and crossing it from their fields to the processing points. Who else other than these processors and transporters would be operating and living there? Nobody, except perhaps for the scruffy, junkie backpackers they saw around – no loss there then!

The sales girls persisted and the Russian team was amused by a tot who approached them, she could not have been more than five or six years old and was offering them a pipe of opium and at a price less than a fifth of what they were paying for beer or local whisky in the bar.

Lev watched them, thinking that these kids would soon be running short of supplies, then what would they have to sell? He had one or two ideas of course, and would perhaps put them to one of the older girls a little later. They all looked alike so it really didn't much matter which one, but not until he'd had something to eat.

# Chapter 66 - *Vientaine, Laos*

The Lao People's Liberation Army had been fully advised and was therefore quick to lend the British team support. Two military helicopters whisked them northwards, following approximately the Mekong's course. A liaison officer was on radio the whole time getting updates as to what was happening upriver.

Much of the course of the Mekong from Jinghong was in an area that was pretty lawless. There were few formal villages or towns that were recognised by whichever nation they just chanced to sit within. The locals had their own economy, their own rules and never sought the assistance of any national authorities. They also had little time for the outside world except as sales potential.

There was no electricity so none would have seen the CNN coverage or been aware of what had happened upriver. News there would travel by word of mouth and this moved much more slowly than the river.

The still water dispassionately took local people, their animals and the local plant and river life. The only element of a lottery was whether an individual stayed away from the water. If there was contact with it there was nothing left to chance, the result was assuredly death.

No newscaster would receive pictures, no authorities would tot up the casualties for a press release, the still water just swept on by, leaving its long dark shadow of death behind it.

There was no formal industry up here to be disabled, only the opium refinery camps. This "industry" started with the growers who slashed and burned the forestry to clear a field, then planted seeds and waited three months, with at most a little light weeding to occupy themselves. The poppies were grown among other taller crops to conceal their presence. The mature opium poppy plant flowered, then dropped its petals.

The pod that was left behind was scored with a multi-bladed knife; these slits seeped a raw opium gum that was collected, the process being repeated four or five times until no further gum emerged. This gum was dried and then sold on. The used pods were then cut and broken to reveal the seeds that were planted for the next season.

At the refinery the gum was first converted into morphine. This was achieved by dissolving the gum in boiling water and straining it through burlap sacking to separate out the morphine. Bricks of the product were then treated with several chemicals to produce either smoking heroin or injectable heroin according to the current demand. The purity from these simple processes was high at around 90%. It was only downstream in the distribution cycle that the drugs were diluted with additives such as baking soda or powdered milk down to the average of 40% purity available at the streets, malls and schools of the world.

The refineries drew water directly from the river and were immediately devastated. The works where the water was delivered from the river in drums had to send out search parties when their teams did not return with these vital supplies.

None of this information reached the authorities, but the presence of the Russians in Muang Sing had been noted and they were being watched carefully as the helicopters homed in on them.

The helicopters separated with one continuing to follow the Mekong, landing as prearranged to deliver Tom and his team, so he could tackle the threat before it swept any further through Laos.

The second helicopter was on its way to deal with the Russians in Muang Sing when liaison took a call informing them they were suddenly up and on the move. As they were still minutes distant, it was decided to pull away so as not to declare their presence until the Russians' intentions were clear. Their people on the ground would have to do the tracking and call the helicopter to the location later.

Down in Ho Chi Minh City, Valéry had found the opportunity to report what was happening in Laos to Kabitsin, he in turn had reached Lev by sat-phone while he was eating. Lev had finished his meal and was just beginning to size up his afters, probably opting for one of the taller girls. He was a big guy and these girls looked flimsy, their lack of nutrition probably compounded by too much use of their own merchandise.

The call had spoilt all that and they had hurried to the vehicle and headed for the location where Kabitsin advised him that the authorities were trying to combat the effects of their insertion and ruin the demonstration.

# Chapter 67 - *Mekong riverside, Laos*

Tom had been dropped off at a clearing perhaps a few hundred metres from the Mekong. The other team members assisted him in carrying his equipment to the bank. His first impressions were that the still water had yet to reach this point, or, a horrible thought occurred to him, might it already have passed? A quick look at the plant life reassured him that this was not the case.

They had no idea how long they had before it reached them so he quickly sized up the river and selected the point where he would attack the damnable stuff. There was a rapid just below them and the river was pinched just before it cascaded on downstream.

It formed into a 'V' shape at the centre of the approach to the fall. He recalled this characteristic V from way back when. He had spent a day canoeing as a child and his tutor had shown him the V from the riverbank and said he should aim his canoe directly at it, but once he was in the canoe careening down to the rapid he craned his neck and never actually managed to see it. He had crashed down the rapids, capsizing and damaging the borrowed canoe, then cracking his knees against the rocks as he swept down the river, trying to avoid the canoe that was following all too closely behind him.

Several trees and handy rocks provided anchors for him to set his equipment out in the flow and to hold it in position just before that V. Here he could position his rotors so that they were located across the central segment of the river. This was the best he could do and he directed the team as they deployed the equipment.

They were set up and the equipment was activated with about ten minutes to spare before the first dead fish started to cascade past them.

Tom worked his way downriver to check if the treatment was proving effective. They had concluded the only way to do this was to dip a container holding a small fish into the water. Tom thought this harked back to the use of canaries in mines when they tested the air quality, but if the test was to prove positive, unlike the canary, the fish could not be withdrawn and revived.

The first fish survived its first dunking and thankfully each of the subsequent series of other locations that Tom tested. Relieved, he returned to the rest of the team and settled down on the bank watching while his equipment did its work. Although it was effective there was no sense of joy and he tried not to look too closely as the death toll of the fish mounted or even a little later as the occasional human body floated by. His nerves were jarred each time there was a change in the noise of the rotors as something passed through it. It sounded a lot like leaving a paperclip on documents dropped into a shredder, but it was not the noise that jarred him with this organic shredding, it was the series of thoughts that it created.

# Chapter 68 - *Roadside, Laos*

Lev had pushed the driver to get to their destination at top speed. As a result he and all the passengers had to take some teeth-jarring bumps and there were terrifying moments when the vehicle appeared to lose all traction as it took off over a large rut, all of them holding their breath until it crashed back safely to earth.

After ten minutes of this he signalled to the driver to stop, to kill the engine. They all listened hard and in just a few minutes were rewarded with the noise of another vehicle crashing along the section they had just passed. He had two of his men dismount and drop into cover beside the road, then started up and drove the vehicle a further hundred metres along the track.

The Laotian team were flying around a bend with all their attention focused on keeping up with their quarry when without warning they were attacked from both sides of the road. The driver tried to avoid the withering fire by pulling off into the trees but they took a huge impact before reaching any worthwhile cover. Bruised and stunned they slumped in their seats, not even compos mentis enough to reach for their weapons as one of the Russians popped up at a window and shot them both.

Lev had worked his way back from their vehicle, nodded his approval at the outcome and reached into the small jeep to scavenge any weapons and seeing their portable radio took this too. He then extracted the ignition keys and threw them off into the woods.

The whole thing had taken just a few minutes and they were able to get back on the road at the same pace as before, pressing on to their destination.

The helicopter called to the jeep radio several times; Lev had no idea what was being said but recognised the thwacking noise as coming from a helicopter. He stopped again and satisfied himself that there was no sound to be heard from outside, so the helicopter was not directly tracking them, was not that close and was now diverted into wondering what had happened to their people. They pressed on.

Tom had checked downriver several more times, apologising to the fish that by now had gamely survived perhaps several dozen duckings, when he decided it was time to check upriver above his equipment to see if the threat had yet passed.

Here the fish promptly died, so he disposed of it and the jar and moved back downriver. He had three more fish ready for these tests and hoped that the other one had been the last casualty.

**Ho Chi Minh city, Vietnam**

Mark was disturbed to hear that the Russians had left the village rather too conveniently for his liking and clearly in something of a hurry, and even more suspiciously this happened only just before the British team would have reached them. It was just too darned convenient, he smelt a rat. It must be that someone inside the team was leaking material to the Russians.

While the events were still unfolding up in the north of Laos, he decided to work up a series of fictitious events that he could report to the team. He dropped the information and watched carefully. After one particularly juicy titbit Valéry was a little too quick to excuse himself on the pretext of needing a cigarette.

He followed him outside a minute or so later to find him talking on his mobile with no sign of a cigarette in sight. Mark lit up showing no apparent interest in Valéry's call. He did not anyway understand what was being said in the French conversation but it was clear that the content was banal, being managed just for his benefit.

He did not act immediately, wondering instead how he might use his knowledge to the max.

**Riverside, Laos**
Lev came upon the British site unnoticed; the Russians had left the vehicle and walked at pace for around fifteen minutes, enjoying the action after having been passively bounced around for too long.

Two of his guys were despatched to find the location of the helicopter and secure it for their own escape in some degree of comfort. He had kept Vlad with him, feeling the need to keep him close for now.

They observed the two Brits by the riverside. They were relaxed, unaware that there was any threat. They could perhaps have taken out these two, shooting them from their cover. But this was not Lev's style, he preferred face-to-face combat and besides they were not sure how their colleagues were faring in terms of capturing the helicopter. He didn't want to spoil that assault and lose his escape route.

They worked their way towards the Brits as stealthily as they could but some instinct made one of them turn and shout out a warning to the other. Caution to the wind, Lev stood and sprayed both of them with bullets; they had been very conveniently grouped from his vantage point.

Downriver Tom dropped into a crouch and crawled off into cover not knowing what the shots might mean. He cautiously inched back upriver to see the two Russians walk over to the two Brits to check they were dead, Lev putting a shot into the head of one of them just to make sure.

Lev then walked to the riverside to view the equipment that was secured out in the river flow; he sprayed the apparatus until his gun ran dry. He mechanically clipped in a new magazine and called out to Vlad to stay at the location while he went to see what had happened with the others and that helicopter.

Vlad, like most experienced soldiers, immediately sat down and relaxed, taking his breaks when he could. Though the Russian had chosen to look out towards the river, Tom dared not move until he had seen who else was present. He had not understood what Lev had said but got the impression these two were not alone.

Time passed before Tom heard the sounds of several people returning. Three men, obviously Russian, were prodding the Laotian pilot ahead of them.

Vlad asked, 'Why don't we just get out of here?'

Lev paused, unsure if he cared to be questioned, but eventually commented, 'We wait for the second helicopter. I've never enjoyed being in those things, and certainly not if there's a risk of another coming out of the sun shooting at me.'

They rooted around among the Brits' packs to find food and water and settled down awaiting the expected arrival.

They obviously heard the noise before Tom did and scattered for cover well before the helicopter came into view. It circled at height surveying the scene, first discerning the two dead Brits, then spotting Tom who was lying out in the open air waving frantically, though remaining well-concealed from the campsite behind good cover. First he showed them four fingers and then pointed out the approximate locations.

Brain ordered the helicopter to swing out first to see the landing site of the other machine. Finding it apparently clear he directed the pilot to drop in hard and fast and had James and one of the Laotian force drop to the ground below, roll away from them, and start back down the river.

The helicopter flew back to hover over the water while Brain strapped himself to an anchor point at the door; with this harness he could hang out over the side in safety. While he scanned the area that Tom had indicated, he asked the pilot to stay high and create enough noise below to hide James's approach.

Brain judged that he still had a few minutes before his colleagues would arrive so he deliberately sprayed the area with gunfire, not expecting to hit anyone, but to encourage them to keep their heads down, and to disorient them with both the noise and the threat.

To Tom it was all happening at a million miles an hour and, unarmed as he was, he had no idea what he could do to help, until he came up with an idea...

Though James was a big guy he could be light-footed and stealthy when he needed to be. Brain was making enough noise for him to get close to the bank before he needed to be too concerned about being heard. He directed the Laotian army guy to go straight ahead while he circled a little, then approached the site at a wider angle through the trees.

The first Russian was cowering behind a small copse and he was able to crawl up behind him, sweep his knife across the man's exposed throat while with his other arm he supported the body and eased it down to the floor. James achieved all this without any obvious movement or noise to alert the others.

Brain had seen the engagement and had the helicopter drop closer to the ground as a decoy.

James then spotted movement, another Russian had been tempted to raise his weapon towards the helicopter but thought better of it as the helicopter lifted again. James made his way across towards this second man.

The Laotian guy lost patience and catching a glimpse of another Russian stood up and started to fire in that direction. Lev from cover saw the man rise and was able to cut him down, before he himself earned some shots from above, forcing him to retreat back deeper into cover before he could finish off the Laotian.

James reached his quarry but this one turned in time to parry the attack and the two men crashed through the undergrowth each seeking an opening to land a telling blow. Brain saw the fight in process, so brought the helicopter very much lower again, to make sure he could cover James from any other interference.

Given this freedom from interruption it was not long before James's bigger body and physique prevailed and he disabled the man with a crushing blow. He judged that he did not need to follow through, he simply disarmed him and tossed the weapon and knife back the way that he had come.

The Laotian guy was mortally wounded but he was not going to die cheaply, he still crawled gamely towards the point where he had seen Lev retreat.

The noise of the helicopter was beginning to annoy them all, particularly Lev who stepped forward and aimed shots at the clattering machine. The pilot took immediate evasive action rising away from the scene, while Brain was urging him to return so that he was better able to assist those on the ground.

Lev let off a few more shots but they were well behind the motion of the craft, failing to hit it. The Laotian saw the big Russian was distracted and took his shot, but weakened from his wounds he could not keep the weapon raised and only managed to hit Lev in the leg.

As this was happening James, still on the move, managed to get in behind a distracted Vlad who was lying on the ground training his gun along the bank. James pulled out his own weapon as he tried to see where Vlad was aiming.

Vlad was in fact watching carefully for Lev to show himself. He had decided that direct action was his best approach. The man had led them badly, was panicked into using the still water early; now they were here, unlikely to get away unscathed. He was damned if he was going to let Lev live if he himself was to die.

Lev, enraged by the wound in his leg, once again pulled on his trigger until he had emptied every shot into the Laotian, then instinctively reaching for the next magazine he realised he did not have one. It was at that moment that Tom stepped out in front of him holding a jar of water. He had hastily thrown out the fish and held the jar threatening to throw it at the big Russian just a few metres away.

Lev froze, looking from Tom's eyes and the jar, assessing the man's resolve, then finally he smiled as he saw a drip of water run down the side and across Tom's knuckles. No way would that man allow that stuff to spill onto his own flesh. Lev drew his knife and painfully on his damaged leg closed the distance between them, daring Tom to throw the water.

Two shots rang out within seconds of each other. Lev looked absolutely shocked; he tried to turn to see who had shot him and dropped to the floor. Tom looked beyond where Lev had been standing to see James rising from the undergrowth. He had not taken the shot on Lev, he had shot Vlad, the final Russian. James had realised too late that Vlad had been lining up to shoot; he was still unsure who had been Vlad's intended target as the angle between Tom and the big Russian was marginal. The Russian was so big, bigger than James himself, so he would have been pretty difficult to miss if he was the intended target, or maybe he had moved into the line of fire as the shot was taken.

Once he had landed and had the opportunity to review the situation on the ground Brain reported the outcome to Mark. Further tests suggested the water passing them was back to normal, though they had no means of knowing if any still water had passed them between the time Lev destroyed the equipment and their tests. Therefore downriver the Laotians arranged to have spotters at intervals vigilantly scouring the river for any signs of a problem, each hastily provisioned with some jars and small fish for the purpose.

Both helicopters were put in the air to follow the river and add their own observations to the task, and of course to scramble to any reported incident.

# Chapter 69 - *Ho Chi Minh City, Vietnam*

This final report was the trigger for Mark to act and he ordered Valéry arrested. Seizing his mobile from him he took some minutes to think what he would say and then last-number-redialled, not at all surprised when it was Kabitsin who grunted, 'Yes, what's happening?'

Mark took a deep breath, 'Hello Mr Kabitsin, it's Mark Elliott here. I don't believe the Chinese will take your proposal very seriously any more. You should know that the damage was completely contained up at the border; after Jinghong I imagine any casualties would be among the local undesirables so you may just have done the world a favour.'

He found himself jabbering, trying to jar the man into some response, 'I doubt there will be any reports or analysis of the incident in the world's press. We've already suggested to the Chinese that they blame Jinghong on a chemical spill. By the way, your insertion team was neutralised with extreme prejudice, pity we can't just do the same with Valéry Sechet, but then we are the good guys. Vasily Manchary will not be released by the Chinese any time soon and we'll round up the other members of your Brotherhood in the coming days and weeks.'

Mark paused for a reaction, then said, 'Your turn to speak?'

'Thank you for supplying me such a detailed report, that certainly saves me some time and trouble. You think this is the end? It's just the beginning. You, the good guys? I always knew we would need to take out the Great Satan at some stage. Your gloating has just brought that moment a little forward in my plans. You will soon appreciate that you are just a little boy trying to play in a man's world!' Kabitsin cut the connection.

# Chapter 70 - *Kent, UK*

Sir Joseph had invited Tom to his home to thank him on behalf of the "free world". Tom was amused by this, wondering quite how the old man felt that he could speak for such a constituency, but anyway took the spirit of his intention seriously.

'So am I now able to resume my civilian life?'

'Are we ever, dear boy, are we ever?' Sir Joseph stared off into the distance through his window. 'We are occasionally allowed the belief that life is about our free will, perhaps creating family and domestic bliss, or single-mindedly pursuing a career wherever it leads us, but that I am afraid is just an illusion. There are evil tendencies in the world, both overseas and here at home. The past structures, strictures and scriptures have served to contain and control, they even managed to breed a sort of contentment, providing us all with a moral compass, a social template for life. But today these are all being stripped away, all the past certainties are revealed as artificial, irrelevant to life as it is now.'

'You sound as though you're contemplating retirement, that your role is passing?'

'No, not that. When the time comes I will have to be forcibly carried away from my desk, or with any luck I'll pass away still in the saddle, who can say? It's just that there is no sound basis for much of what goes on today. No respect for anything. When I was a child, your schoolmaster, a policeman, a local retailer, an adult neighbour needed only to threaten informing your parents of any bad behaviour to gain effective control of any situation, now the parents are more likely to attack you rather than discipline their offensive offspring.'

'You said parents, but so many children of today have only one!'

'Precisely, no family values, no social structure, no further basis of belief in the politicians, royalty reduced to no more than a television soap opera.'

Tom agreed with the older man. 'I am afraid today they all want to become celebrities or sports stars, or the wife of a celebrity or sports star.'

'In my day we were told to get a degree, become a professional or failing that take up a trade. Today no one is prepared to invest time in developing a skill or any knowledge base. They all want everything and want it now!'

'Hm, you're touching on one of my own hobbyhorses. More and more attend an establishment they call a university, but look at the courses they take, media studies, drama, brewing. I can't believe they can actually show up at one and study football!'

Sir Joseph snapped out of his reverie. 'From my perspective you are still very much part of the youth of today, part of what is current. It's people like you and your colleagues who have to set examples, change things. You have to leave the old codgers like me the luxury to sit around and groan about it all. Get out there and change it, for both of our sakes!'

'I think that's where we started this. Am I free to get on now and pursue my own objectives?'

'Of course, of course, but I should like to be able to call upon your advice from time to time. I'd prefer not to have to invoke your reservist status for the future, I'm sure you might prefer that too.'

'So what precisely is it that you have in mind?'

'You may recall that I mentioned plans for an International Environment Defence Corps?'

'I assumed that was just some tactic to get me to agree to help.'

'Very perceptive of you. I'd probably have invented anything to get you to agree, but there are in fact plans for such a team. You can see there is too much news out there and there are too many channels wheeling out anyone and everyone as an "expert" to pontificate on a subject at the drop of a hat. Present company excepted of course, but many of these people are unchallenged as to qualification or experience. Most are there with a vested interest and the damnable journalists interviewing them are such airheads, just smiling and nodding through the conversation no matter how crass or ill-informed the outcome.'

Tom smiled. 'They do try to cram things into tiny slots; they never really allow most interviewees to develop a thought. They press you to come out with some attractive headline-grabbing sound-bite rather than to present any real insight or background. I think it's largely because they don't believe their audience's attention span is greater than a few seconds.'

'Anyway, you'll be aware of the feeding frenzy when the press sniffs a story, camped out on the street like a pack of wolves, tricking the inexperienced into conjecture, cornering the experienced to make them look shifty.'

Tom agreed. 'Certainly, some are so versed in catching you off guard, coming at you from an unexpected direction, using on-air silence as a weapon to make you blurt out something they can twist back against you.'

'Well, less publicly, there's another feeding frenzy that I have to deal with in quite the opposite direction. All this ill-informed news coverage is swallowed whole by politicians too; they don't care to know the detail, just react to the appearance of the issue. Gone are the days when researchers were hired by politicians to make sure their comments were considered and guarded. Bloody researchers today are only there to have sex with their principals or simply to be used as an excuse, a tax dodge, to pay spouses or significant others some income.

'Just take a look at the role models today, they're not statesmen, but a succession of barristers who fix on a rictus grin only to say what they think we want to hear. They make promises and do nothing to deliver. They're more worried about building directorships, making after-dinner speeches, getting column inches and television appearances, working to inflate the advance they can get for their memoirs.'

Tom nodded. 'There does appear to have been a loss of individuality or any basic integrity. I don't think you could slip a cigarette paper between their declared policies.'

'Precisely, you see I knew you were made of the right stuff. That's exactly what's happening with all the global warming and environmental stuff, don't you see? Half-truths built on misquotes, mixed with ill-informed comment, then bent to a particular cause or vested interest and trumpeted in the media by those with deep pockets to make the whole topic have the gloss of truth. Then before you know it, the whole is paraded by politicians as fact. What we need is to have an equivalently media-savvy team that can combat the plethora of nonsense we are force-fed each day.'

'Surely this is where the scientists and the engineers have to step forward and be counted, to tell it how it is?'

Sir Joseph scoffed. 'I think you may have put on some rose-coloured specs there. Even the scientists can't be trusted. Look at those who stood up and defended the tobacco industry, perfectly qualified people purveying a view that kept their salary cheques coming.'

Tom nodded, 'I do know what you mean. Research laboratories need sponsors and commissions, universities need commercial support to build and update facilities. They do try to separate the lay from the professional, have bursars and others who face-up to the money requirement while the scientist can remain objective, and yet…'

'We do part company there I'm afraid. I don't think they are being deliberately suborned, but my view of human nature is that at a very subtle level one's thinking gets inevitably tilted. If you are one of those tobacco experts you would look in the places that show the benefits, have an unconscious blind spot in the direction of the harmful aspects. Just as in my role, some other nation challenges our glorious Albion and I press back at them, never thinking that they might be right, of course we must always be right. Consider our grudging admiration for a capable opponent on the rugger field, yet we can't quite applaud him as much as one of our own.'

'Hm, I have to agree with that sporting analogy. Even when you are watching two sides that you have no particular interest in, the skills on show are not as appreciated as when demonstrated by the team, or the country, you support.'

'So this is what I would be asking of this new team, forget any name for now, committees will probably come up with some awful title and acronym. Your friend the Professor is pressing for Defence International Corps for the Environment, so it can be called DICE, apparently Einstein said "God does not play dice" or some such, all far too artificial for me.'

'I think it was that "God does not play dice with the universe".'

'Whatever. The members of this DICE would have to try to be dispassionate, try to avoid becoming partisan. What we need is a developed expertise that can evaluate global matters and follow through with solutions. It cannot be just some esoteric think tank; we need it to professionally set about issuing the facts, in order to capture the imaginations and column-centimetres of the press, and the hearts and minds of the politicians. And it cannot be without teeth, it must have the resources and capability to strike out at all the misinformation out there. We need it to end up with the reputation the BBC used to enjoy before it was taken over by the PC crowd who manage it today.'

'I hear what you say, but surely DICE will need to stand up against direct and indirect interference by government and intelligence services too. They are bound to try to influence it to take on their views, their ambitions.'

'So, the question is, are you ready to accept the challenge?'

Tom didn't answer this because he was remembering that he had delivered a package from Kabitsin to Sir Joseph; presumably it was a plan like the one the Mafiya man had passed to Mark, probably some franchise proposal – that was what he had supposed at the time. However there had been no mention of this. Was the spymaster also planning to reach an accommodation with Kabitsin? Or was there some other game in play? Certainly Sir Joseph was not offering any insight into this matter.

So he answered, 'Give me some time to mull it over. I need to see that it can fit in with my other activities. Give me a week and I'll come back with my thinking.'

# Chapter 71 - *Litke, Russia*

Paul and his team had been working for days to reveal the deep end of the gouge mark. This required many, many hours every day of painstaking removal of ice and silt, with the nagging fear that they had no clear idea of just what they might find, if anything. It was almost self-defeating, the ice and silt taking it in turns to become the main problem. But finally they uncovered and removed one small rock, the size and shape of a rugby ball, which they brought back to the surface.

It was placed in a large glass container where when water was added it immediately turned to ice. Their caution had proved sensible; as they suspected, the rock was part of the material that was creating still water from $H^2O$.

The team and the rock were moved to a set of very old buildings located just beside a small fishing village at the Gulf of Matochkin Shar back from the coastline of the island along the Kara Sea.

Paul knew this was the strait where many underground nuclear tests had been performed at the end of the previous century. What he had not realised was that they were now being allowed to enter the sanctum sanctorum of the island. In the background Kabitsin was clearly pulling some pretty important strings to get them access to these facilities.

Misha knew a great deal about the test site. He explained that the original test sites had been located in Kazakhstan because Lavrentii Beria, the political head of the Soviet nuclear bomb team, had suggested that the steppe was not populated. When this was clearly shown to be wrong, somewhere else had to be found, away from populated areas and also far from the possibility of Western observation.

In the 1950s the Soviets simply ordered five hundred indigenous people from the islands and then billeted around ten thousand troops there, housed in simple tents, charged with helping to build the facilities. It was not just the cold temperature that they had to contend with, being 'housed' in tents in a location where winds could regularly reach forty knots, but the local polar bear population was then quite large and active too.

During the late 1950s and early 1960s the tests were initially carried out on or under water, but later the emphasis was more on running atmospheric tests. It was the Limited Test Ban Treaty of 1963 that drove them underground. One such underground test, with four devices being exploded simultaneously, was recorded as setting off a greater than 6.9 Richter event. It shifted millions of tonnes of rock that blocked glacial run-off streams and this later formed a lake over two kilometres in length.

The Threshold Test Ban Treaty of 1976 reduced the scope for testing processes even further, though tests of various types continued right up until 1990.

President Gorbachev announced a moratorium in 1991, this was extended by President Yeltsin in 1993 and the Comprehensive Test Ban Treaty was signed in 1996, though it took until the year 2000 to be fully ratified.

The island was to have only a brief respite, by mid-2002 the Russian Defence Minister and the Minister of Atomic Energy were already mooting that testing might need to be resumed in response to world political developments.

Misha's knowledge of this dark history appeared encyclopaedic, but then this was his area of expertise and he explained that he needed to understand nuclear fission in order to fully appreciate the appeal and value of fusion.

He mentioned that there was a nuclear waste site south of the southern island at Bashmachnaya Bay where the waste of the Russian Northern Fleet of nuclear submarines would be stored. Shafts had been drilled on the islands in anticipation of dumping waste 600 metres down, deep in the permafrost where it would be safe from a nuclear strike or a 7.0 Richter earthquake.

Given his knowledge, Paul asked Misha to discuss what was the objective and format for the sub-critical tests that were still being carried out there. Misha explained that during the Cold War the nuclear warheads had to be refreshed with new plutonium every six to ten years and these current tests were checking routinely to evaluate the longevity of existing munitions, one issue being to see if this frequency of update would remain necessary. There were all sorts of theories but the only reality was to take a look and see!

Ellise had only just stopped the routine checks of her badge but this news had her back to fifteen minute appraisals to check any change in colour.

Misha also told them that the building they were using was the base for the current sub-critical tests, the scientists being brought in with any specialist equipment as necessary. Paul became somewhat frustrated that this was exactly what was happening now. The arrival of each new helicopter brought more people, more equipment, and his project was less and less identifiable as his own.

He thought he recognised one or two from Novosibirsk, but these new personnel either professed to have no English or genuinely did not. Whichever it was, it meant that Paul's increasingly truculent requests for data, to be kept in the loop, fell on deaf ears.

So his main focus was on testing the rock brought up from the gouge, but unfortunately the results he obtained were presented in Cyrillic. He could understand any chemical symbols or equations but the rest of the data was made up of dense pages of nonsense as far as he was concerned. He and Ellise would painstakingly try to convert sections of text and then attempt to translate them but they were getting no more than 10% to 15% of it across to English and this was too little to make any sense.

Ellise found an Internet connection and tried to key the Cyrillic into a free translation site but this only produced a garbled set of loose text. Wherever it encountered anything vaguely technical it was unable to suggest a translation, and of course the material was intensely scientific.

They were reduced to grabbing Misha whenever possible to quiz him as to any discoveries, but he had a very heavy schedule; he seldom worked fewer than sixteen hours a day and when he did get off he was exhausted and it appeared that his English faded in direct proportion to his tiredness.

From what little they could gather, the scientists had confirmed that this was indeed a part of a comet or asteroid. It was clearly non-Terran and was giving them a great deal of excitement in terms of its structure and particularly its chemical reactivity in water. Apparently it had always been expected that anything from out in space would have been somewhat more inert.

# Chapter 72 - *Virginia, USA*

Mark had only limited time to contemplate Kabitsin's threat which he had of course reported to Langley. In the meantime while, so far as they knew, the series of demonstrations was over and as the Brotherhood's team had been weakened by death and imprisonment, his own desk had still shown no sign of quietening down.

He had reports from the US Navy. Its submarine had requested permission to leave the Kara Sea and get on with other duties as the activity in the area seemed now to have stopped. The mini-submarine having lifted something from the sea all appeared now to be happening ashore. Agreed.

He had satellite reports. There was an increase in flights and activity on to the island and other records were showing several key individuals from the scientific community with busy calendars had cancelled appointments and simultaneously disappeared from their posts. Interesting.

Communications traffic with the island was increasing. Analysts reported it was not unlike previous occasions when a test was about to take place. Very interesting.

Military communications appeared a tad busier in the region too. Disturbing.

He had also received several further emails from Ellise. Irritating.

Finally he decided to take the time to answer her because she was precisely where all this activity appeared to be centred; perhaps she could enlighten him. Not for him any convolutions, he just plain asked her what was happening. If she was being censored in any way then he would get nothing back, but if not perhaps he could get to the point before they thought to stop her access to communication.

Ellise positively gushed news back at him, with copies to Tom. Clearly she was finding no stimulus on the island, making it clear with a series of whinges that she was not enamoured of Paul who appeared to be completely focused on his role.

Mark pared away all the emotional stuff and asked some follow-up questions about this rock they'd found. What were the Russians doing with it? Could she see any signs of other objectives beyond their trying to understand it?

It was obvious she had no one watching her, no one monitoring the communications between them, so with prompting from several advisors he asked her to seek more information to put them in the picture. He offered to have the Cyrillic text translated but initially she could find no scanner to get the documents to him digitally.

He had forgotten her skill set and was surprised when her next communication indicated that she had managed to copy some data files electronically and had FTP-ed them to a site, providing the address and passwords for Mark to access them. Now they really managed to get to terms with the events that were unfolding in the Arctic.

His questions slowly turned more towards Misha: what was he doing with his very long days? Mark set his analysts the task of reviewing reams of data on cold fusion so that they could provide him with a briefing as to the current status of this somewhat-discredited science.

When a report from his advisors mentioned that Culham Laboratories held a central role with hot fusion, he immediately contacted Tom and asked him to approach their JET facility to find out what the more junior, less entrenched individuals thought about cold fusion.

# Chapter 73 - *Oxfordshire, UK*

Tom had leapt at the excuse to seek out Stevie again and took the ride out to Culham to ask for her help. Over lunch he brought her up to speed with the Danube and Mekong events, not over-dramatising his role in either of them, but showing how their luck had very fortunately held through these encounters, at least so far.

She listened intently as he described the final denouement for her Congo tormentor, smiled at Tom's failed strategy with the water, grimaced at the description of the death of the Laotian who had managed to wound the Russian giant and looked horrified at the chance that the other Russian may have been trying to shoot Tom.

He brought her up to speed with what was happening up in the Arctic and how she might help. She asked him to wait while she approached one of the other tables, and returned accompanied by a good-looking bloke. Tom recognised the pangs of jealousy he felt at this, but managed to dismiss them as he was introduced to Daniel Roberts.

She introduced Tom, though of course Daniel had already recognised him from his frequent appearances on television, and she explained that Daniel was one of the whizz-kids who had worked on JET, MAST and START. When Tom raised an eyebrow, she patiently explained the terms as Joint European Torus, Mega Amp Spherical Tokamak and Small Tight-Aspect Ratio Tokamak.

Daniel virtually dismissed these as if they were old news and spoke enthusiastically about what he was working on with ITER, the International Thermonuclear Experimental Reactor. This, he explained, was planned to be built in France as a joint venture with the EU, Russia, Japan, China, India, South Korea and the USA, the latter he explained having annoyingly pulled their funding from JET. He enthused that this new device would run for longer periods than JET and was designed to manage a constant burn so it would be a properly productive fusion power plant.

His personal hobbyhorse was managing the plasma, avoiding any NTMs, which he explained, without any sense of enlightenment to Tom, stood for Neoclassical Tearing Mode. Apparently it was all about balancing the conditions, ensuring pressure was not over-applied, as this could lead to the plasma reaching and hitting the wall of the reactor. His interest was in ensuring there were no errors or inconsistencies in the electro-magnetic field in order to minimise the chance of these NTMs. The approach was to develop a neural network diagnostic process to control the plasma.

Tom loved his enthusiasm and his commitment to his subject. Although he had been lost from the beginning he didn't like to interrupt his flow, but fearing his lunch break was coming to an end he tried to steer the conversation on to cold fusion. He rather expected Daniel would scoff and be insulted by this change of subject.

Not at all. Daniel launched into his own theories of why it should work and was actually scornful of those in the scientific faculty who were too inflexible to be open to other routes of enquiry. He quickly listed articles and people worth looking up if Tom needed to know more.

Tom arranged a dinner with Stevie for several days ahead and then made his farewells. Back home he followed up the references and chased down all the branches and side-issues that he encountered. Finally he prepared a report on the subject of the current status of cold fusion.

He believed this was where he excelled, taking a complex subject and worrying it down to a clear and succinct statement that could be understood by the man-in-the-street. He went through it several times, chiselling away at the sense and the pace of his words until he was content. He sent it to Mark first, then having added a few pages of introduction explaining Mark's news from the Arctic and the purpose of the report, he forwarded it to Sir Joseph.

He was still a little unsure of the man and didn't know what to think of the proposed new organisation; he'd concluded that it might best be summed up as dicey! But if it could indeed be established as outlined, it would clearly have value. It wasn't so much that he didn't trust Sir Joseph, he seemed a genuinely agreeable guy, a little old-world perhaps, but he appeared to have the right intentions.

He realised his mistrust was the result of years of reading about fictional spymasters and their devious games, plans within plots, bluff, double-bluff and deliberate prestidigitation. Trying to maintain some sense of independence he therefore couldn't resist blind copying it in to Professor Groves too.

# Chapter 74 - *Moscow, Russia*

The surviving Russian from the Laos event was returned to the Russian authorities, who also now held in custody both the General and Vasily. When crimes were heinous enough the usual painful process of extradition proved to be no barrier and there was an unusual degree of cooperation to get the prisoner back to where his information would be of most use. As a result there were no rights afforded for a lawyer to be called, no establishment of a legal team to fight the validity of the extradition treaty, no concept of innocent until proven guilty. In Russia the usual approach in the past would have been a bullet to the head and an unmarked grave but in this case they needed information.

Kabitsin divined that there appeared to be a schism forming, the overt and the covert. Overtly, the Russian administration was keen to show it took the actions of its subjects seriously and there would be a trial and conviction for the mass killings for which they had been responsible.

In the overt group there was also more than a little reaction to the notion that in seeking personal gain this group of prominent citizens had gone against the state's interests. This was a little too similar to the actions of the oligarchs, who had used a resource belonging to Mother Russia but not for the advancement of the interests of their country, their countrymen. Perversely if they had proposed and done this through the mechanisms of the state, and for the state, they would have been heralded as heroes.

So in essence by the overt faction Kabitsin was being considered unpatriotic; it was laughable, his credentials were clear, but it was infuriating too as it was so far from the truth. How could he be turned upon by Mother Russia herself? The lies and rumours must have been spread by the Americans. Wasn't the great patriot himself, the General, confirming the loyal intentions of their group?

Covertly, there were still those in the administration prepared to assist him. Kabitsin was calling in their favours and so far getting what he needed in terms of personnel and materials delivered to the island. But the feelings against him were gathering momentum and he felt he needed to get out of Moscow, away from prying eyes, from young men trying to make a name in the system, from old men who had been snared by him now desperately clutching at this to get their release from his clutches. The bastards, he had more patriotism is a single fingernail that they had in their whole bodies.

He was far from beaten; he could still recover his status in Russia and have his revenge, but he was a great believer in the old saying 'revenge is a dish best served cold'. His street-smarts were still fully functioning and he still had enough pull to set his plans calmly.

To be safe he decided to spirit himself away from Moscow, northward to the islands.

# Chapter 75 - *Virginia, USA*

Mark's alarm bells were ringing again, an arriving passenger from Moscow was being held at JFK. The guy, apart from looking like everyone's idea of a Mafiya gangster, had used a passport that came up on a watch list from the materials seized during his many enquiries which now stretched around the globe from the Congo, via Turkey and the Danube to Asia, the Arctic, and now the States.

When they had opened the traveller's luggage they found a large glass container of liquid that presumably had escaped any close inspection on leaving Russia. But he also had an itinerary and maps that showed him the route into the city together with a detailed map of the Hudson River which had two locations clearly marked with asterisks along its banks.

Mark rushed a trained interrogator to the airport to find out what this was all about and arranged for someone to test the fluid with yet another expendable little fish. They really had to find another way, if animal rights heard about this…

The whole thing smelled completely wrong to him. Kabitsin was a better opponent than this, he would have planned more carefully, would have delivered the water into the States more elegantly. This couldn't be the main attack, surely.

A little later the same alert came in from another Aeroflot flight that had landed at Dulles airport, this time the passenger had maps of DC and the Potomac. By the end of a very long evening there was a third notification from LAX; the guy had an internal flight ticket and a map for San Francisco Bay.

For Mark it was just too simplistic, Kabitsin must be using these three couriers as a feint while the real attack would come elsewhere. But his team was convinced that a three-city attack, mounted simultaneously, would have been a devastating demonstration of the still water's power if they had gotten through.

Each of the three seized containers instantly failed the fish test, so it did prove to be the noxious stuff. But surely Kabitsin could not have hoped to achieve much with these three couriers who had obviously been sent out without any clarity as to their purpose, and were so obvious in their appearance.

Each had been told once he had passed through customs he would be met and supported. Even now there were agents reviewing CCTV coverage from each airport, but it would take days. Anyway, Mark was sure the effort would prove fruitless; these three guys were pawns in a larger game.

He remained unconvinced urging that no one celebrate these captures, they should expect some other attack, and soon.

# Chapter 76 - *Arctic Circle*

The Arctic Circle is arbitrarily defined as the area above 66° 33'N. This approximates to the tree line, beyond which only small shrubs, lichens and mosses survive. It is also the limit of where the true midnight sun and polar night can be experienced.

So this line had some clear logic, but as a result it arbitrarily includes large areas of Russia and Canada, plus parts of Alaska, Greenland, Norway, Sweden and Finland, it doesn't quite reach to Iceland.

The area, often just shown as an amorphous white blob on the edge of most maps, is in fact two large ocean basins, dissected by three submarine mountain ranges.

Global warming is said to be causing this ice to recede, though other 'experts' refer to this as a simple cyclical effect rather than something specifically of mankind's doing. Whichever it is, this and the movement of the sea tend to calve the pack-ice, to crack and break it up. In the 19th century this prompted an explosion of explorers seeking a route to the Polar Sea, a reputed open area located at the pole.

In fact the Arctic, far from being an ice desert located somewhere at the edge of the world, plays a central role in global matters. It generates a circulation of ocean currents that reach right round the world. The warm water coming north from the Atlantic sinks as it becomes denser on passing Greenland and Iceland, creating the catalyst for the movement of millions of cubic kilometres of sea water deep beneath and across the whole Atlantic. Without this process the ocean would stagnate and its marine life forms perish.

**Novaya Zemlya, Russia**
Novaya Zemlya's northern island was almost split in two by this 75°N 'line', perhaps the reason why most of the activity on this island was concentrated towards its middle and south. If the current frequency of the helicopter flights in the south had been noted by anyone other than the intelligence communities, the eco-terrorists would have been emitting their own carbon in an effort to get up there and protest.

Paul was feeling more and more marginalised, off to one side of matters, until he was introduced to a newly-arrived Kabitsin, who for this meeting, contrary to previous occasions, was happy to show he had a good command of English.

'I understand you are the person who started this whole enterprise. I am told you are the one who worked out where the still water comes from?'

'Yes, I'm Paul Wells, but I couldn't have achieved anything without the assistance of Dmitry, Misha and many others. Oh and of course Ellise.' He belatedly felt her gaze on the back of his head and introduced her.

'Charming to meet you too?' Kabitsin's very direct appraising glance was almost indecent and Ellise had to work hard not to squirm. He extended a hand and when she responded cupped her hand between both of his, hanging on just a little too long, looking deep into her eyes.

Then, almost as indecently, he switched his attention back to Paul. 'So let's walk and talk. I so very seldom get up to the north and want to see it in all its glory. Russia has such wonderful scenery that seems to stretch to infinity, don't you agree? Tell me, what precisely have you found for us?'

He had very effectively split up the couple. It was evident to Ellise that she was not included in the invitation, anyway that look he had given her had made her want to give the man a wide berth.

Kabitsin had let Paul lead the conversation initially, now he turned it to his real interests. 'So, are you convinced that it's this comet fragment that's originating the still water?'

'Absolutely, we have this one rock which we just need to place in water for it to change to the variant of deuterium oxide that we call still water.'

'Is the water dissolving the rock to achieve this so it has just a limited life?'

'There is some exchange of mass but it's not disappearing before our eyes.'

'And do you believe that you can find more of the comet to bring up from the seabed?'

'We think so, given the geometry and the gouge in the seabed.'

'Why do you believe that this has only begun to happen now?'

'It's difficult to say, but it may be that climate change has revealed it. I understand from the locals that the location was always permanently iced up until recently. It may be that climate change or even one of the tests here has melted the ice and revealed the comet material.'

'So if I understand where you are: first you have more of your comet to find and recover and then with this comet material you can create this still water on demand. And Misha brought you the device that can convert the still water back to normal water?'

'That's it in a nutshell.'

Kabitsin did not recognise the saying but understood the notion, 'Then what?'

'Well, there is some work Misha is doing…'

'No, you misunderstand me, what do you see as next for you?'

'Back to my tsunami research, I guess.'

'I'm surprised. You're an intelligent man, aren't there other things you could see that you might use this invention of yours for?'

'Strictly it's a discovery, not an invention.'

'Does it matter?' Kabitsin struggled not to snap. 'You are the person who found the source; you could insist that we all call it Wells water for example. With my help you could even seek a patent for your water and control its production, its management, its applications.'

Paul had no idea where this was all leading, but caught the beginnings of a mood which hinted of conspiracy, so he lied shamelessly. 'I've never worried too much about putting my name to things, producing learned papers. I've always been much more practical, more interested in the outcome, its uses and solutions.'

Kabitsin smiled, 'Now that's the right approach, very good answer.'

They walked on a little further, neither of them looking at the scenery, both too immersed in the conversation.

'Have you spent much time considering the offensive capability of this new water?'

'Ellise has mentioned that there seem to have been some further applications of it since Kazakhstan. Of course I realise that, applied carefully, this has huge potential as a weapon. The key is in the "antidote". Until we found that then the fear was that the material could get so firmly into the water cycle that it would effectively wipe out all of life as we know it.'

'Oh, I doubt it. Every significant new weapon down through time has been seen as earth-shattering, but don't discount Mother Nature.' He waved his hand at the scenery around them. 'She has the habit of being able to soldier on.'

'She certainly has done so down through the millennia, but it hasn't always meant that those on earth survived her adjustments. There have been a number of times when virtually all life was extinguished, so she certainly will press on, but maybe we are just destined to be the fossil fuels of the future.'

'I accept your point, but as we have the antidote we need not worry about this. Have you thought of the commercial opportunities?'

'Not really one of my strengths.'

'Then let me suggest some. Currently around the world it is generally assumed that the sun will rise, that the air will be clear to breathe and that the clouds will bring us refreshing water to fortify us and to help us to grow our crops and tend our animals. This has very fortunately been the case for most people, but these are the three huge assumptions that we all take for granted – light, air and water. Am I right?'

'Absolutely, they're about the only things the government can't control, though I guess they do get to charge us for the water if we don't gather it for ourselves, and we're all too lazy now to want to bother.'

'Yes, water is the exception. We have already accepted the notion that there is something to pay to the organisations that gather, purify and distribute the water to our homes and businesses. So why not pay for the services of someone who can assure you that there will be normal water in your pipes and not still water?'

'Wouldn't every water company quickly apply the antidote?'

'So then perhaps the marketing opportunity has quite a short-term life. But just think about the size of the market. It would be the first truly global product, everyone must subscribe, or they die.'

Paul had been seduced by the conversation. Here was this clearly powerful guy who seemed to have time to talk with him, to talk with him as an equal, who appeared to want and appreciate his views on the subject, who seemed to know how to apply the power of still water. But momentarily he glimpsed the horror of what was being proposed. Kabitsin pressed on realising that this was the turning point.

'Just consider the gas for your car. It needs the crude oil that just happens to be where history and geology placed it. Those nations that by chance sit astride these deposits are holding the rest of the world to ransom with their arbitrary pricing, their cartels, their control of production and supply. Not satisfied with that, your government then taxes you for using it, when it's just a naturally-occurring substance. OK, so it's not that easy to get to and perhaps we have to agree to pay something for those who get it out and refine it, but both they and the governments charge us too much on top of what is fair and reasonable – just because they can!'

'You're right. In the UK they charge us around $1 per litre for the fuel and we have to pay a road tax for our vehicles of around $250 to $350 per year too, and all the time they depreciate, rust and break down.'

'And if you can't afford to pay for this, you don't die. So would you pay a $1 a litre for water so that you can stay alive?'

'People already do in buying bottled water. In restaurants they can pay much more than that for a fancy brand.'

'So we will be just like a new business enterprise, with you at the helm, enforcing your patent – we would be a new market force. And, like Mother Nature, the market will just have to adjust, and take our new pricing strategy in its stride.'

They had completed a circular route without seeming to have had any course in mind and were just getting back to the small community.

Kabitsin drew him close. 'We men of vision are very few and far between. We have to stick together against all those out there who are just living day by day. Most of them have no real goals, so it's not at all surprising that they achieve none, you might even say they are a complete waste of air and water.' He smiled exaggeratedly as he said this and Paul automatically responded with a smile of his own.

'We will talk again of your ideas. I find them most interesting.' Paul did not notice the manipulation in his statement; of course he felt they had been his ideas, for it was he who had led this man to the conclusions that they'd just discussed.

'These are powerful notions. Some may come here seeking to interfere, perhaps to disrupt what you are doing. So do not be surprised if I need to move you and the material to safety at a moment's notice. I urge you to recover as much of the comet as you can and keep everything you have ready for rapid removal. And do keep your ideas just between us. Do you trust Ellise?'

'She's out of her depth here, great at computing but with no idea of anything that happens outside the innards of her PC.'

'Then I may need to send her back home so she does not keep the Americans informed of what you are doing. We have been monitoring her emails and she is regularly mailing Mark Elliott,' he paused for effect, 'and Tom Carter .'

Kabitsin looked for, and was not disappointed by, the intended reaction. Paul was fully his now, and Ellise might just provide a little entertainment too.

# Chapter 77 - *London, UK*

Sir Joseph unexpectedly called Tom to meet him at the SIS headquarters at Vauxhall Cross.

As Chief of SIS he continued the tradition, started by the first chief, Mansfield Cumming, and was therefore referred to as 'C' within the service. Although in recent years 'C' was the only serving member whose name was made public, appearing on their official website and regularly cited in media circles.

'Dear boy, welcome to "Ceausescu Towers". Do take a pew,' Sir Joseph ushered him to some easy chairs around a low table and an assistant asked his preferences for coffee.

'I thought we'd agreed I would come back to you in a week or so.'

'Needs must, needs must. No, it's not about that, it's this damnable still water stuff. As you know it seems it's not quite over yet. You've been kindly copying us in on all the material coming from Ellise Walker, thanks for that. But has young Mark Elliott filled you in on the containers seized at three US airports?'

When Tom shook his head he pressed on. 'Thought not, we spooks like to receive every scrap of information from others, but so seldom like to dish it out in return.' He explained what had happened.

'So Mark is not convinced that this is anything other than "selling them a dummy"?'

'Well put. Now their Homeland Security is running around like Chicken-Licken shouting that the sky is about to fall in on their water supplies. We've already been through all that and have concluded we can't, in any real sense, secure our water resources from an attack. Our only course of action is to attack the source.'

'Doesn't Ellise suggest that they've found something in the East Novaya Zemlya Trough that seems to be proven as the origin? I thought Paul was tilting at windmills, but this time he appears to have been right.'

'Yes, but you take me too literally, I mean this Kabitsin character is the source. He appears to still have some pull and has so far eluded capture. We've wrapped up most of his organisation but he seems to have sprung up again on Novaya Zemlya with a coterie of thugs and scientists doing his bidding.'

'Should I warn Ellise?'

'Not a lot we can do from here, I'm afraid. Travel in and out of the islands is controlled by Kabitsin or his cronies so she just has to take her chances. What I have managed to do however is to reply to his proposal that you brought back from Istanbul.'

'I wondered what had happened to that.'

Sir Joseph took his coffee to the window that gave a view along the Thames in both directions. Tom joined him and noted a strange quality in the glass; clearly it had to be bullet-proof and maybe it even had anti-listening qualities. He assumed it was probably the most hi-tech glass he'd seen, given that the IRA's rocket-propelled grenade attack on the building had caused such minimal damage.

'Hm, well we have replied now. Sold him some cock and bull story of our being disenchanted about lost empire, how the colonials have shown us no gratitude for our past munificence, fears of losing status in the world. We even fed him some anti-Chinese and anti-Indian guff, about fearing them supplanting us at the G-8 table. We have some good people, it fair convinced me, didn't know whether to applaud the writers or fire them.'

'To what end?'

'Straight to the point, that's what I like about you. Kabitsin swallowed it whole and agreed that you could go and meet him there to discuss the next steps.'

'Whoa, my last trip at least had some element of science involved, why would I want to enter that island? It sounds foul – cold, irradiated and full of thugs and scientists prepared to work for this gangster.'

'We have to go into the dragon's lair to be able to slay the dragon.'

'You must have some pretty competent people here who are better equipped to do that. I'm no slayer of dragons.'

'That's probably why he insisted on you!'

They discussed the proposal and the strategies for some hours and finally Tom agreed that there was little choice for him but to go.

'So when do I get to meet with "Q"? Surely he can set me up with some remarkable technology to go out and smash SMERSH!'

# Chapter 78 - *Novaya Zemlya, Russia*

Why him? Here he was swaddled in Arctic clothing heading by helicopter out towards the island, and what had they given him? Their advice and good wishes basically.

He had a laptop and a satellite phone and both had obviously been 'doctored' in many ways but no weapons, no killing-machine side-kick, no watches that could saw through handcuffs and not an Aston Martin in sight.

However he had prepared himself well. He knew that humans were only naturally comfortable unclothed at a non-humid temperature in the high 20s centigrade. In this Arctic autumn he could expect it to be somewhere below zero but probably not lower than $-10°C$, and he had learned that it would not be the temperature, but rather more the wind and wet, that he needed to protect himself against.

Just a six kilometre wind speed would lower his body temperature by stripping away the warm air that the body generates around itself. As a poor conductor of heat, air around the body tends to stay warm until a wind whisks it away. However water next to the body, whether from sweat or meteorological events, is a very good conductor and so it would drain away body temperatures very speedily. Plus of course the special water in this 'neck of the woods' might do him even more harm.

Clothing choice was therefore all important. He had been advised not to overdress because then he would sweat and that would chill him. What he selected instead were many layers of loose fitting clothes to trap air and keep it warm. His only compromise was in choosing fingerless gloves as he found even plastic lab gloves made fairly normal manual tasks more complicated. In all other respects he was suited and booted for the weather.

The size of the island was impressive. He realised his previous perception was due to its relative size compared with the vastness of Russia, or maybe it was the Mercator projection's style of mapping that made things on the edge of the map look relatively small. In fact the island's length was greater than the British Isles.

His transfer through Rogachevo had been speedy, now he was landing next to the ever-growing community beside the Matochkin Shar. He had to do a double-take when he ran under the rotors to his welcoming committee. Wondering why everyone ducked their heads when it was quite clear the rotors were metres higher than them, his double-take was because one of the guys meeting him looked just like Lev raised from the dead. He concluded Kabitsin must have a production line of them.

This Lev introduced himself as Fyodor Sidorov, 'But, please call me Fedya.' Minus the sadistic grins, he was clearly a gentler doppelganger of Lev, and the good news was that he was being polite, so far.

Tom was ushered into some buildings and shown into the presence. There was perhaps a 40°C swing in temperatures since their last meeting in a hot, sweaty Istanbul.

Kabitsin had ensured that Tom would arrive while Paul was safely out in the mini-sub that had been brought back to the islands for another session. He was apparently close to recovering another sizeable chunk of his comet and spent much of his day under water.

'How is Sir Joseph?'

Tom was having a day of double-takes – at their last meeting there was a translator and Kabitsin had shown no capability in English. He must have used the artifice to buy himself thinking time.

Tom took a seat, 'He is very well and sends his regards. He hopes you can do something to encourage the Russian authorities to release the General or at least make his imprisonment more pleasant.'

Kabitsin flew out of the chair, but controlled his face and his words with, 'The General is a great patriot and will be treated with respect. They will come to understand that he is still a visionary, that what we are doing is for Rodinya. I understand from Sir Joseph that there is a group of people in Britain who wish to take some positive action to regain its Empire's past prominence in the world.'

'It would be fair to say that all free-thinking Englishmen share that goal. We don't want to slip down the world rankings in the same way as our football team.'

Kabitsin was back in full control of himself. 'Empires – they are always doomed. Look down the ages; they have always been replaced by hungrier, faster, more technologically advanced nations, improved races.'

'That sounds like a pretty good description of the Chinese and the Indians, certainly hungrier, definitely growing in speed and grasping industrialisation and new technologies to their cause.'

'Have you looked closely at any projections of demographic growth? Population is growing exponentially in all the wrong places. We civilised nations are not replacing our own stock, not to mention that we're allowing too much mixing of the genes with lesser nations. We're screwing our way to the extinction of our own identity.'

Tom let the thought hang out there. He couldn't bring himself to support the view, though dared not criticise it; he was here to learn, not to remedy.

'So the British would like the secret of our still water?'

'I'm just Sir Joseph's representative and am not party to the proposal he has sent you. But I personally would like to know what has become of the material since our research back in Novosibirsk.'

Kabitsin thought about this, piercing him with a withering stare. 'I'm sure you would.' Then he seemed to relax a little. 'We both need to resolve a matter first. Your previous lapdog prime minister discredited your nation with his blind acceptance of that idiot Bush. You need to put the Americans back in their place, and I want this too.

'The United States was the beginning of the end for your empire, coming late to both World Wars, ripping the heart out of your nation with their lend-lease schemes. They shipped you materials and demanded the equivalent at today's prices of almost $500 billion, and Russia too, our bill was almost $200 billion. America's future was secured from our misery and at our cost. Like some moneylender, Roosevelt kept his people safe until Pearl Harbour forced him to see that this was his fight too!'

'Yet, Britain and the USA have stayed very close despite that.'

'No, since the war you were always their puppy dog, fed scraps and made to run errands. It was only Blair who made it all too obvious, because Bush didn't have the intellect to keep up the charade that they take you seriously!'

Tom thought it best to concede, 'I agree most Americans see us as just another market, one that's easy to penetrate because of the language.'

'There's my point, they allow you the joy of thinking that they speak English, but the world now speaks American, the language of the greenback, the American dream.'

'How are you suggesting you'd resolve this matter?'

'I'm going to send them a piece of comet!'

# Chapter 79 - *Novaya Zemlya, Russia*

Back at the original campsite Ellise suspected nothing, believing she had been summoned to a meeting. Fedya opened a door for her and stepped back politely for her to go first. As she entered she was pushed forcefully across the threshold and the door was closed and locked behind her.

She found herself in an equipment room with no windows or other doors and it took a while before she could make out the features of the room. She pulled out the torch she used for scanning her badge and by its low light was able to investigate her surroundings.

The walls were obviously made of wood, but a kick at one of them soon made her realise she would not have the strength to make any impression on the thick planks which were closely and firmly interconnected.

She had no alternative but to sit and wait to see what would happen next, though she did find time to check her lapel badge before switching off her torch and settling on to a packing case.

**Matochkin Shar, Russia**
Kabitsin loved to find great men from history whom he thought he might emulate or better still surpass.

He had read every article he could find about Genghis Khan, in particular anything he could find on his predilection for raping captive women. As a result Khan had spread his Y-chromosome so widely that to date there are 16 million people in the world who carry his genes.

Genghis Khan had united his nation behind his cause and from disparate tribes he had forged the second largest empire in history. By the time of his death he had an empire that stretched from the Caspian Sea to the Sea of Japan and by his rapacious actions he had ensured that his seed was spread 800,000 times more greatly than other mere mortals.

First and foremost Kabitsin had thought it necessary to keep this Ellise hidden away from the two British guys while his plans came to fruition. However he had also seen this as his first opportunity to spread his genes with those of a black American.

Just look how the Negro dominated sport around the world. It was fitting that his genes would mix with this fruitful and successful lineage to create a perfect mix of physical prowess and mental strength.

Right now he was engaged in supervising the team much further up the gulf of the Matochkin Shar. It was a mining team that he had managed to "borrow" from across the Kara Sea; they were casual staff who Noril'sk Nickel would draw upon from time to time.

They had been paid a high bonus in return for digging at one of the old nuclear test sites. Of course they had been advised that this was a fresh tunnel and they should not fear the presence of any radiation.

When a couple of the more experienced individuals became aware that they were burrowing through an existing collapsed tunnel they had to be dealt with, and the remaining miners did not fail to notice when they were subsequently supervised by armed guards.

With the ice-covered water behind them and the mountains blocking any other route out, they had little choice but to complete the job and hope to be allowed to leave thereafter.

Kabitsin needed this tunnel of his own, to test what the scientists were preparing for him. He did not want to penetrate too deeply into the ground for fear of what he might release, but he did need to conceal his actions from the satellite coverage that he knew would be prying into the frantic activity here on the island.

Misha had been given every resource to pursue his theories. Now all he needed was to replicate and improve upon the original Fleischmann-Pons experiment that had triggered off the whole issue of cold fusion at the University of Utah way back in 1989.

He had several slices of the comet to provide him with his deuterium. He had also been supplied with a surprisingly large quantity of palladium and palladium chloride; heaven knows where it came from. He had also been given copious amounts of both lithium chloride and lithium itself. This lithium had been removed electrolytically from the lithium chloride and suspended in an oil to stop any tarnishing and blackening of its surface.

His first exercise was to try to reproduce the work done at the US Navy's SPAWAR, Space & Naval Warfare Systems Center in San Diego. Scientists there had developed something they called 'co-deposition' which was an advance on the original experiment.

Essentially SPAWAR had managed initially to 'marinate' a nickel plate in some heavy water, deuterium oxide, with solutes of lithium chloride and palladium chloride, and run a current through it. After time the deuterium atoms inserted themselves into the naturally grid-like structure of the palladium and ended up almost one-for-one, palladium and deuterium.

This co-deposition was further speeded up by constructing the negative electrode from gold or nickel wire held in the same solution.

The mystery of their experiment kicked in when, reassuringly, it was established that there appeared to be more energy coming from the reaction than was being applied, and this energy creation was being achieved at just room temperature and pressure.

The usual particle detector used for measuring alpha radiation from depleted uranium had been used by SPAWAR. In their tests the detectors recorded a pitting which suggested that radiation was present in the cold fusion experiment, but in negligible quantities.

The low-cost detector used was the CR-39 type. The same ones that Russian scientists in the past had as their only option, because their budgets had been so tight. Particles passing through the plastic detector show up as pitting.

A few decades earlier and Ellise would have had to use these, rather than her more instantly obvious colour-changing badge.

The past experiment had noted pitting in the CR-39; they also found more tritium was produced than might have been expected. In addition X-rays were emitted because the electrode warmed up compared to the solution surrounding it. All these factors they believed to be proof of a nuclear reaction. Detractors talked of proximity of radioactive material, of cosmic rays, or perhaps some sort of contamination but more often than not they accused them of poor experimentation.

Hot fusion is about forcing deuterium and tritium atoms together against their natural tendency, which is to keep themselves apart. Each of the protons holds a positive charge and like-charges of course repel each other. But under the extreme temperatures and pressures, fusion can be forced to happen. This creates a helium nucleus and a spare neutron, both emerging from the process with a high kinetic energy – thus delivering useable energy.

Misha had read all the established wisdom but had his own theory. He wanted to try for the middle ground. He would presume that what was observed in cold fusion experiments was genuine, yet he wanted to avoid the huge costs related to hot fusion.

He would attempt to create what he decided to call warm-fusion.

How ironic he thought, warm fusion in the Arctic, but it was here that he had all the materials and a free hand to test his theories. A perfect opportunity to take advantage of a hand-picked team of young engineers and physicists forced together in this place where there was no distraction from the work, no social life to intrude.

As a result one of those creative inspirations had been made, an almost inexplicable quantum leap achieved. Maybe warm fusion's moment had come or they had jumped some time-space vortex. Early experimentation was confirming their thoughts and now they needed to put them to the test.


Paul was still comet-scavenging, committing long hours to the mini-sub and its two-steps forward, three-steps back process of clearing the ice and silt to delve for more portions of the comet. Now he was not worrying about how the others were using his material, content in his mind that Kabitsin was taking care of business while he mined the mother lode.

# Chapter 80 - *Matochkin Shar, Russia*

Tom could learn nothing of Ellise's whereabouts and began to fear the worst, that maybe she had been eliminated. It did not enter his mind that Kabitsin might have had more imaginative plans for her.

With Kabitsin away, Tom was using his skills to mine the scientists for information. As a respected international celebrity-scientist he was generally welcomed and quickly invited to review their activity, what progress had been made. It had taken him less than a day to establish that it was warm fusion that was keeping them all gainfully employed.

Tom of course was attracted to the notion too; it was just his sort of thing. As a result he was not only acquiring information for his spymaster, he was genuinely interested in the potential for this new source of low-cost energy for the world. His reports via his laptop and satellite phone were being filed back to Sir Joseph, where they would have a restricted readership. It was also agreed that he should keep Stevie fully informed at Culham so that he could be provided with direct scientific feedback on the Russian progress that he reported.

Culham's analysis and mirrored experiments confirmed what had been transmitted had genuinely significant new potential. But they also came back with a horrifying warning, there were two possible applications. Weren't there always? The warm fusion could be constrained to become a fuel cell or, if it was allowed to run free, it could be an awesome weapon.

Tom was urged by Sir Joseph to be seen to be 100% committed to Kabitsin's new world order, to ensure he stayed at the centre of the effort so any suggestion that the explosive application was being considered could be fed back.

Sir Joseph also judged this as the time to involve others. He needed the Americans and the Russians to be fully apprised of what was happening so that this madman could be stopped. Kabitsin had already shown a completely cavalier attitude in his use of still water. If he was prepared to kill and destroy innocents and show no sign of remorse, what might he do with this new weapon?

At the islands the first overt signs of Sir Joseph's warnings were the three or four-times daily flyovers of the strait by a pair of MiG-35s, known by NATO as the 'Fulcrum-F'. Each time their approach was timed to pass overhead just as they accelerated to their maximum low altitude speed up beyond Mach 1. They appeared from nowhere and made their presence felt by their sonic booms.

Their return along the route seconds later was slower and from the ground they could be clearly seen to be sporting R-77 missiles, what NATO called their AA-12 Adder. Though these were in fact air-to-air weapons, designed to be used against Cruise and Patriot missiles, at 4 metres long they looked pretty lethal from below.

Kabitsin's contacts also called to advise him that, despite their efforts, the Northern Fleet was despatching various craft to the area. Just as progress was being made he was being isolated, marginalised. He vented his fury during these conversations, which served only to alienate him even more from his fast-declining assets back in Moscow.

He had to act, and act now, to get ahead of the game, to reassure those beginning to desert him, to show them what he was capable of achieving. Even though the tunnel was no more than 80 or 90 metres deep, he rushed the scientific team to take their materials up to the excavation.

At first progress was slow with the miners not wanting to hurry to penetrate the dangerous rocks. They didn't entirely trust that the devices provided would properly measure any radiation present. The regular flyover booms didn't help their attitudes either, each leading to a downing of tools and withdrawal for fear of a tunnel collapse. The previous day the team had refused to work because of the arrival of polar bears; Kabitsin assumed they had been attracted by the dumped bodies of the original troublemakers.

The mining team did relax a little when the scientists arrived, at least there were others prepared to enter the tunnel, but were they too being misled as to the risk?

Tom had come with the group and Kabitsin, seeing him thoroughly engaged in setting up the equipment, showed no signs of concern about his presence. Paul had been summoned as well; he had completed the salvage of a large piece of the comet that they had uncovered, and Kabitsin felt that he should be present for the test.

Ellise had established her plan of escape. She had been provided with regular meals and supplied with fluids, but the last meal had been brought by a younger guy, and he had not been supported by the usual second guard at the door. She was not aware of it, of course, but most of the team were now at the tunnel so numbers at this site were greatly reduced.

She had been keeping herself occupied by exercising and had absolute confidence that she could take this guy if he was the one who came alone the next time. When he swung the door open he was half-turned and so took a few seconds to take in the fact that Ellise was just in bra and pants, the momentary surprise was all she needed to pull him towards her and put the full weight of her knee into his groin. As he crumpled, she swung the door almost closed in case anyone should pass, and then delivered the coup de grâce to his head and neck with a sack she had loaded with anything heavy that she could find. All the pent-up frustrations of her days shut in the room went into the swing and the resultant crunching sound did not augur well for the guy.

She had no time to check his pulse but quickly dressed, then tied him as well as she could with strips of sacking. Leaving nothing to chance she probably over-compensated with too many strips and far too many knots, and all the time she was worried that the slightly open door would raise suspicion.

She emerged slowly and looked around but there was no one to be seen. The key was in the lock and she took the opportunity to fasten the door behind her before she made her way back to her quarters. She was surprised to find the building deserted but decided not to question her luck. She quickly togged up with her outdoor clothes which were still hanging where she had left them, and went outside with no clear plan of action.

Seeing there was a helicopter on the pad, she climbed in and crawled to the back of the area usually used for freight. She would be hidden by the passenger seats in front, but anyone coming to put cargo in the area would be sure to find her. There was no alternative so she settled for creating as low a profile as she could achieve, hard up against the rear of the seats.

Exhausted by her earlier efforts, she must have fallen asleep, but she woke abruptly when the pilot's door was opened and someone got in. Shortly afterwards she heard the pilot going through his routines and starting the engine. Great, her plan was coming together. She assumed they would be flying to Rogachevo Airport and from there she would have more chance to find a way to get away from these awful islands.

The helicopter's destination proved to be not that distant, no great height was achieved and it soon touched down again. Was it further up the strait or perhaps back at Litke? The pilot shut down and departed the craft.

So this was not just a pick-up stop, clearly they were stopping here. If he'd flown empty in this direction he was probably collecting freight and she could not risk being there as it was loaded. She took a quick look around and seeing no one she slipped down from the helicopter and walked purposefully towards nearby buildings that resembled temporarily constructed barracks.

The first one she came to was furnished but unoccupied, for it was used by the shift that was currently working. With limited success she looked around for a weapon, finding only a heavy iron bar, the sort of thing she thought miners would use to drive into a rock face.

Ellise did not dare stay in the room, she had to go and see what was happening out there. There was no difficulty following the strung lights and trodden path up beside the strait and she quickly concluded her best approach was again to walk the route confidently as if she was on some important errand. Her gear was similar to everyone else's and she was no shorter than many of the guys so with a scarf across her face and keeping to the shadows she was confident no one would challenge her.

She eventually reached an area where there was a large canopy raised above benches of equipment; several people were bending over these benches, busy setting up and running checks on kit. She bypassed them and approached a large tunnel. It was probably over 3 metres high and perhaps 5 metres across, certainly big enough for the small tracked vehicles they were using to enter and also to be able to turn to leave.

The tunnel was no smooth-sided road or rail tunnel though, the sides were made of large rocks and rubble, like a moraine thrown up by a glacier. It appeared to slope downwards but Ellise thought this could have been an optical illusion created by the lights.

Towards the far end she could see several more people bending over a smaller bench. As they seemed preoccupied she risked walking into the tunnel where she spotted a recess to one side where the miners had obviously dislodged some loose rubble. The lights from outside and from deep in the tunnel failed to reach into this space so she decided it would be a good place to hide and assess the situation.

Walking with Misha and several others on their way to watch the test, Tom was only minutes behind her. As they reached the canopy the technicians there had completed the rigging of the equipment and they were joined at the control point by the others as they emerged from the tunnel.

Misha waited for the last group to arrive before turning to address all present. He dropped his hood to look around him. He spoke in English in deference to their guests. 'I believe what we are about to witness is the first fruit of a new technology that will bring limitless energy to the world. I think that Mr Kabitsin has earned the right to be the one to start the process.'

Kabitsin walked forward and Misha gave him brief instructions. At this point Kabitsin turned and addressed the onlookers, making his comments in both Russian and English. 'My friends, change is seldom popular because it unsettles the established order. There are always those who will seek to stop any sort of progress that might possibly loosen their grip within the established power base. What we do here will not only change the world of energy, but the world of politics too. This will shake the world from its current axis.' He flicked the switch.

There was a brief pause when nothing happened, then there was a faint glow in an array of light bulbs that were loosely displayed beside the tunnel entrance. Gradually the brightness grew until all the lights were at full intensity. This lasted for several minutes during which time the team cheered and congratulated each other, then suddenly everything went pitch-black.

Misha shouted gleefully, 'Don't worry, I had to put a governor on the device. I was worried that the process might just get away from us; we don't want to add to the damage on the island. It hasn't failed, it just switched off automatically before any harm could be done.' Sure enough the lights came back up from their standard generator within a few seconds.

Tom asked, 'Do you have any idea what power output you could have generated?'

Paul had been unaware of Tom's presence and he pulled Kabitsin to one side, 'What's he doing here?'

Kabitsin smiled. So it was true that these British guys really hated each other, 'Don't worry, he is here as a potential customer for our products. And products is now the word to use, for we have both still water and warm fusion. Relax, you are the CEO of this new organisation, he is just a potential customer.'

'Are you sure of him? I think he's just a bit too John Bull, there's something of the Boy Scout about him. I can't see him conspiring to use still water in any aggressive way.'

'He's here as a representative of Her Majesty's Secret Service to negotiate with us. They want to revisit their past glories, seek to rebuild the Empire. Isn't that precisely what your Boy Scouts did?'

In the meantime Tom and others were being led into the tunnel by Misha to look more closely at the equipment. The group were unaware that they passed close to Ellise who, pressed back within her recess, was at little risk of being noticed; besides their night vision was still somewhat impaired from the device's recent light show.

Misha proudly performed a 'naming of parts' for the others, delighted to tell them the 'ins and outs' of what he had created.


Outside the tunnel Kabitsin was handed a satellite phone by Fedya. A good contact was calling to advise him that a ship had landed in the south of the island and was offloading troops and provisions. He also advised that some of the first arrivals were evidently clearing an area for helicopters to land.

It was all happening too fast for Kabitsin. He needed to get himself more time, but obviously he was not going to be afforded that luxury.

He rapidly turned on his heels and strode off down into the tunnel to join the others, with Paul and the rest of his coterie rushing to keep up.

He requested Misha to repeat his guided tour of the equipment and asked a series of direct questions, particularly focusing on the governor that Misha had referred to. 'So what precisely did the governor do to switch it all off?'

'It was pretty simple stuff, for the future we would need to refine the process extensively. All I did was have it sluice out the deuterium oxide from the cell when the power output reached what I judged to be a high enough level.' He then went in to a long diatribe about how the finished product would need to regulate the flow of the still water to maintain a steady output at useful levels.

'What do you think would have happened if you'd let it run?'

'I feared a reaction that would accelerate until the device over-heated or eventually exploded.'

'Would that have been like a nuclear bomb explosion?'

'No it would just have been a fusing of the lights, at most a small explosion. Cold and warm fusion does generate a nuclear reaction, but I'm not judging or measuring any harmful radioactivity being emitted by the process. But don't underestimate it though, there would be a huge explosion if the reaction got out of control, just not a radioactive one.'

'How long will it take you to refine the device?'

'We need access to some proper engineering facilities where we can clean up the basic design and then integrate the various functions that we have jury-rigged here. Perhaps it will take a month to the first prototype.'

Kabitsin went silent, his mind obviously in overdrive. 'Then we need to get you and your team, plus all of this equipment, to a safe place so that you can be sure to complete your work without interference. Please make it all ready to be transported back to Moscow within the next hour.' With that he left and walked back to the camp with his team hurrying along behind him.

Paul was beside him as they passed Ellise. 'Look, I really don't trust bloody Carter . I feel sure that as a Brit I could find another way to reach out to the British government.'

'Don't worry we'll probably not need him.'

There was a flurry of activity in and out of the tunnel and Tom, finding himself surplus to requirements, thought he might as well leave and head back to his laptop to make some notes. Walking back through the tunnel, he was surprised when someone leapt out from the dark and grabbed him, but was able to see immediately that it was Ellise, she had removed her scarf and hood to make her identity clear.

'Tom, I just overheard Paul and Kabitsin discussing that you're not to be trusted.'

'Was Paul here? Couldn't see who was who with all the hoods and scarves. He kept his presence pretty quiet, I had thought that Misha and Kabitsin spoke in English just for me.'

'Neither of us is safe here, I've been locked away for days in an equipment room. No one told me why, they just shoved me in and locked the door.'

'I had been looking for you since I got here and feared the worst. How did you get out?'

'That's a good point. If they are starting to shut down the camp they'll find the guy I knocked out and left trussed up. We may have even less time than I thought.'

New arrivals passing to and fro forced them both to press back into the recess until the coast was clear again.

Tom said, 'Look why don't you stay right here for a bit while I try to find out where they're going and what the hurry is all of a sudden. I'll be back as soon as I can.'

Kabitsin was calling all of his remaining contacts trying to get these troops held up or sent away but he was finding the flood of opposition was forming up into one of Paul's tsunamis, aimed straight at him. Try as he might he could not get the right answers, no one he reached seemed to know anything about this force arriving at the islands, or at least claimed they did not. They were all lying of course. Clearly the Americans, the British, the Chinese and the Indians were all applying huge pressure on Putin's administration and he, Kabitsin, was losing his control of those back in Moscow. He was simply out of sight and out of mind.

What he needed was to get back there and deliver the news of the still water and get the results of the warm fusion whispered into the right ears. Once they saw and acknowledged that this was all in Russia's interests they would be sure to assist him to continue with his plans. Currently all they could see was the foreign propaganda that he was a rogue Russian stirring up problems for them. Why did politicians always seek the quiet life? They fought to get to power but once there they never seemed to want to rock the boat. Why were they too short-sighted to see the benefits of his scheme?

That's why he had cultivated the General. If they saw him still at the helm then they would listen. Someone from Kabitsin's background was OK, as a fixer, when you didn't want to do your own dirty work, but he wasn't someone you invited out to your dacha for the weekend.

He began to realise how thin his power over them had been. Yes he could pull strings. He could enter the Kremlin and the Duma, but more like a whore in the night – not as an honoured guest, not to be seen with, no pictures taken with him on their 'ego walls'. He was there just to be used and discarded as promptly as possible thereafter.

What a fool he had been to think they could actually appreciate his skills and his ideas. They had just humoured him while he wielded his power, his dirty little secrets. Now they wanted to swat him away like some annoying insect. Well this insect had a bite, a number of bites. He wasn't going to go quietly into the night; he would make them pay for their lack of belief, their lack of loyalty.

Tom had quickly assessed that there were only two helicopters at the camp; perhaps twelve passengers and freight could be moved at a time. He sought out Misha to discover what he knew about this sudden quick departure.

Misha was fretting about his device. 'Having just managed to get it to work, it was no part of my plan to then pull it apart again, in a hurry! Doesn't Kabitsin understand that these things don't just fall together? It takes care and attention to detail, many trial and error phases. It's not an instant success, much more of a progression towards a solution that is always moving forward.'

Now he was being forced to rip it apart just when he needed to be left alone with his baby to help it take its first steps and grow into a fully-fledged device.

He did explain however that he had heard that there was some threat to Kabitsin, that his enemies were trying to interfere with his plans, that they were perhaps coming here. 'But I don't know why or when, and I can't really understand why Kabitsin isn't able to secure the site. He is Mafiya, isn't he? There seem to be quite enough security people here to see off an army.'

Tom offered to help in dismantling the device and was pleased that Misha accepted his assistance. He knew how protective of their ideas scientists could be. When they entered the tunnel he bent to check his laces to allow Misha and his colleagues to move ahead of him, then darted into the recess and tugged Ellise out to join him, whispering, 'Tag along with us. No one will pick up on you if you stay away from the lights along the path.'

'What have you learned?'

'Not much, but let's keep with the group ahead and see what comes up.'

Misha was already draining the residual still water solution into a container and carefully stripping out the precious constituent parts from the cell. Tom stripped off his gloves and threw back his hood to show he was ready to assist. Misha pointed out the way in which he might help with dismantling the electrics, 'Take care with that small piggy-back printed circuit board, it's the governor. We added it to our plans quite late in the process; the next version will have it integrated on to the main board. It's a little fragile at the moment, hand-soldered by me very late last night. I was shattered, not sure I'd want anyone to judge my work on that, but it did its job.'

Tom packed the components into a flight case that was filled with small capsules of polyfoam to cocoon each piece safely. The electronics and electrical portion of the device looked pretty simple. 'Is this all you needed to deliver that power? No, that didn't come out right. What I mean to say is that this is so elegant already, when you integrate it all it looks as if it is going to be a very low-cost item.'

'The only complications really are the chemical components. The means of heating and pressurising them are off-the-shelf. That's the trick, surely? Keep it simple so the whole world can benefit.'

They were so intent on what they were doing that they had not seen Kabitsin returning, and were surprised when he commented, 'Let's get you and your ideas to a safe place then we can worry about the world later.'

Tom looked around to see that Ellise was hanging back deep within the tunnel, appearing to be busy with her head turned away towards some of the jury-rigged lighting. He asked, 'May I ask why this has to be moved right now? Misha could be compromising his device by having to dismantle it.'

'Ah, Mr Carter , always the curious scientist I see! Don't worry, we will take care of it and we will get you your licence agreement as soon as Misha has finished his work. But for now I think that this flight case is mine.' He watched as Tom latched it closed and passed it over to Fedya whom he ordered to take it directly to the waiting helicopter. Then he hustled Misha and his colleagues to finish up and follow, leaving them to it.

Tom walked to the rear of the tunnel to where Ellise was still standing. He drew alongside her to see that the very back of the tunnel shelved away and was filled with water. He couldn't help looking down and caught a glimpse of himself reflected in the surface, and froze.

Ellise was looking into the surface too and saw the same look that she had seen all that time ago on the Galápagos, but this time he did not turn and run away. She went to him and placed her arm around him. 'Whatever is it? What is it that you think you are seeing?'

Tom turned to her, seeming startled that someone else was there. He shook his head. 'It's not quite the same any more. I guess I've changed.'

Ellise persisted, 'I feel sure you could never have done anything to make you so disturbed. Let me help, tell me about it?'

'It's not what I did. It's what I didn't do.'

'We've all had moments like that, but once it's passed, you can't keep going over it again. You have to live with it, you just need to find closure.'

'Save me from that trite American bullshit. Of course I understand that, but it doesn't help, I should have saved him.'

'Who? Who should you have saved?'

'My brother, William. It's like half of me having slipped through my hands.'

'I'm sorry, but you'll need to tell me what you mean.'

'William was my identical twin. He fell overboard when we were sailing and I couldn't pull him from the water. I watched and felt him slip from my hands, sink under the water and drown. It was just like looking into a mirror to watch my own drowning.'

'Horrible, when did this happen?'

'We were ten years old, sailing on a lake at home. We'd done it a thousand times before. It was all a terrible accident. I should have been able to hold on until our father reached us.'

'You were ten years old!'

'But William would have held on.'

'You say you were identical, so he would have had only the same strength as you.'

'He was always the driven one. I know he would have found the tenacity to cling on. I've spent the rest of my life trying to achieve his mental energy, to become him.'

'You said it's not the same anymore?'

'I'm losing the memory of how he looked, back then. In the reflection I've aged. It used to be easy to turn back the years, see him in my reflection, now all I see is our father. I also see the look my father gave me, the look that said why didn't you hold on? Of course he kept insisting that it was an accident and it wasn't my fault, but I saw that first look he gave me, the rest was just words.'

'You have to get past this. That's why you turned away from me in the Galápagos, isn't it?'

'I don't remember what happened. We were having a great day and then suddenly I was running along the beach back to our boat.'

'And the thing Paul keeps on about, you and he in the Navy?'

'We were serving on the Gloucester in Gulf War One, but were seconded across to the USS Tripoli. It hit a mine.'

'Paul said something about you being a coward?'

'No, not that. It was again what I didn't do, rather than anything I did. It was chaos, fire crews dealing with various outbreaks. Everyone dashing around trying to see what damage had been done. Paul and I went through a hatch into an area that had taken most of the impact. It was filling with water, fast, and there were several badly injured down there. All I remember is looking down at the water, seeing William in the reflection and just freezing, I just couldn't move to assist those guys. Later I was told that Paul had to fight his way past me to get to them and help them.'

'That was it? Didn't they know about your brother?'

'No, I've never mentioned him or that day to anyone, ever.'

She took him in her arms and massaged his neck that was seized up, tight and unyielding.

'How very touching!' Paul had come down the tunnel quietly, neither of them aware of how long he had been there, or what he might have heard.

'I wondered where you were hiding for the last few days, Ellise. Had I known Tom bloody Carter had come calling, all would have been revealed.'

'You have that all back to front, your new buddy Kabitsin locked me away. God knows why, but I had half expected that you might have missed me and come to find me.'

Paul raised his arm and was holding a gun, pointed at Ellise. 'You were dragging me down. There I was on the edge of something brilliant, something all mine, and you were whingeing about that bloody badge of yours and bullshit stories about people being flung from helicopters.'

'Don't you see what they're doing to you? You'd never have dreamt of pointing a gun at me before coming to this dreadful place. You've been working flat out for weeks, you've lost all perspective. Can't you see that Kabitsin is Mafiya, a cheap crook.'

'No, he's my partner in all of this. He's the only one who understands the power of this comet, the value of the still water. Just look what he's had these scientists come up with in such a short time. The man is a motivator, a facilitator, he is so well connected.'

Tom said, 'No Paul, he's a mass murderer. While you've been working here on the island he's carried out attacks on the Congo and the Tigris. They killed thousands along the Danube. No one knows how many died along the Mekong, certainly it might have been even more deadly if we'd not stopped him.'

Paul turned the gun on to Tom, 'I don't believe you, he's a businessman. Why would I trust anything that you said anyway? You've always had it in for me, always putting me down. Besides Kabitsin tells me you've sold out, working for the spooks. They think everyone is as convoluted as they are, playing bloody games with the world.'

Tom was trying to move away from Ellise. 'So what are you planning to do?'

'I asked Kabitsin to let me deal with you. Ellise is just a bonus, I didn't know she was here with you, again!'

'Oh, so he's just a businessman is he, so what part of his business requires that you kill us?'

'No, this is not business, this is all pleasure. Leaving you here for the polar bears, never to be bothered by you again, never upstaged, never to have to sit through another of your patronising broadcasts.'

Ellise dropped to the floor, and scooped up some of the water. Paul, who had been psyched up and ready to pull the trigger on Tom, was momentarily indecisive, slow to change his aim.

Tom shouted, 'Look out, Ellise, that's still water.'

Ellise tossed it directly into Paul's face. He immediately dropped the gun as he frantically tried to wipe it from his eyes and nose, keeping his eyes and mouth anchored firmly closed.

Tom, thinking that at least the still water ploy had worked this one time, grabbed for the gun before Paul could work out that he wasn't actually being invaded by the murderous stuff. Ellise beat him to it, producing her metal bar and using all her softball experience to hit Paul on the side of his head. He went down, his legs and arms convulsing.

Waving the gun, Tom said, 'That wasn't really necessary.'

'Yes it was, the bastard was going to kill us, just to build his own reputation!'

'We have to get out of here before they get away with that device and the materials. We can't let them loose on the world with that.'

They rushed back down to the camp site and were relieved to see both helicopters were still there, so Tom went to deal with them first. But how do you disable a helicopter?

He assumed that anyone who knew anything about them would pull off the distributor cap or perform some other simple disablement. If he survived this he promised himself he would read all there was to know about the bloody things. At the time all he could come up with was electrics and fuel, but he had no idea where the battery might be, assuming it even had one.

So fuel was the other option. Presumably diesel, he wasn't even sure that this would ignite if he could find the cap and dropped in a burning rag. Come on think it through!

He ran to one of the tracked vehicles, beckoned Ellise to climb in, and fortunately it started at the push of a button. He drove it directly at the first helicopter and smashed the tail with a satisfying thwack, reassuringly the impact bent the tail and the rear rotor completely out of shape. He pressed on towards the second helicopter but the noise of the first crash had brought people out of the buildings.

Someone was quick to get a pistol drawn on them and started firing single shots. This was enough to make Tom swerve from his original target and he instead hit the second helicopter full on its side. The tracked vehicle tried to stall but he whipped it into reverse and swung away from the firing and down the track quickly getting out of range.

Ellise looked back and saw that he had certainly rocked the second helicopter but it still looked intact. They agreed that they needed to go back and deal with it. Tom used Ellise's bar to clamp the accelerator down and to hold the wheel dead ahead, then they both jumped from the moving vehicle. She had been reluctant to be parted from her bar, which had proven so versatile, but needs must.

They crawled from the road reaching a hollow in the ice just before a vehicle came clattering past in pursuit of theirs. Down the track they heard a noise as their vehicle left the road, probably at a bend, and it could only have gone one way, into the strait. Perhaps that would buy them some time if the Russians assumed they were aboard.

They walked back to the test site with no idea of what was ahead, just knowing they couldn't let this madman escape.

Kabitsin was noisily angry with his security team. How could they have let this happen? Mad with Paul whom he had trusted to kill Tom. He had no further use for Paul now if he couldn't perform a simple task. He had the comet fragments and the warm fusion, he didn't need anyone else. But it was important, before the Russian forces arrived, that Misha and his team were shifted away from here, so they could carry on their work elsewhere.

Kabitsin's thought processes were not assisted by the fact that he was finding himself torn between two courses of action. Use the new technology to place himself at the centre of a global enterprise where his licensing would make him the richest, most powerful person in the world? Or use warm fusion without its governor in order to teach some of his enemies a lesson?

Now he had lost one of the helicopters and his people were looking at the second. They eventually decided that the only available option was for the pilot to suck-it-and-see, try to take off and see if the surfaces and controls worked normally. But the pilot needed a little 'encouragement' first. Kabitsin explained to him his particular penchant for not only killing any individual who displeased him, but also his disposing of any relatives until he was sure that he had completely expunged every shred of DNA that the person might have passed on. Genghis Khan would probably have appreciated this alternative way of making sure that your own seed would predominate.

When they arrived back Tom managed to get into Misha's area without being challenged. They both judged it would be safer if Ellise waited outside; he left her considering ways of immobilising the second helicopter.

Tom swiftly brought Misha up to speed with what was happening and explained about Kabitsin's role in the still water attacks. Misha was shocked but quickly accepted that Tom was telling him the truth; he did know of Kabitsin Mafiya status. Tom promised that in return for his assistance he would make sure that he reached the UK where he would be given every resource to pursue his project. He mentioned having met up with Daniel Roberts at Culham and helpfully Misha had heard of him, had read papers he had produced. It was Misha's idea to remove some vital components from the package so if Kabitsin did take it he would not have a functioning device. He gave Tom the items that he requested.

Tom went outside to catch up with Ellise, to see what ideas she had come up with for them to disable the second helicopter, but she pointed towards it, a pilot was going through his finals before starting it. They watched helplessly as the rotors turned and the pilot lifted off. He tried several of the controls so it hovered perhaps five metres over the camp and then took off in several directions, turning and manoeuvring. The pilot climbed higher and higher going through the same routines, then without any warning set off directly down the strait towards the Kara Sea.

The pilot wasn't going back to the camp. He was going to get a head start and hide his whole family. He'd go overseas, change his name, his appearance, whatever it took until he heard that the Mafiya gang was dead and gone. It was a risk, but putting himself back in that camp would have been a certainty!

Kabitsin was now incandescent. He emerged to establish who was supposed to have been watching the pilot, who was stupid enough not to get into the helicopter to keep an eye on him. The craven idiot had been frightened to get in, in case it crashed. Well, he would have no further worries in this life. Kabitsin ordered his guards to bring everyone outside to see him forced to kneel and be summarily executed for his stupidity. Perhaps finally they would all realise how important this whole enterprise was, why they all had to stay on top of their game.

While outside, Kabitsin kept looking nervously up at the sky. After he had dealt with the 'example' he then ordered Misha and his team back to their work area. He followed them there and explained that given the lack of a helicopter things had changed and they had no more than fifteen minutes to set up the device and have it all working again. They protested that this was too short a time but the look on his face and his previous execution made it abundantly clear that it was better to be seen to be trying to achieve his outrageous request than to argue.

Tom had observed the killing from the shadows, shocked at Kabitsin's actions, and was desperately wondering how he could single-handedly defeat this group. OK, he had a pistol, but he also realised that he had no idea how many shots there were in it, certainly not enough to take out all of the security detail, and he had Ellise to worry about too!

He was a bloody scientist, not a spook and certainly no sort of Jack; no Bauer, Reacher or Ryan! Where did he start? How did he make any impression on their numbers? How could he even get past Fedya to be able to reach Kabitsin? He had no faith but looked up to the sky for inspiration.

As if on cue, they all became aware of an approaching helicopter. In the camp there was evident confusion as to whether it was the pilot returning or, as Kabitsin and Fedya feared, the arrival of the first Russian forces.

Kabitsin called his closest team to gather loosely around him, and they all stared up into the night, or rather into the duskiness that masqueraded as night at that time of the year. The helicopter was not coming directly to the camp, rather annoyingly it was waiting up there, hovering clear of it. As it came closer it became obvious this was a different helicopter. It wasn't the returning pilot, but Kabitsin thought it didn't look much like a Russian military craft either. It looked more commercial, not at all insectile as he would describe the distinctive look of a military helicopter. Who the hell was it? This was no regular flight path for someone to be just passing by; if it was there it had to be intentional.

The helicopter made one fast pass overhead. The scientists scattered when they saw two men hanging from the skids on each side with machine guns at the ready. It made a fast turn and came back to the camp where the two gunmen on the helicopter could now distinguish between security and science. The pilot hovered above the group, rotating slowly so that the two shooters started to take out the security guards who had as yet not begun to respond to the threat.

Tom had no idea who these people were but thanked whoever had sent them. His first 'prayer' had been answered – the sheer number of his opponents was being reduced.

He watched Kabitsin duck back into the buildings leaving Fedya to marshal the remaining guards. They were regrouping and returning fire forcing the helicopter to climb and fly away out of range. But in the brief seconds since it arrived Tom had his second wish on a plate. Kabitsin and Fedya were now separated. Was that all he had to do, wish for things and they'd come to pass? Just who were these guys who had arrived so opportunely?

Again he asked Ellise to wait while he worked his way back to the temporary huts trying to get to Misha's area where he assumed Kabitsin to be headed. He drew the gun that he had taken from Paul as he entered the hut, instinctively acting like every movie cop and spy he'd ever seen, stooping to offer a low profile, both hands on the gun held out straight in front of him. He hoped that these movies weren't just bullshit and that the stance had some beneficial basis in reality, some benefits for him in this current situation.

He managed to stop himself shouting 'Clear!' when he found the hallway empty. Concentrate, this isn't a game. You're not an actor. If you get shot you'll stay shot!

The firing outside was so regular that he could time his movements to coincide with each burst of machine gun; in this way there was no chance that anyone would hear him coming.

He opened the first door he came to, still adopting his crouch as he entered, and saw Misha at his bench feverishly rebuilding his device. Misha either heard him enter or became aware of a change in temperature and turned. He looked first at Tom and then quickly to his right behind the open door, but that warning came too late. Something smashed down on the pistol extended out in front of Tom and it clattered to the floor. So much for watching cop shows as your information source!

Tom reached for the gun only to be kicked in the ribs as he stretched out for it. Kabitsin drove his foot into him several more times as he curled into a foetal position to minimise the potential damage. When the attack finally stopped he saw Kabitsin had pushed his fallen pistol aside and drawn his own gun which was pointing directly at him.

'So, not lost in the Shar after all I see. What of the delightful Ms Walker? I do hope she's still all in one piece too.'

Tom nursed his ribs and declined to answer.

'As you can see, I am planning a little surprise for our uninvited friends. When they take over the camp they may get a little more than they bargained for. We'll set Misha's baby running without its governor and leave them a little welcoming present.'

Misha looked across at Tom and raised his eyebrows almost imperceptibly, but enough to suggest that he was not going to comply. It was clear to Tom that he would sabotage the device rather than achieve Kabitsin's objective. But as soon as Kabitsin realised this, then what would he do? He wouldn't kill the golden goose surely? He might use some of the golden goose's team as an example and then there was always the completely expendable Brit!.

Tom was finding it difficult to breathe and any gentle movement caused a pain like a knife between his ribs. He could see his pistol but it was perhaps five paces away, at least it would have been five paces before his ribcage had met Kabitsin's foot. Now he didn't know if he was capable of reaching it at all.

The gunfire outside had quietened. He had no idea who had won, who might come through the doorway, but Tom felt it was important to get Kabitsin away from the door. He started to crawl, not for his pistol, but towards Misha.

One particular movement almost made him pass out – so don't do that particular movement he screamed internally!

Kabitsin took one step towards him and away from the door, 'Where do you think you are going?'

'To help Misha get the device working for you.' He managed another lurch, which included the same excruciating movement.

Kabitsin took another step, 'I don't think you are fit enough to assist, and why would I trust you anywhere near the device?'

Tom turned to face him, 'Whatever else I might be, first and foremost I am a scientist.' He had to force himself to keep talking and not to glance directly at the door which he realised was opening so carefully that it had to be someone on their side, any of Kabitsin's crew would surely have just walked in. 'This is an important new technology that needs the attention of all scientists to make sure it is used in the correct way, for the general good.'

Ellise launched herself into the room and threw herself on to Kabitsin's back, clinging on to it and grabbing for his gun arm. Kabitsin staggered a few steps forward under the impact but crucially did not lose his footing. With his loose arm he struggled to pry Ellise's arm from around his neck, all the time shaking her from side to side.

He moved towards the hut wall in an attempt to crash her against it to break her grip, but Tom managed to kick out at the back of his leg and brought him down to his knees. Ellise used the momentum to pull him to one side and they both crashed to the floor, still wrestling for control of his gun.

Tom crawled over to them and sat on Kabitsin's gun arm, while struggling for something in his pocket. Kabitsin was twisting free of their combined assault when Tom eventually found what he was looking for. It was a small glass container. He flicked it open and dropped the contents into Kabitsin's open mouth. Tom clamped his hands over Kabitsin's lips so that he couldn't spit out the small fragment of comet that Misha had given him much earlier.

Kabitsin's eyes grew wide with fear and his efforts to wriggle free were frantic, but Tom put all of his effort into keeping his hands clamped over the Russian's mouth. In the mêlée Kabitsin shook his gun hand free and started to turn it towards Tom's damaged ribcage. Kabitsin was winning. The gun was steadily and remorselessly moving towards Tom, then suddenly without warning the villain collapsed – the comet fragment had turned the fluids in his body to still water and drained all the life from him.

Tom crawled up the side of a cabinet and placed his hands into a sink, Misha assisted by pouring water, just plain old water over them as a precaution. He looked over his palms and fingers but found no scratches or gouges that could have come into contact with any still water that might have escaped Kabitsin's mouth.

Tom collapsed to the floor clutching his ribs, but managed to smile at Ellise. 'I thought I told you to wait outside for me.'

'Is it because I am a girl? Or because I'm black?' Ellise laughed.

'Thank you! But what's happening outside? Who was that in the helicopter?'

As he asked the door was flung open and Fedya stepped into the doorway, his bulk completely filling it. He looked down at Kabitsin and across at Tom slightly incredulously. He would have backed Kabitsin every time in a fight, what could have happened here?

Two shots rang out, and Fedya's expression hardly changed as he fell forward into the room and his place at the doorway was taken instead by Brain. 'Someone ordered the cavalry?'

They strapped up Tom's ribs so that he could move without feeling the need to grunt and gently helped him outside. Two of Brain's team were holding the remaining security guards and the final member was watching over the scientists and miners who were sitting on the floor in a separate group with their hands clearly on show.

Brain was explaining, 'Classic piece of misinformation. We used one of Kabitsin's informants, who had turned against him, to feed him stories that the whole Russian armed forces were landing on the islands to take him out. Thought it would make him run with his helicopters and we had the US submarine out there ready to take them out, but when only one of them was detected and forced down we thought we'd better come and see what was happening up here.'

Tom singled out Misha from the seated lines and introduced him to Brain. 'You need to get this man, his equipment and team to safety. Ideally I'd like to see him installed at Culham as soon as possible, he has some important ideas that need to be protected.'

Ellise asked, 'How did you guys get here? Isn't this an invasion of Russian territory?'

'We came in over the ice, made a number of stops at UK and US polar stations to refuel, but it was one of your submarines that knocked out all the communications to and from the island, other than sat-phones that is. We'll drop you back to the sub if you like, back to US territory?'

She asked, 'What about Paul?' She explained where he was and her fears that she might have killed him. One of Brain's guys jogged off to look for him and came back a little later, helping him along – alive, but very groggy.

Tom took Ellise to one side, 'Thanks for saving my skin earlier, and thanks for listening to my silliness about William.'

'As long as you accept that it is silliness, that's a good start.' She reached out to kiss him and he recoiled.

'Sorry I just remember how you followed up, the last time that you kissed me!' then pecked her platonically on both cheeks.

# Chapter 81 - *Oxfordshire, UK*

Tom brought Misha to the Culham Labs after he had been spirited away from the Arctic and arranged that he was fast-tracked for admission into the UK. Misha's gratitude was only exceeded by his excitement over the offer to work at this well-funded research facility with world-renowned colleagues to assist.

On arrival he was formally welcomed by the management and research staff and rushed off to a meeting room where they asked him to present his findings and plans for warm fusion.

As soon as he could, Tom broke away to go in search of Stevie.

*'We're all downstream!'*

www.ingramcontent.com/pod-product-compliance
Lightning Source LLC
Chambersburg PA
CBHW061324170626
46817CB00001B/309